Poison Flowers

Also by Natasha Cooper
A COMMON DEATH

Poison Flowers

NATASHA
COOPER

CROWN PUBLISHERS, INC.
NEW YORK

Author's Note

As everyone knows, there is no such government department as DOAP – the Department of Old Age Pensions. It
and all the characters who take part in the following story
are wholly imaginary and have no counterparts in the real
world.

The quotations from the *Meditations* of Marcus Aurelius
are taken from George Long's translation, first published
in 1862.

Published by Crown Publishers, Inc., 201 East 50th Street, New York,
New York 10022. Member of the Crown Publishing Group.
Published in Great Britain by Simon & Schuster Ltd. in 1991.

CROWN is a trademark of Crown Publishers, Inc.

Manufactured in the United States of America

Library of Congress Cataloging-in-Publication Data

Cooper, Natasha.
Poison flowers / Natasha Cooper.
p.   cm.
I. Title.
PS3553.06215P65   1991
813'.54—dc20   91-21467
                                         CIP

ISBN 0-517-57673-2

10 9 8 7 6 5 4 3 2 1

First American Edition

For
Octavia, Roland and Claudia,
and for the slug,
without which this book would never have been written.

And most of all I would flee from the cruel madness of love -
The honey of poison-flowers and all the measureless ill.

Maud
ALFRED, LORD TENNYSON

Chapter 1

'*A* CEREAL killer,' repeated Willow as she sat opposite Tom Worth in the restaurant in Pimlico. Her green eyes had an uncharacteristic expression of doubtful amusement in them and her normally controlled voice quivered slightly. If Tom had not seemed so serious she might have allowed some of the laughter out. 'What, poison in the muesli?'

Worth's dark eyes narrowed and his nostrils flared. The pale-yellow candlelight lit the engaging bump of his broken nose and the lines of his well-shaped mouth, which usually smiled but was now tucked into a frown. For once the power of his character was undisguised. He looked almost dangerous.

'My God! You are chilling sometimes, Willow. How did you know?'

About to say that she could not think of any other way to kill someone with cereal short of stuffing their mouths and nostrils with it and so suffocating them, Willow suddenly realised what Worth had actually said. Altering her expression from amused doubt to carefully understated confidence, she shrugged and smiled.

'Just a guess, Tom,' she said. 'But I don't think I've ever heard of a serial murderer who used poison.'

'There have been one or two; but it's true that most serial killers use more directly violent means. That's one of the reasons why my superiors take such a dim view of my hypothesis that these deaths are in any way connected,' said Tom, absent-mindedly pouring himself another glass of wine. He put the bottle back on the table and looked across the candle flame to Willow's shadowed face. 'But I'm sure that they are and that we must stop him, whoever he is.'

'What makes you think it's a "he"?' asked Willow, reaching for the bottle and pouring some claret into her glass. She was amused to find part of her mind surprised that Tom Worth had ignored her empty glass when refilling his own. The other man in her life, Richard Lawrence-Crescent, would no more have done that than he would have stripped naked and turned cartwheels in Piccadilly.

'Manner of speaking, really,' said Tom. 'But apart from two isolated American cases, the only genuine serial killers I've ever heard of have been men.'

Willow watched him as he spoke and realised that he was really troubled. Suppressing her lingering amusement over the original misunderstanding, she asked him what made him think that the killings were connected.

Tom looked past her as though she did not exist, as though she were a figment of her own imagination, which in a way she was.

Born the only child of middle-aged, academic parents, Willow had been brought up to be clever, efficient, prudent and perfectly self-sufficient. They had suppressed every sign of emotional dependence in their unexpected child only out of a desire to protect her from crippling distress if they should die before she reached safe adulthood, but they had been so successful that her self-containment became a kind of mental and emotional straight jacket.

For many years she lived reasonably contented in it, having no idea of what she was really like and hardly noticing her own inability to achieve intimacy with anyone. In her early thirties the chilly self-sufficient personality had threatened to extinguish her altogether, and some dormant sense of identity had forced her to take drastic action.

Exchanging her successful full-time Civil Service career for a part-time version, Willow had started to write romantic novels under a pseudonym. In the novels and in the luxurious part-time life they ultimately financed for her, she let all her hitherto suppressed fantasies run free. But even in that life she had still not conquered her fear of letting anyone come close to her.

'Apart from the fact that they're all poisonings?' said Tom, still looking past Willow into the distance. 'It's the way they were done, I think. Listen . . .'

'Start at the beginning,' said Willow, her mind beginning to operate at its professional rather than its social level. They had spent a pleasant couple of hours in the small, informal restaurant, eating an undistinguished but decently cooked meal and chatting inconsequentially of books and films and holiday plans. She was touched – and surprised – that Tom had repressed what was obviously an urgent anxiety in order to entertain her.

'How many murders are you talking about, where did they happen, what are the connecting links, what is the evidence, what . . .?'

'Stop!' Tom said, interrupting her as she had interrupted him. 'I'll give you a brief resumé of what I know. I was called to the scene of a double death in Fulham earlier this year.'

'When? Why haven't you said anything before?'

Tom Worth merely raised his straight, dark eyebrows. Willow came closer to blushing than usual. They had met a few months earlier when he was in charge of an investigation into the murder of the Minister of her department, and an extraordinary moment of passion had flared between them. After the case had ended they had managed to become friends; dining together at about fortnightly intervals, but there was nothing in their relationship to give her any right to expect confidences from him.

'I know, I know,' she said, fighting the small constraint, 'you never discuss your cases. It's just that "earlier this year" sounded as though it must have happened very soon after we first met.'

'Yes, it was a couple of weeks after that,' said Tom, respecting her wish to avoid talking about the murder that had introduced them.

'But there was no reason to tell you anything about it,' he went on. 'The two Fulham victims were an architect called Simon Titchmell and his girlfriend, Annabel Wilna. You may have read about it in the newspapers.'

'I do remember something,' said Willow, frowning in an attempt to reconstruct the newspaper reports, 'but few details. Didn't they think it was suicide?'

'That is the most widely accepted conclusion, although the case hasn't been closed yet. The two of them died after eating muesli that had been contaminated with aconite,' said Tom.

'What, those little yellow flowers?' said Willow, just as the young waiter came to clear away their plates. He asked whether their food had been 'all right' and Worth assured him that it had and ordered coffee.

'I like this place,' said Willow as they waited for it. She looked with approval at the pale beech tables, the plain candle holders, the dark-red felt walls and the unpretentious pictures that hung against them. There were eight other tables, but only two of them in use.

'I'm glad,' said Tom simply, ignoring what he had been about to say when the waiter interrupted them. 'It's nothing particularly special, but I have always felt comfortable here.'

4

'It was kind of you to bring me,' said Willow. Then, as though determined to make up for her earlier ignorance of his problems, she repeated: 'Aconite. Those little yellow flowers?'

'That, my dear Miss King, is a remark worthy of your idiotic *alter ego*,' said Worth caustically. 'I had been going to let it go, but since you've repeated it . . . ' Willow's elegantly dressed red head had lifted at his first words and before he could finish what he had been going to say, she delivered her protest.

'There's absolutely nothing idiotic about "Cressida Woodruffe",' she said, trying not to sound defensive. 'You may not be a consumer of romantic fiction, but there's no need to sneer at it. It gives a great many people a lot of innocent pleasure.'

There were very few people in the world who knew that the austere Willow King, the Assistant Secretary (Finance) of the Department of Old Age Pensions, was the same woman as the glamorous, sybaritic Cressida Woodruffe, but Chief Inspector Worth was one of the few. He had hardly ever spoken about her novels and Willow, who both liked and respected him, did not enjoy having to defend them against his criticism. The fact that she half despised them herself did not give him the right to judge her.

'You're right,' said Tom at once. His smile was mocking, but she had the comforting feeling that it was himself he mocked. 'I've never read any Cressida Woodruffes and it is unfair of me to prejudge them. But, to revert to what we are really discussing, the poisonous aconite has nothing whatever to do with those little yellow flowers. It's astonishing how many educated people get that wrong.'

'Oh really?' said Willow with illusory meekness. 'I never did any biology or botany even at school. But never mind now – tell me more about the murders.'

'My superiors have taken the view that the aconite root, which had been carefully dried and powdered before being added to the cereal, was not properly understood by Titchmell or the girl and was deliberately put into the muesli by one or other of them.'

'Why?' said Willow. 'Why should anyone go to the trouble of drying and grinding up wild flower roots to improve their breakfast?'

'In much smaller doses aconite has been used as a traditional narcotic,' said Tom. 'And it is assumed that they took it as a home-made substitute for marijuana or cocaine.'

'But that's ludicrous!' protested Willow. Tom shrugged. For the first time that evening he looked tired as well as anxious.

Before Willow could say any more or comment on Worth's weariness, the waiter brought their coffee and a plate of hand-made chocolates. When he had gone, Willow picked up a chocolate-coated cherry, ate it and then looked at Worth. Her eyes seemed to be a deeper green than usual in the flickering candlelight.

'Was it a weekday?' she asked. 'Presumably they were on their way to work. No one would take a narcotic before working. Cocaine, perhaps, but not something to make them sleep.'

Worth said nothing, but there was a light in his eyes and a faint smile on his lips that suggested that he appreciated her point.

'Were the other cases as eccentric as that?' she went on. Worth half shrugged his powerful shoulders under the civilised disguise of his well-cut but slightly shabby dark suit.

'Yes,' he said. 'All the deaths were caused by plant poisons taken in food or drink. An elderly spinster died at the end of February after drinking a small quantity of sloe gin every day. Her routine was to have a small glass of the stuff (which she made herself each year when the sloes were ripe) after her evening meal. Unfortunately the bottle she used just before she died had been adulterated with a high concentration of digitalis, from very finely powdered foxglove leaves.'

'I can see precisely why you think the cases are linked,' said Willow. 'How bizarre and utterly horrible! Did she have a bad heart?'

Worth took her slim hand in one of his and gripped it for a moment. The anxious look in his dark eyes was transformed for a moment into an expression of relaxation and amused affection. Whether he was amused at her or at himself Willow was not sure. After a moment she withdrew her hand. Tom drained his coffee and then made a face.

'Too sweet!' he said. 'My fault for putting so much sugar in it. Willow, you cannot imagine how good it is to find someone who is prepared to believe that these murders may be connected. My colleagues and superiors think I'm making a fuss about nothing.' He laughed shortly and there was no amusement in the sound at all. 'They've started talking about "female intuition" and asking whether I'm cracking up.'

'But why?' asked Willow, outraged on his behalf. The amusement crept back into his eyes at her tone.

'Because apart from the type of poison and the fact that it was introduced into food or drink, there is no other connecting link between the deaths. The victims are as unlike each other as they could possibly be and have no apparent connection with each other. Because they live in opposite parts of the country . . .'

'Then how do you know about it? Surely the government hasn't sneaked a national police force into operation without legislation,' said Willow.

Tom laughed again.

'No. Though there are plenty of people who think a national force is the only way forward,' he said. Willow got the impression that he was covering something up.

'Then how do you know?' she asked again, determined to find out.

'There's a system for circulating details of unsolved major crimes among the different forces,' he said a little reluctantly. 'You don't need to know any more about it: just accept that it exists.' He turned to signal to the waiter, who seemed to understand his peculiar gestures and quickly brought the bill.

'Tom,' said Willow, deliberately deciding to leave the subject of the inter-force reporting for the time being, 'may I contribute to this?' She was conscious that she must earn at least ten times his salary from her novels.

'Certainly not,' he said, grinning at her. 'I invited you out to dinner to celebrate my promotion and your finishing the latest book. This bill is mine. You can invite me and pay for our dinner whenever you like, but I won't have unseemly squabbling now.' He put a plastic credit card on top of the folded bill.

'Thank you very much,' said Willow, accepting his rule with ease and considerable pleasure.

He drove her home to Belgravia in his elderly but superbly maintained Saab and parked carefully in a space just a little way from her front door. As Willow King she inhabited a small, dampish flat in Clapham, but Cressida Woodruffe's royalties had bought, decorated and furnished five large and elegant rooms in Chesham Place. Tom did not switch off the engine. Willow looked sideways at him in the mixture of moon- and street-light, liking his eccentric courtesy. She knew quite well that his leaving the engine running was intended to show that he wanted her to be absolutely free to invite him in to her flat or not as she chose.

'Would you like a drink?' she asked, making her voice noncommittal so that he would be as unconstrained in his decision whether to accept her invitation.

'That would be nice,' he said, putting the car in neutral and switching off the engine. 'Thank you.'

When he had locked the car they walked up the broad staircase to her flat side by side. As she unlocked the door

and hurried to switch off the beeping burglar alarm, she thought how much she liked him and trusted him.

'Come into the drawing room,' she said, returning to the small hall. 'It's still a bit bleak, but quite habitable.'

The last time he had been in the Belgravia flat had been after the investigation they had shared into the murder of the Minister of DOAP, when the flat had been broken into, ransacked and vandalised by a man whose successful corruption was threatened by Willow's questions. On that occasion she had been reduced to uncharacteristic tears of rage and fear by the sight of her furniture scored and slashed by a sharp knife, her pictures reduced to heaps of crumpled paper and torn canvas and the whole room covered in feathers from the ruined sofa cushions.

Worth looked around the room, noticing the gaps where pictures had once hung and pieces of furniture had stood.

'Have you heard from the insurance company yet?' he asked as she switched on the lights and removed a guard from in front of the fire that her housekeeper must have lit earlier in the evening.

'Yes. They sent a loss adjustor – a charming man – and if his estimate of the time proves correct, I ought to be getting a cheque from them soon. But now that the book is finished I'll start replacing the stuff in any case. I just hadn't the time to do anything until I'd got it off to my agent. Mrs Rusham tidied everything up and found these temporary sofa cushions and covers. They're fairly ghastly, but I can bear them for a bit. Whisky?'

'Better not,' he said. 'I've drunk enough tonight. Have you any mineral water?'

'Of course,' said Willow. 'Mrs Rusham keeps me well supplied.'

'I must say that whatever I may think of a woman like you bothering to write romantic novels for your living, I envy you your housekeeper.'

Willow handed him a heavy tumbler filled with Vichy water and laughed.

'She's my most indefensible luxury, and yet the one I would be most reluctant to lose,' she said. 'Come and sit down. The sofas aren't as comfortable as they were before that thug dug his knife into them, but it's better than standing up.'

Tom went to sit beside her, carefully leaving two feet between them, and took a mouthful of water. The room might lack ornament, but there were flowers in vases on the mantelpiece and on a small table near the windows. New books lay on a wide stool in front of one of the sofas with the day's newspapers. The small fire burning in the white Adam fireplace warmed the room and its fickle light combined with that of the silk-shaded lamps to create an atmosphere of luxurious peace.

Willow felt completely relaxed as she lay back against the replacement foam-filled sofa cushions, but after a while it occurred to her that Tom did not share her ease.

'What is it, Tom?' she asked. 'Those murders?' He shook his head and the firelight accentuated the shape of his broken nose and the smooth planes of his cheeks and forehead.

'No,' he said, and his voice sounded even deeper than usual. 'I was wondering about that chap, the one you introduced me to the night I came here before Christmas.'

'Richard, you mean,' said Willow, easily identifying her old friend and sometime lover. 'What about him?'

Worth turned away from her to put his glass down on a small table. Then, unencumbered, he turned back to face her. He took her free hand and held it in both of his. This time he did not grip, but she could feel the strength of his fingers and she was at once afraid of the implications of his strength and of the sensations he produced in her. She was afraid that she might be falling in love with him and knew that if she did, she would have no protection left against the hurt her peculiar upbringing had forced her to dread. Richard had never seemed so positive – or so threatening to her self-sufficiency – as Tom Worth.

10

'Willow,' said Tom with difficulty, 'I know that I have no right to ask this – and I don't know that I even expect you to answer – but is he . . . are you and he . . . well, lovers?'

Willow pulled away instinctively, but Tom kept his hold on her hand. Honesty fought with her fear of intimacy and won.

'We were,' she answered truthfully. Even in her own ears, her voice sounded strained. 'But since . . . We have not been lovers – technically – since that night when you and I . . . that night in the middle of the Endelsham case when you stayed with me in Clapham.'

As she spoke Willow thought of Richard's astonished resentment when she had tried to explain to him that the simple, happy arrangement they had shared for the previous three years had ceased to seem simple to her and that she no longer wanted to be his lover, however much she still valued his friendship. She had been nervous about broaching the subject, feeling absurdly that it was considerably more intimate than any of the lovemaking they had shared. Perhaps her nervousness had made her voice and manner colder than she had meant.

'Damn it, Willow! Why didn't you tell me?' Richard had burst out when she had said her piece after they had had dinner together one night.

'I am telling you now, Richard,' she had answered, trying to keep her voice unemotional, knowing that he hated scenes as much as she did.

'I had a right to know. You should have told me when I got here this evening . . . ' Willow had begun to feel angry as Richard sounded more and more resentful.

'Do you mean that you'd have made me pay for dinner if you'd known that I wasn't going to sleep with you? I'll be happy to give you a cheque,' she had said very coldly.

'Don't be a fool,' he had retorted, more coldly still. Willow had waited for him to go on, but he had just stood on the pavement outside her flat, looking as though she had done something unspeakable.

'Richard,' she had said then, trying to explain to him (and perhaps also to herself) why she was breaking up their satisfactory arrangement. 'I . . .'

'Can't we talk about it inside? It's not a subject to be broadcast about Belgravia.'

She had let him into her flat and tried again.

'You see,' she had said at one moment, 'I realise that I've been using you. I like you enormously; I hope that we can be friends; but I have come to understand that I do not love you,' she had finished with difficulty.

'I never supposed that you did,' he had said, looking puzzled. 'I don't know that I love you, but why must that destroy everything? What if I want to go on being used?' Willow had shivered at that question.

'I know that it was convenient for us both . . .'

'Surely more than that?' Richard had said, making Willow feel so unsafe that she longed to take refuge in cold severity. Since she cared about him, she had not been able to do that.

'One of the things that made it all so easy was that unlike other women you never seemed to want to complicate it all with messy feelings,' Richard had said at last.

'I'm sorry, Willow.' Tom's deep voice brought her back to the present.

Willow shuddered as she thought of the full messiness of the feelings she was just beginning to recognise. They seemed much more real than the easy, uncommitted, unthreatening affair with Richard that had been her first essay in the world of passion.

'Was I looking very stern?' she asked, wondering what it was about Tom that had made her take such destructive action against Richard, who had never done her any harm and who had indeed given her much simple pleasure and a great deal of friendship in the years they had been semi-detached lovers.

12

'A little formidable,' he answered. 'But then you often do.' Willow knew that, of course, but however valuable the look was in the Civil Service it was not appropriate to Cressida Woodruffe.

'It wasn't you making me annoyed,' she said with deliberate gentleness. 'Why did you ask about Richard?' Tom smiled at her question, but he looked nervous, too.

'Because I should like very much to . . . ' He shook his dark head and put his hands on her shoulders. 'This is exceptionally difficult, and I cannot think of a way of saying it that is unthreatening enough not to frighten you off but not so coy as to irritate the pair of us. To hell with it!'

At that Willow smiled too, and Tom seemed to take some comfort from her amusement.

'I asked because I want to make love to you – not necessarily tonight and so you needn't look like that and prepare your speech of refusal – and I would not want to embarrass you by asking you to make love with me if you were involved with someone else. What happened between us on that one night was . . . No, never mind.' He took his hands away and picked up his glass again.

Trying to be as honest and sensible as he had been, Willow took a pull at her own drink while she decided what to say.

'Thank you, Tom,' she began.

'For nothing, Will,' he answered, smiling at her properly again.

'I can't deny that I have sometimes thought about that night too – or that it was because of you that I asked Richard . . . told Richard that I couldn't go on as we were. But I don't know . . .'

'It's all right,' he said quickly. 'I wasn't trying to demand anything now. I'll finish this and then be off.'

'There's no hurry, Tom,' she said. 'Let's talk about your murders. Much easier than the other thing.'

'Much,' he said, laughing openly. 'I wish I knew why I find you so irresistible. What more do you want to know about the murders?' Trying to disguise the emotions and sensations Tom aroused in her, Willow said:

'I was just wondering whether I couldn't perhaps help you.'

Worth raised an eyebrow.

'You told me in that restaurant that you're too busy with your new cases to trawl through these filed ones for enough similarities to persuade your superiors that they are connected – so why don't I do it? The book's finished and if I start the next one straight away I'll only make a mess of it,' she went on.

'But what about your interior decoration?' he asked, gesturing around the graceful, half-empty room.

'That won't take long,' said Willow. 'After all, Mrs Rusham will do all the actual organising and dealing with the workmen; I just have to choose the stuff. Do let me help, Tom. I'd really like to.' In her eagerness to do something for him, perhaps to make up for her inability to let him come as close to her as he clearly wanted, she put her right hand on his shoulder. 'Please, Tom. Grisly though the end of that last case was, I thoroughly enjoyed the detecting part.'

'Even though it led to the desecration of your home?' he asked. 'And presumably blew your cover at the department?'

'I'm not certain that it did blow my cover,' she said with a slight smile. 'It's hard to believe that the oaf who followed me here and wrecked the place said nothing to anyone about who I am, but no one has mentioned it to me.' She laughed. 'Perhaps their ideas about my pathetic spinsterhood are so firmly rooted that they can't stretch their stunted imaginations to believe I could be Cressida Woodruffe too.'

Worth looked at her seriously, almost as though he were trying to see past the elegant clothes, the cosmetics and the artfully tumbled hairstyle to the woman she pretended to be as Willow King.

'I'd never have thought make-up could make such a difference,' he said at last. Willow laughed.

'It does of course,' she said. 'And so do the clothes. But I actually think it's mainly the spectacles and the hair. Dragged back in those savage pins it makes my face look completely different. I once passed one of the typists reading a copy of one of my books which had a huge photograph of me on the back, and even stopped to talk to her to test it out. She hadn't a clue. People do tend to see what they expect.'

'Perhaps,' said Tom. 'And the desecration of all this? Are you prepared to risk that again?'

Willow was silent for a long time. At last she said:

'Yes. There's no reason to suppose it could happen again, but even if I am risking it I'd like to help. Couldn't you get me the files on your murders, so that I could do the trawling? I'm sure it wouldn't take long.'

'But what about the rest of your life – the Willow King half?' Tom said. Willow shrugged. He seemed to be determined that she should not have anything to do with his investigation but she was interested enough to protest.

'Obviously I'll still have to go to the department for the middle of each week, but isn't any help better than none?' she said, dropping the cajoling tone and sounding much more like her usual crisp self. 'After all, you needed my help last time. You weren't getting anywhere on your own.'

'You can be a bit of a monster, you know,' he said. 'And you know perfectly well that I can't possibly take police files and hand them out to stray civilians.' He stood up. 'Come on, Willow, be sensible. I must go now and leave you in peace.' He held out a square hand. Willow took it and allowed him to help her up off the sofa.

'It is nice that your palms are so reliably dry,' she said without thinking. Tom Worth roared with laughter, put an arm around her shoulders and planted a friendly kiss on her cheek. Willow hated being the butt of other people's laughter.

'What on earth is the matter with you?' she asked.

'Just that the only compliment you have ever paid me should be so clinical – and so – so unromantic. I find it hard to accept the fact that a woman like you spends half her time writing love stories. I've never met anyone less romantic. I can see that I'm going to have to read some of these books of yours. Good night, Willow. Thank you for this evening.'

'Thank you, Tom,' she said, relaxing again. 'You are exceedingly . . .'

'It's all right,' he said, quickly kissing her lips, 'I didn't mean that I wanted you to make me compliments. I'll be in touch. But if you want me for anything, you know where to ring me.'

He walked out of the room. At the front door, Willow caught him up.

'All I was going to say is that you are an extraordinarily good friend, and I am grateful – really very grateful – for your kindness. Do reconsider about the murders.'

'I'll think about it,' he said and was gone.

Willow shut the heavy front door behind him and slid the bolts and turned the various keys that she had had installed to satisfy her insurance company and her own fears. She could not help thinking about the differences between Tom Worth and Richard as she went to run herself a hot, deep bath.

Richard had always tended to sulk if she expressed any reluctance to go to bed with him or even to dine with him when he wanted to see her, and yet she knew that he had never posed as serious a threat to her detached and satisfactory life. She had succumbed to Tom only once and yet her feelings for him, however much she might sometimes try to deny them, were far stronger than all the affection she felt for Richard.

Determined to banish both the men from her mind, she poured fragrant oils into the hot water and carefully removed her clothes. The shoes she left where they fell for Mrs Rusham to clean, the dress she laid over a chair for Mrs Rusham to press or take to the cleaners as she considered necessary and the rest was flung into the laundry basket. Willow knew that the next time she saw the clothes they would be pristine and carefully hung or folded in the cupboards in her dressing room.

Lying back in the hot, scented water, she tried to remember the little Tom had told her about the murderer, at last allowing herself to laugh at her idiotic misunderstanding of his description of the man as a 'cereal killer'.

Chapter 2

*T*HE FOLLOWING morning, Willow left her alternative identity and her Belgravia flat long before the arrival of Mrs Rusham and set off for Clapham, where she spent the other part of her life. She was anonymously dressed in jeans and a simple black jacket; there was no makeup on her pale, bony face, and her red hair was dragged back into a rubber band. The plain leather shoulder bag she carried contained all the identification necessary for her Civil Service identity and there was nothing in it with the name of Cressida Woodruffe. All Cressida's credit cards were lying in the safe she had had installed at the back of one of her capacious wardrobes. Cressida's watch, too, had been carefully hidden. It would never do for Ms Willow King to be seen sporting a gold Cartier watch in the dusty offices of DOAP.

The expensive, cream-coloured streets of Belgravia were empty at that hour of the morning, and there was no one to witness the metamorphosis of rich Cressida Woodruffe into plain, hardworking Willow King, but she did not want to be surprised by any early colleagues when she eventually got to Clapham. Everyone at the Department of

Old Age Pensions believed that she spent every Thursday evening to Tuesday morning caring for an invalid elderly aunt.

Carrying a red nylon overnight bag, Willow took a bus across the river to Clapham and walked from the stop to her other flat. She let herself in at the street door and walked up the gritty stairs, wondering when she would ever be able to persuade the owners of the other flat to do their share of the hoovering of the common parts. Reaching her own front door, she undid the simple locks, dropped her bag on the scarred but sturdy oak table in the living room, and went to make herself a cup of instant coffee.

The cardboard packet of skimmed milk she had left in the small refrigerator the previous Thursday still smelled of milk rather than sour cheese and so she poured some into the pottery mug on top of the coffee granules and hot water. As she drank the resulting brew, she wrinkled her nose a little, disliking the taste and remembering with regret the wonderfully scented cappuccino that Mrs Rusham made for Cressida's breakfast in Chesham Place every morning. It always took Willow a little while to acclimatise herself when she got back to South London.

Wandering into the slightly damp bedroom to change out of her jeans into one of the inexpensive ready-made suits appropriate for Willow King, she suggested to herself that it might be the contrast between that weekly shock and the subsequent pleasure of returning to Cressida's self-indulgent luxury on Thursday evenings that kept her attached to her double life. Apart from that slightly masochistic reason she could not for the moment think of any other to subject herself to the rigours of her Clapham life.

Remembering the unseasonable heat of the previous day, she chose a beige linen-and-polyester suit from her wardrobe and found tights and shoes to match and a sharply ironed, white, cotton shirt. When she was dressed, she dragged the rubber band off her hair, wincing as it pulled several hairs out of the back of her neck, and brushed out the last of Cressida's curls. With the skill of long practice, she twisted the mass of hair into a neat, vertical roll and pinned it securely against the back of her head.

Even though she had been wreaking similar transformations ever since she had invented her *alter ego*, Willow was often surprised by the efficacy of her disguises. Stripped of cosmetics and revealed in all its angles by the severity of her chosen hairstyle, her face looked years older than it did when it wore Cressida's mascara and blusher and lipstick. Her eyelashes were naturally red, but paler than her hair, and without the definition of liner or mascara the eyes themselves looked washed out and rather small. Her nose seemed sharp and her lips dry. But when she smiled at herself in the glass, she could see the ghost of Cressida looking back at her.

Amused by her mixture of vanity and detachment, Willow stuffed her feet into her beige shoes with their 'man-made, composite' soles, collected her black plastic briefcase and set off for the glass tower that housed the headquarters of the Department of Old Age Pensions. There were a few other early starters waiting for a lift in the hall when she reached the building, but no one she knew particularly well and so she was spared the familiar kind questions about the health of her Aunt Agatha.

When she had first invented the mythical woman, she had revelled in inventing details of Aunt Agatha's life and her struggles with the local hospital, the social services, and the difficulties of life in a small Suffolk village, but over the last few months Willow had found herself less amused by her own joke and was even beginning to wonder whether it might not be time for Aunt Agatha to suffer a terminal illness.

As usual there were piles of paper in several wire baskets on the big desk in Willow's office, and she settled down at once to reading her way through the heaps, throwing some things away, marking others for one or other of her staff to deal with or send for filing. A few she put to one side for more careful consideration. When she had reached the bottom of the pile, she began to draft replies to some of the letters and minutes in answer to questions from the Permanent Secretary and the Minister's office.

At twenty-past nine she heard sounds of movement in her outer office and got up to greet her new typist, an intelligent nineteen-year-old called Marilyn, who got through her work at least three times faster than her predecessor had ever done.

'Good morning, Willow,' she said, turning from the curly coatstand where she was hanging her pale-grey coat. Her skin was pale-grey too, and her hair a dull blonde. She was fanatically neat in her dress as well as her work. Willow admired the neatness, the efficiency and the girl's lack of interest in office gossip, but she wished that she could like her too. There was no reason not to like her, Willow often told herself, but she could not do it. There was a machine-like quality in Marilyn's accomplishments, and the only emotion she had ever shown was pleasure in other people's failure and mistakes.

'Marilyn,' said Willow, making herself smile a little, 'when you've had time to settle down would you bring your notebook?'

'Yes, of course,' said the girl.

Before Willow had dictated more than three letters the red telephone on her desk rang. Irritated with the interruption, she gestured to Marilyn to answer it.

'Yes, yes,' said the girl after a moment. 'Yes, I'll tell her. Thank you.' She put the receiver down on the telephone with all her usual precision, cleared her throat delicately and looked at her chief. 'That was the Permanent Secretary's secretary, Willow. He would like to see you at a quarter to eleven this morning.'

'You might have found out whether that was convenient for me before you agreed on my behalf,' said Willow moderately, considering the unreasonable rage that seethed in her mind at her secretary's assumptions.

'Oh, but I knew you were,' answered Marilyn without discernible emotion or excuse in her voice. 'I always check your diary with Barbara last thing on Monday night.'

'I see,' said Willow, trying to admire the efficiency and ignore the impertinence. 'Well, we'd better get on.'

By twenty-to-eleven, she had dictated all the urgent letters and minutes and planned to deal with the PS as soon as she possibly could, see the rest of her staff and then continue drafting her part of the new White Paper. On her way out, she said something pleasant to Barbara, her Administration Trainee, who appeared to be working busily.

All ability to say anything pleasant to anybody disappeared as soon as she discovered what the Permanent Secretary wanted to tell her. She was often annoyed by his patronising bumbling, but on that particular morning he made her even angrier than usual. The recently appointed Establishments Officer had told her that she was to serve on a selection board for the next two weeks and she had protested about it, eventually insisting that her case should be taken to the Permanent Secretary. Unfortunately the PS had been infuriated that he was being bothered with so trivial a matter and had decided to side with the Establishments Officer.

'You must admit, Willow,' he said in a voice of exaggerated patience that grated on her nerves, 'that the mere fact that you are allowed to work part-time cannot excuse you from the onerous and tedious duties that your colleagues shoulder faithfully.'

'My reluctance has nothing to do with that, Permanent Secretary,' said Willow, sounding annoyingly patient herself, although she did not realise it, 'but with the White Paper. Of course I am willing to serve on selection boards;

22

it is merely that at this particular juncture, I am needed here.'

'I am afraid that you must let your superiors be the judge of that,' said the Permanent Secretary. There was plenty of synthetic kindness in his voice, but his pale, bloodshot eyes looked hopeful and Willow wondered, as she had often wondered before, whether he might be deliberately trying to provoke her.

'Does the Minister know what you're doing?' Willow asked abruptly.

'Despite her feminine desire to be involved with minutiae, Mrs Trouville is quite wise enough not to interfere with my running of this department,' he said through his teeth. Willow shook her head so vigorously that one of the hairpins slipped out of her hair. Furiously, she shoved it back so hard that one of the ends dug into her neck, making her eyes water slightly. She saw an interested expression cross the Permanent Secretary's face and realised that he might suspect her to be weeping. With a voice as cold as snow-buried metal, she said:

'I was not suggesting any such thing. But she is most anxious to ensure that the new legislation gets through during the life of this Parliament. If the White Paper is held up because of this board . . .'

'Important though you are, Willow, you are not the only member of this department to be involved in the new legislation. Mrs Trouville will not be disappointed. Now, I am afraid that I shall have to ask you to leave. I'm rather busy. Bob will give you any details you need of the Final Selection Board.'

'Thank you, Permanent Secretary,' said Willow, determined not to give the man the satisfaction of hearing her being rude to him.

By the end of the day she was asking herself bitterly why she continued to put up with the trials and tedium of her job at DOAP when she could be spending her entire time as Cressida Woodruffe, surrounded by every luxury, with enough money to work or not as she chose, and with no one in a position to give her orders or to question hers. But even as she let the question form in her mind, she controlled some of her feelings. Whatever she had thought that morning while she was still half in Cressida's life and however frustrating the day at DOAP had been, she knew perfectly well that there were several reasons why her double life suited her, just as she knew that to spend all her time as Cressida would eventually bore and stifle her. The contrast between her two characters was in itself a pleasure and she would be prepared to put up with a lot more than the Permanent Secretary's tiresomeness to keep it.

She walked wearily home through the dusty, rubbish-strewn streets of Clapham at seven o'clock, trying to decide whether to cook herself fish fingers or to heat up a frozen pizza for supper, and wishing that there were no dogs in London or at least that they left fewer heaps of excrement on the pavements. As she approached her flat, she saw that there was someone leaning against one of the pillars beside the front door. She recognised him at once and controlled her instinct to run towards him.

'Tom,' she said quietly when she was near enough for him to hear her. The leaning figure straightened up.

'Willow,' he said unsmiling, as though he were not sure of his welcome.

'Come on in,' she said. She felt a little wary of him, but the sanity and intelligence of his familiar face made a welcome change from the hated lineaments of the Permanent Secretary's and even the neat grey features of the efficient Marilyn. 'Are you all right?'

'I'm fine,' he answered, following her up the stairs to her flat. 'I've been thinking about the poisoner and – slightly against my better judgment and conscience – I've come to ask whether you still want to have a look at some of the reports.'

24

'Tom,' said Willow, turning to smile at him in spontaneous pleasure. He stopped on the step just below her and looked up into her face.

'Would you, Will?' he asked.

'I'd love to,' she said, turning back to unlock the door for them both. 'It's precisely what I need to keep me sane for the next couple of weeks. I've just heard that I've got to sit on a Fisbe of all exasperating things.'

'A what?'

'Final Selection Board, FSB, Fisbe,' said Willow, dropping her briefcase and gesturing to Tom to do the same. 'No Leapfrog here, but if you'd like some ordinary whisky I have some – or perhaps a glass of Bulgarian wine?'

'Any beer?' he said, amused by her complete transformation from the glamorous, rich creature with whom he had dined the previous day.

'Snob!' she said. 'Yes, I have some rather dull tinned beer, actually. It's in the fridge: help yourself. I'm going to have wine.'

When he came back into the living room, Willow had taken off the shapeless jacket of her suit to reveal the plain white cotton shirt, open at the neck. Remembering the elegant clothes and the impressive jewellery she had always worn when they dined together during her days as Cressida Woodruffe, he was amused all over again by her appearance.

'Let down your hair, Will,' he said, before he could censor himself.

'You said that once before,' she answered, making no move to take out the hairpins.

'I know,' he said, coming to sit beside her on the old sofa. 'And I hadn't meant to make any allusion to that time. You just look a lot more comfortable when your hair is loose. Go on.'

Shrugging, Willow pulled the pins out of her hair and shook it free. It was much more comfortable.

'I wouldn't want you to think . . . I always do unpin

it when I come home,' she said in a voice bristling with defensiveness.

'Good beer, this,' said Worth ignoring the little scene he had provoked. 'Now, I couldn't bring you the actual files about these murders, but I've made a précis of their contents. You could probably find out a bit more from the local newspaper reports; and if you've any specific questions, let me know and I'll see if there's anything useful in the files.'

'Thank you, Tom,' said Willow, trying to put enough warmth into her voice to show him that she was as grateful for his refusal to pursue the question of her hair as for the information about the murders. 'I'll do what I can for you. I'd like to help you give one in the eye to those wretches – "feminine intuition" indeed!'

'It's not so much for that, Will,' said Tom seriously, 'as to stop whoever is doing this before anyone else gets killed.'

'But there's something else, isn't there?' she said, staring at him. 'You look . . . yes, shifty, Tom. What is really bothering you so much about this case?'

'Isn't the thought of a murderer on the loose enough?'

Willow shook her red head and then had to brush a strand of hair out of her eyes.

'One of the prime movers in the campaign to stop me "wasting time" trying to find a connection between the cases has a personal connection to Titchmell,' he said at last. His voice dragged as though he were fighting a deep reluctance to tell her anything about it.

'His father, who was once a Chief Constable, was Simon Titchmell's godfather,' he said.

'That doesn't sound too bad. Couldn't it be simply coincidence?' asked Willow, trying to understand why he was so worried.

'Possibly. And he is ferociously keen on time-and-motion studies and value for money. And he dislikes me. But his determination to end the investigation into

26

his father's godson's murder strikes me as . . . well, it leaves me uncomfortable.'

'Yes,' said Willow, her novelist's imagination flashing possible plots across her mind like trailers across a giant cinema screen. 'I can see that it might. What's his name, your policeman?'

Tom stood up, towering over Willow and her sofa. She quickly got up herself.

'Bodmin,' he said. 'Commander James Bodmin. He's usually so efficient . . . Never mind that now. I must go.'

'Must you?' she asked.

'I think I'd better,' he said, 'uninvited as I was this evening. Besides, I've got work to do before tomorrow. Good night.'

'Good night, Tom,' said Willow putting out a hand. He gripped it for a moment, kissed her calmly and walked away.

Willow was left to her dingy flat, the frozen pizza, her briefcase full of work, and her difficult acknowledgment that she minded his going.

Pulling herself together with an effort, she cooked and ate her pizza, drank another glass of wine and then turned to the dark-red manilla folder that Tom had left for her. Opening it, she saw a pile of sheets of lined paper covered in the neatest, blackest, most elegant handwriting she had ever encountered.

It was strange, she thought, but she had never seen his writing before. All their arrangements to meet had been made by telephone. If anyone had asked her what she expected it to be like, she would have unhesitatingly said 'schoolboyish, like the writing of someone who doesn't put much on paper and isn't very interested'; yet she was confronted by a hand infinitely more sophisticated and attractive than her own. It gave her a most peculiar sense of disadvantage and stopped her actually reading what he had written for at least five minutes.

When she did eventually make herself concentrate on the content of his notes, she became more and more absorbed in them. By the time she had read the last page, she could understand both why Tom had believed that there must be a connection between the killings, and why some of his superiors had been just as certain that there could not.

As Worth had told her, the victims were quite different from each other, lived in quite different parts of the country, and had no apparent connection between them at all. The first was a sixty-five-year-old spinster, Edith Fernside, who had been living in sheltered housing in Newcastle. Willow saw with a slight chill in her mind that Miss Fernside's address had been only streets away from the red-brick house where she herself had been brought up. She had never been back to Newcastle since the death of her parents some years before and she had hoped never to go there again or even think about it. There had been no actual cruelty or conscious deprivation in her childhood, but it had been bleak enough for her to want to forget it.

According to Tom's notes, Miss Fernside had retired to Newcastle after working as matron in a famous girls' school in Berkshire. She suffered from a weak heart, which was presumably why she had chosen to live in a 'retirement complex' with a warden on call.

'Most doctors,' Tom had written, 'would simply have certified the death as having been caused by cardiac arrest and left it at that, but Miss F. was on the list of a particularly bright – and conscientious – young GP. The symptoms were thought to have arisen very suddenly. She appears to have fainted before the warden could reach her. There had been some vomiting and diarrhoea, but she had lost consciousness fast and her heart had stopped beating before the doctor could get to the house. He noticed various oddities about her condition and refused to sign the death certificate.

'Post-mortem findings included the fact that her blood was a peculiarly dark colour and more liquid than it should have been. There were a few hyperaemic points (excessive amounts of blood in organs) in the mucous membrane of the stomach, intestines and right ventricle of the heart. The GP told the police of his suspicions and with the police surgeon pursued an investigation into every cup and glass in the house for signs of poison. They found a trace of digitalis in the glass from which she had drunk her nightly tot of sloe gin, tested the bottle and discovered an enormous quantity of digitalis in it. They are cumulative poisons and so although each dose in itself would have done her no harm, a week or two of drinking the contaminated stuff killed her.'

Willow looked up from the report, as impressed by the GP as Tom had clearly been, but with other, less comfortable feelings worrying her. To live alone had never struck her as either unpleasant or odd; indeed, from her small involvement with other people, it had seemed infinitely more sensible to live by herself. But the thought of dying alone at sixty-five, after a solitary drink of sloe gin, because some warden could not answer her distress signal quickly enough, was unpleasant.

'But still,' said Willow aloud, searching a rational way to calm herself, 'at least the warden would have been less miserable at what he found than if he had been any child or spouse or lover or friend of Miss Fernside's.'

It was clear from Tom's account of the next deaths that living with a lover was no protection, and Willow read it with care.

Simon Titchmell, a successful architect of 35, and his girlfriend Annabel Wilna, a designer of fashionable gold jewellery, had died on 25 February from eating muesli that had been adulterated with dried and powdered aconite root. The two of them had not known each other long and were not living together although they often spent nights in each other's houses. According to their friends they shared an exemplary devotion and were expected to marry or at least move into a single house. They had apparently had no real enemies and certainly no reason to form any kind of suicide pact. They owed no more money than their large mortgages and monthly credit-card bills; both of them had better than average career prospects and high incomes for their ages. No one could imagine how the aconite had got into Titchmell's breakfast cereal unless either some lunatic had put it in during the packaging or storage of the cereal, as various people had put ground glass and pieces of metal in babyfood a year or two earlier, or the victims had done it themselves.

Neither had come to the attention of the police except after a burglary at the Fulham house two weeks before the murder, when some of Titchmell's cufflinks (made by Ms Wilna) had been stolen, together with a CD player, the video and – of all things – the electric toaster. The junior police officers who had interviewed them had reported later that both Titchmell and Wilna were intelligent, sensible and thoroughly approving of the police. It was thought unlikely by PC Leathwaite that they would have tried to drug themselves with anything, let alone a deadly poison.

Clearly, thought Willow, PC Leathwaite had not been believed. Reaching for a notebook, she scribbled herself a note to remind her to ask Tom Worth whether she could meet PC Leathwaite.

Those of Titchmell's clients who had been interviewed by the police reported that he was an excellent architect, very sensitive to the needs of people living in beautiful seventeenth-century houses (in the restoration of which he specialised), and at least three of them claimed him as a friend. Their names, addresses and occupations suggested that Titchmell had chosen his speciality wisely or at least profitably.

The third victim was a 40-year-old divorced actress called Claire Ullathorne. She had died on 15 March at home in Islington. There was evidence in the flat that she had been violently sick and suffered from diarrhoea. The post-mortem revealed that the blood was thick, dark and cherry-red in colour; there was also hyperaemia of the brain and evidence of gastritis. Colchicine poisoning was ultimately diagnosed.

The post-mortem examination also showed that she had borne a child and that at some stage, probably childhood, she had broken her left arm. It provided no evidence of other illness or trauma except for some very slight inflammation of the hip joints and lower spine. On enquiry, her GP reported that Ullathorne had never sought help for the arthritis. Since she regularly visited the surgery to attend the Well-Woman clinic and had been twice for innoculations before going to Egypt and India on holiday, the doctor assumed therefore that the pain was so slight as to be discounted.

The police view was that Ullathorne had committed suicide having recently failed to get a particularly good part in a television series for which she had been considered. Her friends had refused to believe that she had ever been suicidal and pointed out that with her excellent divorce settlement she had no financial worries and did not actually need to work. She had multifarious interests and had shown no sign of depression.

Willow turned over that sheet to find a note addressed to herself.

'These cases seem to have too many similarities to ignore, despite the differences in the victims' backgrounds. Do you think I'm a fantasist, wasting time – mine and yours – Willow? If you do, bung this lot on a fire somewhere, but don't leave it around for other people to read, please.'

The note of uncertainty made her smile a little. Tom rarely betrayed his tendency to self-doubt, but when he did, the contrast between it and his competence, physical strength and considerable powers of sexual attraction made her feel dangerously protective of him. For years she had counted it as a blessing that she was dependent on no one for anything and no one depended on her except in her official capacity. She had had no practice in feeling protective and did not know what to do with the emotion. Astringently reminding herself that no one who had served with distinction in the SAS for two years – as Tom had done before he eccentrically left the army for the Metropolitan Police – could have any need of protection from someone like herself, Willow read through all nine pages of his notes again.

Then she went into her bedroom to pick up the telephone. Dialling his number, she remembered that he said he would have to work for the rest of the evening and almost put the receiver down again before he could answer. When he did she immediately apologised for disturbing his work and then said:

'I don't think you're mad, Tom. Like you, I find it hard to believe that four people should all commit suicide or kill themselves by accident with plant poisons in such a short time. Surely that's too much of a coincidence?'

'Well, I think so. Cases of poison – accidental and homicidal – do pop up all the time – of course they do, but not as many as that,' said Tom. 'I'm relieved you agree, Willow. I've a certain respect for your brains, you know. Thank you for ringing.'

'Not at all, Tom. Why won't they let you investigate?'

'Because there's not enough evidence to prove any kind of link on which to base any kind of sensible investigation. It is unlikely to be cost-effective.'

'I see. Well, good night,' said Willow, determined to be the first to put down her receiver to give herself the illusion that she was still independent of her feelings for him. Staring down at the telephone, she smiled. Tom's cavalier attitude to her intellectual gifts pleased her, because he was the first person who really seemed to want her for something else as well as her brains. For too many years she had been so accustomed to thinking of herself and being thought of only in terms of her intellect that it was a new pleasure to be liked – apparently – for herself, even though she was still not altogether certain what that self was.

Chapter 3

THE CLATTERING of her alarm clock woke Willow out of a heavy sleep the following morning a little before seven. She lay for a few moments, letting her mind pull itself out of the swamp of sleep in its own time. The polyester-and-cotton sheet had become wrinkled in the night and she was lying uncomfortably across the folds. Sitting up, she swung her long legs out from under the duvet and padded to the bathroom. While the chipped chrome taps dribbled water into the yellowed enamel bath, she went to switch on the kettle and the iron. By the time the bath was full, she had ironed that day's shirt and made a mug of instant coffee, which she took to drink in the bath.

The usual morning routine was disrupted when she caught sight of Tom Worth's folder on the table as she was collecting the various papers she had brought home from the office the previous evening. After she had telephoned him, she had had to put the file on one side and concentrate on her work, but it was too tantalising to ignore again and she picked it up to read Tom's notes once more.

When she had read the few connecting facts again, she secreted the file under her mattress in case the flat was burgled while she was out and hurried to her office, at least half an hour later than usual.

Throughout that day she kept finding herself distracted from the work she had to do by thoughts about the murders, about the kind of person who might have gone around the country putting poison into other people's food and drink, and about Tom's vague but uncomfortable suspicions of his superior. So preoccupied was she that Barbara had to knock twice before Willow even heard her at the door.

'Come in, Barbara,' she said as soon as the girl opened it. 'Have you finished those drafts?'

'Not yet, Willow. I'm just waiting for some statistics from John; but it won't be long now. I've just heard about the board next week. Why are they making you do it? I always thought the Civil Servant on FSBs was a Principal. He was when I came before the board.'

'That is usually the case,' said Willow coolly. She thought that Barbara, who undoubtedly expected early promotion, would probably have enjoyed taking her place on a board as a change from the hard work of the office. 'But this is a board for Direct-Entry Principals and so they need an Assistant Secretary.'

'But how are you going to manage if it really takes up the whole of Tuesday, Wednesday and Thursday?'

Willow shrugged. 'I shall just have to come in before and after it each day and leave you piles of stuff to distribute. Will you be all right, Barbara?'

'Yes, I think so. If not, I'll leave large pleas for help all over your desk,' said Barbara cheerfully.

'Or force the P . . .' Willow stopped herself in mid-sentence. Whatever she thought about the Permanent Secretary, it would be grossly unsuitable to complain about him to the junior staff. 'Never mind. I have great confidence in you, Barbara.' The black-haired Scottish girl beamed.

'Really?' she said. 'I'm glad, because my last assessment

in this job is just about to crop up, isn't it?'

Willow wished that she could raise a single eyebrow as Tom Worth had done to her, so that she could express her disapproval of Barbara's bouncy comment. Then she reminded herself that the girl had in fact proved to be one of the best trainees Willow had ever had, and that there would soon be a new one to be taught her particular ways and persuaded to leave office politics alone and office gossip too.

'I expect it is,' she said more kindly. 'Don't worry too much about it.'

Barbara's expression of pleased surprise made Willow realise how sparing she had been with her compliments, but she reassured herself with the fact that her staff worked harder and more loyally than many of her peers' even without compliments. When she and Barbara had discussed the day's work, Willow said:

'By the way, Barbara, I have to find out about a woman who died recently in Newcastle. Could you put through a request for a trace? I need to know all her employers. Shouldn't be too difficult, because she died only about five or six years after retirement. She died two months ago. The file must be reasonably accessible. Her name was Edith Fernside. Can you do that for me?'

'Certainly, but why do you need to know?' asked Barbara, quite reasonably under the circumstances. Nothing in the work she did with Willow implied a need for any detailed information about individuals. They were concerned only with the policy of pension payments. Willow raised both eyebrows and tried – successfully – to make her green eyes look frosty. Barbara blushed and hastily departed.

Feeling mildly guilty and thinking that her growing friendship with Tom Worth was making her dangerously introspective and absurdly inclined to question the certainties that had always made her life bearable, Willow tried to banish both him and his murders from her mind.

She was determined to investigate all the DOAP problems that would need solving before she was rid of the tiresome selection board and able to get back into her normal working routine.

As soon as she reached her flat that evening, she retrieved Tom's file from under her mattress, found an A4 pad of plain paper and black and red felt pens. With a glass of the previous day's bottle of wine to assist her she started to jot down in black ink all the things she wanted to know about the victims.

When her list was as complete as she could make it she began to annotate it in red with suggestions as to how she might find the answers to her questions. She was still hunched over her lists when the chiming clock in the flat downstairs tinkled out ten strokes. Dropping the felt-tipped pen, Willow put both hands round the back of her neck and stretched against the stiffness in her shoulders and spine.

The wine glass had been empty for some time and it dawned on her that she was both hungry and thirsty. The cardboard boxes of fish fingers and pizzas and plastic sacks of vegetables in her little freezer looked unappetising when she opened its insulated door, and for once she rebelled against her self-imposed frugality.

There was a rather good French restaurant only about fifty yards from her front door and although she had no desire to sit alone at one of its white-clothed, flower-decked tables, the thought of its delectable cooking made saliva rush into her dry mouth. She found the restaurant's telephone number in the book, picked up the receiver and dialled. When someone in the restaurant answered, Willow asked whether they would be prepared to deliver a meal to her flat. Perhaps because it was a slack night, or perhaps because they genuinely wanted to provide an efficient and customer-friendly service, the restaurant undertook to supply three courses from its *table d'hôte* within twenty minutes.

Determined not to waste those minutes, Willow started to dial Richard Crescent's number. Half-way through, she stopped. It seemed a little unfair to badger him for information after she had ended their affair. On the other hand, he was the only person she knew well who moved in the kind of circles about which she wanted information. Richard was a successful merchant banker and, apart from Willow, his friends all seemed to be rich, ex-public school and fairly coventional. Reminding herself that she had always wanted – and told Richard she wanted – them to remain friends, Willow redialled the number.

'Richard Crescent,' said the voice that came on the line when the ringing stopped.

'Richard,' she said mellifluously. 'It's Willow here. How are you?'

'I'm all right. But what on earth's happened to you?'

'Nothing. Why?' she said, disconcerted that he should have taken the initiative in the conversation.

'Never, ever – even when we were still, you know – have you telephoned me on a Willow King day. What's up?' said Richard with some acerbity in his usually pleasant voice.

'No, I suppose not,' conceded Willow. 'My routines seem to be slipping a bit. Trouble in the office, I'm afraid. But Richard, I wanted some help.'

'What can I do?' he asked. Considering their last meeting, Willow wondered whether the question might have been intended to be sarcastic, but she remembered Richard's basic good nature and took it at its face value.

'I need to know about a man who died recently, called Simon Titchmell. He was an architect and from the little I know of his clients and his background, he sounds like someone you might have come across,' she said.

'I've always known his sister better,' said Richard, confirming Willow's assumption that he would have known someone connected with the man. 'But why on earth does DOAP want to know about Titchmell? And why can't they find out for themselves?'

'DOAP?' repeated Willow sounding almost stupid. 'What are you talking about, Richard?'

'You said you had trouble in the office. Willow, are you all right. You don't sound at all like yourself.'

'I'm perfectly well,' she said hurriedly, hating the thought that something might be destroying the self-sufficiency and rationality that had helped her survive content for 39 years in a world that had always seemed alien and sometimes actually hostile. 'There is trouble at the office, but this is something different. Can we meet, Richard?'

'So that I can tell you about Titchmell? I thought the reason we stopped seeing each other was because you thought that you were using me and couldn't bear it.' There was no doubt about the hostility in his voice as he said that.

'This is different,' said Willow. 'This is the kind of request for help that any old friend might make. Besides,' she added honestly, 'I've missed you. It would be pleasant to have a meal together. What about it?'

'Have you?' said Richard and there was an echo of his old pleading in the words. 'Then let's meet. There's been a big hole in my life, Willow, and I'm prepared to forego dignity to fill it. Tomorrow's your first Cressida day of the week: what about dinner at Belgrave's as in the old days?'

'Why not?' she said, wondering whether the things she had said could have constituted 'leading him on' and whether to be fair she ought to tell him that much as she wanted to see him she still did not want to go to bed with him. But that would have been presumptuous, and she did not believe it decent to do or say the things that in other people made her spit with rage, and so she said no more.

Her dinner arrived soon after she and Richard had said 'good night' to each other, and, having paid for it and tipped the young waitress who had brought it to the flat, Willow settled down at her sturdy oak table to a meal that was almost as good as the one she expected to share with Richard the following night.

On Thursday evening, after a tedious and frustrating day at DOAP, she arrived late and harrassed at the hairdresser she had patronised ever since her first book had been published. Struggling to find her way into the pink cotton overall that the receptionist was holding out to her, Willow saw the owner of the salon coming towards her with a most reproachful expression on his sharp-featured, swarthy face.

'I know, I know,' said Willow more sharply than she usually spoke in the scented pink-and-green-and-silver bower over which he presided. 'I'm very late, Gino. I'm sorry. I couldn't get away before. Do your best, will you?'

'But of course, Miss Woodruffe,' he said, shrugging and pouting as he fingered a strand of her dirty red hair. 'Don't I always?'

Willow smiled for the first time in hours.

'Yes, Gino, and I'm grateful. It feels horrible. Is there someone free to wash it?'

The Italian gestured to one of his apprentices who led Willow away like a prize heifer garlanded with pink towels to the basin, where he proceeded to batter her stiff neck against the white porcelain edge of the basin and pull her hair as he tried to untangle it with his fingers and a powerful jet of over-hot water. Her eyes were watering slightly as she was eventually released from the minor torture and she looked curiously at the apprentice.

'You must be new,' she said.

He nodded. Willow left him to go and sit in Gino's chair awaiting his ministrations. His experienced touch on her head and neck was far more gentle than his young assistant's and by the time he had finished cutting, drying and tweaking Willow's hair, she felt soothed. Looking round the gleaming room, she saw that there was only one other customer left and that all the hair clippings had been laboriously swept from around her feet.

'Thank you, Gino,' she said. 'I'm sorry I've held you up.'

'No problem, Miss Woodruffe,' he said. 'For me, that is. But the manicurist has had to go home. Shall I make another appointment for you tomorrow?'

Willow shook her newly sleek head.

'No. My nails can stay unpainted until next Thursday. It won't kill me. Thanks, Gino.'

He escorted her to the front door himself and carefully helped her out of the floating pink garment and into her own jacket. She reflected with amusement on the effect of cossetting and its price. An hour of Gino's time had wrought the transformation between Willow's almost constant exasperation and impatience and Cressida's easier-going attitude to her luxurious life; and all for the cost of an admittedly expensive *coiffure*.

Freed for the moment of Willow's puritanical burdens, she walked slowly home through the warm April evening, noticing the burgeoning leaves on the plane trees of Sloane Square and looking forward to the summer.

Her Chesham Place flat seemed to welcome her as she arrived and even as she noticed the sentimentality of her pleasure she revelled in it. Part of the ritual of her weekly transformation was to have a bath as soon as she reached the flat and so she went quickly to the yellow-and-white bathroom. It was extravagantly large, having been converted from what would otherwise have been the spare bedroom, and luxuriously appointed.

The water gushed out of the brass taps and Willow poured in an unnecessarily large quantity of Chanel No.19 bath oil, breathing voluptuously as the fragrant steam reached her nostrils. Mrs Rusham had laid four clean, thick white towels on the heated rack in front of the old chimney breast and put out new bars of soap in the niche beside the taps and on the basin. A simple bowl of early yellow roses stood on the windowsill, and there were new novels lying on the table by the side of the bath.

Sighing in relief and delight, Willow stripped off her clothes and, wrapped in a pale-yellow towelling dressing gown two sizes too big for her, went to fetch a glass of sherry. Returning to the bathroom, she put the glass down on the table with the books, shed her dressing gown and sank into the bath. Lying there, sipping her sherry and feeling the water gradually heating up her long, thin body, she looked around the pretty room and wondered whether it would be too absurdly extravagant to have the old chimney opened up again so that she could have a proper fire in the bathroom. She was never cold in it because there was a huge radiator as well as the heated towel rail, but there was something about actual flames in a good grate under a well carved white marble chimneypiece that added the final touch to any room.

Half an hour later, so relaxed that she had forgotten her sherry and had not even picked up either of the books, she heard the front door bell buzz. Reaching out with her left hand, she found the button of the intercom and pushed it.

'Willow? It's Richard.'

'Heavens I'm late,' she said. 'Sorry, Richard, come on up.' Having pressed the button that would release the electronic lock of the front door, Willow heaved herself out of the bath, wrapped herself up in the yellow dressing gown again and went out into the hall. She noticed that she was leaving foamy damp marks on the bathroom carpet and the hall parquet, but knew that Mrs Rusham would do whatever had to be done to get the marks out in due course and refused to worry about them.

'Richard,' she said opening the door to his knock. 'So sorry to be like this. I was held up at DOAP. Come in.' He leaned down towards her and she, thinking it unnecessarily churlish to spurn his gesture, reached upwards so that their cheeks touched.

He was a good six inches taller than she, but something about him, some inner disengagement perhaps, made his size far less obtrusive than Tom Worth's. Richard gave no

42

impression of physical power, despite his reputed prowess on the squash court and cricket pitch. As always he was well dressed in an impeccably cut, conventional dark-grey worsted suit, a shirt of widely spaced claret stripes on white, an Hermes silk tie and a pair of heavy gold cufflinks.

His eyes were an indeterminate, very English mixture of green and grey and blue, and his thick hair was the dull brown of a sparrow's breast. His long face was clean shaven and usually held an expression of vague amiability that disguised his formidable intelligence. Willow had known him look tender, ecstatic, occasionally sulky and sometimes wildly amused, but it was when he was half smiling that he looked most familiar to her. All in all, he looked what he was: a kind, clever, successful, not particularly forceful or imaginative child of a conventional southern English family with a profitable job in the City.

'You look glorious,' he said. 'I've never seen you in that colour before. It suits you – yellow.'

'Haven't you?' she said, looking down at the dressing gown in some surprise. 'Yes, my dressing gowns always used to be white. I suppose Mrs Rusham must have bought this one to match the bathroom wallpaper. Never mind. Will you help yourself to a drink while I go and dress?'

Richard obediently walked in the opposite direction from her bedroom. Willow was relieved by his docility and annoyed with herself for the unfair provocation of opening the door to him clad only in a dressing gown. She went quickly to put on a very unrevealing, though quite flattering, dark-blue silk dress. A little makeup on her face anchored the pinkness produced by the hot bathwater and plenty of mascara gave her eyes their Cressida-like allure instead of Willow's discomforting pallor. The finishing touch was provided by an antique diamond brooch that she pinned at the apex of her modest neckline.

'My God but you're glamorous,' said Richard when she went into the drawing room. 'Sorry. I'd just forgotten the extent of it. New brooch? Have I been supplanted?'

Her glossy lips tightening a little at his assumptions, Willow poured herself another small glass of sherry.

'Yes, it is a new brooch. I bought it in the Burlington Arcade as a present to myself when I finished *Simon's Simples* and the American publisher doubled the last advance,' she said, ignoring his last question.

'Have I been supplanted?' Richard repeated obviously, determined not to let her get away with it.

'No, Richard,' she said, looking frankly at him. 'There is another man whom I see sometimes, but he and I do not have the same relationship that you and I had. No one else has that. Must we do this? Can't we be civilised? You like overt emotion as little as I, even when it's your own,' she added.

Too intelligent to dismiss that reminder as malicious, Richard shrugged, but when he next spoke, his voice and his yearning eyes were under control again.

'I've booked the table for nine o'clock. Is that all right for you, or would you rather have a bit more time?'

'No, thank you, Richard. That's fine,' she said. 'Shall we go?'

They were greeted in the dark cosy restaurant with slightly nauseating cries of welcome, recognition and relief and shown to the 'table you always used to have'. When the elaborate menus were presented, Willow made up her mind to choose something she had never eaten before in order to stop the nostalgia before it choked her, and before it reinforced Richard's obvious determination to retrieve their old relationship. Eventually she chose sorrel soup and grilled lobster.

When Richard had ordered their food and chosen the wine, without any reference to Willow, he turned back to face her.

'If I'm not to talk about the past or ask you questions about the present, what about your asking me about Titchmell?' he said.

44

'Thank you, Richard,' said Willow, once more accepting the sense of his words rather than his tone. 'I suppose I want to know everything about him. Why don't you just talk and if I have a specific question, I'll interrupt you.'

'As you perfectly well know, I hate being interrupted,' he said, with the first gleam of real humour he had shown that evening. 'But I'll do my best to put up with it.' He picked up a handful of the almost unbelievably delicious, warm, salted nuts that had been put between them in a small glass dish.

'The family is middlingly well-off and based in Sussex, Waltrincham, I think. Papa was in the wine trade – but at the rather smart end of it. Simon qualified as an architect some time ago and started out, I think, to work in one of the big practices doing mainly local government work. He went solo about five years ago, since when he'd forsaken tower blocks for slightly precious restorations of derelict country houses. The property disaster and mortgage-interest rises cast a bit of a damper on his practice, but most of his clients were rich enough not to mind too much.'

'Quite successful, then?' suggested Willow.

'Oh yes. Caroline always talks – or rather talked – of him as her "rich big brother".'

'And what is she?' asked Willow, picking three nuts for herself.

'Patent agent. Probably going to be a lot richer than most architects in the end, but it takes a bit of time,' said Richard, smiling. Something in his smile made Willow wonder whether Caroline could have supplanted her in Richard's life, but she could hardly ask directly.

'How do you know them?' she asked instead.

'Oh, I met her around. As one does. I can't actually remember where. It was several years ago. I like her.' He grinned suddenly. 'I think you would, too. She's very down-to-earth, and doesn't let anyone get away with anything. A bit like you, now I come to think of it.' Richard looked across the crisp white damask cloth to where Willow was picking some more nuts from the dish.

'You haven't painted your nails,' he said suddenly.

'No. I just couldn't get away from the office in time to get them done and I'm incapable of doing it myself,' said Willow, looking up at him. 'The sister sounds interesting,' she added, suddenly seeing a way to useful information. 'I'd love to meet her. Why don't you have a dinner party, Richard? You must owe lots of people: you're always dining out.'

'Dinner party? I don't give dinner parties,' he protested. 'Come on, Willow, I have neither the time nor the talents for that sort of thing. And I don't owe anyone. *I* always pay my debts.'

His emphasis on the pronoun made Willow smile before it occurred to her that he might mean that she still owed him a debt.

The *sommelier* appeared and went through his ritual of presenting the corked bottle to Richard for his inspection of the label, opening it, cleaning some invisible residue from the neck and pouring an inch into Richard's glass. Richard, grasping the glass by its foot, held it up to the light for a moment, swirled the wine round, sniffed and eventually took a sip. After a moment's judicious thought, as he moved the wine around his mouth like mouthwash, he nodded at the wine waiter, who sighed as though in relief and poured a glassful for Willow.

Sometimes the mutually-massaging performance amused her; sometimes she thought it entirely idiotic. If there had been something wrong with the wine, the smell alone would have given it away to all three of them as soon as any had been poured and she very much doubted whether Richard knew the taste of the wine he had chosen well enough to detect any fraud. Even if he had, she could not believe that he would be able to conquer his disinclination to complain.

'I wasn't suggesting you were being mean, Richard,' she said when the *sommelier* had left them again. 'But do think about it. I'd like to meet her. I'd lend you Mrs Rusham, Richard. She's been pining for you these last four months, and she'd do all the shopping, cooking, flowers. Come on. It would be good for you. I'll even pay for the dinner and then there won't be any debts between us.'

As she said that Richard's pleasant face changed until he looked really angry.

'Why are you so obsessed with money at the moment?' he demanded, showing her a side of his character she had never encountered before.

'I'm not,' she said, making certain that she did not sound defensive. 'But you've been so emphatic about paying your debts: I didn't want to be any less punctilious.'

Richard fiddled with the salt cellar for a moment and then looked up at her with accusing eyes.

'There are other debts, though, Willow: more important than monetary ones.'

Willow smiled in order to relax her facial muscles and so prevent her voice from coming out harsh.

'I know that,' she said. 'It was recognising it that told me I had to stop what I was doing to you. Don't let's talk about all that now. What about having a dinner party?'

'Well I suppose . . . ' Richard was beginning when their first courses arrived. Willow watched him slurping up the first of his oysters and put her spoon into the frothy green soup she had chosen to draw a line between all the dinners they had shared in the past. It was quite pleasant, if a little sharper than she would have liked.

'You're making a mistake,' said Richard, enthusiastically licking his fingers. 'These are wonderful and we're not likely to get many more until the autumn.'

'What about it? I'm sure Mrs Rusham could get you oysters just as good as those,' said Willow cajolingly.

'I've never been able to resist you when you were determined on anything,' said Richard, picking up another

of the thick grey shells, squeezing lemon juice on to the
quivering blob it contained and tipping it into his mouth.
'I might as well give in gracefully. When am I to have this
dinner party?'

'As soon as possible,' said Willow. 'Next week? Thursday or Friday, perhaps?'

'All right,' said Richard amenable at last, 'but in return
I want you to tell me what this is all about.' He sucked up
another oyster and drained the liquid its shell contained
straight into his mouth. When he had dropped the shell
on his plate, he looked at her. She was relieved to see that
there was a smile back in his greyish eyes.

'I can't do that, I'm afraid,' said Willow, deciding that she
had eaten enough soup to last her for some time. She put
down her spoon.

'You're not playing your old game, are you? Racing that
policeman to the solution of some mystery? Presumably
he can't work out who caused Titchmell's death and you
. . . ' He paused, but Willow was far too experienced to
be rushed into speech by someone else's silence. She only
smiled, wondering whether her mouth looked as much like
the Mona Lisa's as it felt.

'Well in that case, I can see that I shall just have to help
you out,' said Richard with a self-satisfied smile. 'You
wouldn't have got anywhere last time without me.'

Remembering that she had said something very similar
to Tom Worth, Willow decided to allow Richard his
triumph and laughed with him.

Chapter 4

*E*ATING ONE of Mrs Rusham's best breakfasts the following morning, Willow ran through her list of questions
to ask about the four victims and thought about the people
who might be able to answer some of them. She decided
that if she were to telephone them to put in her various
requests for information, she could then reasonably ignore
the investigation for the rest of the day and go shopping.
There was to be a sale of fine English furniture at Christie's
the following week and she would be able to view the lots
any time that day.

She had just finished eating when Mrs Rusham came in
with the newspapers and a second cup of coffee.

'Thank you, Mrs Rusham,' said Willow, looking up.
'That was perfect. You really are a splendid cook.'

'I'm glad you think so, Miss Woodruffe,' said Mrs
Rusham. For some reason Willow had never understood,
her housekeeper had always treated her with cool formality although she had shown Richard an almost confiding
devotion, and her severe features lightened into a real
smile as Willow told her about Richard's plans for a dinner
party.

'And since he has very little time and not a lot of expertise, he wondered whether you would be prepared to help him out,' said Willow at last.

'Well of course, Miss Woodruffe,' said Mrs Rusham happily. 'It's always a pleasure to do anything for Mr Lawrence-Crescent.'

'Splendid,' said Willow, wondering what Richard had ever actually done to arouse the affection she could see shining in her employee's usually dull brown eyes. 'Why don't you ring him up at his office – here's the number – some time this morning and sort it all out with him?'

Willow would not have been surprised if pressure of work had made Richard quite forget his promise to entice the patent agent to dinner, and a little gentle reminder from the besotted Mrs Rusham would do no harm. The housekeeper agreed and asked whether Willow would be lunching at the flat.

'Yes, I think I probably will,' she said. 'But don't do anything very elaborate. I ate enormously with Mr Crescent last night.'

'Very good, Miss Woodruffe,' said Mrs Rusham formally and departed for her immaculate kitchen, carrying the egg-smeared Minton plate with her.

Willow leaned back in her chair, picking up her coffee cup in one hand and *The Times* in the other. When she had read the home news, the letters and the 'Friday page', she put the newspaper down and instead leafed through the *Daily Mercury*. Sensational, badly written and smudgily printed, it was not a newspaper she had ever read until she had met one of the journalists who worked on its diary section during the course of her investigation into the murder of the Minister. Willow had felt rather bad about having cheated information out of Jane Cleverholme, the journalist, and as a sop to her conscience had taken the paper ever since. Willow rarely read much of it, but was occasionally entertained by the different ways it reported the same items she had read in *The Times*.

That Friday the *Daily Mercury* had its usual complement of death, disaster, failure, petty malice and sex. Willow dropped it fastidiously into the wastepaper basket, as she usually did, and thought of an excuse to telephone Jane Cleverholme.

When she answered, Willow announced herself, adding:

'I've just been reading the *Mercury* and wondering all over again why on earth you . . .'

'Don't say it,' said Jane bitterly. 'I know; but it pays well and I still haven't had the break I need to get out. Never mind that now. How are you, Cressida? Still planning to write your romance-among-the-tabloids book?'

'Well actually,' said Willow slowly and feeling guilty, 'I'm not sure that it's going to work. My agent is a bit doubtful about it and the more I think about it, the more worried I get. I imagine that there'd be even more elephant traps than usual.'

'What are you talking about?' demanded Jane briskly.

'Elephant traps,' Willow repeated in an obliging voice. 'Oh, you know, Jane, ghastly opportunities for wholly unconscious libel and that sort of thing. And newspapers are so used to being charged enormous sums when they libel people that they might be a bit vindictive. I'm an appalling coward about libel, I'm afraid.'

'So what can I do for you?'

'How shaming that you think I'd only ring you if I wanted something!' said Willow. 'But in fact you are right; I wondered whether you knew anything at all about an actress called Claire Ullathorne? She died just over a month ago: suicide, I think.'

'I'm not sure I've ever heard of her,' said Jane. 'Why d'you want to know? A backstage romance?'

'That sort of thing,' lied Willow calmly. 'The strains and stresses of that life. You see, I've heard that she was reasonably well-off and attractive, and so it seems that she must have killed herself just because of a part she didn't get. Where could I find out about her?'

'Hmmm,' said Jane. 'I could look through our clippings library if you like; but you'd probably get as much information from the reference books, although they wouldn't have our inimitable style and gloss.'

'Good idea,' said Willow foreseeing that her self-indulgent day was going to be more taken up with the investigation than she had planned. 'But what are they? I don't suppose she'd have made *Who's Who.*'

'No,' agreed Jane. 'But she's bound to have been in *The Stage.*'

'You are a mine of information, Jane. Thank you.'

'I'll ring you if I find anything in the library,' she said.

'And then we can have another of our dinners,' answered Willow gratefully. 'Good bye, Jane.'

As soon as Jane had replaced her receiver and Willow could hear the dialling tone again, she tapped in Tom Worth's home number. As she expected she was answered by his machine and carefully dictated into it the message she had planned:

'Tom, Cressida here. Can you get me in touch with the PC who dealt with the Titchmell burglary? I need to find out everything he heard and thought about Titchmell and his girlfriend, and his house and the break-in. That's all for the moment. Oh, and would you like to come to Sunday lunch here?'

That done she decided to go straight to Christie's to see whether there was anything in the sale that might take the place of her ruined furniture. The sale rooms were conveniently close to the London Library, of which she was a member, and so she could consult whatever reference books they had while she was in St James's.

It hardly seemed worth while getting her car out of the garage just to drive it ten minutes across London only to struggle to find a parking space, and so she asked Mrs Rusham to ring for a taxi while she herself went to tidy her face and hair and get a jacket. The weather had been almost miraculously warm for April, but it might well change.

On that thought Willow pulled a straight-cut navy blue coat out of the cupboard instead of the jacket she had planned to wear and slung it round her shoulders.

It occurred to her as she took a quick, derisively admiring look at her reflection in the long glass in her bedroom, that a longish string of pearls would have gone well with the dress and lightened the heavy colour mixture, but she had none. When she had first been able to afford real jewellery she had wanted gold and diamonds and emeralds; the quieter charms of pearls had seemed less attractive. If the new book sold well, perhaps she should give herself some pearls at last.

'The taxi's downstairs, Miss Woodruffe,' called Mrs Rusham, and Willow went down to the street.

The large first-floor room in Christie's main building was full of dealers, sightseers and a few private buyers when Willow arrived. She bought a catalogue and unscrewed her fat black Mont Blanc pen ready to mark anything she liked.

Some of the estimates were way out of her price range, but she found a charming eighteenth-century folding card table made of kingwood that she liked and fell badly in love with a superb seventeenth-century walnut secretaire. It was of much better quality than the bureau bookcase she had had before, and according to the catalogue the cloudy looking glass on its doors was original, as were the two perfectly preserved candlesticks. The estimate in the catalogue was high.

Quickly working out in her head precisely what she would receive of her publisher's latest advance after the Inland Revenue had had their share, Willow decided that she could afford an extravagance and went to leave bids for the two pieces.

Shaking a little at the prospect of spending so much money and feeling for a disconcerting moment more like the frugal Willow King than the freely extravagant Cressida Woodruffe, she walked out of Christie's and turned left along King Street and left again into St James's Square. She had joined the London Library after her first book had been published and loved the stateliness of it as well as the enormous convenience it offered.

Taking the creaking, groaning lift up to the first floor, she walked into the reading room as quietly as possible so as not to disturb the elderly gentlemen reading newspapers and journals in the low red-leather chairs. Willow herself had once spent a morning in one of those chairs and had fallen into the heaviest and most comfortable sleep she could remember enjoying out of either of her beds.

Austerely laying her handbag and large notebook on a small table in front of a hard, upright chair, she then walked to the racks that ran down the middle of the room in search of the reference books Jane Cleverholme had recommended. To that pile she then added the *Architects' Yearbook*.

From her loot she discovered that there was no immediately obvious connection between the 40-year-old actress and the 35-year-old-architect. They had been born and brought up in quite different parts of the country. Simon Titchmell had lived in Fulham and Claire Ullathorne in Canonbury. They were of different ages and sexes. It struck Willow that Claire Ullathorne's divorced husband might have been the connecting link, but when she took a chance and looked him up in *Who's Who*, she found that he was a distinguished soldier, twenty years older than Simon Titchmell and on the point of retirement. They had had no children, which made her wonder about the evidence of childbirth she had read in the post-mortem report.

Simon Titchmell did not figure in *Who's Who*, but his godfather, the retired Chief Constable, did. The entry was not particularly illuminating, although it did list his recreations as 'fine wine, good conversation, bridge and the theatre'. Willow filed that information away in her memory and made a note to try to find out whether the Chief Constable's interest in the theatre had ever led him to an acquaintance with Claire Ullathorne. His son, Commander Bodmin, did not appear.

Willow replaced the fat, red book on its shelf and instead turned to the *Architects' Yearbook* in search of information about Simon Titchmell. There was no indication that he had ever done any stage design, but Willow thought it just possible that he might have designed a set or two and perhaps even met Claire Ullathorne that way. Willow resolved to ask his sister that at Richard's dinner party. Before she abandoned the reference books, she looked up the entry for the architecture practice which had first employed Simon Titchmell.

She saw that among the projects they had completed was a complex of buildings for the Metropolitan Police and at once she began to wonder whether Commander Bodmin might have had a hand in selecting the architects, giving the work to his father's godson's firm and consequently believing himself vulnerable to a charge of nepotism. That information, too, was filed both in her memory and her notes, although she could not quite bring herself to believe that anyone would refuse to pursue a murder investigation because of so vague a threat.

Having gutted the reference books, Willow tidied up her papers, took the heavy volumes back to their shelves and then made her way down to the sepulchral basement where the back copies of *The Times* and *Country Life* were kept. It was often hard to stop herself browsing through the really ancient copies of *The Times*, but for once she was interested enough in her current enquiry to go straight for the volumes for the past few years. Heaving the great dark-red books on to the high metal table, she read through vast numbers of theatrical, film and television reviews, finding only four that referred to Claire Ullathorne. All were favourable and the most recent was positively eulogistic. Even though she had failed to get the part she evidently wanted, she was quite successful.

There was nothing in any of the few architectural columns about Simon Titchmell. *Country Life* proved more fruitful, but only to the extent of a pair of articles about large country houses that he had restored. Looking at the photographs and reading the accompanying text, Willow thought that she understood precisely why Richard had called Titchmell's work 'precious', but there was nothing there to throw any light at all on why he might have been murdered, or even have stupidly taken a fatal dose of aconite for some peculiar purpose of his own.

The thought of aconite sent Willow upstairs to the 'Science and Miscellaneous' shelves for a book on poisons. The only one she could find had been published in 1906, but she thought it unlikely to be badly out of date.

'Poisons can't have changed much in eighty years,' she murmured, much to the surprise of a young man leaning against the stacks further into the gloomy room.

Willow took the fat book down to the front desk and signed for it. Checking the catalogue, she discovered that the library did own a more modern book on poisons and so she put in a request to borrow it when it was next returned.

When she emerged into the sunlit green-and-whiteness of the square, she decided to walk back to Chesham Place. There was half an hour to spare before lunch and the exercise might stimulate her brain.

She planned to go via Jermyn Street and found herself seduced into a little self-indulgent window shopping, which soon turned into the real thing when she let herself buy a luxurious yellow silk shirt in one shop and a pair of soft black-leather shoes in another. Once again her long-entrenched frugality protested at the extravagance. She partly salved her agitated conscience by dropping into Hatchards in Piccadilly for a book about English wild flowers, which she thought might help her avoid making another mistake like the one she had made over the aconite. She also asked in the non-fiction paperback department whether there were any books about serial killers. To her surprise the assistant went immediately to an American study of the phenomenon and offered it to her. Willow read the blurb and, deciding that it might be useful, paid for it and took it away.

When she reached the flat, ten minutes after one o'clock, Mrs Rusham greeted her with patent disapproval and a clutch of telephone messages. Ignoring the first, Willow thanked her for the messages and, having washed, walked into the dining room for lunch. When she saw what had been laid out for her, she thought that Mrs Rusham's disapproval of her lateness was a bit absurd, for all the food was cold. There was a perfectly arranged salad of radiccio, goat's cheese and olive oil to start with and a miniature game pie to follow.

Mrs Rusham was a past-master of the art of making raised pies, and since Willow was not particuarly keen on pork pies, her housekeeper always had plenty of game in the freezer instead. As usual the pastry was crisp on top and delectably chewy beneath the surface and the partridge, pheasant and hare filling was a small miracle of flavour, presumably moistened with something beyond the jellied stock that glistened in all the interstices. Willow washed it down with a glass of Vichy water and completed her lunch with a ripe pear.

When she had finished that, she carried her plates out to the kitchen to thank Mrs Rusham.

'I'm glad it was satisfactory, Miss Woodruffe,' she said. 'As you will have seen from your messages, Mr Lawrence-Crescent telephoned this morning, and he also asked me to tell you that his guests have all accepted for Thursday next week.'

'Excellent,' said Willow, genuinely pleased. 'And have you and he decided on a menu?'

'He said that he would leave everything to me,' said Mrs Rusham, beaming with remembered gratification. 'Is there anything you would like this afternoon, Miss Woodruffe?'

'This afternoon? No, I don't think so. Do you want some time off?' asked Willow.

'Oh no. But I thought I would deal with the laundry and take your dry cleaning out if you didn't want me for anything else.'

Willow shook her head and took her small sheaf of telephone messages to her small writing room. The only unexpected call was from Eve Greville, her literary agent, asking her to ring back. One of the others was from Tom Worth. In reading Mrs Rusham's laboriously neat writing, Willow discovered that Tom could not possibly introduce her to 'the young man', but would do what he could to find out 'the information' for her. The message ended: 'Please tell Miss Woodruffe to be very careful and very discreet indeed.'

Willow sat looking at that message for some time, before trying to telephone Tom to ask what he meant. For once he was in his office and she was quickly put through to his extension. But it did not help her much. All Tom would say when she pressed him for an explanation was:

'I can't talk about this now. We're very busy here. But I cannot stress enough that in such a situation you must take great care. It could be . . . People are not likely to appreciate questions and may take . . . evasive action. I must go. Goodbye.'

As she listened to the empty buzz produced by her receiver and thought about the grey formality of his usually expressive voice, Willow realised that he must have been afraid that he was being overheard and so she tried to fill in the gaps in what he had actually managed to say. He was clearly afraid for her safety, which seemed absurd. Even if there really were a poisoner on the loose he or she could hardly have become aware that Willow had any interest in him or her. Only Tom and to some extent Richard Crescent had any idea of that. She could not believe that either of them posed any threat to her.

The only other people who could know anything at all were Tom's colleagues and superiors. Someone at his office might have noticed that he had had the relevant files out when they ought to have been consigned to some defunct-case storage. It was just possible, she supposed, that they might then have tapped his telephones and discovered that Willow was helping him uncover the poisoner. Could Tom really be afraid of something like that?

On reflection, Willow decided that he could, and, knowing his bottomless store of commonsense and courage, she could not help feeling shaken.

Deliberately deciding to ignore her weakness, Willow opened the toxicology text book she had brought from the library. Cross checking its references to plants with the English flora she had bought, she grew more and more appalled at how easy it was to obtain lethal poisons from the bogs, meadows, woods and gardens of Great Britain. She had always assumed that apart from the odd fungus and, of course, deadly nightshade, only tropical plants were poisonous. Her own absurdity made her laugh for a moment, but as she thought about the omnipresence of poisonous plants she began to question her own and Tom's conviction that there must be some connection between the deaths. She also began to wonder how she could protect herself if the person she were trying to unmask really did discover her activities.

After a while she went back to the book and discovered from the statistics quoted that surprisingly few murderers had used such methods. She felt slightly comforted.

'But it is eighty-odd years out of date,' she reminded herself. 'And perhaps detection of poison is more efficient now.'

Before she could get any further, she heard the front door bell ring. There was no sound from the kitchen and so Willow went out to answer it herself, realising that Mrs Rusham must have already gone to the dry cleaners.

'Package for Woodruffe,' came the crackling voice through the intercom.

'I'll come down,' said Willow and, taking her keys, she walked downstairs to open the front door. When she got there she looked around for the expected man in motorcycle kit wanting a signature, but there was no one. A shabby, often re-used padded envelope had been propped against the top step. Willow picked it up and saw that it was addressed to her in ill-written pencilled capitals.

She looked once more up and down the street for the messenger but eventualy shrugged and took the package upstairs. It was not until she had reached her own front door that she began to wonder about the parcel. Knowing that she was not expecting anything, she tried to think who might have sent it to her. Her publishers and agent often sent her manuscripts in recycled padded bags, but they always had her address typed on labels bearing the name of their company. Handwritten packages sometimes came her way from struggling authors wanting advice on the writing of bestsellers, but those always came through her publishers. Very few people indeed had Cressida Woodruffe's private address.

She held the parcel out in front of her to try to decipher the various postmarks that had been stamped on it at one time or another, but most were blurred or incomplete and did not help. Her skin began to prickle as an explanation presented itself to her. At first she would not let herself believe it, but it came to seem more and more likely. She sniffed the thick, dark-yellow envelope, but the only smells she could distinguish were cigarette smoke and dust. But she did not think that she would have recognised the smell of an explosive even if it was there.

Her hands were suddenly slippery with sweat, her tongue felt dry and swollen and her throat ached. She dropped the package and flinched violently as it hit the floor.

It was some moments before she realised that the ringing sound that came from somewhere behind her was the telephone and that the parcel was lying innocently where it had fallen. Walking with some difficulty, as though her terror had ruined her co-ordination, Willow went to answer the telephone.

'Cressida?' said a voice she could not recognise.

'Who is it?' she said urgently in a voice made hoarse by tension.

'Jane Cleverholme. Are you OK?'

'Oh . . . Jane. Yes. Yes, I'm fine. I've just had rather a shock. What can I do for you?' said Willow, struggling to regain her equilibrium.

'I just rang to say that I've asked one of the messengers to bring you a bag of cuttings about your actress. He said he'd drop it off whenever he had a gap in his legitimate jobs.'

'What?' said Willow, hardly able to grasp the fact that all her fear had been for nothing. 'Cuttings. Oh I see. Thank you, Jane. Yes, they've come. He dumped them on the front doorstep a while ago. I'll ring you when I've had a chance to look at them. Thank you.' She put down the receiver without waiting for Jane to say anything more and went to brew herself a soothing cup of cocoa.

When she had drunk it and banished all but the last echoes of terror, she went to collect the parcel from the hall and took it into her writing room. There she abstracted the staples from the padded envelope as carefully as she would have done in her Clapham life, forgetting that there was a stack of nearly fifty untouched padded bags in the cupboard beside her desk, and pulled out the bundle of photocopied newspaper cuttings.

Clipped to the top one was a note from Jane.

'Dear Cressida,

I hope these are some help. If you're looking for a reason for the suicide perhaps the top two cuttings hold a clue.

Good luck with the book. Jane.'

With increasing eagerness, Willow pulled the note away and concentrated on the cutting it had hidden.

'Actress discovers long-lost daughter,' said the headline of the article, which was dated about nine months before Claire Ullathorne's death. As she read down the column, Willow discovered that Claire had had an illegitimate child, whom she had given for adoption at birth. On her eighteenth birthday the child had exercised her rights and tracked down her natural mother. Claire Ullathorne was quoted as having said: 'This lightens all the sadness I felt when I had to give Amanda up at birth. It's the best thing that has ever happened to me.'

Wondering why Jane thought that that could have led to Claire's suicide, Willow turned to the next cutting, where she read of a horrible car crash in which a stolen van, driven by a drunk, had ploughed into a line of stationary traffic on the opposite side of the road, killing the driver and two passengers of the leading car. One of the passengers was named as Claire Ullathorne's daughter.

'Oh, poor woman,' said Willow aloud. Looking at the date, she saw that the crash had been reported the previous autumn, at least six months before Claire's death. Willow asked herself whether the loss of the child she had known for only about three months could have made the actress kill herself, and if so why she should have waited so long to do it and why she should have chosen so unlikely a death as colchicine poisoning.

It struck Willow that perhaps like aconitine, colchicine might be used as a narcotic, in which case the actress might

62

have brewed it to help her deal with her unhappiness. Willow looked up colchicine in her toxicology textbook but discovered only that it had been used in patent medicines for gout, which was not much help.

Turning to the account of aconitine, Willow could find nothing to state what its medical use had been and had to fall back on Tom's theory that it was used as a narcotic. The more she thought about it, the less she could believe that a Fulham architect in his mid-thirties would believe that such a drug would give him and his girlfriend a 'high'. Even if he had, she told herself, he would not have chosen to take it at breakfast.

Her ruminations were interrupted by the ringing of the telephone and she absent-mindedly lifted the receiver, saying 'Yes' into it.

'Willow, is that you?' came Tom Worth's voice, sounding alive and warm once more.

When she agreed that it was, he told her that hers was a 'damn silly' way of answering a telephone. Willow laughed.

'I developed it in terror that I might one day say "Willow King" as I do at DOAP,' she said. 'Now, what about PC Leathwaite? Why can't I meet him?'

'Because there is no reasonable excuse for my getting hold of a junior officer in another branch of the force and inviting him to meet a famous romantic novelist. Come on, Willow, be sensible,' said Tom, sounding almost exasperated. 'But I dropped into the Fulham station and had a word with him in the canteen. He couldn't tell me anything very interesting, but I'll bring my notes on Sunday – that is if the invitation still stands?'

'It stands, Tom. I . . . 'she began, wanting to tell him about her bomb scare so that he could remove the last of her fear and comfort her.

'Good. See you then, Will . . . And thank you.'

He put the receiver down without more ado and Willow was left holding hers in her hand, asking herself whether he was trying to tantalise her on purpose or whether he had as little interest in talking to her as he seemed.

'Perhaps,' she told herself bracingly, 'he is merely a busy policeman with no inclination for telephonic dalliance. There wasn't a bomb and I have no reason in the world to be afraid.'

Impelled by some not-very-obscure impulse, Willow then dialled the number of Richard Crescent's office and received all the endearments and comfort for which she had the stomach. She also agreed to dine with him the following evening.

'By the way,' he said, just as she was about to say goodbye, 'Caroline Titchmell is engaged.'

'To whom?' asked Willow, interested that there was nothing in his voice but pleasure and interest.

'A teacher of English Literature and creative writing at various adult education establishments, called . . . She did tell me, because she wants to bring him to dinner. Ah yes, Ben Jonson.'

'He can't be, Richard,' said Willow, thinking of 'Drink to me only'. 'Oh perhaps he's got an h in the middle.'

'Why not? Oh, oh I see. I always forget that you're literate as well as sparklingly numerate. No, the Jonson's spelled the same, but he's Benedict rather than Benjamin, though always known as Ben, apparently.'

'Well no wonder he teaches Eng Lit! But at least he hasn't called himself Will Shakespeare. I suppose that's something to be said in his favour,' said Willow.

Richard laughed and told her that he was looking forward to the dinner party she had forced him to plan.

'I'm glad,' she said, wished him goodbye and then put down her receiver.

She spent the rest of the day inventing stories that would weave connections between the four dead people, but nothing she could think of seemed at all convincing. Eventually she gave up in despair, ate the supper Mrs Rusham had left for her in the Aga, watched an old Dashiell Hammet film on the television, and then picked up her book about serial murder and tried to remember that she had no reason to be afraid for her own safety.

Chapter 5

*H*AVING SPENT most of Saturday trawling through shop after shop looking at curtain and upholstery materials and paint colours for her drawing room, Willow was exhausted by the time Mrs Rusham performed her last duty of the week by bringing a tea tray into the drawing room. As well as the Georgian silver tea pot, the inlaid mahogany tray held a blue-and-white Minton cup and saucer and a matching plate of sandwiches.

Willow, who had kicked off her elegant but by then tight shoes and was lying at full length on the sofa, looked up to thank her. Mrs Rusham wished her a pleasant Sunday and then departed, leaving Willow in full possession of the flat. She poured herself some tea and meditated on the impossibility of achieving unalloyed pleasure. Every delight had to be paid for in one coin or another. Mrs Rusham's superb cooking and unobtrusive cleaning, tidying and pressing were benefits to be treasured, but having her in the flat, knowing that there was another person with keys and rights to it, was a fairly high price to pay for them.

When she had recovered her energies she got up off the

sofa and took the tea tray back to the kitchen. She ran a sinkful of hot water to wash up the china and then dried it carefully. Mrs Rusham guarded the kitchen jealously and so it was a rare weekend treat for Willow to be allowed to do anything in it. With the crockery put away and the sink emptied and dried, she fetched her bag from the hall and laid out all the bits and pieces of silk, chintz and wool and the paintcards that she had collected during the day.

The drawing room decoration had not itself suffered from the burglars, but since she was going to have to have new cushions and covers made for the sofas, she might as well take the opportunity to change the whole room. Its duck-egg walls and old French chintz curtains had always pleased her, but since the break-in she found that they reminded her of that too vividly to be ignored.

The new chintz pattern that she liked most was French again, but this time the predominant colours were a mixture of gentle yellows, creams and white. As she looked at it and held it up both against and then to the light, she began to visualise the room painted in a careful slightly yellowish ivory, the colour of a particularly rich, thick clotted-cream. Her silk Persian carpet would go as well in such a room as it had in the blue, violet and rose of the previous scheme, and she could have the sofas upholstered in a deeper yellow, perhaps, with the Louis XV elbow chairs (which had survived the thugs' depredations) in some kind of small pattern or stripe that would combine the creams and yellows of the rest.

Either of the pieces of furniture for which she had left bids at Christie's would look wonderful against such a background, and if the loss adjustor were to agree to pay for a replacement Chippendale looking glass, its gilt frame would be perfectly set off by the cream colour she visualised. She doubted whether she would ever find another Turner watercolour to replace the one that the thugs had ripped to pieces, but she would find a painting to take its place in the end.

There would need to be some richer colour in the room to provide accents, she thought, and until she found a picture it would have to be provided by cushions and flowers: a carefully chosen orangey-pink somewhere between salmon and copper, but paler, might work, or perhaps a green of some kind.

Cheerful, with her feet no longer burning and her legs no longer aching from the afternoon's standing and walking on the pavements of Knightsbridge and Chelsea, Willow packed the bits and pieces away and went to dress for her dinner with Richard.

They shared their food in perfect amity until Richard said with an unusually satirical inflexion in his voice:

'You have been very polite, Willow, but you can start asking your questions now.'

Her thin face had tensed as he began to speak but she deliberately relaxed into a smile. She took a sip of wine.

'Ah, Richard,' she said, watching him over the rim of the glass, 'you can't really think I want to see you only when I need information. I like you. I enjoy your company.'

Richard's taut shoulders slackened slightly and the derisive smile on his narrow lips relaxed into a warmer version.

'Really?' he said.

'Really,' she answered with some emphasis. After that they finished the evening in such good spirits that she asked him into the flat for a drink when he had driven her back there.

He chose whisky as he had always done and poured himself a modest tot while she lit the fire.

'Willow, what's changed, really changed?' he asked as he came to sit beside her on the sofa, carrying his whisky and her mineral water. She looked at him and wished that he could have left their new friendship unthreatened for a little longer. To lose him completely would be a pity, she thought, and believed without vanity that it would be a pity for him too. They had many of the same tastes and enjoyed each other's company. Surely the fact that she no longer shared his desire did not necessarily mean that they had to waste everything else?

'I know you've found someone else,' said Richard, without showing any particular resentment. 'But you're still quite happy to dine with me and you say you've only slept with him once. Why can't we carry on as we were? Surely he's not that possessive?'

'He's not possessive at all, Richard,' said Willow, amused to think of Tom Worth's quite different qualities. 'But I find that I owe more to my non-conformist upbringing than I ever knew. I can't bring myself to accept the proposition that it is possible to . . . well, to have those kind of dealings with two men at once.'

'And you want them more with him?' said Richard, not looking at her. To her distress he sounded unhappy and she did not know what to do about it. The mixture of feelings it aroused in her was upsetting and made her feel both inadequate and unkind.

'I know you hate my pleading, Willow,' Richard went on after a moment, 'but what difference would it make to him if you and I occasionally did what we've spent the past three and a half years doing so happily?'

'God knows, Richard. But it would make a difference to me. And surely it would to you too?' she said, thinking that if he were in love with her he could never propose such an arrangement, and that if he were not her refusal to sleep with him could not hurt him even if it annoyed him or damaged his pride. She was disconcerted to find how much she minded that he should not be hurt, despite her carefully inculcated detachment.

'And yet you seem to have enjoyed seeing me again this week,' he said. The tone of injured innocence in his voice stiffened Willow's determination.

'Of course I have,' she said in a voice her Civil Service staff would have recognised. 'And you enjoyed it too. It seems perfectly clear, therefore, that we can continue to give each other pleasure provided that we stay within the limits of friendship.'

'Your limits, you mean,' he said crossly. Willow smiled at his petulance.

'Yes. Come off it, Richard. Our arrangement was peculiar but it suited us both. You must admit that you liked the semi-detachedness as much as I.'

His long, handsome face broke into a rueful smile then and he shook his head.

'I suppose I did,' he said. 'And I suppose there is no particular reason why my wants should take precedence over yours.'

Liking his ability to say that, Willow took his whisky glass away and bent down to plant a sisterly kiss on his high forehead.

'You're an honest man, Richard, and I've always liked that,' she said. 'Now you'd better go before nostalgia and affection get the better of me. Thank you for dinner tonight.'

He got up obediently and kissed her hand flamboyantly.

'Your wish is my command, my dear,' he said, 'and I'll try this friendship lark, but I don't know how good I'll be at it.'

'See you on Thursday,' said Willow. 'Let me know in Clapham if Mrs Rusham isn't coming up to scratch.'

'Oh she will,' he said with a return of the arrogance which Willow often managed to find amusing. 'See you on Thursday. I hope you get what you want out of Caroline Titchmell.'

'I hope so, too,' said Willow to the closed door after he had gone. It had occurred to her that it was going to be quite difficult to raise the subject of the girl's dead brother in the middle of a social occasion.

Finding herself disinclined for fiction but not yet ready to sleep, she found her collected copy of the original Ben Jonson's works and took it to bed with her. But she put it aside almost pettishly when she read:

70

'Follow a shadow, it still flies you,
　　Seem to fly it, it will pursue:
So court a mistress, she denies you;
　　Let her alone, she will court you.
Say are not women truly, then,
　　Styl'd but the shadows of us men?'

'Talk about arrogance!' she said aloud as she turned over with her face in the linen-covered, goose-down pillows. 'As if men aren't exactly the same! It's enough to make a feminist of anyone.'

She turned over on her back to laugh at herself as she discovered in her mind a barrier against Benedict Jonson, whom she had never met, and a wholly prejudiced sympathy for Caroline Titchmell.

The amusement must have worked some beneficial relaxation in Willow, for she fell asleep almost at once and woke later than usual, almost happy. She spent the morning pottering about the kitchen, reading the Sunday newspapers and planning what to have for lunch with Tom Worth.

He arrived soon after twelve bringing her a written account of his casual conversation with PC Leathwaite, a bottle of undistinguished claret and a huge bunch of scented, seasonal narcissi.

'How lovely, Tom!' said Willow, inhaling the almost unbearably sweet scent of the flowers as they walked back into the kitchen. 'Could you bear to find a va·e for them, while I get back to my pots and pans? I think i ·rs Rusham keeps them in that cupboard over there.'

Worth obediently opened the immaculately clean doors until he found a cupboard full of vases, selected a plain glass jar, filled it with water from the tap and stuffed the flowers into it. Unfettered, they fell naturally into a free shape that appealed to Willow. Without bothering to dry the bottom of the jar, Tom dumped it in the middle of the pale beech table in the centre of the room.

Willow immediately left her work and mopped the resulting damp ring. When she saw Tom watching her in considerable surprise and curiosity she made her shamefaced admission:

'Mrs Rusham would be furious with me if I left a damp ring. And don't bother to tell me that it's my table and she's my employee – it doesn't help.'

'All right, I won't. Shall I open the bottle?'

Thinking of the distinguished Montrachet chilling in her fridge, Willow had a small struggle with herself.

'Lovely,' she said, not wanting to force him to accept the fact that she was so much richer than he. 'Or if you prefer, there is some white in the fridge. We're going to be eating fish.' She tried to keep her voice absolutely neutral, but out of the corner of her eye she saw a gleam of amusement in his. He went straight to the fridge, found her bottle and uncorked it.

Later, when they had eaten the fish and the apricot flan that Mrs Rusham had made and were drinking coffee, Worth broached the subject that he had come to discuss.

'And are you still of the opinion that the murders are part of a series?' he asked.

'Yes,' said Willow, twirling her coffee cup round and round as she watched the viscous debris at the bottom cling to the fine bone china and then release itself to sink slug-like to the other side. 'I can see why your colleagues disagree, but I do wonder about their determination to shelve the Titchmell enquiry.' She had decided to tell him nothing about her misplaced terror of being bombed, but she did add:

'By the way, why did you send that message about my being so careful and discreet?'

Tom's dark eyes held hers for a moment and then looked away.

'I was afraid,' he said, 'that your zeal might be overtaking your discretion. When you left that message about talking to PC Leathwaite . . .'

'For heaven's sake, Tom!' said Willow, surprised by his assumption that she would be silly enough to ignore the need for secrecy. 'I thought you must be afraid of reprisals or violent warnings-off.'

'I'm sorry, Will,' he said, touching her hand lightly. 'Things are very sticky at the moment with cuts and wildly different ideas about the purpose and style of policing London, and I'm anxious not to rock the boat unnecessarily.'

'But not so anxious that you could let the investigation go by default?' she said, finding herself more interested in him and his ideas than in almost anyone else she had ever met.

'That's right,' said Tom. 'And I'm sure that there is some connection between Titchmell and Commander Bodmin.'

Willow thought of her researches in the London Library and told him of Titchmell's firm's work for the police. Tom thought it unlikely to have anything to do with Bodmin, but he promised to check for her.

'Good,' said Willow calmly. 'And while you're doing that, all I have to do is to find out what connection there is between the poison victims and leave it to your undermanned force to arrest the killer.'

'Yes. Your difficulty is going to be that there is no obvious connection. It's possible that they merely re-minded the killer of specific people who have frustrated him, in which case you'll never find the link. Or perhaps the poisoner just likes killing and chose them quite at random,' said Tom, looking as nearly defeated as she had ever seen him.

'I find that hard to believe,' said Willow in a judicious voice. 'I don't know much about serial killers in general, but this one seems too clever, neat and cool to choose victims except for some real purpose. After all, whoever it is is bright and controlled enough to find out about the poisons, collect the necessary plants, extract a fatal dose from them and get it into the food and drink of the victims. If the killer spent that much time and effort it suggests that the victims must have been chosen for some quite powerful reason: after all, it's not as though they were simply strangled or shot.'

Tom got up from the table and strode up and down the long kitchen as though the act of sitting still would make it even more difficult for him to contain his frustration. He reached the window, looked out for a moment over the dustbins ranged in a small yard behind the tall house, and then wheeled round to face Willow again.

'And yet it is difficult to see what possible connection there could be between a young architect, an almost middle-aged actress, and an elderly retired nurse,' he said.

'I know,' said Willow, leaning forward to pour more coffee into both their cups. 'Presumably you – or your opposite numbers in Newcastle – have already eliminated the obvious motives in each case?'

'Oh yes. There are no jealous lovers, blackmailers or anything like that in any of the cases,' said Tom.

'Or individual grudges? I've heard of lots of people feeling nearly murderous towards their architects.' Tom shook his head, but he smiled too.

'We've got to start somewhere,' said Willow, 'and the things I want to know are: whether they had ever lived in the same place at the same time; shared the same doctor, shared the same bank, worked together in any circumstances whatever, been in the same hospital at the same time . . .'

'We've been through all the obvious questions and the rest would be almost impossible to establish,' said Tom gloomily. 'It's just those sort of enquiries that take an enormous amount of time and produce nothing very useful in the end. No, I wanted your help for something different.'

'Come and have some more coffee,' said Willow, 'and try to explain what you think I can do if I'm not to ask those sorts of questions.'

He came back to the table, pulled out his chair and sat down. He picked up the cup she had filled with coffee and sat, holding it to his lips, with both elbows propped on the table.

'I suppose that I thought you'd be able to see some link that never occurred to the rest of us,' he said rather hopelessly. 'I can't imagine what.'

Willow saw that his face had taken on the tight unhappy look she had first noticed in the Pimlico restaurant. She was surprised by how personally he was taking the case and she wondered whether there was something he had not told her.

'Well, I'll just have to find something a bit more subtle then. We agree that there's too much coincidence in so many deaths from plant poisons. That being so, there must be a link.'

'May I make some more coffee?' Worth asked, pushing himself up off his chair. 'This is cold.'

'Yes do,' said Willow, pleased with his informality and his refusal to assume that as a woman she would make the food and drink available for him. 'I've already put some ferrets down various holes, but I doubt if I'll get any rabbits for a few days.'

'Ferrets?' repeated Tom, turning to watch her face. His voice sounded amused again, which pleased her. 'Such as?'

'I've arranged to meet the architect's sister, so that I can find out more from her about him and the girlfriend. I've sent a trace in to find out about Miss Fernside's previous employers – information which I suppose you might well have already, now I come to think of it – and . . .'

'Yes, I suppose we have. But I haven't got it here,' said Tom.

'But at your flat?' asked Willow.

'No. I'd have to get it from the office. The earliest I could get it to you would be Monday evening.'

'In which case I might as well wait for the trace. Tom, you are a bit tiresome: you might have thought I'd need to know that,' said Willow mildly. 'Will you at least try to get answers to my other questions?'

'Very few murders are caused by events or emotions from the distant past, Willow,' he said, and then added a little crossly: 'What are you smiling at?'

'I didn't realise that it showed,' she said.

'Well it did. You looked transformed by it,' said Worth, as though the compliment was being dragged from him. 'It made you look happy.'

'I am, except when I think about the murderer, the victims, or you as the victim of your colleagues' malice,' she said, smiling more openly at him. 'I was just thinking that you are the only man I know who could say something like that – about murders not being caused by things from the past – without sounding patronising or contemptuous.'

As she spoke, Tom Worth's craggy face also relaxed into a smile, and his right hand stretched out towards her. Willow put her own into it.

'Well, Will? What about it?' he asked, as though he were suggesting a walk in the park. Willow was not deceived, but she was not pressed into a decision either.

'Why not?' she said at last.

As he was shutting the door of her bedroom, Willow turned back, suddenly aware of the risk he represented to her peace of mind.

'Don't say it, Will,' said Tom, gently brushing one hand across her lips, leaving a trail of sensation where he had touched her. His certainty and the feel of his skin on hers made her breathless.

'Yes,' he said. 'I remember, too. Come to bed.'

She put out both hands and he gripped them, leaning forward to kiss her. His hands left hers and she felt him pull her closer until she was leaning against him. Her muscles seemed to have turned to jelly and something had happened to her mind. She could think of nothing but him and the dizzying sensations that his hands and his lips and his body sent through her.

By the time they were lying on her huge, soft bed, she knew that any risk was worth taking and reached for him, to take and to give.

Two-and-a-half hours later Willow got quietly out of bed to run a bath. When she went back into the bedroom she saw that Tom was still asleep, flat on his back, his dark hair falling over his forehead and his right hand lying on top of the linen-covered duvet, palm upwards. He looked vulnerable and almost unbearably attractive as he lay against the brilliantly white linen. Willow stood, clutching the primrose dressing gown around herself and looking at him.

Love had not been an element in either of her lives before Tom had appeared to smash through her self-sufficiency and the perfect arrangements she had made to keep herself protected from difficult and frightening emotion. Looking back to her peculiar childhood, she understood why her parents had treated her as they had, but having discovered how completely incompetent she was in the real world of feelings she found it hard to forgive them.

Richard, who had his own distaste for emotion, had been the first person in whom she had ever confided or for whom she had allowed herself to feel any affection at all. Now she was confronted by feelings that were far stronger than that and she was terrified. She did not know how she would react or what she would do, whether she could survive a real passion and whether she could give enough. It was obvious that unless she sent Tom Worth away her life would change, and yet the idea of its changing worried her still. Nothing could be clear-cut any more; everything seemed dangerous and frightening in a world where she cared so much for someone else.

A changing note in the sound of the bathwater rescued her from her introspection and she went to turn off the taps. Lying back in oiled and scented water wrought its usual calming influence over Willow's mind and by the time Tom appeared in the doorway, she was able to smile at him with some of her self-protection back in place.

'Did you sleep well?' she asked. He nodded with a schoolboy grin.

'Did you mind my going to sleep?

'No, Tom,' said Willow. 'It is, I understand, a normal physiological reaction to . . . you know.'

'I love your primness, Will,' he said, laughing and coming to sit on the edge of the bath. 'It seems so out of character.'

Willow could feel herself blushing and hoped that he would put it down to the steam from her bath, but was fairly sure that he would not.

'You know an awful lot about women,' she said irrelevantly, washing her right foot. 'I suppose that just means that you've had a lot of experience.'

'I like women,' he said, and she believed him. 'I really like them. Can I have that bath after you?'

'Why not have a new one?' she said. 'There's plenty of hot water.'

When they were both dressed again, Willow asked him about his talk with PC Leathwaite, adding:

'I know you've given me those notes, but tell me what you remember. It'll be fresher like that.'

'He's a bright lad,' said Tom, leading the way out of Willow's green-and-white bedroom towards the kitchen. 'D'you want a cup of tea?'

'Not really,' said Willow. 'But do help yourself.'

Tom went to switch on the kettle, while Willow sat in her old chair at the kitchen table.

'So? What did he tell you?' she prompted.

'He said that Titchmell struck him as being thoroughly sound, what he called a "solid citizen", and perfectly responsible.'

'What did that mean? Responsible for what?'

'I think he meant that Titchmell had done everything he could, short of installing a burglar alarm, to make his house burglar-proof, and when asked why he didn't have an alarm, he explained that he thought they were anti-social and in any case did very little good.'

'Do you agree with that?' asked Willow, diverted into leaving the investigation.

'No, on balance I think they are worthwhile,' said Tom.

'How did they get into Titchmell's house?'

'Chucked a brick through the kitchen window,' said Tom. 'And no locks are going to protect anyone against that sort of thing.'

'But didn't anyone hear anything? Breaking glass makes a hell of a racket.'

'No one's admitted to it, but you know the great British public. They hate reporting anything. Besides, most people who live in those streets work all day, and it seems likely that the window was broken at about half-past three in the afternoon.'

Willow got up as soon as he had finished speaking and went into her writing room to fetch her notebook.

'What's so important about that?' asked Tom, fishing a tea bag out of his mug.

'Do you really want that sort of tea?' asked Willow. 'There's plenty of China tea in the cupboard, and about six tea pots.'

'Yes, my dear Will, I do. I need the oomph of an Indian tea-bag. Now what is so important?'

'Obviously the break-in must have been when the murderer put the poison in the museli,' she said. 'And . . .'

'Not obviously at all,' said Tom, sipping the scalding tea and wincing slightly. 'Do you know how many afternoon burglaries there are every week in bits of London like Fulham and Clapham?'

Willow shook her head.

'Nor do I, but there are plenty, believe me. It could have been the murderer, or it could have been truanting schoolchildren or professional thieves from the area, or from outside it . . . could have been anyone. And if it had been the murderer, he or she would have taken an unnecessary risk of getting done for burglary by lugging away a video and all the rest,' said Tom.

'I think it would just have shown that the killer was intelligent,' answered Willow, beginning to form a mental picture of her quarry. 'A bit elaborate, I agree, but clever. How long before the deaths was it?'

'Two weeks,' said Tom, 'give or take a day.'

'Then a poisoned packet of muesli must have been substituted for the spare in the store cupboard,' said Willow. 'Do we know whether Titchmell was a good housekeeper?'

'No, we don't,' said Tom, raising his left eyebrow.

Willow suppressed her envy of his skill and scribbled down a question to ask Caroline Titchmell if she got the chance.

'And what about Claire Ullathorne and Edith Fernside? Were they burgled in the weeks before their deaths?'

'No. I did check that, you see,' said Worth with a smile that turned to laughter as he saw her expression.

'I don't see why you were so sure that I could help you,' said Willow with mock crossness, 'when you've already thought of everything I've come up with and when you're so certain that you're cleverer than me.'

'You're slipping, Ms King,' said Tom, draining his mug, 'it's "I" there, not "me". I suppose that it was your novelist's imagination I wanted,' he went on. 'Ordinary policework can't help in a case like this with no physical evidence, no apparent motive, and no pattern to the murders. I thought you might be able to pick out something none of us pedestrian thinkers has considered.'

Willow almost laughed at that. For years her pride had been in academic brilliance and intellectual rigour. Now she was being applauded for intuition and imagination by a man who apparently despised the sort of books that had made her fortune. It was both funny and oddly heartwarming.

Chapter 6

THE FOLLOWING Tuesday Willow was at her desk at DOAP at six-thirty in the morning, determined to get through her baskets of papers before she had to leave for the Selection Board, which was to be held in a building just off Trafalgar Square. There were all the usual constituents of her working day and she ploughed steadily through them, leaving notes on most of the letters and minutes for Barbara, and eventually making a small pile of things for Marilyn to type. When she had finished all the urgent work she allowed herself to pick up the result of her trace request on Edith Fernside.

Before she started to read it, she looked at the plain gilt watch on her left wrist and saw that it was already half-past eight. Stuffing the papers into her black handbag, she collected her mackintosh in case it rained and set off to catch a bus up to Whitehall.

When she was standing uncomfortably in the third bus that had drawn up at the stop, trying to balance against its bumping and swaying, she thought about the miserable specimens of humanity who had to travel to work by public transport every day. The frustration of seeing two buses drawing up at the stop and being unable to get on because the bus was already packed to bursting point was intense. As well as making her head ache with fury it drove all thoughts of Edith Fernside out of her mind.

Enough people got off the bus at Vauxhall to allow Willow to sit down. By then there was an ache in her back and she was sweating from the stuffiness and the energy she was using to control her frustration. Sighing as she leaned back against the back of the seat, she fished in her bag for the trace papers.

There was a certain satisfaction on her pale, unpainted face when she reached the end of the report. Edith Fernside had once been matron at the Hampshire girls' school where Claire Ullathorne had been educated.

'So that's the connection,' she said, looking straight ahead of her and trying to imagine where the architect fitted in.

'Sorry?' said the burly man at her side, who was taking up far more than his fair share of their double seat.

'For what?' asked Willow vaguely.

'I thought you said something,' said the man, beginning to sound aggrieved.

'No, nothing,' said Willow with a frosty smile. 'Ah, this is my stop. D'you mind?'

He heaved himself out of the seat and she squeezed past him, clinging on to the handrail and wondering how many other dirty, sweaty hands had fingered it before she had to use it. When the bus stopped and its pneumatic doors had sprung back with an enormous hiss, like the sigh of some quite vicious animal, Willow stepped decorously down on to the pavement and made her way to the forbidding Civil Service building. Once, nearly eighteen years earlier, she too had been a candidate, waiting in nervous silence for the final interview to begin. It had seemed desperately important, then, to succeed.

Like so many earnest others from the world beyond the service, Willow King had thought of the solidity of the job and its index-linked pension, of the responsibility Civil Servants carried and the power she believed they had to change the administration of the country. She had known or suspected nothing of the boredom she had discovered in DOAP, or the frustration of being held back and snubbed by those superior in office but not in brains, or of the malice and triviality engendered in some of her colleagues by the narrowness of their world. It struck her as she gave her name to the uniformed man at the reception desk that the kindest thing she could do during her stint in the interviews would be to warn the brightest of what was in store for them and shepherd the dullards through the interview, knowing that they would probably be happier than the rest if they actually made it into a department.

She was given directions to the selectors' room and made her way upstairs to meet them. A quick look around the room told her that none of them was familiar, which was not strange given the size of the service but was a considerable comfort.

It was easy to distinguish the chairman of the board, one of the senior Civil Service Commissioners. His fine-boned face suggested enough intelligence to give Willow some hope of sensible decisions. She went up to introduce herself to him. He shook her hand firmly.

'William Westover,' he said. 'And this is Mrs Culmstock, headmistress of St Cecilia's Kensington, Jonathan Silverthorne of ABX International, and Michael Rodenhurst of the Department of Prisons and Rehabilitation.'

'Aha,' said Willow, identifying him immediately, 'the psychiatrist.'

'That's me,' he said, cheerfully, and then added in answer to a small stiffness in her voice: 'Don't tell me that in common with a vast proportion of our colleagues you disapprove of psychiatry and think that it is wholly misconceived as an academic discipline.'

'Something like that,' said Willow, smiling slightly and thinking that he must be as bored by the prospect of the next three days as she was if he plunged so quickly into such friendly badinage. She decided to prolong it. 'But I'm quite good at keeping my ideas to myself, so you need not be afraid of arguments about such things. Besides, since DPR was hived off from the Home Office after the riots, I think you've all been doing a good job, which will no doubt outweigh my unfair prejudices.'

'That's a relief,' he said, and she was not too entrenched in her Civil Service character to wonder whether he were deliberately trying to provoke her. 'I can see that you would be very good at suppressing your feelings – and indeed your anger.'

'If you . . .' she began furiously and then belatedly remembered the gleam in his grey eyes. 'If you are going to tell me that I need to find my anger in order to become a whole person,' she went on much more moderately, 'then we will fall out.'

'I promise not to do that,' he said. The gleam in his eyes brightened.

'Ladies and gentlemen,' said the chairman. 'I think we should begin.' He led the way to the large round table and sat down. There was a blotter, a glass water carafe and tumbler in front of each place, together with a folder.

Opening the one in her place, Willow began to read the lists of the candidates' backgrounds and achievements, together with the results of their earlier tests and interviews. By the time she had finished she was fairly certain which of the candidates she would be prepared to fight for, and she was absolutely certain that the others had decided too. Only an outstandingly frightful or impressive performance could change those first assessments.

The commissioner began the day's proceedings with a little speech in which he explained that they were there to select candidates who would be leaders of the service over the next twenty or thirty years, people of intelligence, obviously, but also of professionalism, steadiness and above all loyalty. The service needed people who could faithfully carry out the policies of whichever political party was in power, whether or not they personally thought the policies correct. Willow had heard it all before and let her attention wander. She vaguely heard the commissioner pay tribute to the headmistress's long experience of judging the potential of her pupils and the industrialist's knowledge of modern management techniques and talents. Her own encomium and the psychiatrist's were short but fair, and Willow acknowledged hers with a tight smile.

The first candidate was summoned, questioned and quickly dismissed. Her departure was followed by an admiring chorus from the entire board, all alike impressed by her mixture of brains, culture, good record and admirably expressed views on the future of the civilised world. Only Willow voiced a small objection, that it was hard to see why such a paragon should want to join the service. Her caveat was dismissed and the second candidate summoned.

He proved to be a young man who had done well in one of the northern offices of Willow's department as a Senior Executive Officer. She had been impressed by the account of his achievements in his home town and thought he would make a good administrative officer at the DOAP tower, but as soon as she heard his unconfident voice and saw the damp marks his hands left on the glossy table she knew that she would have trouble persuading the rest of the board.

While they were asking their questions and apparently trying to increase the poor man's nervousness, Willow started to concentrate on the questions she would ask when the chairman had finished his. She made notes of the candidate's answers to the other selectors' questions and jotted down her immediate impressions so that she would have plenty of ammunition in any conflict that followed. When the frightened man had been sent out of the room, Willow listened with interest to the other selectors' views.

They were fairly evenly divided between those who liked his brains and good academic record and those who found his presentation of himself lacking in confidence and his voice too 'regional' for their taste.

The argument went backwards and forwards, with Willow several times wanting to tell the representatives of 'the great and the good' on the panel that their expectations of the candidates were too high, until the selectors were freed for lunch.

In the dining room Willow was gratified to see that she was to be seated beside the psychiatrist, partly because he had been the only other member of the panel unequivocally in favour of the nervous man from Manchester, but also because she thought he might be useful to her. Having tasted her soup, she turned to him.

'I hardly remember anything of my Fiske. Do you?' she asked.

'Virtually nothing,' he said, shaking his head, 'but the mind does tend to blank out particularly stressful memories.'

'Yes, I'm sure it does,' said Willow, sounding as though she did not believe it. Then she corrected herself. 'Sorry, that was probably a Pavlovian reaction of mine to that wretched word "stress". It's so fashionable. I sometimes think that if one broke a leg there would be people around to say that it was stress that had cracked the bones.'

'I doubt if it was a Pavlovian reaction,' he answered, but there was a smile in his eyes.

'Never mind. I wanted to ask you about something I read recently. It's this new discipline called "Psychological Offender Profiling". Have you come across it?'

'Of course,' he said. 'Well developed in the States; not used so much over here yet. The police do tend towards conservatism in such things.'

'I'm sure they do,' answered Willow. 'But how can I find out about it? It sounds thoroughly interesting.'

'There have been one or two papers in the journals recently, but not an enormous number of books. Why are you interested?'

Finishing a mouthful of tomato soup, Willow looked speculatively at the young man. It was obvious that he might be very useful to her, if she could confide in him, but she had no way of knowing whether he would treat any confidences as privileged.

'It simply struck me,' she said when she had swallowed her mouthful, 'that a skill like that would really justify the existence of psychiatry. If you were able to look at police notes of cases for which they had good reason to think there was a connection, and tell them what kind of person to hunt, you would be worth having. "You" in general, I mean.'

'There are a great many skills psychiatrists have that are of considerable use,' he said with more seriousness than he had shown until then, 'but I agree about offender profiling. The difficulty is that it is still relatively new and there aren't enough people with enough experience over here to persuade the police to use them much. And . . .'

'Without being used by the police they can't get the experience,' said Willow, committing one of her besetting sins in finishing his sentence.

'More or less,' he said. 'But . . .'

Before Michael Rodenhurst could tell her what his caveat was, the soup plates were cleared away and some perfectly acceptable lamb and vegetables were handed round. When the waitress had gone, the psychiatrist's attention was claimed by the headmistress, which left Willow to make conversation with the industrialist. There was no pudding, and as soon as they had all drunk their indifferent coffee the chairman began to round up his team and take them back to the interview room. On the way Willow said casually to Michael Rodenhurst:

'Frustrating to be interrupted like that, isn't it? I've got to go back to my office in due course, but would you like a quick drink when this is finished for the day?'

'Why not?' he answered. 'But it will have to be quick.'

At the end of the day's session Willow could feel herself on the point of losing her temper with the headmistress, who seemed to have an unrealistic view of both the Civil Service and the kind of candidate such boards could expect. Once or twice Willow caught the eye of the psychiatrist and felt a little better for the amusement she read in it. When they were at last released, he came straight over to her.

'You look as though you need that drink,' he said, ushering her towards the door.

'Does it show that badly?' asked Willow and then, in case he had misunderstood her need, added: 'Not that I particularly want alcohol.'

'Just escape,' suggested the psychiatrist. 'Yes I could see that. But why was it so bad?'

'Because, I suppose, I dislike being contradicted by people who know less than I do about the subject under discussion,' she said, half turning towards him. Catching a derisive gleam in his eye, she added: 'And please don't tell me what that betrays about my subconscious or I'll tell you a story I heard in my youth about a psychiatrist who spent his life under a bed.'

'Because he was a little potty,' said Michael cheerfully. 'Yes, I heard it, too. But don't worry, I learned fairly soon in my psychiatric training that I would have no friends left if I gave rein to my impulse to tell them all how well they fitted the various mental disorders about which I was learning. There's a peaceful pub just round here. Come on.'

When they got inside he asked her what she would like to drink. That rather stumped Willow. It was a very long time since she had been in a pub. She hated beer, which in any case reminded her of her undergraduate days at

Newcastle; she did not feel like risking the wine or sherry; and the idea of ordering mineral water seemed bizarre in that small, smoke-ridden temple to alcohol.

'Cider, I think,' she said eventually. 'Dry cider. Half a pint, please.'

'I won't be long,' said Michael. 'Why not grab a table before the rush starts.'

Willow obediently made her way to one of the round tables, pleased to see that it had been mopped recently. She picked up the heavy ash tray and put it on a different table before sitting down.

'Here,' said Michael a moment later, handing her the drink.

'Thank you very much.'

'Now, why do you really want to know about psychological profiling?' he asked, before taking a gulp of his beer.

'It interests me,' she said, skating neatly over the thin ice of half-truths. 'I just wonder how effective it would be if, say, you were presented with three or four crimes probably committed by the same person. Would you really be able to give the police a realistic description of the offender?'

'We'd be able to give them suggestions as to the type of person to look for, and possibly where to look,' he said moderately. 'But if any of the data they'd given us were wrong – or of course if the crimes had not after all been committed by the same person – then nothing we could offer would be any use. And in any case, we could only give them pointers, not an actual identity. Why?'

'Can you give me an example of how you'd set about it?' asked Willow, drinking some cider, which she found pleasant and effective at clearing the dust and fury out of her mind and throat.

'OK,' said Michael, shrugging slightly. 'You give me descriptions of a few crimes and I'll explain what we'd do.'

'I?' said Willow, slightly nonplussed to be presented so quickly with the opportunity for which she had been angling. Michael laughed.

'Yes, you. If I set them out, you'll accuse me of planning them to show what we can do in the best light and mock,' he said. 'Come on.'

'All right. What about . . .? I suppose it's usually murder?'

'Usually,' said Michael.

'Right: then murder by . . . oh, poisoning. Three unlikely victims, say: an elderly woman in the north of England; a younger one, richer, prettier, more in tune with the modern world, in the south; and a man, youngish, professional, successful, in London.'

'This,' said Michael, 'reminds me of the beginning of *The Three Hostages.*'

'John Buchan?' said Willow. 'I've never read it.'

'Good heavens!' exclaimed the psychiatrist, putting his large, dimpled glass tankard down on the table and turning round to face her. 'How extraordinary! You should, you know. Apart from being an exciting thriller, it's an instructive account of how an intelligent man-of-action of that date regarded the fossicking about in people's minds of hypnotists and, by extension I've always thought, psychiatrists.'

'I'll look it up,' said Willow drily, not intending to do any such thing. 'But come on, tell me how you'd set about the profile.'

'I'd need to know a lot more. On the surface it strikes me as unlikely that three such different crimes would be connected. Give me a reason why the police might think they were committed by the same person?'

'Oh, the *modus operandi*,' said Willow. 'I suppose they'd have to have had evidence of that.'

'In that case, I'd look carefully at the social position of all the victims in case there was a pattern. There's been a study of American serial killers that suggests most are from the lower-middle and upper-working class who kill representatives of the class they consider has frustrated their ambitions in life.'

'All right,' said Willow, fishing in her briefcase for a notebook and pencil. 'Social class. What about personal connections between the victims?'

'Presumably the police have already ruled that out or they wouldn't be coming to us. If it's a genuine serial killer, they're unlikely to have any personal connection. Either they would not have known him or they would have been only the slightest of acquaintances. If it's not, then of course they will have been in some way involved with him.'

Willow considered that. Before she could ask another question, the psychiatrist went on:

'But on the face of it, with such different victims, I'd put my money on his not being the classic serial killer. They tend to wreak their vengeance on unknown people as symbols. In the circumstances I'd advise the police to search diligently for some connecting link, however tenuous or apparently absurd, and then look for a person with a grudge.'

'What kind of person?' asked Willow, thinking of her still-shadowy picture of the killer's mind. She drained her cider and put the glass down on the table, knowing that she would have to leave soon if she were to get any work done at DOAP that evening.

'Someone riddled with a mixture of vanity and inadequacy,' he said slowly. 'I know that a large proportion of the population suffers from that, but I think the police should look for it. Someone determined to exact vengeance, convinced of his – or her – right to it, and without the resources to gain any kind of satisfaction from other means.'

'Man or woman?' asked Willow. Her instinct, which she was determined not to trust, was that the person she was hunting was male. 'How could you tell that?'

'Difficult with something like poison,' he said, 'particularly with victims of both sexes. I think you've cheated, you know, producing such an unlikely scenario. There's generally a sexual motive of some kind in serial killings, but none that I could imagine with the victims you've dreamed up for me. And with murders that need no physical strength it's hard to say . . .'

'I think I remember reading somewhere that poison always used to be considered "the woman's method",' said Willow.

'Coward's, you mean,' said Michael. '"The coward's weapon, poison." Phineas Fletcher writing in 1614, when presumably causing someone else's death was only manly if it involved some physical risk to the killer.'

'There you are, you see,' said Willow with rather depressed satisfaction, '"manly" is the opposite of "cowardly", therefore coward equals woman . . . I must go.'

'I don't actually believe that coward equals woman,' he said mildly. 'Must you really go? I was rather enjoying myself and I'd hate you to disappear on such a sour note.' Willow relented slightly.

'I was enjoying myself, too,' she said. 'It's just that I've a deskful of work back at DOAP. Good night. Thank you for the cider. It was good. See you tomorrow.'

As she walked back to the bus stop, she decided that she had learned very little except that her determination to find a connection between the victims was correct. She did not blame the young psychiatrist for being so vague in his suggestions, because she had not been able to give him the full story. He might be genuinely useful to her if she could get Tom's permission to enroll him in their conspiracy to discover the murderer, she thought.

When she had eventually battled her way back to DOAP and riffled through all the work on her desk, she went quickly back to the flat, picked up her telephone and dialled Tom's number. All she got was his answering machine.

'Willow here,' she said, trying to hide the disappointment she felt. 'I've discovered someone who might help us and would like to tell him the background. May I? Ring me when you've time.'

Then, thinking of the only connection she had yet discovered, she rang Richard Crescent. He, to her surprise, answered.

'Richard,' she said, sounding pleased, 'I'm glad I've caught you between work and social life.'

'Willow, my dear,' he said, 'what a surprise! All these calls during your Clapham days!'

'It's just that I wanted to ask you a question before your dinner party,' she said, relieved to hear him sounding cheerful.

'I might have known it,' he said. 'All right, let's have it.'

'Where was Simon Titchmell at school, do you know?' she asked.

'Blockhurst,' he said. 'Why?'

'Where is that? I don't think I've ever heard of it.'

'Scotland. His mother is Scottish and wanted him to have a taste of life up there. Good school, if not absolutely in the front rank.'

'So it has nothing to do with Hampshire Place?' said Willow, disappointed again.

'Nothing at all,' he said, laughing at her. 'But Caroline was there. You can talk to her about it on Thursday if you want. If that's all, Willow, I must go.'

'Nearly,' she said quickly. 'You won't forget that I'm Cressida Woodruffe on Thursday, will you, Richard?'

'Have I ever forgotten?' he said and put down his receiver.

Admitting to herself that although he had once or twice worried her, he had in fact always called her Cressida when there was anyone else there to hear, Willow dialled the number of her Chesham Place flat. When the machine answered she played her remote-control bleeper down the line and listened to her messages. There were two: one from her agent asking why 'Cressida' had not answered the earlier message and one from Christie's announcing that neither of the bids she had left for the auction that day had been successful.

Sadly Willow put down her receiver and went to see whether there was anything in her freezer that she could bring herself to eat.

Chapter 7

O N THE DAY of Richard's dinner party, Willow did not think that she would be able to get all the way back to Clapham, look in at her office and be back in the West End in time to have her hair done, dress and be at Richard's by eight o'clock. Against her principles she rang her Administration Trainee to ask whether there were any urgent matters that would need to be dealt with before the following Tuesday.

'Nothing tairrrminally urgent,' said Barbara, sounding very much more Scottish than usual. 'The Permanent Secretary has been agitating for the figures on pensions for widows below retiring age.'

'Has he?' said Willow, wondering what he was up to. Elsie Trouville, the Minister, was as anxious as Willow to reorganise the payments of pensions to widows of working age and she knew that the Permanent Secretary disagreed with their ideas.

'Yes. John's been preparing them for him,' said Barbara.

'Good,' said Willow, wishing that she could suggest her staff sit on the figures until she could get back to the office. 'Anything else?'

'Nothing we can't manage, Willow.'

Relieved to know that there was nothing vital she had to do at DOAP, Willow extricated herself from the telephone box and set out on her weekly transformation into Cressida Woodruffe.

Two and a half hours later, sleekly coiffured, discreetly made up and clothed in an understated but very expensive black dress, she rang the bell of Richard's huge, Holland Park flat.

'Good evening, Miss Woodruffe,' said Mrs Rusham, obviously delighted to be welcoming her employer into Richard Crescent's house. 'Mr Lawrence-Crescent is in the drawing room. Shall I take your coat?'

'Thank you, Mrs Rusham, I'll go and find him. Everything going all right?'

'Perfectly, thank you,' said Mrs Rusham, carrying Willow's jacket upstairs. Willow walked into the immense, pale, bay-windowed drawing room, where she found Richard pouring two glasses of very superior New World Chardonnay.

'Glass of wine, W . . . Cressida?' he said. Willow accepted one with a minatory frown. As she moved towards a pale-grey sofa, her eye was caught by the number of glasses on a tray beside the drinks.

'Isn't it going to be just us, Caroline Titchmell and Ben Jonson?' she asked, dismayed.

'No, I ran into little Emma Gnatche the other day and she looked so forlorn and asked so urgently about you that I thought I'd ask her too, and then to balance the numbers James Montholme, who works with me.'

'I see,' said Willow, remembering the charming eighteen-year-old she had met during her investigation into the murder of the Minister of DOAP. Emma's family had known him for years and he had given her her first job. Her artless confidences had given Willow some useful clues then and she thought they might well help to elicit information from Caroline Titchmell. 'Well, it'll be pleasant to see Emma again.'

'Oh and by the way, you ought to know: Ben Jonson writes novels as well as teaches English. I've never heard of anything he's written, but Caroline says they're fantastically literary and well thought of, but not frightfully popular.'

'Oh Lord!' said Willow. 'And I'd hoped to persuade them both to like me.'

'Why shouldn't they?' Richard was asking when the doorbell rang again. In a moment a young woman in her early thirties stood in the doorway of the drawing room, laughing over her shoulder. Willow could see a taller man standing behind her, but because his face was out of the direct light it was hard to see what he looked like. The woman, whom Richard soon introduced as Caroline Titchmell, was short and almost plump. Her dark hair was cut quite short and gleamed with frequent washing and conditioning. It was cut with a half fringe to keep the bulk of it away from her face, which was what old-fashioned novelists would have called 'heart-shaped' with its broad brow and pointed chin. Her eyes were a peculiarly dark blue and looked arresting in her pale face. She too was wearing black, but Willow was not sure whether that was merely because it suited her so well or as a sign that she was mourning her brother's death.

Willow held out her hand and smiled when she was introduced. Caroline Titchmell shook it, saying:

'What a pleasure! I enjoy your books so much.'

'Really?' said Willow, genuinely surprised. It had never struck her that her romantic confections would appeal to professional women like this one, who had confidence and intelligence blazing out of her blue eyes. 'I am glad.'

'Do you know Ben Jonson?' She took her fiancé's arm and led him forward. In the light his face was revealed as square and pink. His nose was snubbed and his mouth wide, making him seem both young and ingenuous. Willow thought he looked friendly and as unlike the author of literary novels as it was possible to be. If she had met him on neutral ground and been asked to guess his profession, she would have suggested farming or perhaps sport, or even teaching in an old-fashioned boys' prep school.

Remembering his critically-acclaimed novels, she braced herself for polite contempt, smiled at him and shook his hand.

'I must confess that I haven't read them myself,' he began, and Willow expected the worst. 'My own tastes in genre fiction run more to mystery. But I admire anyone who can write as reliably as you do and appeal so widely.'

'That's very generous of you,' said Willow, thinking that he not only looked unexpectedly pleasant but sounded it too with his remarkably light gentle voice. 'I think Richard's got some cold white wine. He's disappeared, but may I pour you some?'

Both of them accepted and Willow brought them each a glass of the Chardonnay.

'Richard told me that you are a patent agent, Caroline,' she began. 'It sounds idiotic, but I'm not certain that I know what that implies.' That was a lie, but Willow could not think of another way to get Caroline talking, and she could hardly launch straight into questions about Simon's death.

'If you invent a wonderful new mousetrap and want to patent it, you would come to someone like me, who would look at it and then either tell you that there are fifteen dozen similar things already on the market, help you to improve it, or faint in amazement at its originality and register the patents for you all over the world,' said Caroline Titchmell.

'I see,' said Willow. 'Do you have to do much re-inventing for people?'

Caroline was about to speak when Richard reappeared from the direction of the kitchen with a plate of pastry boats filled with one of Mrs Rusham's sea-food mixtures in pink mayonnaise. He must have overheard the question because he said quickly,

'Have you heard about the patent agent and the razor-blade mousetrap?'

Caroline sighed but shook her sleek head. Willow looked curiously at Richard, for he had never been a man to tell jokes.

'Tell us, Richard,' said Ben Jonson, giving him the necessary permission.

'The inventor brought his chosen patent agent a narrow rectangular piece of MDF . . .'

'MDF?' repeated Willow, puzzled.

'Medium-density fibreboard,' said Caroline, leaving Willow not much the wiser.

'. . . with a razor blade embedded three quarters of the way down it, sharp side upwards,' said Richard. 'He laid it down on the patent agent's desk, fished in the pocket of his brown suit and brought out a piece of fluffy cheese, which he placed on the short side of the board. The patent agent asked wearily how the trap worked. The inventor proudly ran two of his fingers down the long side, pretending to be the mouse, you understand . . .'

'Yes, we understand that,' said Caroline as wearily as the patent agent in Richard's story.

'. . . and then said, "the mouse looks over the razor blade, sees the cheese and, in reaching over the blade for it, cuts his throat." The patent agent sent him away.'

'Good for her,' said Ben, patting Caroline's shoulder and grinning at Willow.

'Yes. But the inventor was back six months later, jubilantly, with a refinement. This time there was no cheese, just the board and the razor blade. But now the razor blade had a serrated edge. The patent agent asked the usual question and the inventor gleefully explained that this time the mouse would run along the board, look over the razor blade and, shaking his head from side to side along the serrations, say, "No cheese", and die of a cut throat as before.'

'What a horrible idea,' said Willow before she saw the joke. Richard's story seemed to have broken the ice and by the time the door bell rang again, Willow and Caroline were talking easily about the difficulties professional women faced in their dealings with male colleagues who had preconceived ideas of femininity, of toughness in women, and, perhaps most tedious of all, of the best ways of "managing" women.

They were interrupted when Richard brought a very young fair-haired woman into the room. Her fine blond hair was caught back in a velvet hairband, there were pearls in her ears and round her neck, and she was wearing a simple dark-blue dress.

'Emma!' said Willow, getting up to shake her hand. 'How nice to see you again. How are you?'

'I'm fine, actually,' she said. 'I loved your new book, and so did Mummy,' said the girl.

'Oh good,' said Willow inadequately. She was usually embarrassed when people praised her books and never knew how to take their compliments gracefully. 'Emma, do you know Caroline Titchmell? Caroline, this is Emma Gnatche. Oh, and Ben Jonson.'

Richard brought Emma a glass of wine and then said:

'These two harpies here were discussing ways of subduing their male colleagues so why not come and talk to Ben and me. He's just been test driving a new car.'

Rather to Willow's surprise, Emma gave her a grin full of complicity and then went off to chatter about cars with Ben and Richard, but later she realised that Emma had been listening to the other conversation too.

After Caroline had relayed one hair-raising episode of a misogynist inventor, who had been appalled to discover that he had to listen to criticism from a woman, Emma turned away from the men to say:

'I wish I was like you two.'

'You may well be when you've been about the world as long as we have,' said Caroline Titchmell, noticing how young she was. 'I'd hardly heard of misogyny when I was your age and certainly hadn't a clue about dealing with it. What do you do at the moment?'

At that question Emma blushed and confessed that she was marking time and could not quite decide. She was helping out at a private catering company, she explained, cooking for parties and weddings, and would probably go to Scotland when the shooting season started. When Caroline heard the name of the company, she laughed,

'I've just asked them whether they'll do my wedding – what fun!'

'Have you decided against university, then?' said Willow, disappointed in Emma, who had been on the point of breaking with her family's tradition the last time they talked.

'No,' said Emma. 'I haven't given up at all. In fact I have applied for a place to read History and Economics. Apparently my A levels are probably good enough, but I'd left it so late that I won't be able to go until the year after this – even if they'll have me.'

'Good for you,' said Willow. 'If you get bored with cooking in the meantime, you could always come and do some research for me.' Emma's face of delight gave Willow pause, but having made her offer she was prepared to stick to it. She herself felt delight a moment later as Caroline asked Emma where she had been at school. In no time at all Emma had elicited the fact that Caroline had been at Hampshire Place and said:

'What was it like? I've got lots of friends who were there who absolutely hated it.'

'Did they? How extraordinary. I didn't mind it at all,' said Caroline, holding up her wine glass to Richard, who refilled it. 'Not that I was particularly happy there; but I think that was boarding school in itself rather than Hants Place.'

'It's so strict . . .' Emma was beginning when Richard interrupted her to introduce the last guest.

'Here's James Montholme at last. Shall we eat? Mrs Rusham is getting a little restive,' he said. Willow could have kicked him. They all wasted the next five minutes getting themselves to the red dining room and being told where to sit by Richard. She forgave him only when she found that she and Caroline had been placed opposite each other with Richard between them. While he was popping out to the kitchen, Willow put her elbows on the polished mahogany table and leaned across to say,

'Wasn't the school strict when you were there?'

Caroline shook her head.

'Not really. Of course most schools have eased up since those days; perhaps Hants Place got a bit left behind. No, the only person there who was at all strict in any unpleasant sense was the matron,' she said.

Once again Richard interrupted, coming back to sit down and saying brightly,

'Now what plot are you two hatching? I've never seen anyone look so conspiratorial.'

'No plot, Richard,' said Willow. 'Caroline was just telling me about a sadistic matron at her school. What did she do?'

'She wasn't precisely sadistic,' said Caroline helping herself from the dish Mrs Rusham offered her. 'Well, perhaps she was. There was one day when I felt absolutely frightful – sick, blinding headache, photophobia – and she told me I was making a fuss about nothing. It turned out that I had meningitis,' she finished drily.

'How ghastly!' said Willow.

'Yes it was, particularly being told that I'd imagined my symptoms because I wanted to get out of some minor punishment I'd landed myself with. I don't know that I'll ever forget the feeling of total powerlessness mixed with those horrible physical symptoms. You see, I *knew* there was something wrong with me, and I was terrified of what it might be.'

'I should think so,' said Richard indignantly. 'Who on earth was she? She sounds most unsuitable to be a school matron.'

'Fernie, we called her,' said Caroline, her eyes holding that blank look of concentrated memory. 'Miss Fernside. Yes, I think she probably was most unsuitable.'

Willow could have kissed Richard for his last intervention and was smiling at him so warmly that she did not notice that Mrs Rusham had got right round the table and was now offering her the dish of hot salmon soufflé. A slight cough from her housekeeper brought Willow's attention round smartly. She helped herself to a modest amount of soufflé, knowing from experience that it was both unctuous and very filling.

'This is delicious,' said Caroline when Mrs Rusham had gone. 'You are lucky to have such a wonderful cook.'

'She's Cressida's really,' said Richard. 'I've just been lent her for this evening. Now tell me, Caroline . . .'

Willow did not hear Richard's question because Ben, who was sitting on her left, asked her what stage she was at with her new book.

'Nowhere really,' said Willow with a smile that was supposed to be disarming. She finished her soufflé and put down her fork. 'I've just finished one and I'm taking a few weeks off before I start the next.'

'It's a foul stage, isn't it?' said Ben in his peculiarly gentle voice. 'I always hate it. All that anguish and emotion locked up in a typescript that has to be picked over by strangers who may well misunderstand what you've been trying to do and, worst of all, reject what it . . .' He paused to take a mouthful of the soufflé. 'I once had the most frightful row with a young editor who had dared to rewrite whole chunks of a book he had entirely misunderstood.'

'I don't go through such agonies myself,' said Willow, rather amused to hear a bite in his otherwise gentle voice. Even so she could not imagine the editor in question being particularly worried by the row. 'I don't write that sort of book – just entertainment.'

'But don't you put any of yourself into your books?' asked Ben, with a frown that looked out of place on his friendly, obvious face. 'I find that hard to believe.'

'I don't think so,' said Willow, wondering which of herselves she might put in. Even Cressida was sharper, more self-determined and more confident than the emotionally droopy but commercially perky girls who sighed over their love lives and their businesses in her novels; and Willow King would never find a place in a novel designed to appeal to the more obvious fantasies of its readers.

'I suspect you do though,' said Ben. 'I find that I do even when I'm writing about people quite different from myself, say, a female Eskimo huntress.'

'Do you really write about the Eskimo? I must read some of your books,' said Willow with a smile.

'I have done, but you may find that one a little hard to get hold of,' answered Ben. 'I think it sold about three hundred copies five years ago, desite remarkably good reviews, and was remaindered by the publishers as soon as my contract allowed them to do it. They're not like your books.'

'No,' agreed Willow. 'Mine are never reviewed at all.'

'But they sell,' said Ben with a laugh. 'How they sell!'

'Oh yes, they sell,' Willow was beginning when Richard interrupted.

'Books, books, books,' he said, from Willow's other side. 'I should never have sat you two together, but I thought you were such different sorts of writers that you'd manage to avoid the subject.'

'Never,' said Ben. 'We'll be on to royalties in a moment.' Willow watched Caroline's rather intense, serious face light up and half turning back to Ben saw an extraordinarily affectionate expression on his face. On the face of it they seemed a rather surprising couple. Caroline was exquisitely neat in her clothes and hair, whereas Ben's floppy brown hair was untidy and his corduroy jacket rubbed and creased. There was a small round patch of dark blue in the corner of one pocket, as though he had let a pen leak, and the cuffs were frayed.

Willow wondered how they had met and what it was they had found in each other that they had not found elsewhere. That there was something was obvious, because of the way they caught each other's eyes even when they were talking to other people and looked every so often to see that the other was content. She rather envied them their obvious certainty of each other.

'I think it's wonderful,' said Emma Gnatche from the other end of the table, where she had been monopolised by the young man from Richard's office who, in Willow's eyes, was simply a junior banker without a thought or expression of his own. 'To be a published writer!'

There was so much innocent awe in her voice that both Ben and Willow laughed. Mrs Rusham removed their fish plates then and returned to offer them a casserole of guinea fowl with prunes and port, which was another of her specialities. When she had gone Ben turned back to Emma Gnatche.

'You mustn't mind, Emma,' he said kindly. 'We're not mocking you; we're only envious of your innocence.'

Willow let them get on with it and talked idly to Richard while eating her guinea fowl and keeping half an ear on Ben's conversation. When she realised that it was all about Jonson trying to stage one of his namesake's court masques and reproduce the Inigo Jones design for it in miniature, she ceased to pay attention.

Much later, when she and Caroline had gone upstairs to find their coats, Willow said:

'Ben seems an unusually kind man. You are lucky.'

'I know,' said Caroline with a sigh. 'Finding him is really the thing that's kept me sane recently.' Willow must have looked completely blank as she tried to think of something to say, for Caroline went on: 'I thought Richard might have

106

told you that my brother died recently in rather horrible circumstances. Without Ben I'm not sure how I'd have coped.'

Willow was distressed to see that there were tears in Caroline's eyes.

'How frightful!' she said. 'You must . . . I mean it's no wonder you value his kindness.' As she spoke, Willow knew that neither her surprise nor her attempt at comfort had been at all convincing. Caroline did not seem to have noticed, absorbed as she was in her memories.

'He was really rather wonderful,' she said, blinking them back. 'He let me talk about Simon and what happened for hours on end, which must have been very difficult for him and dull, because they'd hardly known each other. I think it's got to him a bit in the last week or so, because he's been rather tense, but he always listens and is kind.'

'What did happen?' said Willow, ignoring Ben Jonson's feelings as she sat down on Richard's plump, blue-covered bed.

'He was poisoned,' said Caroline, still standing, both hands on the buttons of her coat. 'He and his girlfriend. She was a sweet girl, but I didn't really know her all that well and so her death doesn't seem to . . . I'm sorry.'

Willow got up and went to Richard's blue-and-white bathroom, coming back with a handful of tissues, which she offered to Caroline. After a short, silent mopping Caroline faced Willow again.

'I'm sorry, it keeps happening. It was just all so frightful. Not only his dying, but knowing that he'd been killed, murdered, and all the fuss with the police.'

'Were they unpleasant?'

'No more than they could help. Half the time they were actually quite sympathetic. But it was perfectly obvious that they suspected all of us. It's really been pretty grisly. That part is over now, but Simon is still dead. I can't really get used to it; that's why I seem to need to talk and talk about it. I can't go on loading it all on to Ben now that it's started to worry him, and yet I still have this compulsion to talk.'

'Then talk to me,' said Willow. 'I don't mean now. He must be wanting to get home. But why don't you and I meet and you can talk or not talk as you please? We could meet on Sunday and go for a walk or perhaps an exhibition, depending on the weather? What about it? Would you like to?'

'I'd love to,' said Caroline after a moment's obvious surprise.

'Good,' said Willow. 'What about coming to my flat after lunch on Sunday? Come at twoish?'

'Thank you. That's really kind,' she said. Willow dictated her address and telephone number and they went downstairs again.

When everyone else had gone Willow thanked Richard.

'Did you get what you wanted?' he asked.

'A bit of it,' said Willow. 'And I may get the rest later. Thank you for arranging it.'

'She's a nice girl, Willow,' he said. There was a hint of warning in his voice.

'I know. I liked her a lot, and I feel very sorry for her indeed,' said Willow with genuine sincerity. 'I'm not about to exploit her,' she added, and when she saw Richard looking doubtful, went on: 'Did I harm Emma Gnatche? You were worried about her last time this arose.'

'No, I have to admit that you've done Emma nothing but good. I like the fact that she's off to university.'

'Do you, Richard? I'm glad,' said Willow, reaching up to kiss his cheek. 'You're a sweet, kind man when you're not too busy. Good night.'

Chapter 8

*T*HE NEXT morning Willow was wakened by the shrilling of the telephone near her bed. Feeling as though she had been dragged forcibly out of a thick bog, she tried to focus on the table where the telephone stood. At last she pulled herself together enough to pick up the receiver.

'Yes?'

'Willow,' came the vigorous voice of Tom Worth.

'Yes. What time is it?'

'Seven o'clock. You're usually up by now. What's the matter?'

Willow noticed that there was no apology for having woken her up, but all she said was:

'Nothing. I was heavily asleep, that's all. What do you want?'

'There's been another poisoning. It ought to be in your paper this morning. That's how I learned about it. I'm going to find out more, but from what I've read it sounds horribly as though it's another of ours. I'll be in touch as soon as I've talked to the people in charge of the case in Cheltenham. By the way, I'm sorry I woke you.'

'It's all right, Tom,' said Willow, mollified as much by his news as by his belated apology. 'My papers aren't delivered for another half hour, but I'll scour them as soon as they arrive.'

'I love you, you know,' he said and put down his receiver before she could say anything.

'What a man!' muttered Willow as she got out of bed and walked slowly to her yellow-and-white bathroom. 'But at least he doesn't cling,' she added to herself.

She had had her bath and dressed before she remembered that she had given Mrs Rusham the day off so that she could tidy up Richard's flat. Not at all sure that she could manage the cappuccino machine, Willow made herself a pot of filter coffee and toasted two slices of the previous day's bread. Just as she was sitting down at the kitchen table, she heard the newspapers arrive and went out to the hall to pick them up. Buttering her toast, she scanned the front page of *The Times* and found nothing. But she discovered the small paragraph on the last page of home news:

'A Cheltenham doctor was found dead in his home last Monday evening. The post-mortem found that he had been poisoned and the police are interviewing all the patients he saw before he left his surgery that evening.'

Turning to the *Daily Mercury*, Willow found stronger meat. Averting her eyes from the oddly posed teenage nude on the third page, Willow's eye was caught by a moderately sized headline: 'Gynaecologist poisoned. Patients being questioned by police.'

Reading the article, Willow discovered that a youngish doctor, James Bruterley, had died at his home in Cheltenham soon after he had finished that evening's surgery. His wife, referred to by the newspaper as 'the sad, beautiful, young, blond widow', had arrived back home from ten days away and found him dead in his study. She summoned one of his colleagues in the practice, who quickly discovered that Doctor Bruterley had died of acute poisoning. There were no details of what kind of poison had been used.

In default of facts, the article gave its readers to suppose that there was a scandal as well as a death in the full story, which could not be told 'for legal reasons'. According to the *Mercury*, the police were anxious to talk to a young woman with a history of mental disturbance, who had been 'close' to the dead man.

In an apparent *non sequitur* the article informed its readers that it was a striking-off offence for a doctor to have 'an intimate relationship with a patient'. References to the sad, beautiful widow, to the doctor's many devoted patients, to his youth and his extreme good looks all tended to suggest that he could have been the victim of a designing woman. The slightly muddy photograph, obviously blown up from a small print, supported the paper's contention that he was handsome. He had sharply defined cheekbones and large dark eyes set under slanting brows, and he looked both intelligent and desperately romantic. Willow thought that if she had had to pick a model of the perfect romantic hero, a little cruel perhaps but even more irresistible for that, she might have chosen Dr Bruterley.

As she sat staring down at the photograph and wondering whether there could be any connection between him and the elderly spinster nurse in Newcastle, the telephone rang again.

'Tom?' said Willow as soon as she had picked it up.

'Yes. Willow, it looks as though this really is another of ours. I've been on to the Cheltenham police discreetly. They're willing to consider anything, but expressed the usual doubts that this murder could have anything to do with the others.'

'How was it done?' Willow asked.

'Nicotine in his private bottle of malt whisky,' said Tom. 'Apparently they're inclined to the suicide theory. It seems that he had been having an affair with a woman – rather disturbed apparently – who was a patient of his practice. She'd apparently only been to the surgery twice in the last five years and never seen him, but strictly she could be said to have been his patient. He was trying to end the affair, either because he was bored or because of his belated discovery that she was a patient; it is thought that she was trying to blackmail him into keeping it on by threatening him with the General Medical Council or even the police.'

'But a man as ruthless as he looks – and sounds – isn't going to be driven to suicide by something like that, surely?'

'I don't know,' said Tom. 'Loss of livelihood, loss of social status, power over patients, that sort of thing – it might drive a highly-strung man off his rocker.'

'Goodness, how scientific you sound!' said Willow in a voice of wholly synthetic admiration. Tom laughed.

'No, I can see that if he really were highly strung, suicide might seem to be an option for a man like that, but I can't see him boiling up a box of cigarettes, distilling the resulting liquid and pouring the poison into his bottle of whisky. Why not just a single dose into his glass and then add the whisky . . .?'

'In any case,' said Willow quite sharply, 'he was a doctor with access to every drug in the entire pharmacopoeia. Why bother to make his own poison? And he'd have risked killing his wife or guests by poisoning the whole bottle.'

'Apparently not,' said Tom. There was an unkind note in his voice for which Willow could not account until he told her the rest. 'He was particularly partial to a very expensive, single malt whisky. But he thought it too good for either his wife or guests, who had to make do with a supermarket's own brand of blended whisky.'

'What a shit to be so selfish – and so self-regarding!' exclaimed Willow.

'Yes, despite the glamour of that photograph and the sorrow of the "lovely young widow", he doesn't sound an attractive sort of man,' said Tom. 'By the way, I heard that there is to be a memorial service in Cheltenham tomorrow.'

'Odd!' remarked Willow. 'Why no funeral? Memorial services are usually held about a month after the funeral, I thought.'

'You can't bury a body like this until the police are satisfied that it can't tell them any more. Presumably the family want to do something now. I can't possibly show up at something like that, but you could.'

'At the memorial service of a total stranger?' said Willow in outrage. 'I couldn't force myself on that poor woman and spy.'

'You amaze me,' said Tom. 'I never thought you were so sentimental. You wouldn't be forcing yourself on her; you wouldn't need to speak to her and you certainly wouldn't spy . . . You just might discover something. Couldn't you think up an excuse to be there? What about the famous romantic imagination?'

At that barrage of insults, Willow was almost determined to tell Tom Worth that he could take his investigation and bury it, but she disapproved of people who let their emotions get in the way of work they had undertaken. Besides, the person she was tracking had begun to take on a vague but compelling identity in her mind, and she was becoming increasingly determined to find out more.

'Where was this doctor at medical school?'

'Dowting's,' said Tom, 'in South London.'

'Right. I must go now,' said Willow. 'Ring me if you get any more information. Goodbye.' She put down the receiver with more than a slight snap.

His suggestion of her going to the memorial service was not stupid, she had to admit, and her instinctive distaste for it was easy to rationalise away. Having explained to the shrinking part of her mind that there were many things she might discover at the service without at all inconveniencing or worrying any of Dr Bruterley's family, Willow went to sort out some suitable clothes.

The next day, clad in a straight-cut black coat, thin black tights, black calf shoes, and carrying her gloves, bag and Cossack-style hat, Willow caught the 11.05 am train from Paddington to Cheltenham. As Cressida Woodruffe she always travelled first class, and so she made her way along the dirty platform until she reached the first-class carriages. As usual they were cleaner than the rest, perhaps because the people who travelled in them were less inclined to fling their mess around. The first no-smoking carriage she reached was empty and so she went in, put her hat carefully on the luggage rack, took a slim book out of her handbag and sat down in the window seat facing towards Cheltenham.

Opening the book, she found that she had picked up the wrong one. She had meant to bring a second-hand copy of one of Ben Jonson's novels she had bought after her conversation with Tom Worth the previous day. Instead she found herself with an equally battered hardback edition of Marcus Aurelius's *Meditations*. Willow could not even remember having bought it, but she was quite certain that she had never read it, and must have had it lying in the bookshelf where she had put Ben Jonson's novel when she brought it home.

Like everyone else, Willow knew about the meditations and had even referred to them in conversation as though she knew them well, but flicking through the pages at random, she was surprised by the simplicity and the common sense of the exhortations the Roman emperor had written to himself. Her eye was caught now and again by ideas that seemed particularly apposite to her condition and she read on and on. 'If thou workest at that which is before thee, following right reason seriously, vigorously, calmly . . . expecting nothing, fearing nothing . . . thou wilt live happy', she found at one moment and nodded emphatically as though the Stoic emperor was sitting there opposite her.

The train stopped at country stations every so often, but Willow hardly noticed as she read, taking more and more time to think about what she was reading. She had just reached the words, 'Let no act be done without a purpose, nor otherwise than according to the perfect principles of art', when the door of her blessedly empty compartment was slid open with considerable force. Willow looked up. A very large man in a formal dark suit and black tie stood in the doorway. There was an uncertain expression on his face, and it seemed to Willow that he was not accustomed to feeling any lack of certainty.

'Sorry,' he said shortly. 'I thought this one was empty.'

'That's all right,' said Willow, remembering that she was in a public conveyance and not her own car. 'I haven't reserved the whole compartment. Come in and sit down.'

'Thanks,' he said, lowering himself on to the seat diagonally opposite Willow's and extending his long legs. He looked at her as she sat there in her black coat and shoes and then let his eyes flick upwards to look at the luggage rack above her head, where she had put her elegant hat. 'You look as though you are going to poor Jim Bruterley's service too,' he said, gesturing to his own funereal clothes and black tie.

'What an extraordinary coincidence!' said Willow, shutting up Marcus Aurelius. Despite her natural inclination to avoid talking to chance-met strangers, this one offered an unexpected opportunity to hear about the dead man and to pursue her task according to 'the perfect principles of art'.

'Not really,' said the large man. 'The train's full of us. I just got rather pissed off with the bunch I was with and thought I'd pay a bit extra for some peace and quiet.' He sat in brooding silence, staring at his knees for a while, and then lifted his head again to add: 'They seemed to think it was a party. Poor Jim. I really . . .' He broke off once more and stared out at the brown-and-green smear of country that shot past the sticky-looking windows.

'Did you know him well?' asked Willow politely, but with her mission in mind as well.

'I used to,' he said, still looking out of the window nearest to him and presenting the back of his head to Willow. 'We haven't seen much of each other these past few years, but . . . well, he was always there.'

He turned back to Willow and for a moment she thought that there were signs of tears in his eyes, which seemed unlikely.

'You know,' he went on, 'when one of you gets married you think everything'll be pretty much the same and for a year or two it is: both the friend and the wife work hard to like each other for the husband's sake, but then either it all comes to seem too much trouble and they move away, or something happens and you drift.'

Willow thought that she could recognise in the man's babble the loquacity that comes from a severe and sudden shock. Before she could say anything, he had started again.

'But I never thought that just because I didn't push hard enough to see him old Jim would go and die on me like this.' He sighed. 'I haven't even seen him for nearly two years.'

'Were you at Dowting's together?' asked Willow.

'Dowting's and school before that . . .'

'Blockhurst?' asked Willow, remembering that that was where Simon Titchmell had been educated.

'God no! Nothing Scottish about either of us. We were at Michaelson's. We really became doctors because of each other, spurred each other on, competed with each other . . . My wife could never really stand old Jim, but at the beginning she tried to pretend.'

'Oh,' said Willow surprised, 'I thought it was his wife you meant when you talked about drifting apart.' The large man shook his head, took out an enormous white handkerchief and gave his nose a thorough blow.

'Hay fever starting early,' he said defensively. 'No, old Jim only got married about six years ago. I did it as soon as we qualified.'

'Is your wife on the train?' asked Willow.

'Yes, she's with that crowd down in the bar . . . having a whale of a time,' he said bitterly. 'What are you reading?'

Willow obligingly held up her book.

'Ah,' said the man surprisingly, 'And "Of human life the time is a point, and the substance is in a flux, and the perception dull, and the composition of the whole body subject to putrefaction, and the soul a whirl, and fortune hard to divine, and fame a thing devoid of judgment." Well, that applies to poor old Jim all right.'

'How strange that you should know Marcus Aurelius so well,' said Willow, suprised without quite knowing why. Plenty of doctors were well read in subjects beyond their own. Perhaps it was his air of success and gins-and-tonics and hearty games that made the idea of his studying the musings of the ancient emperor-scholar so odd.

'I find the old boy's thoughts help when things get rough – like now. I say, d'you mind my interrupting you like this when you're probably wanting a bit of peace to think of old Jim?'

'No,' said Willow smiling. 'I feel a bit of a fraud coming to his service, actually, and was even thinking of turning straight back to London.'

'Why on earth?' asked the man, showing a little more interest in her. Willow shrugged in her well-cut black coat.

'Well, you see, I only ever met him once. But he did me a singularly good turn and so . . .' She made her voice tail off artistically, as she tried desperately to think of something the dead man might have done for her and a likely place for them to have met.

'Old Jim was a bloody good man, whatever they said,' said his erstwhile friend. 'Pulled me out of more than one scrape. What did he do for you?'

Willow suddenly smiled brilliantly.

'He stopped me from trying to go to medical school as a mature student,' she said. 'And instead I started to write romantic novels and found my métier. I'd have been an awful doctor. When I read about his death, I thought it was the least I could do to come to the service. D'you think his wife would mind?'

'Should think she'd be delighted. Damn good of you to bother. Not many people would,' said the man. He straightened up and held out his right hand. 'By the way, my name's Andrew Salcott.'

'Cressida Woodruffe,' said Willow, shaking hands with him. As soon as she saw the doubtful look on his face, she hurried to reassure him. 'Don't worry, I'm sure you've never come across my books. They're not at all your sort of thing.'

His face cleared and he even smiled.

'It's true I don't read much except science fiction and Dick Francis,' he said. 'Except for medical journals, of course.'

Willow thought his smile rather attractive and approved of his wish for quietness on his way to his dead friend's memorial service. She admired his obviously genuine regret for Jim Bruterley's death, and wished that he did not present such a good opportunity for interrogation.

'D'you think it's true what the papers are saying?' she asked.

'Which one?' he asked, and there was both anger and bitterness in his voice. 'I'm perfectly certain that Jim would never have committed suicide – and certainly not over some trollop . . . sorry, some girl who was a patient. If anyone like that had started to blackmail Jim he'd have seen them off pretty damn quick, believe you me.'

'And yet murder seems so unlikely,' said Willow, making her face puzzled. 'Could it have been an accident? Or one of those frightful maniacs who go round putting ground glass in tins and packets of food, do you think?'

'Couldn't have been that. First thing I thought of too,' he said, smiling admiringly at Willow. 'I asked Miranda if it was a new bottle, but she said no: only about a quarter full.'

'And no one but he ever drank from it?' said Willow. 'I find that hard to believe.'

'Not many people,' admitted Andrew Salcott. 'I dare say he'd have unscrewed it for me and one or two others, but he wasn't a great one for offering single malts to w . . . all and sundry.' His voice tailed off as he reached the unfortunate word. Willow, tiring of his relentless 'manliness', spoke it for him.

'Women and such like, I take it?' she said, gritting her teeth and making herself smile.

'That's right. Had rather old-fashioned views about women, did Jim. I didn't altogether share them,' he hastened to add, 'but they were part of him.'

'Such as? I thought he was a gynaecologist; surely he can't have disliked women. Did he disapprove of women doctors?'

'He wasn't really. That was the papers. He'd done various gynae jobs but he was a GP these days. He didn't much like women as doctors. You see,' he started, trying to explain his friend, 'he had awfully high standards of feminine . . . charms, say, and he hated to see really lovely women wearing themselves out and making themselves ugly in the cause of work.'

'So only ugly women should work?' suggested Willow, again with the clenched smile. Andrew Salcott smiled too, rather sadly she thought.

'Well they don't get much choice, do they? Poor things,' he said.

Willow brushed her left hand over her eyes for a moment, trying to hide from him the despair that his assumptions aroused in her. When she looked at him again, she saw that he was embarrassed.

'I say,' he said, looking obviously at her ringless left

hand, 'I didn't mean to suggest . . . I mean a smashing-looking bird like you . . .' His voice died completely.

'Choice comes into it sometimes, you know,' she said, and then deciding to take advantage of his confusion added, 'Tell me about Jim's girlfriends . . . before he was married, I mean.'

'He played the field a bit,' said Andrew. 'Always had his pick, you see. The most gorgeous creatures used to flock round him – and the other sort of course . . .'

'What,' said Willow, making herself sound disinterested, 'the ugly ones?' Andrew nodded.

'He was so goodlooking and didn't care a hoot for any of them until Miranda turned up again,' he said. 'Did you ever meet her?'

'Miranda? No,' said Willow. 'He and I only met on that one occasion. What's she like?'

Dr Salcott's heavy face took on an affectionate light.

'She's a duck,' he said unexpectedly. 'Pretty, well-dressed, sweet, lovely mother, super wife, gentle, oh you know . . . We all wanted her in the old days, but she only had eyes for him. He just didn't notice till later.'

'I see,' said Willow, wondering how to put her next question. 'She must have been awfully hurt by the things the papers have said. Presumably if she's that special there's no truth in their innuendoes.'

'I say,' said Salcott, staring out of the window, 'we're nearly there. I must go and collar my wife. I dare say I'll see you at the service. Thanks.'

'For what?' asked Willow, surprised.

'Providing a spot of peace and quiet and minding about Jim,' he said as he left the compartment.

Willow felt guilty for having disliked his attitudes towards women. She was sorry for his wife and felt forming in her mind the single dismissive syllable 'men!' that so infuriated Richard whenever she had said it after he had provoked her by silliness or arrogance. But then she thought warmly of Tom Worth for a moment and of

Ben Jonson. Neither of them showed any signs of the 'women are really only good for one thing' habits of mind, and Tom was . . . Willow could feel her face relaxing into a smile and she wondered what was happening to her. Until the eruption of Tom Worth into her life she had never, ever, caught herself daydreaming about love.

She stood up and, balancing one knee on the opposite seat, examined her face in the rectangular mirror that was screwed to the wall too low to be used in any comfort. Adding a little extra mascara to her eyelashes and another coat of lipstick helped to deal with the slightly travelled look her face had taken on, and a light dusting of powder removed it altogether. Then she lifted the expensive hat from the rack and tried it this way and that until she had achieved a becoming angle, when she skewered the hat in place with a long Edwardian jet-tipped pin. By the time the train stopped she was ready, both for the memorial service and for her enquiries.

Having taken a taxi to the church, Willow was rather early for the service, but went in and allowed herself to be shown into a pew fairly near the back. That suited her because she could watch the rest of the congregation. They came in singly and in couples and family groups. It was easy to recognise Andrew Salcott's group for they had obviously enjoyed themselves on the train and, although they were compelling their faces into suitably sad expressions, their eyes were too bright and their cheeks too flushed to hide their excitement.

The church smelled of damp, slightly rotting flowers, mildewed hymnbooks and expensive scent. The flowers were all white, as though for a wedding, and curiously there were pink candles in all the holders. Willow had never seen pink candles in a church before and wondered about them. She sat in her hard seat, watching the mourners and waiting for something, anything, to strike her as revealing. Various other people were shown into her pew and she stood politely to let them shuffle apologetically past her. None of them looked as though they might be particularly useful. There were a few single women in the church, but none who looked desperate enough to be a spurned mistress, and several men on their own. The dead man's colleagues were obvious, as were his family. Willow was rather shocked when at last the widow arrived, with two small children clinging to her hands. A memorial service did not seem to her to be at all suitable for children as young as three and five.

In one respect the tabloid newspapers were right, she thought, the widow was extremely beautiful. As tall as Willow, but a lot more graceful, she had thick blond hair that had been brushed up into an elaborately plaited bun, rather like a Viennese loaf, on which she had perched a small black hat with a veil. Her suit was made of thick corded black silk and it seemed to have been made for her, so closely did it follow her excellent figure. The children were not dressed in black. The younger boy had a navy-blue duffle coat over his shorts and jersey and the elder was dressed in grey flannel, perhaps his school uniform.

As soon as the widow and her offspring were settled the vicar appeared, dressed in black and gold vestments over his white surplice. The organ rolled and the congregation stopped whispering and stood up to sing, 'Fight the good fight, with all thy might.' Willow, who had always liked the tune, sang cheerfully. She rather admired Mrs Bruterley for choosing such a rousing hymn. As she was looking round, singing the words by heart, she caught sight of the first familiar face and stopped singing at once.

Willow could not think of any reason on earth why Emma Gnatche should be at the service, but there she was, wearing a prettily cut black dress with slightly puffed sleeves; her large-brimmed black hat was tilted on the back of her blond head, making her face look even more innocent than usual.

The burly, white-haired man standing next to Willow politely handed her a service sheet, as though he thought her sudden silence had been caused by lack of words to follow. She smiled to thank him and started to sing again.

There followed prayers, two readings and an address, which was of more interest to Willow than all the rest. The vicar stood in his pulpit and addressed his congregation in a pleasantly authoritative voice. It became clear during his first few sentences that Jim Bruterley had been a reliable member of the church. Willow found that surprising and listened with increasing attention. The vicar referred to 'the tragic accident that has deprived Jim's family of a devoted husband and father, his colleagues and his patients of an excellent doctor, and the rest of us of a much cherished friend.' He talked, too, of the dedication of a man who could have become a rich Harley-Street specialist, but had decided instead to serve unspectacularly as a general practitioner; and he talked of the universality of sorrow.

At that, the man sitting beside Willow gave a convulsive start and she heard him whispering to the woman on his other side:

'Sorrow for Bruterley won't be exactly universal, will it, m'dear?'

Willow could hear only a 'shhhh' sound from his wife. With the rest of the congregation she stood to sing 'Christian dost thou see them?', which seemed an even odder choice of hymn than the first. The elderly man by Willow seemed to take exception to the hymn as well as the address, for when the congregation sang, 'Christian, up and smite them, Counting gain but loss;' he muttered to his wife, 'Damned accountants' hymn.'

A suppressed smile tweaked at Willow's lips as she heard the *sotto-voce* comment, but as they reached the last verse, she thought that perhaps she understood why Miranda Bruterley had wanted to have that particular hymn sung:

'"Well I know they trouble,
O My servant true;
Thou art very weary,
I was weary too;"'

At the end of the hymn they all knelt again for more
prayers for the dead man, for his 'family and friends' and
for the peaceful future of mankind. Another reading, this
time from *The Revelation*, allowed the congregation to sit.
As the words rolled down the stone aisles of the great grey
Gothic church, Willow thought that she could understand
the vast anger of the woman who had arranged the service.

'But the fearful and the unbelieving, and the abomin-
able, and murderers, and whoremongers, and sorcerers,
and idolators, and all liars, shall have their part in the
lake which burneth with fire and brimstone: which is the
second death.'

After that, the last hymn – 'God be at my head' – came
almost as balm to the rasped nerves of all those sensitive
enough to share the anger. When they reached the final
verse, 'God be at mine end/And at my departing', Willow
felt a lurch of genuine emotion, a mixture of regret that
anyone so young should be dead and fury that if, as
she and Tom suspected, Bruterley had been murdered,
anyone should have thought their private satisfaction or
revenge worth the loss of his life. Her quest was beginning
to seem almost personal, and she wished that she had
some more direct way of tackling it.

At the end of the service, she let all the others past her
and waited by her pew until she saw Emma coming down
the aisle and then said quietly:

'Emma?'

'Hello? Goodness, Cressida. How extraordinary! Mummy, this is Cressida Woodruffe: you've heard me talk
about her. Cressida, my mother.'

'How do you, Lady Gnatche?' said Willow, shaking
hands. 'Emma, I didn't know you knew Jim Bruterley.'

124

'I didn't really, but Mummy knew him on the Conservatives. She's chairman of the local party, you know,' she added, seeing that Willow was lost. 'And since I'd come home for the weekend, I've come with her.'

'Of course, you live near here. I'd forgotten.' They walked together down the long aisle and out into the sunshine. Lady Gnatche left them to fetch her car.

'Are you coming up to the house, Cressida?' asked Emma as they watched her go.

'Lord no,' said Willow. 'I didn't know them that well. It was nice to see you at Richard's the other day, Emma.'

'I liked it, but I did feel very young,' she said. Willow laughed.

'By the way,' she said, telling lies again, 'that school you were talking about with Caroline Thingummy seems to be awfully famous; the people in my pew today were talking about it, too.'

'Well, Miranda Bruterley was there,' said Emma. 'Oh golly, there's Mummy with the car; she loathes being kept waiting. I'd better go.'

'What was her surname before she married, do you know?' asked Willow, making sure that she did not grab Emma's shoulder to keep her as she wanted.

'Northcote,' called Emma over her shoulder. 'See you in London, I hope.'

Chapter 9

WILLOW telephoned Tom Worth as soon as she got back to London.

'Tom?' she said in relief as she recognised his human voice rather than the recorded version. 'I'm back from the funeral; I haven't discovered much, but I've come across something that seems to be one connecting link between them all. Can we meet, or are you busy?'

'Let's meet,' he said. 'Would you like to come here?'

'To your flat?' said Willow, rather surprised because she had never crossed his threshold. 'Yes, all right. Thank you.'

He gave her the address in Pimlico and directions, and for once she took her car, an almost vulgarly luxurious Mercedes that she had bought very soon after she first made money. She was curious to see Tom's flat, but even more eager to discuss with him the possible relevance of Hampshire Place, the expensive and fairly exclusive school for girls.

When she reached the flat Tom would not let her tell him anything until he had taken her black coat and poured her a glass of wine. She sat sipping it and looking around the room, which was large, and peaceful. The walls were painted white, the carpet was a subtle, slightly bluish, dark-grey, the lamps black with white shades, the upholstery white and the cushions startling pink. There was no pattern anywhere except in a large abstract painting that hung on the wall opposite the empty fireplace and in a colossal pink-and-white azalea planted in a nineteenth-century *famille rose* pot. The room was the complete antithesis of everything that Willow had tried to achieve in her own flat, and yet she liked it: the calm, the order and the emptiness pleased as much as they surprised her.

'You look better in that green,' said Tom, referring to the dress she had been wearing under her funereal coat. 'Now, tell me: what is the link you have discovered between the victims?'

'All of them in one way or another are connected with Hampshire Place – the boarding school for girls in the New Forest,' she said, adding caustically, 'and there's no need to look as though you think I'm a lunatic.'

'I hadn't realised that I was,' he said, smiling slightly. 'I'm interested in your conclusions, if not particularly hopeful. Tell me more.'

'Edith Fernside was matron there for sixteen years. Claire Ullathorne was a pupil. Simon Titchmell's sister was there and so was Bruterley's wife. It's too much of a coincidence to be merely – well, coincidence. But I'm a bit stuck now. I can't think of any way to go down there and grill the staff . . . except,' Willow said as she thought of an excuse, 'as a prospective parent. Perhaps we should go together?'

'Perhaps we should,' said Tom, looking at her so seriously that Willow quickly changed the subject.

'There's one other thing, Tom. May I tell one other person about all this?' He shook his head straight away. 'There is a reason,' Willow went on.

'What?'

'The DPR psychiatrist on my board is interested in something called offender profiling. I've talked to him about it and I think it's possible that he could help. If . . .'

'Willow, he's a Civil Servant,' said Tom. 'Very few of them are like you, in my limited experience, despite their fearsome oaths of secrecy. I really don't think it's a good idea. Besides, I'm not sure profiling would be much use on this case; ours are not classic serial killings.'

'So I understand,' she said. At the look on Tom's face, she added: 'He explained the American studies and the kinds of cases they've worked on over there.'

'I see.'

'I also,' added Willow, not wanting to lie by omission or even by implication, 'tried him out by pretending to invent some of our cases. What he said was that we should look for someone – probably a man – with an unusually high mixture of vanity and inadequacy.'

'That's bloody helpful! I can think of lots,' said Tom with a laugh in his voice. 'But none come to mind who have anything to do with schools like Hampshire Place.'

'Do you know anything about it?' she asked. 'Everyone except me seems to.' Tom grinned and rubbed his broken nose.

'Well, yes, Willow, in fact I do,' he said. 'One of my nieces is there at the moment.'

'That's the answer,' she said. 'Why don't we go down there tomorrow and take her out to tea? Oh no, I can't; I'm committed to Simon Titchmell's sister tomorrow. But you could, Tom.'

'Giving me orders, eh, Willow?'

'Yes, I am. You shouldn't have turned the investigation over to me if you didn't want me to lead it,' she said a little stiffly.

'All right; though it's difficult to imagine what I could possibly find out. I'd better give my sister a ring and set it up. The school would probably have me arrested as a child molester if I turned up unannounced. There's a casserole in the oven; why don't you go and give it a stir while I telephone?'

About to say that she did not want to interfere with his cooking, Willow realised that he wanted privacy and went silently into his little kitchen. It was as spotlessly clean as the rest of the flat and much more individual and better equipped than she would have expected of a bachelor. Willow mentally kicked herself. Until Tom's presence in her life had forced her to think about her own attitudes she had always thought of herself as wholly untainted by sexism; but in his company she was becoming aware that in her own way she was almost as bad as the Dr Salcott she had met on the train to Jim Bruterley's memorial service.

When she heard the final 'ping' of the telephone, she went back into the drawing room. Tom was standing by the telephone, looking down at the floor.

'Trouble?' said Willow. He looked round at the sound of her voice and shook his head.

'Not trouble, merely that it's the school holidays at the moment. Curious how one forgets that sort of thing,' he said. Willow laughed.

'My sister was surprised at my unwonted avuncular concern and suggested that I go and have lunch with them instead tomorrow,' Tom went on.

'You sound reluctant.'

'Not really,' said Tom. 'Oh, to be truthful, I suppose I am. Her husband takes a dim view of my current occupation and I find myself very bored by his attitudes – and, worse, his jokes. Never mind; I like her and it's a long time since I've seen her. I don't imagine I'll discover anything about the school, but I'll listen to my niece's prattle and see what happens. How's the stew?'

'Smelling delectable,' said Willow. 'Where did you learn to cook?'

'At the Sarah Kensington School,' he said, daring her to laugh at him. Willow dared.

'Among all the debs? I somehow can't imagine it. But what an imaginative mother you must have had,' she said.

'You are outrageous,' said Tom. 'It had nothing to do with my mother, who died before I even joined the army. When I came out I knew I'd have to look after myself, and I thought I'd rather learn to cook that sort of food than the brown-rice healthy variety. Now, let's go and eat it.'

As they ate Willow was touched by the care Tom had put into his hospitality and even more impressed by his culinary skills than she let him see. The casserole was as good as anything Mrs Rusham produced, with perfectly tender beef, nuggets of bacon that had somehow stayed crisp despite their long cooking, mushrooms, carrots and a thick sauce that tasted of wine. There was garlic in it somewhere, but in carefully moderate quantities. There were baked potatoes with crisp skins and a salad. It seemed strange that anyone of Tom's energy and violent past should have the patience to cook like that.

When she had finished, Willow refused a second helping but with regret.

'It was wonderful,' she said sincerely, 'but I'm full.'

He helped himself to more without making any sort of fuss and settled down to eat again.

'Tom,' said Willow after a moment. He looked up and nodded.

'I'm sure we could use some of the profiling techniques even if this poisoner isn't a real serial murderer. I'm not nagging you about letting me tell the psychiatrist, but suggesting we borrow the technique.'

'OK. How would you start?'

'The killer is obviously reasonably well educated,' began Willow, thinking of the shadowy character who was beginning to obsess her. 'It's relatively easy to find out about these poisons, but it would be far easier to bludgeon, throttle or even set fire to people . . . Have you got any paper?'

'Plenty. Why?'

130

'Like most Civil Servants I think more easily with pencil and paper than without,' answered Willow. She watched as Tom walked over to a plain matt-black desk in the corner of the room. It was curious, she thought, how his strength was apparent in every movement. He came back with a large plain-paper pad and a selection of writing implements. Willow chose a black felt-tipped pen with an italic tip and wrote the numbers from one to twenty in a neat line down the left-hand side of the top page.

'Being a bit optimistic, aren't you?' said Tom.

'I don't think so,' she answered. 'There must be at least twenty characteristics we could deduce from the evidence left in these killings. Here, this one's for you.' She handed him the numbered sheet and then proceeded to draw up another for herself, thinking that if she were to pin down some aspects of the vague character of the killer, it might become more definite in her mind and easier to project into real suspicion.

'I need coffee to deal with this,' said Tom. 'I won't be long.' Unhurriedly he collected the plates and dishes and carried them off to the kitchen, leaving Willow to her numbers.

1. Intelligence. Familiarity with scientific terms. Ability to calculate fatal dose. ?Some scientific training.
2. Inadequate/vain.
3. Belonging or aspiring to upper-middle class.
4. Angry. ?Misfit.
5. Connection with Hampshire Place School.
6. Efficient. Careful.
7. Ability to play social worker/health visitor convincingly.
8. Interest in detective fiction.
9. Not necessarily physically strong.
10. Therefore, if a man, not particularly concerned with machismo.
11. Daring.

'Here you are.' Tom's voice interrupted Willow's cogitation. 'You drink it black after meals, don't you?'

'Yes, thank you,' she said. There was a deep crease between her eyebrows.

'What have you got?' asked Tom, standing behind her and reading her list over her shoulder. After a while he said, 'I agree with some of them, but I don't quite see how you've arrived at 3, 4, 7, 8 and 10.'

Willow turned in her chair to look up at Tom's intent face. His eyes were focussed on her list but as she moved he looked instead at her. A smile creased the corners of his eyes and widened his mouth. He bent and very quickly kissed her.

'Three is easy,' said Willow coolly, thinking it inappropriate that he had interrupted a serious discussion with a kiss and yet unable to pretend that she had not liked it. 'Three of the four victims so far belong to that class – and if the only book I've found on offender profiling is right it is likely that these murderers choose their victims from the class they consider has injured them or somehow thwarted them.'

'Possible,' said Tom, returning to his own chair on the opposite side of the table. 'And the others?'

'Four is because I cannot imagine anyone going to the trouble of killing anyone else if they were not angry in some degree. Seven is because Miss Fernside must have had lots of visits from rent-control officers, social workers, meals-on-wheels people, and they are the only strangers I can imagine her letting into her bungalow. If our murderer did not break in, then the only way I can see that he could have got in to substitute a poisoned bottle of sloe gin for hers is by pretending to be someone like that,' said Willow, drawing a neat picture of her coffee cup on the list of characteristics.

'I suppose that's possible. The killer would have had to have come at least twice, though, to discover her routines and decide what to poison,' said Tom, amused to watch her doodling.

'True enough. Can you talk to a neighbour or friend of hers to discover whether anyone new came to see her a little while before she died?' asked Willow as she abandoned her drawing.

'We could try, I suppose,' said Tom gloomily, 'if we had a bit more to go on. 'Unless I can get up there myself . . . No, I don't think we can tackle that yet. If we get near identifying a suspect then we've a chance. Now, what about eight?'

'Eight is because something about the methods suggests a literary interest in death: that's not a reasoned point, but I do feel it. The method is extraordinarily simple and yet apparently rarely used. It suggests imagination more than violence.'

'Arty, you mean. Perhaps,' said Tom. 'I'm not sure that I've much to add to your list. Oh, except . . .' He began to scribble. When he had finished he passed his list to Willow and sat back in his chair, sipping coffee. She looked with interest at what he had contributed.

1. No police record.
2. Probably 30 – 35 years old.
3. Probably white.
4. Agile.
5. Neat fingered – ?some experience of model-making.

'Are you laughing at me?' asked Willow, sounding almost angry. 'I'm not doing this for amusement.'

'God forbid!' said Tom. 'What bothers you?'

'Number five,' she answered. He smiled kindly and for once she enjoyed someone else's kindness without finding anything patronising in it.

'No, that's genuine. Our killer makes the poisons and inserts them into his victims' food and drink in a way that leaves no trace on packet or bottle. I think that suggests someone who is used to dealing with inert materials –

as well as the plants themselves – on a fairly small scale: ergo, model-maker.'

'And some experience of botany,' added Willow. 'Could you recognise colchicum seeds if you saw them?'

'Yes,' said Tom apologetically, 'and digitalis and . . .'

'I know, aconite,' said Willow, with a mocking smile in her green eyes. 'And you know that the poisonous one is not the little yellow flower. But I don't suppose many ordinary people are so botanically aware. How do you know?'

'I rather like gardening,' he admitted. 'I have a roof garden here and I plant it up with all sorts of things. One gets to know plants quite quickly. Anyone brought up in a house with a big garden – as I was – learns that sort of thing without even noticing.'

'So we should add "Familiarity with flowering plants. Query brought up in the country",' said Willow. 'Well, between us we have seventeen points so far. Not too bad. Now tell me why you don't think there's a police record.'

'Various finger prints have been found at one or other scene-of-the-crime, and none matches any in the files. It may be coincidence, but I imagine the killer has left prints and we just haven't one to match them,' said Tom.

'Are there any prints at any of the scenes that match any at the others?'

'No,' said Tom. 'I had hopes of Cheltenham, but there aren't any yet.'

'In that case,' said Willow, 'it's just as likely that all the extraneous prints are innocent and our quarry may have a record after all and know enough to wear surgical gloves.' She added a question mark to the first point on Tom's list. 'I just wish we had some way of knowing whether it was a man or a woman.'

'Any gut feeling?' asked Tom. Willow shook her head. The figure in her mind was nearly always male, but having no evidence of the killer's sex she was wary of putting her instinct into words. 'All I am certain of,' she said slowly, 'is that man or woman, the killer must be able to hide behind a civilised front.'

'I think you're right about that,' said Tom.

'It's a vile thought,' said Willow, shivering unconsciously. She stood up. Tom looked up at her.

'You sound frightened,' he said seriously. Willow shook her loose red hair away from her face and tried to work out what she really did feel.

'It's just the thought that it could be anyone . . . someone I've talked to . . . someone I've liked, even. It's the thought of all that hidden malice – wickedness – that's so horrible, and . . . oh, it's like dry rot I suppose: creeping, fatal evil hidden behind an apparently healthy solid exterior. Ugh!' She shook her head again and remembered the discovery of dry rot in her parents' austere home in Newcastle when she was a child and how she had stood at the edge of the afflicted room, staring down at the innocent-looking, mushroom-smelling white threads that were destroying the fabric of the house. She had known long before then that she could not rely on people's benevolence; it was after the dry rot that she had learned not to trust inanimate things either.

'I suppose I ought to be going,' she said, looking at her watch. 'It's nearly eleven.'

'Unless you'd like to stay?' suggested Tom. 'I make quite nice breakfasts too.'

'No, thank you, Tom,' said Willow, but both her face and her voice softened as she spoke. 'I . . . I need to . . .'

'Be alone,' he supplied. 'It's allowed. Thank you for coming. If I get anywhere tomorrow I'll let you know.'

'And I,' said Willow. 'Good night, Tom.' She held his face between her hands for a moment and then kissed him. 'Don't bother to come down. I'll see myself out.'

'Willow,' he said as she reached the door. She looked back. 'If you do get frightened, will you send for me?'

'All right,' she said. 'Don't come down.'

He did as she asked, but when she had unlocked her car and looked quickly up to the windows of his flat she saw him standing there, one curtain held back in his right hand. He raised the other and waved. Willow waved back. She drove away thinking of how many weaknesses she was compelled to show him. It struck her as very odd that she did not mind. Ever since she could remember she had battled to hide them all, from herself as much as from anyone else.

The next day Willow kept thinking of her quarry and the two lists of possible characteristics. With a lurch in her stomach, she acknowledged that there were many things in both lists that could be said to be true of the woman she was expecting within the next quarter of an hour. On the other hand, they could probably be said of Miranda Bruterley, Andrew Salcott, Ben Jonson and probably dozens of other people of whom she had never even heard yet.

Willow heard her front-door bell ring. Running her hands under the kitchen tap and drying them on the thick clean towel Mrs Rusham had laid out, she went to open the door.

'Did you really mean me to come?' asked Caroline Titchmell like a child uncertain of her welcome.

Confronted with the sensible, unaggressive charm of the woman herself, Willow almost laughed at her unfounded and half-formed suspicion. The murderer must be able to present an acceptable face to the world, but even so Willow did not believe that anyone could behave as Caroline did if she had murdered her own brother. Besides, she thought, as she searched for a reason to support her intuition, Caroline probably had keys to her brother's house and would never have had to break in to plant the poisoned cereal in his cupboards.

'Of course I meant it,' she said, smiling. 'Come on in and we'll decide what to do. Would you like some coffee?'

'No thank you. I've just had some,' said Caroline. That afternoon she was dressed in jeans and a navy-blue jersey patterned with tulips. There was the frill of a red-and-white striped shirt poking out above the neck of the jersey. She looked just as sensible and attractive as she had at Richard's dinner and less intense.

'What would you like to do?' Willow asked, leading the way back into the warm, sunny kitchen. 'I'm afraid that the drawing room isn't really habitable. I had a rather bad burglary a few months ago and I haven't got round to replacing everything they damaged yet.'

'Poor you. I've always thought it must be foul – really one of the worst things – to come back and find your home ransacked,' said Caroline, dropping into a chair by the scrubbed table. 'It's never happened to me, but Simon . . . A while before Simon died it happened to him, and he was more shaken by it than he'd have expected, he told me. It . . . That was the last time I saw him, and I think I'll always remember him unhappy and even afraid instead of the way he usually was.'

'How was he usually?' asked Willow as she leaned against the sink. Caroline looked at her speculatively.

'You don't have to listen to my outpourings about him, you know,' she said a little stiffly. 'We could just go to an exhibition and . . .'

'I know,' answered Willow, 'but I'm interested – although the last thing I want to do is to pry.' Caroline shook her head, and looked away from Willow's face.

'He never seemed afraid of anything,' she said at last. Willow was distressed to hear a quiver in her voice. 'Until then. He passed every exam with ease. He had hosts of friends. He worked astonishingly hard, although he . . .' Caroline's voice broke completely then.

'He sounds remarkable,' said Willow. 'Did you get on well?'

Caroline looked directly at Willow.

'Yes,' she said, 'we were inseparable as children. What about you? Did you get on well with your siblings?'

'I never had any,' said Willow, making the corners of her lips turn down in a rueful grimace. 'I often wished I had and assume – probably irrationally – that if I had we would have been friends. And yet I know lots of people who hardly ever see their brothers and sisters.'

'We were friends,' said Caroline sadly. 'Not particularly close ones, but we usually saw each other every week. The only reason I didn't see him after the burglary was that I had to be in the States for a fortnight, and then he died. It seems so unfair . . .'

'I'm so sorry,' said Willow.

'Yes,' said Caroline drearily. 'The most difficult thing is knowing that there is nothing – absolutely nothing – to be done about its hurting so much except to wait until it hurts less.'

'I suppose,' said Willow trying to pick her words with extreme care, 'that there must be a certain consolation in knowing that at least he is not hurting now.'

'You're right of course,' said Caroline, trying to smile. 'But it's not wholly selfish to mind that he died . . .'

'I didn't mean to suggest that,' said Willow quickly.

'There are so many things he would have – could have – done. He had so many talents and he was so much loved by so many people. My mother's been almost broken by his death. She absolutely adored him, you see.'

Willow stood up straight. There were a lot of questions that she wanted to ask, but could not without sounding as though she suspected Caroline of something and was trying to interrogate her.

'Now, what would you like to do? It's a glorious day. We could go anywhere,' she said instead of asking anything about Simon's relationship with his mother.

'Do you know Ham House?' asked Caroline. Willow shook her head.

'It's bliss,' she said. 'Simon first took me there when I came to London. It wasn't restored then, but it is now – and the garden's fun, too.'

'It sounds perfect,' said Willow. 'Do you know the way?'

'Yes, but I haven't got my car. Ben drove me here. I hardly ever drive myself.'

'Why not?' asked Willow. 'Not that it matters at all,' she added hastily in case she had sounded unpleasant. 'My car's outside.'

'I rather disliked the man who taught me to drive and it put me off a bit. Of course I do drive when I have to. One of the perks of the partnership is a good car. Ben loves it. He even chose the colour; he once told me in a rather misguidedly sentimental moment that it matches my eyes.'

Caroline's voice had taken on a warmth of affection that touched Willow.

'Ben's lucky – and not just in the car,' said Willow.

'Oh it's two-way luck,' said Caroline softly. 'He's done . . . I can't tell you how much he's done for me.'

Her face was lighter and happier than it had been since she had arrived at Willow's flat.

'So shall we go to Ham?' she said cheerfully. Willow, who did not mind where they went provided that they would be able to talk about Simon there, nodded. Ham sounded as good a place as any.

When they got there, having talked only trivialities on the half-hour drive, she found that it was better than that: an enchanting, small seventeenth-century house, built of dark purplish-red brick with creamy stone coigns, set in a garden of charming formality. As Willow parked the car, the sky began to cloud over and so they decided to look at the house first and explore the garden later if the sun came out again.

They walked into a small hall, which was floored with black-and-white marble, and paid for their tickets. A fire was burning in the fireplace and the atmosphere effectively suggested a private house.

'It's terribly cosy, isn't it?' said Caroline, looking up at the portraits ranged round the double-height hall. 'Simon always said that this period was the very pinnacle of domestic architecture in England and that this was one of his favourite examples.'

'Did he take you about much?' Willow asked over her shoulder as she bought a guide book. 'It must have been very nice to have a ready-made companion when you first arrived in London.'

'It was,' said Caroline, looking straight ahead of her at a piece of blank wall. Then she turned to Willow with a sympathetic smile. 'Were you very lonely when you first came here?'

'Yes,' said Willow honestly. 'Although I didn't realise it until later. I put my depression down to my gloomy flat, my unexciting colleagues, my dull work and so on. But I think I was – very lonely.'

'What work did you do then?' asked Caroline. It was a reasonable question, but Willow was not inclined to answer it.

'A lot of dull, dead-end jobs,' she said. 'I wish I'd thought of something like patent-agenting. Had you always planned to do that?'

'Not really. I was simply working to qualify as a solicitor first, but found it dull. Simon suggested I might prefer patent work,' said Caroline. 'He seemed to think that he was responsible for me, which was sweet of him, because he needn't have bothered.' She walked over to the large white chimney piece and peered at the mouldings. 'We did grow apart a bit later,' she added, almost as though something had forced the information out of her.

Willow thought that she recognised in Caroline the almost fanatical truth-telling of a person who was terrified of her instinctive desire to cover up unpleasantness and rearrange memories of her own and other people's failings to make them seem less bad.

'Did you quarrel?' asked Willow, making her voice very gentle so that the question did not sound like an accusation. She followed Caroline, guidebook in hand.

'Not exactly; but he had his friends and I mine. And we . . . we both had different ideas about social life and things.' She turned to look at Willow, her heart-shaped face tormented. With obvious difficulty she started speaking again. 'I suppose that's one reason why I feel so bad about his death.'

Willow said nothing. A simple 'Why?' would have sounded crass and she could not think of anything else to say. After a long silence, Caroline said in a painful voice:

'We never had a chance to make peace.'

Willow wandered away towards the main staircase to give Caroline time to recover. There had obviously been some serious falling-out between them even if Caroline had said that it did not really constitute a quarrel. But Willow could not imagine anyone with any intelligence killing her brother because as young adults they had liked different people and had disagreed – or even quarrelled – about their opposing ideas of how to spend their spare time. Besides, no one who had been involved in a murder would lay bare her own motive even to someone as apparently uninvolved as Willow.

'Isn't it amazing?' said Caroline, staring up at the portraits that lined the staircase walls. She had mopped her tears, restored her eye makeup and was apparently determined to entertain Willow. 'But let's go up and see the State apartments. They're a charming mixture of cosiness and stateliness.'

'That sounds contradictory,' said Willow, following her across the hall in the opposite direction from the main stairs.

'Wait and see,' said Caroline over her shoulder. She even had a little discreet mischief in her bright, blue eyes and Willow liked her more and more. It seemed admirable that despite her recent collapse she could take the trouble to entertain someone else as she was doing, and that she could apparently enjoy herself. Willow was interested in a way beyond her investigation: having for years avoided being contaminated by her own or anyone else's emotions, she was beginning to want to know more about other people's.

'Caroline,' she said as they climbed the dark, narrow back stairs.

'Yes?'

'What did you quarrel about? You and your brother, I mean.'

Caroline was silent for so long that Willow thought that she might not answer.

'It was so silly really,' she said eventually. 'Although it seemed desperately important at the time. At university Simon had got in with a rather druggy crowd and thought them sophisticated and fun. Even after they'd all come to London they carried on with it and when I was in a state about some of my exams, he took me to one of their parties to distract me.' She stopped and brushed the back of her small hand against her eyes.

'What happened?' asked Willow, sounding gentle but feeling quite remorseless.

'It's probably quite a common story,' Caroline said, shrugging her plump shoulders. 'Someone thought it would be funny to put LSD in Simon's prissy, dull, little sister's drink. I had a bad trip and was affected by it for ages. Quite unfairly I blamed Simon, although he knew nothing about it beforehand and was furious when he discovered what had happened.'

'I think your fury is understandable,' said Willow. 'You mustn't blame yourself for it now that he is dead.'

At that piece of attempted comfort, Caroline turned her face away from Willow, but not quickly enough to hide the expression of intense, bitter disagreement. Willow was

142

momentarily shocked by the power of the emotion she saw in Caroline's face.

'It seems so petty now,' she said calmly after about three minutes, in which she had obviously wrestled to hide her resentment. 'Letting an old grievance like that spoil what Simon and I had had together as children . . . What must he have thought of me?'

'Perhaps part of what made you so angry was his having turned away from that to waste his time, his money and his health on drugs,' suggested Willow. When Caroline did not answer, she half changed the subject.

'He was lucky to get away with it. The few people I've come across who've been involved with drugs have all been in trouble with the police at some time or another,' said Willow not altogether truthfully.

'Simon did have one narrow escape,' said Caroline, 'but yes, I suppose he was lucky. I didn't know much about it at the time, but my mother discovered what he was up to soon after the awful party and engineered a meeting between him and his godfather one Christmas. Uncle Tom was a policeman, you see, and he gave Si the most dreadful rocket and threatened him with prison if he didn't swear to give up. I think Si was quite frightened, because he seemed to have dropped it after that.'

Willow thought that at last she understood exactly why Commander Bodmin had believed the aconitine in Simon Titchmell's muesli might have been self-administered and changed the subject again by suggesting that they look at the rooms they had come upstairs to see. Once more Caroline buried her emotions and reverted to the charmingly instructive guide she had been earlier.

They walked all over the house, admiring and criticising as they went. Willow enjoyed Caroline's measured enthu-siasm as much as the pleasures of the house and, finding herself unable to put any more of her questions, she tried to banish the investigation from her mind. When they reached the Queen's Bedroom, Willow stood entranced in front of the bed. A very grand four-poster upholstered and curtained in pale-blue brocade, it was tiny; yet even so, each of the four posts was topped with a pot of fluffy white ostrich feathers.

'I wish I'd come to places like this before I planned my flat,' she said, 'although I can't quite see myself in such a gold-encrusted confection. What about you?'

Caroline considered the elegant bed for a moment.

'Somehow I don't think it would quite suit Ben,' she said at last. 'He's quite a one for plainish living, having been brought up pretty poor and still being less well off than . . .'

'I can imagine so,' said Willow with sympathy in her voice, 'if all I've heard about academic salaries is true.'

'Alas, yes,' said Caroline, turning her back on the luxurious furniture and going to look out at the green park. 'I think it's probably quite difficult for him that I'm already making about three times his earnings and that the division can only widen, but he says he doesn't mind if I don't.'

'He seemed far too sensible to resent something like that,' said Willow, remembering the gentleness of his voice and the intelligent tolerance of his views. Caroline turned her back on the view to face Willow. Very seriously she rebutted the suggestion of resentment.

'But what is difficult is knowing that I could so easily afford to buy the things he has to struggle for; that if he were earning the same as me we could get a much more luxurious house in a far nicer bit of London. That sort of thing . . . He doesn't resent it, but he's too sensitive not to mind the fact that he can't give me the material things I could give him. He gives me plenty of the rest, of course,' she added earnestly.

Willow thought of her recognition of a similar discrepancy between herself and Tom Worth over the bottle of wine he had brought her the previous weekend and understood something of what Caroline faced.

'It's beautifully sunny now,' she said. 'Why don't we go out for a bit?'

Caroline agreed and they made their way down the main staircase and out into the garden. Walking down one of the *allés*, Willow idly admired a particularly fine plant. Caroline identified it, surprisingly giving both Latin and ordinary English names for it.

'Goodness, how learned you sound,' said Willow, impressed by Caroline's unexpected knowledge and trying not to remember the lists of the murderer's characteristics.

'Well, my parents have a garden and my mother is pretty keen – I used to help her and learned a bit that way. It's coming in quite useful now that Ben and I have our own tiny garden to plan. We go to Kew and Wisley quite often at weekends for ideas.'

'Did Simon help as well?' asked Willow.

'Not much. He was usually too busy.'

'Didn't your mother mind that?' asked Willow in genuine curiosity. Caroline's voice took on a tiny amount of bitterness as she answered the question.

'My mother did not consider that it was Simon's business to help with anything in the house or garden: he was too important to be bogged down with domestic tasks,' she said. 'No, the only thing mother minded was his devotion to girls she did not like. She could get quite cross with him sometimes.'

'Good heavens!' said Willow. 'I'd never have imagined that that sort of thing still went on.'

'What, mothers criticising their children's lovers? Definitely! Luckily she likes Ben,' said Caroline.

'I'm not surprised,' said Willow, 'but I really meant assuming that daughters will help domestically while sons are exempt. Didn't you mind?'

Caroline managed to laugh.

'Yes, when I was in my rebellious teens I minded very much indeed,' she said, 'although oddly enough it didn't change any of my affection for Si.'

'In your school holidays, I suppose,' said Willow, dragging the conversation back to her suspicions rather clumsily. 'Talking of school, I've been meaning to ask whether you or Simon ever knew Claire Ullathorne.'

'Who?' said Caroline, looking and sounding genuinely puzzled. 'Ullathorne? I don't think I've ever heard of her. Why?'

'I just wondered,' said Willow lamely. 'She was at Hampshire Place and became an actress. But she must have left some years before you got there.'

'No,' said Caroline. 'I've never come across her and I can't imagine how Simon would have, unless of course she was one of that beastly set. I suppose she could have been. Is . . .?' But before she could finish her question, Willow forestalled her.

'Did you like his girlfriends?' Willow asked. 'Or did you share your mother's views?'

'I loathed the druggy ones, but I thought Annabel was sweet,' said Caroline, rather repressively, Willow thought. Caroline turned away and said in a voice that sounded as though someone was throttling her: 'That's another thing that makes their deaths so bloody unfair: at last he'd found someone to love who was really worth it and worth him and now . . . they're both dead. I'm sorry, Cressida.'

Willow saw that she was in tears again and thought that once more she had misjudged Caroline. Willow asked no more except about the flowers and trees they saw, but her mind was full of questions. Would it be too far fetched to think that a woman who was besotted with her own son might decide to murder him and his latest mistress because she hated her? Yes, Willow decided a little regretfully, it would.

'Did your brother always eat healthy things like muesli?' she asked suddenly, unable to suppress a question that did not seem at all dangerous. Caroline looked startled as well she might, but she answered straightforwardly enough.

'No. He'd always rather despised that sort of thing, but Annabel was a real health-freak and insisted that he have a proper breakfast full of grains. She even bought it for him, I think.'

Willow drove them both back to Belgravia with plenty on her mind. When she had parked the Mercedes outside her flat she remembered that Ben had brought Caroline there and asked whether she would like a lift home.

'Actually, Ben said he would pick me up at half-past four,' said Caroline with a slight smile. 'I warned him that we might be later than that but he swore that he didn't mind waiting. He's parked over there,' she added, waving towards a large dark-blue BMW on the opposite side of the road.

Through the windscreen Willow could see a figure reading a newspaper. Quite involuntarily she said:

'Doesn't it drive you mad to have him hanging about for you?'

'No,' said Caroline, looking surprised. 'No one has ever looked after me like this before . . . it's a wonderful feeling being collected from stations or airports after exhausting meetings with inventors or lawyers, and parties are infinitely better when you don't have to worry about taxis or parking. And besides, he likes doing it and my miseries have been getting him down, so . . . But he's begun to cheer up again in the last few days.'

'I think you're very kind to put up with it. It would make me terribly twitchy to know that there was someone else who knew exactly where I was and what I was doing all the time,' said Willow, quite unable to imagine giving anyone else so much control over her. Caroline laughed.

'I don't mind that much, although I would have in the past,' she said. 'It must be love softening my brain – or at least my independence. I do sometimes feel as though I've succumbed to some peculiarly beguiling temptation that will lead to all sorts of trouble in the future, but it's all right at the moment.'

'I'm glad,' said Willow. It was all she could bring herself to say in the face of something that would be anathema to herself. 'And do you reciprocate?'

'You mean, do I collect him from things? Not really. His working hours are so much more flexible than mine. I'm nearly always stuck in my office when he gets back to London. He . . . he's much kinder to me than I am to him,' said Caroline with a rather wistful smile.

'Well, I think he's lucky,' said Willow politely.

Chapter 10

M UCH AS she had enjoyed the expedition to Ham and
much as she had liked Caroline Titchmell, Willow
could not let herself ignore the links she had discovered
between Caroline and three of the four victims. Caroline
had a reason at least to resent both her brother and Miss
Fernside. On the other hand, Willow still could not fit
Caroline into the murderer's space in her mind. And unless
she were mad, Willow told herself again, Caroline had had
no reason to kill anyone, least of all her brother, even if he
or his friends had once played a cruel and dangerous trick
on her.

Reminding herself that for other people at least 'the
heart hath reasons reason knows not of,' Willow went
into the kitchen to make herself a cup of tea. Feeling
momentarily tired from the expedition, she took the tea
to her bedroom and drank it propped up against a bank
of down-filled pillows. As she put the empty cup down
on her bedside table she heard in her mind an echo
of Caroline's cultivated, sensible, well-articulated voice
saying, 'I don't think I shall ever forget the sensation of
complete powerlessness . . .'

The telephone buzzed in Willow's left ear, making her start. She put out a hand to pick up the receiver, but the small shock had made her clumsy and she pushed the telephone off the bedside table on to the floor. Reaching over the side of the bed to pick it up off the grey-green carpet, she felt the blood thumping unpleasantly in her head and when she straightened up again with the telephone securely held between both hands, she was slightly breathless.

'Willow?' came Tom Worth's voice, vibrating with energy and strength, 'what's the matter? Did I get you out of your bath?'

'No,' she answered shortly as she regained her self-control. 'I have a telephone in the bathroom.'

'So you do; how absurd of me to imagine the greater spotted Woodruffe flying to answer a bell,' said Tom. Willow thought irrelevantly that only Tom Worth would be able to tease her without either hurting or annoying her.

'I was asleep,' she said, smiling to herself. 'How was your lunch?'

'Pleasant but not frightfully instructive. And yours?'

'It wasn't lunch,' she answered literally, 'but . . .'

'You actually sound worried, Willow,' he said. 'I wish I could see that face of yours. Are you all right?'

'Yes. But I am a little concerned. Can you tell me whether the Fulham investigation went into the question of who might or might not have had expectations under Titchmell's will?'

'He hadn't all that much to leave,' said Tom readily. 'A mortgaged house, a life-insurance policy that paid off the mortgage, the proceeds of a self-employed pension policy, and about ten thousand pounds.'

'The house must have been worth a bit,' said Willow, 'if the life insurance paid off the mortgage.'

'A fair bit,' agreed Tom. 'As to who might have had expectations: we didn't get very far, because he left no will. No one was admitting any private expectations and there was no reason to suppose anyone had any.'

'So who did inherit?'

'His parents – which is what happens if you die intestate unless you have a spouse or children,' said Tom.

Willow thought that of all people Caroline Titchmell would have known the intestacy rules; after all, she had qualified as a solicitor before becoming a patent agent. And if it was improbable that she would have killed her brother for revenge for the drugging, it was even less likely that she would have killed him for the price of a house in Fulham.

'Willow?' said Tom into the silence.

'Yes?' she said, thinking of all the other people whose miseries and motives she had yet to explore.

'I wish you'd tell me what it is that's bothering you so much,' he said.

'There isn't really anything to tell,' she said. 'Just a feeling: and I'm damned if I'm going to be accused of relying on female intuition even if that happened to you. Did you really discover nothing about Hampshire Place at your sister's?'

'Nothing. She's almost as neurotically conscientious as you are when it comes to her children, and she made stringent enquiries before she chose the school for her precious daughter,' said Tom. 'It's stricter than most under this headmistress, having been relatively liberal under the one before.'

'In what way?' asked Willow, remembering Emma Gnatche's announcement that her friends thought it horribly strict.

'Oh they used to be allowed to wear their own clothes at weekends and even have contact with carefully chosen neighbouring boys' schools,' said Tom. 'Dances and shared debating societies, and so on. But the dragon in charge now considers that too many girls wasted time and energy on premature romantic entanglements and stopped all that. She had a lot of support from parents when she let it be known that one of the girls had got pregnant after an encounter in the bushes with a sixth-former from Michaelson's.'

'Good Lord! I wonder,' said Willow, remembering that Andrew Salcott had said that he and Bruterley had been at Michaelson's. Salcott had definitely given her the impression that his friend had been given to accepting the eager pursuit of beautiful women.

'Wonder what?' asked Tom.

'I haven't worked out the idea enough to talk about it yet,' she said quickly and was relieved when he did not press her. She seemed to be floundering in a welter of disjointed, irrational, unsustainable suspicions of probably wholly innocent people and she had enough respect for Tom's brains not to want to display her muddled thoughts. 'Thank you, Tom. I'll let you know if I get any further. Thank you for ringing. No, before you go, there is one thing: you must have come across Titchmell's sister when you were dealing with the case . . .'

'Yes, I had quite a lot of time with her. Why?'

'What did you make of her?' asked Willow. She trusted Tom's judgment and thought that his verdict might help to clear her brain of suspicion of Caroline.

'I liked her,' he said slowly, 'although I never felt that I'd quite got to the bottom of her.'

'Did you ever suspect her?' Willow asked quite sharply. There was a pause.

'Not of murder,' said Tom with ease. 'But there was something she was holding on to . . . something she was ashamed of. But that's a reaction we often get. The most innocent people often find that the presence of police officers makes them remember some peccadillo or other and act guilty. Did you like her?'

'Yes I did,' said Willow, 'although there are reasons for her to have resented both her brother and Fernside. Perhaps that was what you sensed. But I mustn't hold you up. Thank you for ringing. Good night, Tom.'

'Willow . . .' he was beginning when she cut the connection.

She took herself off to the kitchen to see what Mrs Rusham had left in the fridge. Finding a fresh loaf of granary bread, half a cooked lobster, some Little Gem lettuces and a bowl of mayonnaise, she made herself a sandwich and sat at the kitchen table eating it. The sandwich was so deep that pieces of lobster and blobs of mayonnaise kept escaping as Willow bit into it. As she wiped some mayonnaise off her chin, she thought how easy it was to live alone, and how luxurious.

Even through her satisfaction, she could not forget the person who hid his or her murderous character from the world, carefully plotting to wipe out people who had frustrated him – or her. Willow wondered rather unhappily whether it would be possible to sense the evil in a murderer she met unawares. Regretfully she decided that it probably would not. And yet whenever she thought of the person who had gone to such trouble to poison other people's food and drink she felt an echo of vicious malice.

Suddenly she pushed away the bowl of mayonnaise and got up to fling the rest of the sandwich in the rubbish bin. If she had already met and alerted the murderer by her questions, then her own food might not be safe. Trying to control the first sensations of incipient hysteria, Willow made herself list the various anti-burglar devices she had had installed in the flat. She told herself that she had no need to fear contamination of any food she ate there unless there had been a burglary, but she could not quite get rid of her fear. Eventually she went angrily to bed, determined to stop herself speculating until she had some more solid evidence on which to base her suspicions. She took Marcus Aurelius's *Meditations* to bed with her in the hope that their calm good sense would soothe her.

Having slept badly and dreamed wild dreams of pursuit and flight, Willow woke the following morning in an odd mood of uncharacteristically low self-esteem. Her lack of progress in unmasking the killer was upsetting her. She could not help thinking of the violence she had unleashed against her possessions during her last investigation and the risks she had so lightheartedly accepted when she had involved herself in this one.

Telling herself that the only way to ensure that she was not at risk would be to unmask the murderer for the police, Willow went to bathe and dress. By the time Mrs Rusham let herself in through the front door to start her week's work, Willow was almost too distracted to enjoy her breakfast. But when Mrs Rusham took away the melon skin and substituted a plate of perfectly cooked fishcakes, Willow managed to ignore the notebook of questions that she had put beside her coffee cup.

When she had finished, Willow laid down her knife and fork with a small sigh, and when Mrs Rusham reappeared with a new cup of cappuccino, Willow complimented her with real fervour. Mrs Rusham's usual coolness warmed a fraction.

'Mr Lawrence-Crescent mentioned last week that you liked fishcakes, Miss Woodruffe,' she said, leaving Willow amazed that her predilection for the humble frozen fish-finger had been so oddly translated, and rather touched at Mrs Rusham's efforts to accommodate her tastes.

When she had got over the unusual sensations and finished her coffee, Willow retreated to the drawing room and sat in one of the French chairs beside the telephone, trying to think of a way to exonerate Caroline completely so that she could be dismissed and Willow could concentrate on her other suspects. The obvious way would be to find out whether she had any cause to resent the doctor who had been killed in Cheltenham, but she could hardly ring up his widow and ask such a question directly.

After some thought, Willow decided to try to kill two birds with one stone and looked up the number for Dr Andrew Salcott's house. Apart from Emma Gnatche, whom she did not want to involve, Salcott was the only person Willow knew who had known Dr Bruterley. Having spoken to Salcott's wife, Willow eventually tracked him down to Dowting's, the big teaching hospital where he worked for part of each week. Reluctant to disturb him in the middle of a ward round or some urgent case, Willow refused the telephonist's offer to 'bleep him' and left a message asking him to telephone her when he had time.

Almost as soon as she had put the telephone down, the bell rang and she picked up the receiver again, expecting to hear his voice. Instead she heard Caroline's pleasantly deep one inviting her to supper on Thursday.

'Richard is coming, and Ben and I would both be so pleased if you could come too. Not a formal party like Richard's, but just us and perhaps one other couple for supper in the kitchen.'

'I'd love to,' said Willow, not sure she liked the implication that she and Richard were 'a couple'. Caroline gave her address and asked Willow to come as soon after eight as she could manage.

Writing the appointment in her diary, Willow was struck by the fact that Mrs Rusham had never once asked her any questions about the days her employer spent away from the flat. It was partly for the housekeeper's lack of curiosity that Willow so greatly prized her, but it seemed odd all the same.

There was not much that Willow could do to take the investigation any further until she had talked to Andrew Salcott. She had no reason to suspect him, beyond the fact that he knew Jim Bruterley, had had at least tenuous connections with Hampshire Place, was probably neat-fingered (most doctors were) and had access to such things as surgical gloves and the high-precision tools that might help him to adulterate boxes and bottles without leaving a mark. He had also given her the impression that he was an angry man, but that did not add up to much. She decided to ignore the investigation for the moment and go into her writing room and start playing with ideas for her next novel.

The early stages of producing a synopsis for her publishers usually pleased her: it was the last moment of perfect freedom, in which she could invent whatever characters she liked, give them whatever names, disasters, happiness and fulfilment she wanted. Later, once part of the book was written, she became its prisoner, struggling to make what she was writing work consistently within its own limits and often hating it before she was done with it.

On that particular morning, though, the usual light-hearted planning seemed less fun than usual. Whenever she started scribbling notes on a character's appearance or predilections, she found herself thinking of the murderer she was seeking.

The post arrived before Willow could become too bogged down in fruitless speculation and anger with herself. Among the bills and fan letters was a post-card from the London Library, informing Willow that the modern book on poisons that she had reserved had been returned to the library and could be collected at any time within the next fortnight. Unable to sit still any longer, Willow went through to the kitchen, where Mrs Rusham was cooking something that smelled wonderfully of new olive oil and sweet onions, to say:

'I have to go out for about half an hour. If a Dr Andrew Salcott telephones, could you ask him for a telephone number where I can reach him and the most convenient time for me to ring?'

'Certainly, Miss Woodruffe,' said Mrs Rusham, not even sounding surprised. Willow whisked herself out of the flat, into a taxi and round to St James's Square. She asked the taxi to wait while she went into the library to collect her book, and then made him drive her home.

Mrs Rusham told her that the only telephone call had been from her editor. Willow thanked her and then went to telephone her publishers. Having dealt with a few small questions on the typescript, the editor then asked Willow how her new book was going.

'I've hardly done anything yet,' said Willow. 'I need to let it come to me rather than try to force it.'

'Good idea,' said Susan Walker. 'You probably need a bit of a rest, too. What about a holiday?'

'I don't much like them,' said Willow with a smile in her voice. Having no 'Cressida Woodruffe' passport, she could hardly go abroad with any of the luxury she could have afforded and so preferred to stay in England. 'But I've been going out and about a bit,' she said, anxious not to let Susan feel sorry for her. 'I met a delightful writer the other day: Ben Jonson. Do you know him?'

There was a short silence at the other end of the line and then Susan said:

'No, but I've heard that he can be difficult.'

Remembering Ben's own account of his anger with an intrusive and insensitive editor, Willow said:

'No need to find a man's valet for a true character assessment – just ask his editor.'

'You're absolutely right,' said Susan with a rueful laugh. 'The nicest people turn out to be dragons in defence of their writing. Anthony Williams has just joined us from Manx and Herman, and he was regaling us with some of the habits of the literati the other day. He used to work with Ben Jonson and had quite a rough time.'

'How odd. He seemed so gentle,' said Willow. 'What are the books like?'

'Never read them,' said Susan. 'But they're said to be very well written. Anthony was full of admiration for the *books*. Look, Cressida, I've got to go. We've got that wretched weekly meeting. Let's have lunch soon. May I ring you?'

'Please do,' said Willow and then settled down to read her account of the plant poisons of the world. The book she had just collected was very different from the learned if old-fashioned tome she had already pored over, although it dealt with most of the same poisons. The modern author appeared to have tried small doses of many of them and could describe his symptoms in graphic and often horrifying detail. He also added one or two intriguing snippets of information, such as the fact that various species were immune to poisons that could kill a human: rabbits, snails, slugs, blackbirds and monkeys, for example, could eat quantities of deadly nightshade without ill effects and there was even one beetle, *Halca atropa*, that lived solely on its leaves.

By the time Andrew Salcott did telephone Willow, she was deep in the mysteries of poisons, having learned among other wierdly fascinating things that carrot is fatal to white mice, but as soon as he gave her his name, her mind switched straight back to what she needed to know.

'I'm doing some research for my next book,' she said, blessing that all-embracing cover story, 'and I wondered whether I could possibly buy you a drink or a meal and pick your medical brains.'

'What a splendid idea!' he said. 'My wife's about to take the children back to school and going on to stay with a . . . a friend for a week in Shropshire. Why don't we have dinner one night next week?'

'How very nice,' said Willow. 'Thank you so much.'

'For nothing,' said Salcott. 'You were so good to me on that train I'd planned to ring you up anyway. You just got in ahead of me. We'll have a splendid dinner and you can ask me anything you want.'

'You are kind,' she said with a coo in her voice. 'Might I ask you something now that hasn't anything to do with my book? It's a rather odd question.' There was a moment's thoughtful pause before Salcott answered:

'You can certainly ask. Whether I can tell or not is another matter.'

'Thank you. It's nothing medical or confidential. Do you remember a scandal at Hampshire Place? I suspect that it may have happened while you were at Michaelson's.'

'When one of the girls got pregnant?' said Salcott, with a laugh in his rollicking voice. 'Of course I remember, but why on earth do you want to know about that?'

'It's a rather private matter,' said Willow feebly. 'I'm afraid of making unintentional mischief with a . . . a friend of mine through ignorance. I'm awfully anxious to know who the father was.'

'Ummm,' he said, stalling as she had feared he might.

'I gathered, you see,' said Willow as carefully as she could, 'that it was either poor Dr Bruterley or . . . well, someone else, if you see what I mean.' There was such a long silence that she eventually added, 'are you still there?'

'I don't see what you mean at all,' he said, sounding almost angry. 'Are you pumping me for information to feed to those disgusting newspapers? I really do think that poor Miranda has had enough to put up with, without ancient scandals . . .'

'Good heavens no!' said Willow loudly enough to stop the flow. 'Can you really think that of me?' She put a lot of injury into her voice.

'No. I'm sorry,' said Salcott abruptly. 'If it'll stop any kind of mischief I suppose I ought to agree that it might have been Jim. Probably was, in fact. Does it matter?'

'Not if it was him,' said Willow reassuringly. 'I'd heard . . . well, that . . . never mind. If it was Bruterley then I can forget it. Who was the girl?'

'Sarah something,' said Andrew Salcott so readily and with such a kindly note in his deep voice that Willow thought he must have interpreted her incoherent, meaningless words as uncertainty about some man in whom she was romantically interested.

'Not Caroline Titchmell?' she said, just to make sure. There was a gale of laughter at the other end of the telephone.

'Spotty Little Titch? Good heavens, no!' said Salcott, obviously quite happy now that he was no longer worried about a scandal involving his old friend. 'I'd have remembered that. And if it had been her the father certainly wouldn't have been old Jim. He could have had his pick of them all – and probably did – and he wasn't the least interested in Titchmell. He always liked them tall and thin. No, this was a leggy creature with wild blond hair called Sarah. I honestly can't remember her surname. What's Titchmell doing now? I haven't thought of her or heard her name for years.'

'I have no idea,' said Willow, lying without compunction. 'So, she never had any kind of fling with Dr Bruterley.'

'Absolutely not! I say, I must go now. But let's make a date for next week. Monday? It's my first night of freedom.'

'Monday would be fine,' said Willow. They agreed to meet at a restaurant in Chelsea, where she had never eaten. She said goodbye and put down the telephone, feeling happier than she had for some days. Her investigation had progressed to the extent that she could banish her unrealistic suspicions of Caroline Titchmell. With a source of information about Bruterley all ready to talk to her, Willow had plenty to do.

She went back to her synopsis, determined to polish it off before she talked to Andrew Salcott, so that she could free her mind for her inquisition. She had completed the notes for two chapters before she thought of the woman who had been thought to be blackmailing Dr Bruterley. Had her name been Sarah? Willow could not remember whether the *Daily Mercury* had gone so far as to put a name to the 'disturbed' patient, but into her novelist's brain flashed a complete synopsis for a novel – or a crime.

If leggy, blond Sarah had been made pregnant at school by Bruterley, she would presumably have come under the untender care of the matron who had been so unsympathetic to Caroline Titchmell. That matron was Miss Fernside. An unsympathetic, unimaginative matron of the old school – probably a virgin herself – might well have caused a pregnant schoolgirl terrible unhappiness. And perhaps, terrified of having the child and ruining her life, she had in the holidays gone to see an old girl of the school, known to have had an abortion. That could have been the actress Claire Ullathorne, who might have recommended an abortionist.

Working back, using the known ages of the people involved, Willow decided that the pregnancy scandal must have happened some time between 1972 and 1977. She grinned at herself suddenly, having forgotten how old she was; her imagination had been suggesting some pre-Abortion Act, backstreet practitioner. Nevertheless, it was possible that something had gone wrong with Sarah's operation for which she had blamed the matron, the actress and the father of her unborn child. Perhaps she had buried the hurt and anger at the time and they had resurfaced only when Bruterley once again led her into a sexual relationship and rejected her.

The only trouble with that unhappy but forensically promising scenario was that Willow could not imagine how Simon Titchmell and his girlfriend might have played parts in it.

After lunch she accepted a cup of espresso coffee from her housekeeper and said:

'By the way, Mrs Rusham, what happens to the newspapers I leave on the breakfast table?'

'I take them to the recycling bins near my home on Monday evenings,' answered the housekeeper, looking rather affronted. 'Have you some objection?'

'Good heavens no!' said Willow. 'I'm impressed by your concern for ecology. I'd just hoped that last Thursday's *Mercury* might still be readable.'

'I'm afraid not. If you wish me to keep the papers in future . . .'

'No. No, thank you, Mrs Rusham,' said Willow with a polite smile. She carried her coffee into the drawing room, silently cursing the housekeeper's efficiency. In her small irritation, the bleakness of the room annoyed her and, forgetting both coffee and investigation for the moment, she opened one of the drawers in the Pembroke table that carried the telephone and took out her paint and fabric samples.

Having held them up against the walls and squinted at them through ninety-per-cent closed eyelids, she confirmed the tentative choice she had made the week before and telephoned the interior decorator who had organised the original decoration of the flat.

He sounded delighted to take on the chore of finding decorators and upholsterers to tackle the work, and asked whether 'Cressida' wanted him to select paintings and furniture to substitute for the irreplaceable things she had lost.

'No, don't worry about that, Martin,' Willow said. 'I'll gradually find them myself. Of course, if you happen to see anything nice you could let me know about it . . . but I rather enjoy the final choosing and buying myself.'

'That's understandable,' he said. 'I'd hate to live surrounded by furniture chosen by someone else, but you'd be amazed by how many people do.'

'Perhaps your other clients are lazier than I,' said Willow, amused as she always was by the foibles and absurdities of the very rich and thinking 'good copy'.

'Actually, my dear,' said Martin, exaggerating his languid voice, 'I think a lot of them are just rather unsure about their taste.'

'Oh, bitchy, bitchy, Martin,' said Willow, even more amused. 'Well, I like mine and so I've chosen the colours and the fabrics. Would you like me to send them?'

'Why don't I come round and pick them up. It would be lovely to see you, and . . .'

'And you could just check on my taste and send me a big bill for your professional time?' said Willow, sounding to her slight dismay more like the Civil Servant than the rich novelist.

'Bitchy yourself,' said Martin, but he was laughing. 'All right, send them. I've got all the old measurements on file and so I can put in the orders without coming to measure up. But the cutters will have to cut the covers on site, you know.'

'Yes, I know,' said Willow. 'But you could fix that with Mrs Rusham for any time on a Tuesday, Wednesday or Thursday,' she went on. 'I'm out all those days and so it won't hurt me.'

'And the decorating? Do you expect me to have that done within three days?'

'Absolutely,' she said, sounding like Lady Bracknell. 'And don't tell me it's not possible. The panelling is in very good condition, so all they'll have to do is wash it down and then apply three coats of paint.'

'There's always the ceiling and the woodwork, dear,' said Martin. 'But I suppose I could arrange it so that they work three days one week and three days the next if you insist.'

'You are a little treasure,' Willow informed him. 'And I'll pay your bill with exemplary promptitude. It should be quite nice for you, because the chintz I've chosen is ludicrously expensive. Your thirty-three per cent – or however big the commission is nowadays – will come to quite a lot. Let Mrs Rusham know when you need access to the flat.'

'I will. Thank you for the order; I may say, in spite of your rather – shall we say acerbic? – attitude, you are one of my easier clients,' said Martin. 'Goodbye.'

Feeling refreshed by the interchange, Willow drank her cold coffee, shuddering from the strength of it, and then dialled the number of the *Daily Mercury*.

'Jane Cleverholme, please,' she said, and then a moment later: 'Jane? Good. Cressida Woodruffe here. Thank you for those cuttings. I'm afraid that I need to pick your brains again.'

'I think I still owe you, Cressida, for your discretion last year after I'd spilled the beans about my boss's wife,' said Jane. 'What can I do for you?' Willow could hear the millions of cigarettes she must have smoked in the huskiness of her voice.

'Mrs Rusham has thrown out my last week's *Mercuries*,' she said, 'and I've forgotten the details of the disgruntled mistress of the glamorous murdered doctor. D'you remember the piece?'

'Cheltenham, wasn't it? Yes I remember. But why do you want to know?' The suspicion was even clearer in Jane's voice than the cigarettes.

'You've never quite dropped the idea that I might be freelancing for a rival gossip column, have you?' Willow said. 'But I promise that I am not. Did you read anything anywhere after our last discussion? No, you did not. I just need to know, and I'm too discreet to tell you why.'

'Will you promise that when discretion is no longer necessary you'll tell me all?' Jane asked. 'And give me the story a micro-second before everyone else?'

'Yes, I promise that,' said Willow when she had had time to think it over. Then she spelled out her promise: 'When discretion is no longer needed, I'll tell you before any other journalist has had a chance.'

'Good. I'll go and look up the story. Do you want to hang on or shall I ring you back?'

'I'll hang on,' said Willow, who was long past the stage of minding how high her telephone bill was in Chesham Place. Her Abbeville Road telephone was quite another matter, of course, and if it rose above her budgeted maximum she was seriously displeased.

'It's not surprising you didn't remember much,' said Jane. 'We hardly printed any of it. Damned lawyers, you know. All we said was that she was blond, a former mental patient, beautiful and unhappy.'

'Leaving your charming readers to fill in the gaps: ex-mental patient equals mad equals homicidal; blond and beautiful equals promiscuous and so on. Tell me what you didn't put in the article.'

'Come on, Cressida,' said Jane crossly. 'That's more than my job's worth. Haven't you heard of slander? It's just as bad as libel . . .'

'But less easy to prove. Don't tell me your telephone calls are all taped?' said Willow.

'I wouldn't put it past my paranoid chief, the famous Gripper-the-pig. Oh Lord! Well, if he's listening to all our conversations, he'll have known long ago that we all loathe him. Got that?' she called in a different voice. Reverting to her normal tones, she went on: 'You could always ask specific questions and I'll see whether I can answer them.'

Willow felt once again the bitter envy the amateur feels of her professional counterpart. Unlike the police, Willow would never be in a position to subpoena anyone or demand their files or make them give her a signed statement.

'Is her name Sarah?'

'Yes.'

'What is her surname?'

'Can't say.'

'Blast!' said Willow with un-Cressida-like primness. 'Has she ever had an abortion?'

'No record here.'

'Where does she live?'

'Cheltenham,' said Jane, sounding happy to be able to give her friend something.

'I know that, you idiot. Where in Cheltenham?'

'Honestly, Cressida, I *cannot* tell you things like that.'

'All right. Is there anything you can tell me?' asked Willow, burying her irritation because she thought she could hear real sympathy in Jane's smokey voice.

'Nothing else, I'm afraid. Sorry. Oh well, perhaps it would be OK to let you know that we can't find her. She seems to have done a bunk. The police are probably looking for her and we certainly are. But that really is all.'

'Don't worry. I'll get it somewhere else. Thanks, Jane. I'll see you soon, I hope,' said Willow. They said goodbye to each other and Willow was left with an ever-growing bundle of loose ideas in her mind and a sense of horrible frustration. She decided to walk it off and went to change out of her soft black suede shoes into something more suitable for out of doors.

It was a short walk through Lowndes Square and across Knightsbridge into Hyde Park, and Willow was soon picking her way across the grass towards the Serpentine. The grass was almost dry, but still freshly green, and the trees were much further advanced than she had realised from her forays among London's streets. The horse-chestnuts already had their soft cones of white flowers out among the leaves, but other trees showed only a fuzz of greenness among their still-sharp black branches.

As she circled the ornamental lake, Willow was surprised to see that there were still uniformed nannies pushing waist-high, swan-necked, prams in glossy dark-blue or black. One passed her and she noticed a pristine broderie anglaise canopy attached to the pram to shield the baby from the sun. The whole equipage looked as archaic as those house-party photographs from the Indian summer before the First World War. Willow looked away and was relieved to see a far more familiar group of children on bicycles and skate-boards, shepherded along by two nannies of the new school, who were dressed in skin-tight leggings and sweatshirts and had pink flashes died into their spikey hair and heavy black makeup around their eyes.

She walked on, thinking of nothing very much but hoping that her mind would clear eventually, until she had crossed into Kensington Gardens and found herself amid the fountains at the end of the Long Water. The symmetry of the formal arrangement of pools pleased her and she decided to sit for a while to rest her feet.

The fountains' spray was blowing wildly in the wind. Willow watched in detached amusement as a group of children charged through the wettest of the paths, getting soaked in the spray and squealing in mixed delight and terror, but she became less amused when the wind suddenly changed direction and a gust blew a cold shower over her.

Perhaps it was the cold or perhaps the exercise had its usual beneficial effect on her mind, but whatever it was, by the time she had walked past the statues and round the Round Pond, she knew that her next move in the investigation had to be to interview Miranda Bruterley. However much Willow disliked the idea of intruding on a woman so recently widowed, she knew that she could get no further without asking questions to which only Miranda could know the answer. Willow hurried back to her flat and telephone.

Chapter 11

A S SOON as Willow got back inside the flat she went
into her pale, pretty bedroom and, without taking off
her coat, picked up the telephone and dialled the number
of Tom Worth's office. When she was told that he was
talking to someone else on another line, she left a message
for him to ring her back urgently, took off her coat and
shoes, and lay flat on her back on the antique Irish lace
counterpane.

Staring up at the ivory-coloured ceiling, she waited for
Tom and thought about the person she was pursuing.
There must be a sourness and a sick delight in the
murderer, she thought, as well as the vanity and the
inadequacy of which the psychiatrist had warned her.
She could imagine the murderer taking pleasure in
the sense of power the killings must have provided,
both during the long, intricate planning and in the
aftermath. Willow tried to imagine what that aftermath
must have been like. Would satisfaction have been
uppermost or fear or even a kind of sick hangover?
What outward signs could those feelings have created in
the killer?

'And what hurt or insult could ever make an intelligent person kill?' she asked herself, and then realised the naivety of the question. From her reading of the one psychology textbook she had found that mentioned serial killers, Willow knew that for those who had provided the case studies for the book the smallest rejection had been enough to make them want to kill. On the other hand the person she was tracking was not precisely like them; of that she was absolutely sure. They had selected their victims according to physical types. Her poisoner had chosen the victims for some other reason, and she was determined to work it out.

Delving into her own psyche in search of some feeling that might have propelled her into homicide, Willow decided that of all the emotions she had ever felt, only frustration would be strong enough. The impotent rage she felt in her Civil Service life when colleagues would not listen to her rational demolition of their arguments and accept it made her feel more nearly murderous than anything else except the filth, inefficiency and over-crowding of transport in London. But she knew that she was eccentric where strong feelings were concerned.

If there were a spectrum of emotion akin to the rainbow, she thought, and she represented violet, the poisoner would be red, although probably giving other people the impression of violet coolness. Willow put both hands behind her head, tilting her face towards the opposite wall instead of the ceiling. There was an anonymous eighteenth-century French painting hanging there in lieu of the Watteau she would have liked if only she could have afforded it, showing a picnic in a grassy glade, with two pairs of silk-dressed lovers flirting with each other amid all the romantic impedimenta of swing, ribboned mandolin and flowers.

'Love,' said Willow aloud, remembering that love, money and revenge were always said to be the classic motives for murder. She tried to fit them to what she knew of the poisonings. Money could be dismissed straight away, because Edith Fernside had had nothing to leave but a few knick-knacks and some pathetic savings in the Post Office Savings Bank. She had had an adequate pension, which paid the high service charge on her bungalow, but that had died with her. Even Simon Titchmell's fortune had been limited to the price of his house. Tom had provided no information on Claire Ullathorne's will, but Willow could remember that she was said to have had a good divorce settlement. That did not sound like untold riches, even if Ullathorne had had enough money to keep herself when she could not find work.

The telephone rang before Willow could get any further.

'Willow? You wanted me,' said Tom. 'I hope it's important because I'm in the middle of a hell of a case.'

'It is,' she answered, unworried by his brusqueness. 'I need to know the name and address of Dr Bruterley's mistress and I need to talk to his widow. Can you fix that for me?'

'The first, probably: I expect I can get her name from the Cheltenham people; the second, no: I can't pass you off as a police officer and even if I could the Cheltenham boys would never put up with my sending someone to interfere in their case,' said Tom, sounding irritable for once.

'Then I'll just have to take a risk and go and see her as myself,' said Willow.

'She won't talk to you,' said Tom. 'And don't you dare suggest that you are there officially. If you must go, you can be a novelist or a pensions investigator or a journalist or anything you like, so long as it has nothing to do with the police. Understood?'

'Yes, I quite understand,' answered Willow with complete sincerity. 'Even though it's frustrating. Is your case going to keep you in the office all night or could we have dinner? Mrs Rusham's been cooking something that smells amazing and there's always plenty for two.'

'That's nice of you, Will,' said Tom, softening his voice, 'but I don't think I'd better accept, because I've no idea when I'll get out of here.'

'Don't worry about that,' she said. 'Come if you can. I . . . I'd like to see you.' That was as far as she could let herself go, despite her sharp moments of terror and her absurd feeling that Tom would be able to protect her from the poisoner.

'Would you?' Tom's voice was almost wistful, but it firmed as he added: 'Then I'll do my best, but I can't promise.'

When his voice had gone, Willow slowly replaced her receiver and tried to imagine her small disappointment magnified to an extent that could make her want to kill Tom Worth. She could not do it, but then, she hastily tried to persuade herself, she did not love him. He was a friend, a dear and trusted and wanted friend, but no more than that.

'Love, money or revenge,' she was saying to herself as she fell asleep.

When she woke three hours later, surrounded by the slanting golden light of a late spring evening, she could not understand what had happened to her. She didn't approve of afternoon rests, and she had always despised people who lay about when they ought to have been working.

She got off the bed, feeling groggy, and saw to her surprise that it was after eight o'clock. Mrs Rusham must have left the flat with deliberate quietness so as not to disturb her employer. Willow rubbed her eyes, forgetting that as Cressida she was wearing black mascara on her pale-red lashes. The doorbell rang and she wandered out to listen to the intercom.

'Will? It's me, Tom.'

'Come on up,' she said, still sounding half-asleep, and pressed the buzzer.

Two minutes later he was knocking at the door of her flat. Willow opened it. He looked at her face and took her into his arms.

'It's all right. Please don't let yourself get so upset. What's happened?' he said into her hair as he stroked her back. 'I should never have involved you.'

'What on earth are you talking about?' asked Willow, waking up fast and pulling herself out of his embrace.

'Whatever it is that's made you cry,' said Tom. 'I've never known you do that before, except the night they wrecked your flat. I knew you were upset from the things you said on the telephone yesterday, but I hadn't realised that it was so bad. I'm sorry I was so brisk when we spoke this afternoon.'

'What makes you think I've been crying?' asked Willow, all at sea. For answer he put both hands on her shoulders and turned her round so that she was facing the pretty, gilt-framed mirror that hung on the hall wall. Willow saw the smudges of mascara below her eyes and laughed.

'You're a kind man, Tom, and all-too experienced,' she said. 'But you ought to learn the difference between smudged mascara and the wept-over sort. I was asleep until a few minutes ago and knuckled my eyes like a child, forgetting the makeup. I do not cry.'

'I see,' he said, blinking at the finality of her pronouncement. 'I do occasionally – generally with rage. Can I have some whisky?'

'Yes of course. Go and help yourself while I clean up my face,' said Willow, surprised by his admission.

'All right, but don't bother to make it up again. I like you as Willow sometimes.'

She left him, toying with the idea of telling him that she made up her face for her own pleasure and not for anyone else's; but when she had washed off the black smudges and the rest of the half-dissolved make up, she did not replace it. When she went back to him, Tom was standing by the window, a heavy glass tumbler in his hand.

172

'May I pour something for you?' he asked, starting towards her.

'Don't worry,' Willow answered, pouring herself a glass of amontillado sherry. 'I think I can manage.' Tom's quick smile answered all the implications of her five words, but he did not comment, instead asking:

'Despite the lack of tears, you have been upset, haven't you, Willow?'

Looking carefully at him, Willow could see nothing but concern for herself and so she told him many of the things she had thought, said and been disabused of by Caroline Titchmell. Her irrational fears of being poisoned Willow kept to herself.

'And you were miserable because you liked her so much?' suggested Tom.

'Partly,' she said. 'But more because if someone like that – with all those talents and attractions – could kill people because they had once been unkind to her, my few optimistic assumptions about humankind would have been disproved. But most of all it was because of the vileness of the thought that someone who could poison people like that could project such niceness. You see I really did like her. Funny,' she added, 'until I started this detecting business I had no idea how many people I'd find in the world whom I could like. It's rather unsettling . . .'

Tom looked as though he were about to speak, but then he drank some more whisky instead and waited for whatever Willow might say next.

'Never mind that, though,' was what came, in a far crisper voice than the one she had used before. 'What we need now is more information about Bruterley's mistress. Did you get anything from your Cheltenham "boys"?'

'Not a lot,' he answered, 'except that she's disappeared.'

'Aha,' said Willow. 'So my informant was right. Well, that must be a hopeful sign. What clots the police there must be . . .'

'Be fair, Will,' said Tom. 'By the time they had discovered

the existence of the woman she had gone, and it was a bit late then to put a watch on all routes out of Cheltenham. Besides . . .'

'They presumably suspected the widow at first,' suggested Willow. Tom's face gave her the answer even before he put it into words.

'Most murders are domestic, Willow,' he said. 'But it seems not in this case. At first sight, it looked as though Mrs Bruterley had had the opportunity of poisoning that bottle of whisky at any time she wanted to. She could easily have extracted the necessary nicotine with the most basic kitchen equipment . . .'

'Does she smoke?' asked Willow, sitting on the sofa and twirling her sherry glass between her fingers.

'No, but that would not have stopped her from buying boxes of cigars, would it?' said Tom, looking amused.

'And so what has given them the idea that she didn't do it? I imagine they'd have arrested her by now if they thought they could prove anything.'

'Apart from the fact that she had no apparent motive she was away staying with her mother in Northumberland for about ten days before her husband died, and . . .'

'Have they any proof that he drank from that particular whisky bottle in those ten days?' asked Willow sharply. She disliked hearing the shrill urgency in her voice, and so she made herself calm down, breathed deeply and drank a little more sherry.

'Yes, the senior partner of the practice was one of the people who was allowed to share Bruterley's single malt, and he has told the police that he and Bruterley had a couple of drinks from it three days after Mrs Bruterley left with her children. That is seen as pretty conclusive,' said Tom. 'That and the lack of motive.'

'Unless she knew about the mistress. Jealousy is a bloody strong motive.'

'Apparently she knew nothing about his infidelities,' said Tom. Willow was not certain whether he believed his

174

own statement or indeed whether it was believable. She made a mental note to ask Andrew Salcott about Miranda's attitudes to her husband and her marriage.

'Then what about money?' she asked, putting her doubts to one side for the moment. 'Didn't she stand to inherit anything after his death? Most widows get something.'

'He had no life assurance . . .' Tom was beginning when Willow interrupted him again.

'But what about the mortgage? The building society must have insisted on life assurance.'

'No mortgage,' said Tom. 'The house was bought outright by Miranda Bruterley herself. She owns it. She has plenty of money of her own. Bruterley had put all he had into buying his share of the practice and building up his collection of pictures.'

'Who did know about the mistress?' asked Willow, leaving the question of money.

'Apparently very few people knew. There was the girl herself, Bruterley, and the malt-whisky-drinking senior doctor, to whom Bruterley had talked when he discovered that the girl was a patient. They'd managed to keep it pretty quiet, you see,' said Tom. He got out of his chair and came to sit beside Willow on the sofa. She smiled at him. He laid a hand on her knee for a moment, but she had too many questions to let the pleasant sensations aroused by his hand distract her.

'Really? How long had it been going on?' Willow asked.

'About three months apparently,' said Tom, accepting her questions and removing his hand. Watching Willow's doubtful expression, he went on, 'but there's nothing whatever to suggest that the widow might have done it even if she had known about the affair. There's no evidence she knew how to extract nicotine from cigars or that she ever bought any tobacco at all. She has a nanny living in the house all the time and the girl has made a statement saying that she never smelled anything

175

untoward there and saw no evidence of experiments in the kitchen.'

'And had there ever been a burglary in their house?' asked Willow. Tom smiled ruefully and drank some more whisky.

'Yes. That was one of the things I asked the boys to check. The Bruterleys were burgled the day before Mrs Bruterley went away. The police there don't think that was particularly significant because there has been a spate of breaking and entering in Cheltenham and it was the classic sort: video and television, jewellery and loose money,' said Tom.

'And perhaps a fatal dose of nicotine added to the malt whisky,' said Willow, sounding thoughtful. She sipped her sherry. 'Oh damn no. If the burglary was before Mrs Bruterley went away and someone else drank some from the relevant bottle after she had gone, it can't have been done during the burglary. Are your boys certain that there wasn't another burglary?'

'Positive – unfortunately for our investigation.'

'Did Bruterley drink whisky every evening?'

'Apparently not; only when under particular stress.'

'Ummm,' murmured Willow. 'Shall we eat? It's getting pretty late.'

'Whatever you say,' answered Tom, getting off the sofa and offering her his hand. She managed to stand up without his assistance.

They discovered that Mrs Rusham had already laid the dining room table for one and so Willow went to fetch more cutlery, plates and glasses while Tom took a heavy cast-iron pot from the slow oven in the Aga and found a bowl of salad waiting in the refrigerator beside a jar of dressing. He fatigued the salad and took both dishes into the dining room.

'There's probably some kind of potato somewhere,' said Willow, passing him in the doorway. 'I'll go and investigate.'

176

She found an oval gratin dish full of potato slices cooked in a very little stock with onions and garlic, and carried it back to the dining room, where Tom was waiting. Willow helped herself to what proved to be a stew of squid in tomatoes and its own ink.

They ate for most of the time in companionable silence, occasionally making a remark to each other, and it was not until they were sitting over their coffee and small glasses of 1962 Armagnac that Willow brought up the subject of the case, by saying:

'I meant to tell you. I think I've discovered why Commander Bodmin might have believed that batty suggestion of Simon Titchmell's having put the aconitine in his own cereal.'

Tom looked up from his glass, his dark face taut and watchful.

'Why?' he said abruptly. As she told him what she had learned about Titchmell's drug habits from his sister, Tom's face relaxed into an expression of satisfaction.

'Yes, that could explain it. And his slight shiftiness is presumably caused by his thinking that his father ought to have reported Titchmell. Well done, Will. Thank you for clearing that up. It had been worrying me.'

'By the way, did you get the mistress's name?' said Willow, childishly pleased by his approval.

'Sarah Rowfant,' said Tom, breathing in the sharp warm scent of the brandy.

'Maiden or married?'

'Maiden, I understand,' said Tom. He reached into the inner pocket of his tweed jacket and brought out a small black-leather-covered notebook. Flicking through its pages he said, 'Never been married. Nothing known against her until this . . .'

'Which can't be said to be "known" yet, can it?' said Willow, suddenly afraid for the absent woman. If Miranda Bruterley had been away for ten days, then the doctor would have been free to devote all his time to his mistress. Perhaps she had even moved into the house, in which case she could easily have substituted the poisoned whisky.

'True,' said Tom, watching her with an odd expression in his dark eyes. 'Willow, are you all right?'

'Yes, of course, I am,' she said crossly. Then she let herself smile at him. 'I do find it all a bit depressing, though, this searching people's lives for enough misery to make them kill each other,' she said, determined not to let him know how frightened she was.

'Yes, but that's always been part of the job,' answered Tom. 'The skill is in finding a way to involve all your mental faculties and none of your emotions.'

Willow looked down at the nut-brown liquid in her glass.

'But if you don't let your emotions get involved, how can you ever discover what might have motivated your murderer?' she asked.

'Ah yes,' said Tom. 'In real – I mean ordinary – police work, motive always comes a poor third to means and opportunity. The difficulty with this case – if it is a single case – is that neither means nor opportunity are narrow enough categories to help. That is why I wanted you involved . . . I suppose,' he added slowly, watching her face, 'that I have been exploiting you.'

Willow thought about that for a moment and discovered to her surprise that even if he had been she did not mind. Uncertain what to tell him about that, she asked another question instead:

'Is there any way that you can find out whether Sarah Rowfant knew Simon Titchmell?'

'I'm not sure. The Titchmell case is officially closed. Can't you ask his sister?'

'Tricky without explaining why I want to know. She probably already thinks that I'm unspeakably nosey after all my questions on Sunday. And there're her feelings, too. I don't want to keep reminding her about her brother's death just as the raw patches are skinning over,' said Willow.

Tom smiled across at her.

'But you could at least discover whether Rowfant was the girl in the Hampshire Place scandal,' suggested Willow. Tom nodded and that was the last either of them said about the murders that evening.

They spent the night together happily and, as they parted in the empty street just before six o'clock the next morning, Willow felt relieved to recognise how little of an invader Tom had proved himself. They had made love, but he had not crowded her emotionally or demanded any undertakings from her. She found that she trusted him.

Willow crossed the Thames from one life into the other in a mood of peaceful happiness that lasted until she reached her Abbeville Road flat. Discovering that her internal front door swung open as she pushed her key into the lock, she was visited by a horrible sense of *déjà vu*. Expecting to be faced with the devastation she had seen in Belgravia, she pushed the door wide and walked into her flat. There was a dreadful smell of damp wool, but none of the mess she expected. A quick glance around her living room showed her that the old black-and-white television she had hardly ever watched had been removed, but nothing else seemed to be missing. In the kitchen she discovered that she had lost her cheap food processor and toaster. She walked on towards her bedroom, congratulating herself that she could have suffered far more badly.

It was there that she discovered the worst damage. There was a large square of some kind of board attached to an obvious hole in her ceiling; the damp smell was coming from a large patch of wet carpet just below the board. Before she could decide what had happened there was a ring at the front door.

'Yes?' she called in what she hoped was a confident voice.

'I heard you and thought I ought to come up and explain,' said the voice of her ineffectual neighbour from the flat downstairs.

'Thank you, Mr Smith,' said Willow. 'What happened?'

'We got back last night to discover that we'd been burgled and when the police came they couldn't find any sign of forced entry except through the hall door. They came on up here and discovered that they'd got in through your roof, forced their way out and gone on to us. I got a man I know to do something to keep the rain out of your bedroom and we've a locksmith coming this morning. Maggie's going to wait in for him.'

'Thank you very much indeed,' said Willow, really grateful. 'Have you lost much?'

'All Maggie's jewellery,' he said sadly, 'and things like the electric drill. You?'

'The television, that sort of thing. I don't have jewellery. I suppose I'll have to get a roofer. Why couldn't they have broken a window like every other burglar?'

'I know,' said Smith sympathetically. 'The police would like to talk to you. I've written down the number of the Crime Desk and the reference number you'll need for your insurance company.'

'Thanks,' said Willow. 'I wish I had time to see to it all this morning, but I've got to be in Whitehall in . . .' She looked down at her watch, 'an hour and a half. I'll ring the police. Do you think your wife could ask the locksmith to put new locks on my door? I'll leave a blank cheque with her.'

'She was planning to do it anyway,' said the neighbour. 'She's planning to join the Neighbourhood Watch, too. Would you like some of the leaflets?'

Willow shook her head and as soon as she had got rid of the man she went to telephone the Crime Desk of the local police station.

When she had told the officer who answered what she had lost she said:

'Isn't it a bit peculiar that they should have gone to such trouble to get into a house with nothing very much to steal?'

'Not really,' said the intelligent-sounding policeman at the other end of the telephone. 'Roofers working on the house next door to you had left ladders unsecured and the scrotes just climbed up and hopped over the parapet wall. They've been doing it quite often in Clapham in the last year or so.'

Scrotes? thought Willow to herself, but she said no more.

Going to make herself a cup of coffee before setting off for DOAP, she suddenly thought of the possible significance of the burglary and all desire for coffee left her. Feeling sick, shivering and unable to stop looking behind her every few minutes, she found a black plastic bag from the kitchen drawer and flung into it every tin, bottle and packet of food in the house. She ransacked her small freezer and threw everything into the bag along with the salt and pepper and all the bottles of gin, whisky and sherry from her sidetable. Having carted her heavy burden down to the dustbins, she switched off the fridge to defrost it, emptied the kettle and, having washed her hands with great thoroughness, proceeded to scrub it out. Then she thought of the water tank in the roof and wondered whether the intruder could – or would – have poisoned that.

She ran into the bathroom and turned the taps full on, leaving the plug out of the bath, so that she could empty the tank, and she resolved to drink water only from the kitchen cold tap, which led directly from the mains.

By the time she had finished scouring the flat of anything edible or drinkable that might have been contaminated, it was far too late to go into DOAP. She hastily changed out of her jeans into a thin grey suit and white shirt, dragged her hair back from her face, signed and dated a cheque and took it downstairs to Mrs Smith, who promised to get a receipt for her, and then rushed out of the flat to catch the bus to Whitehall.

As she was running to the bus stop, Willow realised how hungry she felt and even managed to smile as she remembered one of the few remarks Tom had made as they had been eating Mrs Rusham's luxurious pudding the night before. He had asked her how on earth she kept her straight slim figure if she ate such food all the time.

'You've been to supper in Abbeville Road. Doesn't that explain it?' she had said then. Determined not to let herself think of who might have been the mysterious and efficient burglar until she had a chance to talk to Tom Worth, Willow kept her mind on questions of diet and slimness as the bus lurched over the potholes towards Whitehall.

When she reached the dull, grey building in Northumberland Avenue, she was relieved to see that she was not the last of the selectors to arrive. Both the commissioner himself and the headmistress were absent. Michael Rodenhurst, the psychiatrist, looked up from his newspaper at the sound of Willow's arrival and gave her a smile of cheerful friendliness. She responded with a small wave and went to fetch herself a cup of coffee and a bun. They at least must be safe, she told herself.

Having greeted the industrialist, who was also sitting reading a newspaper, Willow went to sit beside Michael.

'You look tired,' he said.

'It is rather a strain,' said Willow, 'having to keep my work under control before breakfast and after dinner and then sit here all day, listening to . . .' She did not specify what it was they had to hear, but saw from his quick grin that he understood much of her frustration.

'Is there so much pressure at DOAP then that you can't deal with the urgent things on Mondays and Fridays?' he asked.

'Didn't you know? I'm a part-time Assistant Secretary. I work there only on Tuesdays, Wednesdays and Thursdays, which is why this board is such a nuisance,' answered Willow.

'How odd that they should have put you forward for it,' said Michael. Willow laughed bitterly.

'When I was first told that I had to do it, I assumed that it was the Perm's way of punishing me for something he disliked, but it's just dawned on me that he may have wanted me out of the way while he tried to get something past the Minister,' said Willow, thinking with some satisfaction that Elsie Trouville was more than a match for the Permanent Secretary. 'Ah, here we go. Let's hope this week's candidates are a more inspiring lot than last week's.'

They got up and fell in behind the industrialist, who led the way to the committee room, and settled down for the day's interrogations.

That night, as soon as she got home, Willow dictated a message on to Tom's answering machine, retrieved her bicycle from behind the dustbins and rode off to a large supermarket in the Vauxhall Road. There she loaded a trolley with replacements for the food and drink she had thrown away. As she waited in the queue to pay, she saw that it had started to rain heavily and she began to dread the exhausting bicycle ride back to the flat.

So involved was she in her own thoughts that she unloaded her trolley-full on to the check-out conveyor belt without even realising what she was doing, and handed over her Switch card like an automaton.

'What a pretty name!' said the motherly woman at the till as she took the card. 'How do you pronounce it?'

'Cressida,' said Willow absently and was surprised when the woman looked worriedly back at the plastic rectangle.

'I don't think so, dear,' she said, knitting her brows. Willow managed to laugh despite her horror that she was beginning to mix the two separate halves of her life.

'I'm sorry,' she said, making herself smile. 'I wasn't thinking. It's pronounced Will-a-meena. But I've been called Willow ever since I was at primary school.'

She loaded everything back into the trolley and pushed it out into the car park, where she had chained up her bicycle. Turning up the collar of her mackintosh, she transferred the bottles and packets into both panniers and the front basket of her bicycle, buckled the straps and unlocked the padlock. Pushing the bicycle out into the Vauxhall Road, she felt the rain beginning to trickle down the back of her neck and cursed the burglar who had forced her out on such a night. She had to stop at the first zebra crossing and thought it unfair of the pedestrians, who all had umbrellas, to make her wait in the rain without any covering at all.

Almost as though her feelings had touched one of them he looked round. In the yellow glare of the streetlights, Willow recognised Ben Jonson and felt a moment's panic. He looked at her without recognition and merely raised his free hand in the direction of all the drivers and riders who had stopped at the crossing. Having recognised him so easily, Willow wondered whether she really looked as different from 'Cressida Woodruffe' as she had always assumed. Peering at herself in the nearest shop window and seeing a white face, draggled with hair that looked dark brown in the rain, she was reassured.

Cars hooted behind her and she pulled herself up on to the bicycle again and pushed against the pedals. As she rode laboriously back up the hill towards her flat, she tried to imagine what Ben Jonson could possibly be doing in Vauxhall. For a while she managed to persuade herself that she must have been mistaken when she thought she recognised him, but then she remembered that there was a huge adult education building close to the supermarket.

As soon as she had unloaded her shopping and dumped it on the kitchen floor, she went out again and walked to the nearest tube station. At the bookstall she bought a copy of *Floodlight* and searched through the multifarious adult-education courses on offer until she came to the one that explained his presence. Every Tuesday evening during

184

term time, Ben Jonson taught a class of aspiring writers in Vauxhall.

With that small mystery cleared up, Willow unpacked her shopping and started to stow it away in fridge, freezer and cupboard. It was not until she had repacked the small freezer so that all the boxes and packets fitted neatly in that she thought of the dark-red file Tom had left with her at the beginning of her investigation.

Sweating slightly, with a dry throat and empty mind, she fled to her bedroom and pushed the heavy mattress off her bed. There was the file, lying where she had left it. When she flicked it open, she saw Tom's elegantly written notes of the few clues to the murderer's identity. For the first time since she had seen the evidence of the burglary, Willow allowed herself to believe that it might have been no more than that. She could not believe that anyone searching her flat for signs that she might be involved in pursuing a murderer would have missed the file.

With the effects of shock and fear receding from her mind and body, Willow replaced the mattress and walked slowly back into her kitchen to cook and eat a frozen pizza while she waited for Tom Worth to telephone.

Chapter 12

B Y THE LAST day of the board, Willow was pining to get back to her office and do some real work again. She had agreed to have lunch with Michael Rodenhurst in a fish restaurant he knew on the far side of Trafalgar Square instead of joining the other selectors in their official lunch, but when the time came she regretted it.

The last candidate to be interviewed before lunch was a young woman who had explained that her first choice of department would be the DPR, because she was particularly interested in the mechanics and moralities of policing and the rehabilitation of offenders. Instead of listening to the questions put to the candidate by the other members of the board, Willow had uncharacteristically allowed her attention to wander back to her own investigation. When the chairman turned courteously to invite her to put her own questions to the candidate, Willow thanked him and asked:

'What would you do if, through the "Regional Unsolved Crime Reporting System", you came across a group of crimes – murders, let us say – that had taken place in quite different parts of the country that seemed to you to have been committed by the same person?'

'I'd report to my superior,' said the candidate in a soft West-country voice, 'who would, presumably, contact the relevant police forces if he thought it suitable.'

'And if your superior or the police sneered at your ideas and told you that you were indulging in nothing more than female intuition?'

Most of the other interviewers looked crossly at Willow, whose questions were not the sort that were usually asked in such interviews. The candidate looked merely puzzled. Eventually she decided on her answer:

'By informing my superior, I would have done what I see as my duty. I don't quite see what else I could do,' she said, allowing a little sound of injury into her voice. 'I'm not a police officer. Even if I were working in DPR, I should have no crime-solving responsibilities. If my impression was thought to be wrong by the police . . .'

'Then do you believe that the police are always right?' asked Willow in a disinterested but by no means uninterested voice.

'Not always . . .' the candidate was beginning, looking hot and flustered.

'I think we'd all agree that the evidence bears that out,' said the chairman with a reassuring smile at the candidate, forestalling any more eccentric questions from Willow.

At the end of the interview, when the candidate had been released, the chairman reprimanded Willow for exceeding her brief. Willow smiled coldly at him.

'With respect, Chairman,' she said, 'I was trying to find out whether, like some of our other candidates, she had inflated ideas of the powers of Civil Servants; and how realistic she might be about the kind of moral choices that may well face her if she succeeds in her ambitions to join DPR and move up the ladder there.'

'I see,' said the chairman with slightly less disapproval in his thin, grey face. 'And what have you learned?'

'That she is thoroughly realistic, reasonably conscientious and ought to make a good officer,' said Willow to the manifest surprise of the rest of the board, who had clearly thought her antagonistic towards that particular candidate.

The rest of them added their views and at last the chairman released them for lunch, adding that the man they were expecting to interview that afternoon was ill and so the session would be cancelled.

Wishing that she could go straight back to DOAP, eat a sandwich at her desk and get on with some work, Willow instead walked with the psychiatrist to the restaurant where he had booked a table. Just off Piccadilly, it was upsettingly close to the world she inhabited as Cressida and for a moment Willow was worried that she might be recognised. A quick look at her reflection in a big mirror in the ladies' lavatory assured her that no one accustomed to Cressida's luxurious curls and subtly painted face would see anything familiar in the pale, slighty freckled skin, sandy eyelashes and severe hairstyle.

When she went back to the table Michael was tasting a glass of white wine and nodding appreciatively at the wine waiter. As Willow sat down, Michael half rose from his seat, offered her a glass of Chablis and then said:

'Let's choose what we're going to eat and get it ordered before we relax. I know that we both have an unexpectedly free afternoon, but . . .'

'There's too much work waiting in the office to waste it in idle chatter,' said Willow, interrupting without conscience.

'Precisely,' said the psychiatrist and handed her a large maroon menu. Willow read it carefully and then said:

'Oysters, I think.'

'Oysters, and what then?' asked Michael.

'Grilled sole and some spinach, please,' she answered.

'How austere!' Michael signalled efficiently to the waiter and ordered himself potted shrimps and then an elaborate lobster dish. When all the questions had been asked and answered and the waiter had eventually disappeared, Michael turned back to Willow.

'Now, tell me what all this is about,' he said.

'You sound rather severe,' said Willow. 'What are you talking about?'

'Your questions: the ones you asked me last week and the ones you put to that poor flummoxed girl this morning. What is going on?'

Willow took a gulp of the sharp, cold wine to give herself a moment to think.

'At first I thought that you must be writing – or planning to write – a detective story in your spare time, but after this morning I am beginning to think that you must really be worried about some actual deaths,' said Michael.

Wishing that she could blush to order, Willow put down her wine glass and looked at Michael, making her eyes widen slightly as those of Cressida Woodruffe's heroines tended to do when they were faced with unexpectedly attractive men.

'I suppose,' she said slowly, lowering her undarkened eyelashes, 'that being a psychiatrist you are taught to look for unlikely motives.' If she had been a toucher she would have patted his shoulder or hand. As it was, even as Cressida, she never went in for casual touching except with Tom Worth.

'It is a bit embarrassing,' she went on, 'and I'll have to rely on your discretion. I'd hate my colleagues to know about my secret ambitions. You could be very useful to me, you know,' she added.

Michael Rodenhurst leaned back in his green leather chair, with an amused and rather knowing smile. Willow was prepared to put up with it to continue her placatory campaign, although she did feel the humiliation of some subordinate member of a tribe of gorillas presenting her backside to be groomed by the silverback chief.

'You can't really mean that you are writing a murder story,' he said.

'Well, "trying to write" would be more accurate,' she answered with a deceptively frank smile. 'And I'm anxious to get as much verisimilitude in it as possible – hence my questions. I have got one or two more, in fact.'

'What is the plot?' he asked, looking even more amused.

When Willow had sucked one of the gelatinous molluscs from its smooth-lined shell, she produced the information she thought necessary to convince him of her own imaginary veracity.

'The book is all about a woman who poisons the men who have spurned her.'

'Rather far fetched, I would have thought,' said the psychiatrist, obviously enjoying his potted shrimps.

'What about all those ancient saws?' asked Willow and was pleased to see his face crease up into a real smile.

'"Hell hath no fury like a woman scorned",' he quoted.

'Yes, but you and I know that that is long out of date even if it ever held true.'

'Well never mind that,' said Willow before swallowing her last oyster and laying its heavy, gnarled grey shell back onto the seaweed-decorated ice on her plate. 'What has been bothering me particularly is that from the only useful book I've managed to find it seems that most serial murderers are male, and I particularly want to have a female killer in my book.'

'I wonder why,' said Michael. 'You know, Willow King, you interest me very much indeed.'

'A case study?' she suggested, sounding coldly dismissive. 'A case study in repression, perhaps,' she added, remembering all the snide comments and jokes she had ever overheard about her undoubted virginity, her sexlessness, her joyless life, her unattractivenss and the terrible deprivation of living life without a man. For years she had persuaded herself that she was entirely indifferent to them, but recently she had been beginning to consider the possibility that she had actually minded

190

being so despised. Perhaps her determination to make more money than her colleagues could ever earn had been her way of taking revenge for their contempt.

'No,' he said, drawing out the vowel to what Willow thought excessive length. 'But you are not at all what I expected from what I've heard about you in the department or from my observations of you on that first day; you present yourself as one sort of person when you are quite obviously very different.'

Willow turned her face away, suddenly stricken by the thought that the two characters she inhabited so satisfactorily – and separately – might be drawing closer together. No one who had met her as Willow King had ever suspected that she was not altogether what she seemed until she had been confronted with Chief Inspector Worth. Somehow he seemed to be having a discernible effect on her. That worried Willow considerably.

Damn Tom Worth, she thought bitterly, and then remembered how much she liked him.

'Perhaps,' she said carefully, having schooled her face back into chill formality, 'you were simply guilty of judging by appearances – and of prejudice.'

'Perhaps,' said the psychiatrist, nodding to the waiter who was hovering near the table with their main courses. When everything was arranged and Willow was already calmly eating her sole and spinach, Michael went on:

'What . . .?'

'Michael,' said Willow, using his name for the first time, 'I can't stop you speculating about whatever neuroses and unreconstructed complexes you think I may suffer, but I'd rather you kept your conclusions to yourself. Whatever is wrong with me – and I am quite prepared to believe that there is plenty – I am a functioning human being and I'd rather not investigate the aspects of my character that might make me stop functioning. Do you understand what I'm talking about?'

He nodded, ate some lobster drenched in rich, dusky-pink sauce, and when he had swallowed said:

'All right, no questions from me. Why don't you ask the rest of yours? Or shall we merely talk about the last time we went abroad?'

Wanting to kick him, but determined to take his suggestions at face value, Willow asked him everything else she wanted to know about the tracking down of killers through psychological assessment. Unfortunately she learned nothing that gave her any clues.

When they had finished their fish, Willow declined both pudding and coffee and insisted on paying half the bill. Gracefully accepting her contribution, Michael asked her whether he had offended her.

'You've given me a good deal to think about,' she said accurately. 'It would be pleasant to continue the discussion, but I've too much work waiting.' She stood up, collected her bag and held out her hand. 'I've enjoyed our various talks,' she said, shaking his hand.

'So have I,' he said, holding on to her hand for longer than necessary. Willow could feel it sweating slightly. 'I hope that we can have more – and that if you need any more copy for your detective story you will ring me. Here's my extension number,' said Michael, offering her a small piece of paper. Willow took it, thanked him and left the restaurant without reciprocating.

As she walked down the Haymarket towards Trafalgar Square and the bus stop she wanted, she thought that the last person she would contact of her own free will would be Michael Rodenhurst. He saw too much and was too free with his questions to be a safe source of information or even friendship. That was a pity, because she had both liked him and found him interesting, but it could not be helped. Willow was not going to admit anyone else into the secrets of her double life if she could help it.

She reached her office in a mood of determined efficiency that made her voice sharply crisp and jolted her staff out of their post-lunch languor. Without letting any of them make excuses for dilatoriness or sloppy work, she spoke to most of them, looked at what they had been doing for the previous two weeks, reprimanded those who needed it, complimented one or two and retreated to her own laden desk to process all the papers that had accumulated there.

By the time she remembered her hair appointment at Gino's salon and the dinner party she was supposed to be attending afterwards, it was twenty-past six. Hurrying to lock away her classified papers and write a list of things for Barbara to deal with over the next two working days, Willow then ran out of the building and back to her flat.

When she got there, she remembered with a lurch of dismay that she had done nothing about finding people to mend the roof and cursed herself, wondering whether some of Cressida's frivolity and reliance on Mrs Rusham were infecting her in her Clapham life. There was no time to do anything that evening and so she changed into her jeans and sweater and set off for Sloane Square.

That evening she did not gain her usual relaxation from the self-indulgence of the hairdressing and manicure. As she sat down at the basin to have her hair washed, she began to wish that she had gone home to Chesham Place first and cross-examined Mrs Rusham about who had been to the flat while she had been away. It was not so much burglars that worried her, because the alarm and all the locks ought to keep them out, as spurious officials from the council or meter-readers or anyone else that Mrs Rusham might have allowed through the front door.

Gino, the lively gossiping owner of the establishment who always dealt with 'Miss Woodruffe's' hair, was silent as though he understood that she was preoccupied. While one of his apprentices was dusting the prickly ends of hair from her neck after the cutting, Gino laid a hand on her shoulder.

'Please don't let it get to you so much,' he whispered into her ear. 'Whatever it is will cure itself and worrying about it gives you ugly lines all over your face.'

At that Willow's frown broke up into a laugh and the lines fell into place.

'Thanks, Gino,' she said. 'I needed a little common sense to sort me out. I must go. I'm late.' She left a larger than usual tip for the apprentice, paid her bill and left in order to change into something suitable for Caroline Titchmell's dinner.

Remembering that it had been described as 'informal', she eschewed the dresses she wore when she and Richard dined together and chose a pair of comfortable black trousers made by Issey Miyake and a loose shirt of fine black-and-white-striped double poplin. Large baroque pearls set in gold in her earlobes and a heavy gold chain round her neck added the necessary touch of ostentation for a successful romantic novelist, and quickly but carefully applied makeup banished all signs of the Civil Servant.

She had ordered a taxi as soon as she reached Chesham Place and before she could so much as read her letters or listen to the messages on her telephone answering machine, the driver rang the doorbell. Grabbing a black suede jacket and shoving money and keys into the pocket, Willow let herself out of the flat, set the alarm and double-locked the door behind her as she had done ever since her burglary and ran down the stairs.

The taxi found his way easily to the house in Notting Hill and she was relieved to see that she was only twenty minutes late. She rang the front-door bell with an apology ready, but Ben Jonson gave her no chance to say anything.

'Cressida!' he exclaimed, as though her appearance were a wonderful surprise. She thought that he was looking a lot happier than he had done when they met at Richard's. 'How good that you've got here.

194

I'm afraid that Richard is going to be late.' Willow laughed.

'These bankers!' she said, but then added more seriously, 'Surely you were expecting me?'

'Yes, we were,' he said, ushering her into a brightly lit hall, 'but I can never manage to get over the feeling that guests won't turn up after all: that they will have forgotten, decided that they didn't want to come, or even that I never asked them.'

'But in this case you couldn't have worried about the last, because it was Caroline who did the inviting,' Willow said over her shoulder, laughing kindly at him. She rather liked the honesty of his admission of insecurity, but could not quite understand the face he made at her then.

'Caroline, hello,' she added, seeing her hostess in the open doorway of what turned out to be the drawing room. 'How nice to see you.'

'And you,' said Caroline, who was wearing a short dress of deep violet linen that set off her dark hair and made her eyes look brilliant in her pale face. 'Come and meet Mark and Sarah Tothill. Sarah is going to do the food for my wedding.'

Willow shook hands with Sarah, a tall handsome woman in her early thirties, and, remembering the conversation at Richard's dinner, said something about knowing that Emma Gnatche had been working for her company.

'She's such a good girl, and all the clients like her,' said Sarah, smiling. 'I hate the thought of losing her when she goes off to university.'

'I can imagine,' answered Willow, and was about to ask a question about the economics of private catering when Sarah's husband interrupted.

'I think she's about the most irritating girl I've ever met,' he announced.

'Little Emma?' cried Willow. 'How can you think that? She didn't annoy you, did she, Ben?' she went on, turning to include her host in the conversation. He looked nonplussed for a moment until Willow reminded him that he had met Emma at Richard Crescent's dinner.

'No,' he said after a moment's thought. 'I think that as an example of the over-privileged and under-educated classes who own everything in this country, she was remarkably inoffensive.'

There was a sourness in that answer that Willow would not have expected from someone as kind as Ben, but, remembering her own reaction to Emma's unearned privileges when they had first met, she smiled at him. At least he had defended her protégée from Mark's gratuitous unpleasantness. She could not imagine what Emma could have done to provoke it.

'What would you like to drink, Cressida?' asked Caroline, who clearly thought that they had talked enough about someone she hardly knew.

'A glass of wine, please,' said Willow and looked interestedly round the room. She had seen that the house was a flat-fronted, early Victorian building as she was hurrying up the four steps to the front door, and had rather expected it to have been furnished in the familiar stripped pine and swagged curtain school of interior decoration.

The double drawing room was quite different from all her expectations. The walls were as starkly white as those of Tom Worth's flat, but there were no other similarities. Where his rooms were austere and minimally furnished, this one contained some remarkable things. There was a very fine marquetry chest against one of the long walls, rows and rows of books along the other, some exquisite Jacobite wine glasses arrayed along the chimneypiece, and some old-fashioned, overstuffed chairs and a sofa covered in dim cretonne. There was a fender stool upholstered in some attractive petit point, and as a final touch of eccentricity the curtains were of worn but superb antique silk brocade in a colour between red and orange and pink, which Willow recognised as 'carnation' from her visit to Ham House.

'What a wonderful room!' she said, looking up and down it.

'Rather a jumble, I'm afraid,' said Caroline. 'Simon would have hated it, but we both enjoy having things we like around us, whether they go together or not, don't we, Ben?'

'It seems sensible,' he said, his voice gentle again. 'And combining my glass and your tapestry would be impossible in any other kind of decor.'

'Your tapestry?' said Willow curiously. 'Do you do it yourself?'

'Yes,' said Caroline with a slight blush. 'I find it enormously therapeutic after days dealing with infuriating people. It calms me and slows me down and makes me sane again.'

Ben touched her cheek in a gesture of extraordinary tenderness and went out of the room saying something about fetching the wine.

'There's lots more stuff to come, though,' said Caroline, recovering her complexion. 'This is really the only room we've finished. We only moved in a month ago and haven't yet decorated the room where we're going to keep Ben's masque sets; they're exquisite and it's important that they don't get damaged.'

Willow was just about to ask more when Ben reappeared and handed her a glass of red wine. At Caroline's invitation Willow sat down in one of the big chairs between Sarah and her heavy-faced husband, who was smoking a small cigar, which Willow thought was quite as offensive as his remark about Emma had been.

'I'm afraid it's only Bulgarian Cabernet Sauvignon,' said Caroline, watching Willow sip her wine.

'There's nothing wrong with that,' said Willow, who always drank it herself in Clapham. She assumed that Caroline, who could obviously well afford better wine, had adjusted her tastes to her fiancé's means so as not to underline her financial superiority. On her left Mark said *sotto voce*:

'Typical.'

Willow decided that he was either drunk or determined to be unpleasant and so she ignored him. Ben perched on the arm of Sarah's chair just then and told Willow that he had been reading one of her books. She smiled and said:

'I don't think I'll ask you what you thought of it.' But he told her and she was both surprised and rather pleased that he had found in it several things to admire.

'I thought you rather ran away from the possibilities of your heroine's relationship with her father,' he said after they had discussed the difficulties and delights of their craft.

'I suppose I did,' answered Willow. 'And I suppose that was because I get so bored with writers like me trotting out their fifth-hand psychobabble. I wanted to tell a story without any delving into childhood neuroses to explain adult motivation; but perhaps that was a mistake. Perhaps we're all so used to that now that we can't accept emotions as realistic unless they're rooted in such things.'

'Surely all present emotion must be rooted in the past,' said Mark in protest. It was the first time he had spoken politely and so Willow looked at him with interest. 'Whether you accept the views of psychoanalysts or not, you must agree with that. We must be what our pasts have made of us,' he went on.

'I'm not sure that we are necessarily,' said Willow, relaxing. 'I hate – and reject – the idea that the person that is me, the individuality, the core of me, is merely a product of what was done to me in childhood.'

'It can't be only that,' said Ben, picking up a bowl of cashew nuts and offering them to Willow. 'I'm as different as you could possibly imagine from the boy my mother brought me up to be. She lost both her brothers in the war and taught me to be as tough and manly and athletic as they were. But look at me!'

He gestured down at his gangly, rather shambling figure and laughed. The others laughed with him.

'But the way that you think and react as an adult must have something to do with the way your parents treated you,' he went on. 'That's only common sense.'

'But it suggests that babies are born without characters . . . Can that be right?' asked Willow.

'I wouldn't have thought so. Mark,' said Ben, turning to him, 'you're the doctor. What's your view?'

'Most people nowadays accept that certain aspects of personality are genetically determined,' he said, just as Willow was thinking: another doctor; I wonder if he knew Bruterley and Salcott. I wish I could ask all these people what I need to know directly instead of playing around with mock questions and speculation.

'If they're right,' Mark continued, 'then what Cressida believes is true . . .'

The ring of the doorbell interrupted him and heralded the arrival of Richard Crescent, hot and tired from a meeting with some of his clients and their lawyers. Willow would have been interested to dig deeper into what everyone thought about psychological motivation for actions in adulthood, but had to leave the subject.

'No. I'd better not hold you up any more,' Richard said when Ben offered him a drink.

'All right, let's eat,' said Caroline. 'I ought to have asked you both, do you eat snails? I know that Sarah and Mark do, because she gave me the recipe; and Ben and I particularly like them, but I know lots of people don't.'

Richard enthusiastically and Willow politely assured her that they were happy to eat snails and all six of them went in to the kitchen to eat.

The snails were served in individual pottery plates, which Caroline said she had bought in Italy, and so Willow had no excuse to limit her helping. She choked down all six of her snails and quickly followed them with nuggets of hot french bread soaked in the garlic-and-parsley-flavoured butter that was the only pleasant aspect of the dish. A deep gulp of the smooth Bulgarian wine banished the memory of the chewy, wriggly-looking snails and she felt able to concentrate on conversation again.

It occurred to her that if she had not picked up Marcus Aurelius instead of Ben's book she would have been able to return his compliments about her novel. Thinking that he had little enough vanity not to mind that she had not read any of his books and that he might be amused by the story, she told him what had happened. He laughed happily and in his soft voice said:

'Marcus Aurelius, how that takes me back! We had a master at school who was a devotee and used to chalk up one of his precepts on the blackboard each week for us to learn. I don't know that it did me much good.'

'I was struck, though,' said Willow, 'by how sensible his ideas were.'

'As far as I can remember he was a great one for swallowing his emotions and presenting a calm front to the horrors of the world,' said Caroline from the other side of the table.

'That's right,' said Ben. 'That was what our English master so greatly admired. We all tried to do it too – an earnest class of grammar-school Stoics. Well I'm glad that you had something else good to read in place of one of my novels, but I hope you'll let me give you a copy of the latest.' He got up then to remove the snail plates and Willow wondered whether she would have found his book as instructive as she had found the emperor's *Meditations*.

After the snail shells had been taken away Willow asked Mark where he had trained and, learning that it was not at Dowting's, she deliberately abandoned her investigation and settled down to enjoy herself, which she did until he reverted to his earlier form.

Willow was talking to Sarah across the table when she heard Caroline say something about the iniquities of consultants paid by the National Health Service skimping their duties in favour of their private patients and huge fees. As she spoke Mark slammed his glass down on the scrubbed pine table so hard that a wave of purple wine washed over the edge of the glass and dripped down its stem.

'That's bloody offensive nonsense,' he said, 'and it just shows how ignorant you are, despite your airs and your wretched arrogance.' Willow was astonished at his passion and at his rudeness. She looked across the table at his wife, who merely rolled her eyes upwards and shrugged. Caroline looked stunned and rather sick, and it was Ben Jonson who spoke, in a voice that was still soft and gentle and yet utterly implacable.

'May I remind you that you are a guest here?' he said. Without waiting for an answer, he went on: 'Since Caroline is here I shan't tell you exactly what I think of you, your character and your behaviour, but I think it would be better if you left.'

'No, Ben, really no,' said Caroline, white-faced. 'It's not important.'

'Yes it is,' said Ben. He dropped his napkin on the table and pushed back his chair. 'Tothill?'

'This is a joke, I take it,' said Mark, looking as surprised by Ben's softly spoken onslaught as Willow felt.

'No joke,' said Ben. 'I think it would be better if you were to leave.'

'Ben, please,' whispered Caroline, but her plea was half-drowned in Sarah's saying:

'Come on, Mark.' She got up, asked Ben for her coat and then waited in the hall for her husband, who eventually left without saying another word. His face was clenched and Willow saw that he was shaking with anger. She

felt extraordinarily embarrassed by the whole scene and
had no idea what to say or do. To refer to the scene
would merely prolong Caroline's distress, but it seemed
impossible to ignore it.

'What a frightful chap!' said Richard cheerfully. 'Could
I have some more wine, Caroline?' He held out his glass,
and Willow admired his technique. Caroline started
but then pulled herself together and reached for the
wine bottle. By the time Ben came back, oddly looking
both triumphant and ashamed, the other three were
calmly talking about the prospects for Eastern European
prosperity.

The rest of the evening passed pleasantly enough and
Willow became more and more convinced that Caroline
and Ben had a fair chance of making each other happy,
even if he was rather more protective than he needed
to be. When Willow eventually got up to leave, Richard
offered her a lift home and she accepted. As they were
saying goodbye to Caroline in the narrow hall, Ben
suddenly remembered that he wanted to give Willow a
copy of his book and ran lightly up the stairs to fetch
it.

Watching him, she thought that he had done himself an
injustice in denigrating his athletic prowess. He seemed
to move with considerable springiness. He was back
within a few minutes and held out a glossily jacketed
book.

Willow took it, thanked him and then raised her eyes
to his as she said:

'Would you sign it for me?'

He laughed, found a fountain pen and scribbled a
message on the title page. When she was sitting in the
passenger seat of Richard's car as he drove down towards
Kensington High Street, she looked to see what Ben had
written:

'Cressida: From one novelist to another, with best
wishes, Ben Jonson.'

'What did you think of him?' asked Richard, watching Willow out of the corner of his eye as she put the book in her capacious handbag.

'Intelligent, gentle, sensible about most things,' she said. 'Unlike that boorish doctor, whom I loathed. I think Caroline's chosen quite well.'

'No money, though,' said Richard, 'and not a lot of background either.'

Willow turned to look out of the car windows at the damp streets, trying to think of a way of answering him that would not sound rude.

'Really Richard, you are absurdly hidebound. There are more important things in a husband than either money or public school education,' she said eventually.

'Good Lord! Are there really?' asked Richard, and Willow was disturbed to discover that she could not be quite certain whether or not he was joking. She was silent for the rest of the journey, thinking about Caroline and Ben and their shared talent for dealing with strong emotions and defusing them before they could explode.

When Richard drew up outside her flat, she was preparing to thank him for coming so far out of his way when he started to speak.

'Willow,' he said quietly, 'are you really looking into poor Simon Titchmell's death?'

'Not precisely,' she said, 'but it has a bearing on what I'm trying to discover. Why?'

'Well,' he began and then fell silent, picking at some loose skin near his right thumbnail. 'Caroline is by way of being a friend of mine, and she's had a hell of a lot to put up with one way and another. I'm a bit bothered about her and about whether I ought not to have warned her about you,' he finished in a rush. Willow was fair enough to take his objection calmly.

'I don't think you need worry, Richard,' she said. 'Caroline is quite safe from me.' At that moment she believed what she said.

Richard turned towards her and in the light of a streetlamp she saw his face slackening into a real smile. He leaned forwards and kissed her cheek.

'Thanks, Willow,' he said and put an arm across her to open her door. 'Shall I see you soon?'

'Oh, I hope so,' she said. 'I'll let you know when it's all over and I can tell you all about it.'

Richard grinned and switched on the ignition.

Chapter 13

W ILLOW fell asleep almost as soon as she got into her bed that night. As usual, Mrs Rusham had made the bed up with clean sheets. Sliding between the cold, crisp smoothness of the two layers of fine linen, Willow thought of the unironed polyester bedding she used in Clapham and blessed the day she had invented Cressida Woodruffe. She supposed that Ben Jonson and probably Michael Rodenhurst, too, would put down her unlikely love of luxury to the emotional and material austerity of her childhood. It was true, she acknowledged to herself, that her scholarly parents would have disapproved profoundly of the way she lived in Belgravia, but she would go no further than that.

Smiling a little and letting her mind drift, Willow lost consciousness, only to wake four hours later with the most appalling pain under her front ribs. Thinking for a moment that it must be a bad attack of wind, she turned over to lie on her front, hoping that the pain would subside. It was only a few minutes before she realised that it was not going to and that it was not wind either. Flinging aside the linen-covered duvet she ran to the bathroom and reached it only just in time to be terribly, digustingly sick down the lavatory.

When the retching spasms had eventually stopped, Willow knelt for a moment longer, her elbows propped on the mahogany seat, trying to find the strength to get up. At last she did so, pulled the chain and staggered over to the basin to wash out her mouth and wipe the sweat off her face. Staring at her reflection in the mirror, she saw that her skin was the colour and texture of mashed turnips, that there were immense mushroom-coloured bags under her sunken eyes and that she looked about a hundred years old. She thought that she knew what had happened to her and turned to walk to the telephone.

Before she could reach it she was sick again. Recognising some hardly chewed snails amid the vomit, she tried to tell herself that there must have been something wrong with the snails or even that all the garlic butter in which they had been cooked was responsible for her unusual indigestion. But she did not believe herself. She could not remember ever having been so sick, even in childhood. She tried to get up, but saliva spurted into her mouth and her throat burned and she was sick again. The paroxysm exhausted her. Sinking back on to the floor, her last conscious thought was: 'I need help.'

Coming painfully back to consciousness nearly two hours later, she was sick again, bringing up nothing but thin, bitter-tasting fluid; she was in worse pain than ever; and she felt desperately, frighteningly weak. Taking a towel with her just in case she was overtaken again, she crawled in pain to the telephone on the wall at the other end of the bath.

Her mind felt woolly and stupid. It was almost impossible for her to remember the telephone number, but at last she did, and punched the relevant keys. She noticed that something had happened to her vision: it was hard to focus on the buttons of the telephone and green-black spots danced before her eyes. Putting out a hand to see whether she could focus on it, she noticed that it was covered with a nettle-like rash. In sudden terror, Willow waited for Tom's comforting voice.

It did not come. All she heard was the formally-spoken message on his answering machine. Gasping, 'It's Willow. I need help,' she had to turn towards the bath to be sick yet again.

Sweating, with involuntary tears seeping out of her eyes, she picked up the telephone again, dialled 999 and managed to ask for an ambulance.

Dimly through the pains, confusion and fear, Willow heard bells ringing and a knocking at the door, and dragged herself there to open it. Somehow the ambulance men must have persuaded one of the other tenants to open the street door. Willow just looked at them.

'There now, love. You'll be all right now,' said one in the most fatherly tones she had ever heard. Her own father had never risked softening her character with endearments. The ambulance man shook out a bright red blanket and wrapped it around her shoulders. Willow tried to tell him what had happened but as soon as she opened her mouth the gasping spasms began again. There was nothing left in her stomach to bring up, but it was a while before she could stop retching. The ambulance man held her against him with one hand and wiped her forehead with the other, murmuring comfort to her. When she was quiet again he told her that his colleague had gone to fetch a stretcher.

A few minutes later, Willow was securely strapped on to the stretcher, one of the ambulance men had found her handbag and keys, locked the front door of her flat and laid the bag beside her. They carried her down the stairs between them. She knew that she ought to ask which hospital they would take her to, but she could not summon up the energy. They were in charge and for once she was content to have no part in her eventual fate.

As they were pushing her stretcher into the back of the ambulance, there was a shout from across the road.

'Wait!' A man came running and the senior ambulance man said:

'Yes, sir?'

'She telephoned me. What's happened?'

'Are you a relative, sir?' asked the ambulance man. Tom Worth took his police identification out of his pocket and was admitted to the ambulance. Sitting down, he took Willow's clammy hands between his own and asked her what had happened.

'I've been sick and sick and sick,' she said, slurring her words. 'I think they've poisoned me.' She shut her eyes and her head lolled away from him. Tom and the ambulance man looked at each other.

'Willow, wake up!' said Tom, forgetting or ignoring the fact that she was supposed to be Cressida Woodruffe in that part of London. 'Who? What have you eaten?'

'"Eels and eel broth, mother",' she sang half under her breath. Tom shook her, despite the ambulance man's restraining hand on his sleeve.

'Wake up, Willow! What have you eaten? Where have you been?'

She opened her eyes and he saw that her pupils were widely dilated and sucked in a deep breath. Taking out his handkerchief, he wiped her sweaty face and brushed the long dark-red hair back from her forehead.

'Willow, tell me,' he insisted. 'Where have you been and what have you eaten?' Something in his voice got through to her fading consciousness and she recognised his dark eyes. Struggling with the nightmare thoughts in her mind, she tried to tell him what was making her so afraid.

'Snails,' she said. 'Snails at Titchmell's. The book says snails can live for weeks on belladonna. Can they . . .?' Before she could finish her question she starting retching again. When the spasm was over she seemed not to remember what they had been talking about and lay with her eyes closed, breathing deeply, and holding her hands across her stomach.

Through the only half-sentient receiver that was her mind, Willow was vaguely aware of being hoisted and wheeled and carried and transferred to a bed. Someone pulled open her eyes and shone bright lights into them, felt her pulse, put a cold stethoscope to her chest and pushed and pulled and dug their fingers into her skin. She heard voices and every so often one would make sense even to her:

'I shouldn't have thought that was possible,' said one strange, deep voice. Then came Tom's, reassuringly familiar:

'What poison could it be? Is there any plant that could do this?'

'Lots, I'd say. But there's plenty else,' said the strange voice. 'It looks quite like oysters to me. Does she eat oysters?'

Tom said something then that Willow could not understand and she forced herself to break out of her own weakness to say:

'Oysters for lunch.'

'Did she say something?' said the doctor.

'Willow,' came Tom's voice, 'say it again, please.' She lifted her eyelids with as much effort as though she were heaving up a cabin trunk filled with rocks, and said as distinctly as she could:

'I . . . ate . . . oysters . . . for . . . lunch.'

'Aha,' said one of the men and Willow heard no more.

Nightmares mixed with people doing things to her, asking her questions and telling her things for several hours and Willow was not at all sure what was real and what was not, but at eight the next morning she woke in her right mind to discover herself in a high white bed, lying in a shaft of sunlight from a vast modern window.

'Hello,' said a cheerful voice to her right. Willow turned her head lazily to see herself being watched by a young nurse in a blue-and-white striped uniform.

'Hello,' said Willow herself. 'It wasn't poison, then?'

'An allergic reaction to the oysters you ate, the doctor thinks. You'll be fine in no time at all. How do you feel?'

Willow thought about it for a bit.

'Fragile,' she said at last. 'Fragile but . . . alive.'

'Do you want anything to drink – or eat?' asked the nurse, watching her closely.

'No,' said Willow, feeling her eyelids closing again. She vaguely heard the sound of rubber-soled shoes squeaking against linoleum and slept.

When she woke again Tom Worth was standing beside her, looking down at her with an expression of profound relief on his familiar face.

'You frightened me, Will,' he said when he saw her eyes focusing.

'You're not the only one,' she said with the beginnings of a return to her familiar self. 'I was convinced they'd poisoned me.'

'Tell me what happened,' he said, dragging up a chair. 'You said something about Caroline Titchmell last night.'

'It was probably slander,' she said, rolling her head from side to side on the pillow to make sure that all her nerves and muscles still worked. Miraculously they did. 'But it seemed so pat. After we'd met last Sunday and I'd asked her questions, she rang up and invited me to supper. I'd already decided that she couldn't have had anything to do with the deaths or I'd never have gone near any food she'd prepared. But then once I was being so vilely ill last night, I thought I'd got it wrong somewhere and that she must have been frightened by something I'd said, and decided to do away with me by means of snails that had been specially fed on belladonna.'

'Far fetched,' commented Tom with what Willow considered not nearly enough sympathy for someone in her condition, 'and unlikely to work.'

'Not at all,' she said in the voice she used to her most tiresome subordinates – and superiors – in the Civil

Service. 'The snails were served in individual dishes, six for each of us. The belladonna ones could easily have been given to me without risking anyone else. It doesn't seem any more far fetched to me than putting nicotine in malt whisky or foxgloves into sloe gin.'

Tom looked for a moment as though he were going to change the subject to something more soothing for an invalid, but eventually he changed his mind.

'What made you suspect Titchmell in the beginning?' he asked. 'She inherited nothing from her brother, and . . .'

'But until Bruterley, she was connected with two of the three people who died,' said Willow, 'and there is even a tenuous connection with him in that his wife was at school with her.'

'But why should Titchmell have wanted to kill the spinster in Newcastle?' asked Tom in protest. 'I know that she was the matron at Titchmell's school and didn't believe that the girl had meningitis. But that's hardly enough, surely?'

'One wouldn't have thought so, but Caroline did say that she had felt terrible rage and frustration then. . . . Anyone mad enough to murder must blow minor hurts up into major tragedies, or they'd never get as far as murdering. Perhaps it was enough.'

'Not twelve years on,' said Tom mildly. 'And there was nothing connecting her to Claire Ullathorne.'

'Except that they had been at the same school,' said Willow. 'The trouble was that they can't have known each other there, and Caroline did say that she had never heard the name. Of course she would if she'd actually killed Ullathorne. And it is just possible that Claire knew Simon Titchmell. But . . .'

Willow sat up suddenly, ignoring the ugly hospital nightgown she was wearing, which had no usable buttons and flapped around her nakedness.

'Wait . . . Something's occurring to me. Tom, you put something in your notes about Ullathorne and her doctor.

What was it?' Willow asked. Her cold green eyes were shining with enthusiasm and her voice was lighter and livelier than at any time since her dramatic sickness. Tom Worth smiled and delved into his memory.

'I can't remember saying anything, but the information we got from the doctor was that Ullathorne never consulted her except for matters of innoculation, contraception and cervical smears,' he said.

'There was something else, though,' said Willow. Suddenly she did become aware of the stiff, ugly, rust-stained nightgown she had been dressed in and slid back beneath the bedclothes. 'Something about inflammation of the joints.'

'That's right. She was suffering from the early stages of arthritis. But the doctor confirmed that she'd never . . . Don't tell me that your belladonna snails book . . .'

'It does,' said Willow. 'The first book I got out said that colchicine was often used in patent medicines for gout, but the more modern one says that although an infusion of colchicum seeds has been used since time immemorial for treating gout, recently it has been discovered to help arthritis as well. I bet she was interested in herbal medicine and made the dose herself.' Willow laughed.

'She probably had window boxes of the stuff growing outside her flat and you bobbies never noticed,' she said.

'We did in fact check the contents of her window boxes and roof garden,' said Tom with a certain satisfaction. 'It was thought that she might have taken the stuff by mistake . . . people do, I gather.'

'And what about her allotment?' asked Willow. To Tom Worth then she looked almost like a witch, her green eyes wild, her skin paler than ever and her red hair crackling with electricity and flying about her thin face.

'What makes you think she had an allotment?' he asked, looking at her sideways. 'I can't think of many actresses who have, particularly not rich ones.'

'I don't know whether she did or not. But she might

212

have done, mightn't she? People do, I gather,' said Willow, neatly mimicking his own patronising intonation. 'And when you think how much time most actors have to spend resting, an allotment would be a very good idea – cheap vegetables and flowers, exercise . . . and she did live in North London after all.'

'You, my dear Miss Woodruffe,' he said with a smile she enjoyed, 'are feeling better. I think it's most unlikely, but I shall look into the allotment question.' He stood up and replaced the plastic chair on which he had been sitting.

'By the way,' he said, coming back to her bedside, 'we've found Sarah Rowfant.'

'Ah,' said Willow, 'and from your expression of pity I take it that she's not the girl in the school scandal and her flight from Cheltenham was entirely innocent.'

'Precisely,' he said. 'She left Cheltenham as soon as she heard that Bruterley was dead because she needed solace and had no idea that he had been murdered, and she took refuge with a friend in a croft on a virtually deserted Scottish island.'

'Where there is no telephone, they received no newspapers and never listened to the radio,' supplied Willow in the sing-song voice of a lift attendant in a department store.

'That's right. And apparently accurate, too. She's never had an abortion and has been entirely frank with the Cheltenham boys about her affair.'

'So that's that,' said Willow, sounding ill again. 'We're back at at the beginning. 'I don't quite know where to go from here, except that I must talk to Miranda Bruterley. When am I going to be let out of here?'

'I don't know,' said Tom.

'Well go and find out,' said Willow as though he were a particularly dilatory and idiotic typist. 'Here am I – quite literally working my guts out for you – it's the least you can do in return.' Laughing, Tom went to carry out her orders.

He came back with the white-coated doctor, who looked her over, took her pulse and blood pressure again and told her that she could leave on Sunday unless she had any kind of relapse.

'Right,' said Willow when he had gone. 'Now find me a telephone and get the Bruterleys' number for me.'

Tom raised an eyebrow and smiled his irresistible smile and Willow relented.

'Please, dear, sweet Tom . . . not that I approve of sexual harassment,' she said.

'I beg your pardon?'

'It's sexual harassment to use patronising endearments in your efforts to persuade people to do things for you,' she said, laughing at him.

'And I'd taken the endearments as their straightforward selves,' he said, turning away. 'Ah me.'

When he came back, pushing a yellow telephone trolley in front of him, Willow first demanded change from him, and then dismissed him, saying in an off-hand voice:

'There, there, I do love you – really I do.'

Tom, who had been walking away, spun round on his heel and looked down at her as seriously as he had done when she was ill.

'Really?'

Something in his voice or eyes terrified her, but before she could say anything, he grinned again.

'Don't worry about it,' he said. 'I shouldn't have asked. Don't go eating any more oysters, will you?'

'That I can promise you,' she said and tried to smile, but the recognition of how near she had come to committing herself was too awful to be treated lightly. As she picked up the telephone receiver she suddenly remembered her poor housekeeper and the mess that must have greeted her when she arrived for work at seven-thirty that Friday morning. Instead of dialling the number Tom had given her for Mrs Bruterley, Willow rang the number of her own flat in Belgravia.

Mrs Rusham sounded genuinely relieved to hear from her employer and expressed considerable sympathy when she heard that 'Miss Woodruffe' was in hospital. Willow thanked her, apologised for the unpleasant mess in the flat and assured her that she would be back there as soon as the doctors released her on Sunday. Once Mrs Rusham was pacified, Willow pressed the 'follow-on call' button on the telephone and dialled the Cheltenham number. She was answered by a young foreign female voice and assumed that it must belong to the nanny.

'Could I speak to Mrs Bruterley?' Willow asked, taking care to speak clearly, but not so slowly as to insult the girl's unknown command of English.

'Who is speaking, please?' came the competent reply.

'My name is Cressida Woodruffe,' said Willow, wondering whether Miranda would have read the letter Willow had sent after the memorial service or remember her name.

'Please to wait, please,' said the nanny. Willow watched the figures on the liquid-crystal display screen on the telephone flash down from the two pounds she had pushed into the machine. They had reached 50p before another voice, tired and somehow wary, said:

'Cressida Woodruffe? This is Miranda Bruterley. Thank you so much for your sweet letter.'

'You did get it, then,' said Willow. 'I am glad. And I'm sorry to be intruding at such a time; it's just that I have to be in Cheltenham on Monday and I wondered if I could possibly come and talk to you. I promise not to take up too much time.'

There was silence at the other end of the line, which did not surprise Willow very much. Before she could plunge on with explanations of her odd request, Miranda Bruterley said:

'I'm not very good company, you know.' Willow thought that an odd remark under the circumstances.

'It's just that I need your help, although I can't really explain it on the telephone,' she said.

215

'How well did you know Jim?' Miranda said with some animation in her voice at last. There was suspicion in it, too, which Willow was quite glad to hear. The black figures on the little screen started to flash nought and Willow fumbled amid the small heap of change Tom had left for a fifty-pence piece to thrust into the slot. It dropped with a loud clunk and the screen ceased to threaten.

'Hardly at all,' Willow answered, almost honestly. 'And I hadn't seen him for years.'

'Ah, then you're not . . . sorry, I did warn you I'm not at my best. Well,' Miranda went on, sounding only tired by then, 'come if you want. But I don't know how much I'll be able to do to help.'

'May I come just after lunch?' asked Willow. 'About half-past two?'

'Yes, all right. I'll see you then,' said Miranda. 'I did like your letter, you know,' she finished and then put down the telephone.

Chapter 14

W ILLOW was still feeling rather shaky when she reached Cheltenham in her large and comfortable Mercedes at half-past one on the following Monday afternoon. She drove around until she found the Bruterleys' house, parked in the road beyond their gates and decided to order her thoughts and questions in the half hour before she could go in.

She had been convinced for a long time that the murders of Miss Fernside, Simon Titchmell and Dr Bruterley were connected. The type of poison – easily made from readily available 'natural ingredients' – and the method – a burglary, or perhaps in Miss Fernside's case a decoy official visit, a short while before the death and the remnants of poison found in the victims' food or drink supplies – were too similar to be coincidence. Claire Ullathorne's death, on the other hand, she was more and more inclined to put into a separate category. There had been no burglary and there were no remnants of poison to be found.

As far as Willow could remember, the forensic pathologist had found a mixture of red wine and colchicine in

Claire Ullathorne's stomach and it had therefore been concluded that the poison might have been mixed with the wine. The few dregs left in the wine bottle had shown no traces of poison, but the quantity of wine was so minute that it might have been impossible to isolate any poison from them even if it had been there.

Willow tried to think of ways to open a bottle of wine and recork it to look as though it had not been touched. The poison could have been introduced into an open bottle that had been re-corked either with the cork itself or a patent stopper, she thought, or by means of a hypodermic. She wondered how likely it was that someone opening a bottle would ignore a small puncture in the lead or plastic cover over the cork. A hypodermic would suggest a nurse or doctor, or perhaps a diabetic or drug addict.

'Or even,' she told herself drily, 'a DIY expert. After all, the best way to obliterate air bubbles in newly hung wallpaper is to inject paste into them with a syringe.' And then she suddenly remembered reading of a fashion during the early 1980s for home-made wine; she had even seen the necessary kits and supplies in chain-store chemists. There were packets of corks there and coloured lead covers. Armed with those, anyone could have tampered with a bottle of wine in such a way that it looked untouched.

Even so, she decided stoutly, there was a real possibility that the Claire Ullathorne case was not linked to the other three. Looking at her watch she saw that she had ten more minutes in which to concentrate on the coming interview and dropped all thought of everything except James Bruterley and his wife.

By the time her watch gave her permission to get out of the car, Willow had decided to be relatively frank in her approach to the widow: after all, not being able to ask Caroline Titchmell any direct questions had, she was certain, meant that she missed a lot of useful information and built up a wholly artificial suspicion in her mind. Willow did not see how talking frankly to Mrs Bruterley could cause trouble or give anything away to the poisoner. Willow felt sure that she knew aspects of the killer's character: murderousness concealed behind a bland exterior, manipulativeness, resentment, and a sick pleasure in revenge.

She still found the knowledge that all that hatred could be successfully hidden behind a civilised front extraordinarily uncomfortable, and wondered as she examined the few people she had met on the case, whether the front consisted of joviality, social aggression, kindness or arrogance. There was nothing to tell her and she looked from one to another of them in her mind, at one moment unable to believe that any of them were capable of killing and at the next afraid that all of them might be.

Bracing herself against her fear and reminding herself that Miranda Bruterley had been declared innocent by the police, Willow got out of the car, walked up the crunching gravel drive and rang the old-fashioned black iron bell outside the front door.

It was opened by Miranda Bruterley herself, looking far paler and even more ill than she had been at the memorial service. Perhaps her pallor was accentuated by the oddly unbecoming green sweater that she wore over her black trousers. Her long blond hair was lank and rather greasy and her skin looked dead, except for a few raw patches that looked as though she had been picking at incipient or imaginary pimples.

'Mrs Bruterley, it is good of you to see me,' said Willow, holding out her hand. Miranda took it in a limp, damp clasp and invited Willow into the house.

'I've sent the children and their nanny back to my mother's house,' she said as she led the way to the drawing room. 'There have been too many journalists trying to get in here and too many policemen about.'

'It must be hard enough for such young children to come to terms with losing their father without that,' said Willow with genuine sympathy. The woman in front of her turned her head and shrugged.

'They hardly saw him, actually,' she said. Willow saw that there were new tears welling into her reddened eyes. 'And he was quite tough with them when he was around . . . you know, wouldn't let them make any kind of noise in case it disturbed his rare rest, that sort of thing.'

'Dear me,' said Willow inadequately, thinking that he sounded rather a difficult man.

Miranda opened the door of a large sunny room decorated prettily if conventionally in apricot, white and pale green.

'Come and sit down. Would you like some coffee?' Willow shook her head, thinking that the fewer things that were put into her scoured stomach the better. She sat on a fat sofa and was surprised to see Miranda open a heavy silver cigarette case and take out and light a long cigarette.

'Have you always smoked?' Willow asked, with a distinct memory of Tom's having told her that the widow was not a smoker.

'No,' said Miranda, taking a deep mouthful of hot smoke. 'Not since my marriage. But I've needed something to help me control things since Jim . . . Sorry, would you like one?'

'No, thank you,' said Willow and waited to be asked why she had come. Miranda Bruterley said nothing, just prowled around the room dragging on her cigarette as fervently as though she were a navvy used to sixty a day. After a while Willow took the initiative.

'Mrs Bruterley,' she began.

'I do wish you'd call me Miranda,' said the widow a little plaintively.

'Miranda,' said Willow, staring again, 'I've come on an errand that is going to sound odd.'

'You said you wanted help,' she said, interrupting her guest. 'I'll do what I can. In fact I really could do with a job just now. Which charity is it for?'

At last Willow understood the widow's lack of curiosity and outrage at the invasion of her house by a stranger. As a woman of independent means, without a career and with a nanny and plenty of other help in the house, Miranda Bruterley would have been an obvious target for anyone wanting either voluntary workers or money raised for a good cause.

'It's not quite like that,' said Willow. 'I've come to ask you questions about what happened to your husband.'

'Oh God! You're not another journalist, are you?' said Miranda, anger taking over from the unhappy weariness in her face.

'No,' said Willow. 'I'm a friend of Caroline Titchmell's.'

'Titch? Good heavens! What's she got to do with any of it? What ever happened to her?'

'She herself is all right,' said Willow, 'but about two months ago, her brother was killed.'

'Poor old Titch,' said Miranda. 'I vaguely remember him, I think. But how can I help?'

'I'm not sure,' said Willow, ready to take the plunge into indiscretion, knowing that Tom Worth would be furious, 'but the way he was killed is horribly similar to the way that your husband died. The police apparently don't think that there is a connection, but I can't help wondering about it, and I do want to help Caroline if I can. Of course I haven't said anything at all to her about your husband's death.'

At last Miranda Bruterley stubbed out her cigarette, flung open a tall window as though to let out the smell of smoke, and came to sit on a low stool in front of Willow.

'I'm concentrating now,' she said, sounding much less limp and almost intelligent. Even her lacklustre eyes seemed to have sharpened. 'What do you want to know?'

'First,' said Willow scanning her mental notes, 'whether there was any connection between your husband and Simon Titchmell. Had they ever had any business dealings together? That sort of thing.'

It had occurred to her that Titchmell must have bought his drugs from someone, who might just conceivably have been Dr Bruterley.

Miranda stared at her black patent-leather pumps as they rested on the moss-green Wilton carpet and twisted her huge diamond engagement ring round and round her finger.

'I don't think they'd ever met,' she said at last. 'We've . . . we'd been married for six years and Simon Titchmell has certainly never been here in that time. Jim never mentioned his name as far as I can remember, and I don't see how they would ever have met.'

'You say that you met him, though,' said Willow.

'Yes. Years ago – while we were still at school – Titch's parents brought him to one Speech Day, I think. He wasn't at any of the boys' schools we used to do things with so he was quite a curiosity. But it was as casual as that,' said Miranda, smiling at Willow and blinking a little as though to demonstrate her innocence of any malice or subterfuge.

'You mean that you never knew him properly, never went to stay in the school holidays or anything like that?' asked Willow, trying not to stare into Miranda's tear-stained face.

'Oh God no,' said Miranda, actually laughing at the absurdity. 'Titch was one of the clever ones and I was a thicko. The only thing I was ever any good at was biology and that wasn't very useful.' She stopped laughing but there was an odd, reminiscent smile on her face. For a moment Willow could see past the pastiness of her complexion and the red swellings around her eyes to the beautiful woman she must be in normal circumstances, and indeed had appeared to be at the memorial service.

'You look as though that pleases you,' Willow said, letting herself sound puzzled. Miranda's pale skin flushed slightly.

'No; I was just remembering unkindly how superior we used to feel to the clever ones,' she said. It took Willow a moment to understand what she meant.

'You mean because you were prettier?' she suggested. The blush deepened, but Miranda raised her reddened eyes. Looking at Willow directly, she said:

'It is a bit shaming now, but at the time it seemed normal. There was a group of us – five or six I suppose – who all had quite a lot of money of our own – trusts and things – and were really quite good-looking and had nicer clothes than the rest and knew lots of people. . . . Not that it's done me much good,' she finished with a small shrug.

'You must have known Dr Bruterley then,' said Willow, not feeling quite up to commenting on the assumptions Miranda had betrayed in her unpleasant little confession. 'Wasn't he at one of the schools close by?'

'Yes,' she said. 'That's really what I meant. He was always terrifically sought after – at those grisly school dances and at home, of course – and he was always very sweet to me. . . . And look what happened in the end.' She forgot her amusement and burst into tears, burying her face in her smoothly manicured hands. Willow waited until Miranda had regained some kind of control and then suggested that they had some coffee after all.

When it had been made and poured into Royal Worcester cups, Miranda looked recovered enough for Willow to mention the old school scandal. The huge grey eyes filled with surprise.

'You mean when one of the seniors got pregnant? Wasn't it ghastly? But what's it got to do with any of this?' she asked.

Willow was staggered by the idea that Miranda might not have known that her husband had been the culprit, but she could not quite bring herself to make the announcement.

'I just wondered,' she said instead, 'whether you knew who the father had been.'

Miranda shook her blond head.

'Goodness, no! It was kept the most deathly secret. We thought it must be one of the boys from Michaelson's, but I don't know which. You don't mean that in fact it was Simon Titchmell, do you?'

Willow merely shook her head and shrugged.

'Did you see much of your husband while he was training at Dowting's?' she asked, trying to approach the subject from an easier angle.

'No, not really at all. I was still at school, of course, when he started there and then I went to Paris for a bit and did various things and we didn't meet up again properly until he qualified.'

'But you didn't marry quite then, did you?'

'Not for ages,' said Miranda with a smile hovering around her pink lips again. 'He was a bit of Don Juan, you see, and I was pretty certain that if I'd let him know how much I wanted him then I'd be on the scrapheap with all the others in no time at all.'

She turned away and stared out at her immaculate garden through the rapidly dissipating haze of cigarette smoke.

'He was awfully sweet when he finally came round to the idea of wanting to marry me,' she said. 'He told me that he'd seen how silly and unhappy that sort of a life was and that . . .' Her voice trembled and she turned away again. After a few moments she tried again: 'That falling in love with me had made him change completely. And I believed him – until this.'

The name of Sarah Rowfant had not been spoken, but Willow knew quite well that it was sounding as loudly in Miranda's mind as in her own. Willow wished that she could offer the woman some kind of comfort, but there was none.

'That was why it was so particularly awful to discover that he was having an affair, you see,' said Miranda after a while, still staring away from Willow. 'It made me wonder how many others there had been, whether Jim had ever in fact had any of the thoughts about me he'd talked about, whether he had ever loved me, whether it was just my money he wanted, whether the things I thought were important about myself meant nothing at all, whether I'd have been better to have been quite different.'

She swung back to face Willow again and shrugged.

'Whether, for instance, I'd have been better and happier if I'd been more like poor Titch.'

'Why do you despise her so much?' asked Willow, so curious that she ignored her interrogation for the moment.

'I don't think I do,' said Miranda, sounding much more social and self-conscious than she had before.

'Oh yes you do,' said Willow with a false gaiety. 'Why? Because she wasn't pretty at school?'

'No!' protested Miranda. 'Well, no . . . I suppose it was the fashion to be a bit dismissive of people who worked that hard and looked like that. I'm sure she's not at all like it now, but in those days she was awfully fat as well as embarrassingly short and she had revolting spots – absolutely revolting.'

At that moment Willow gave up any attempt to like Miranda Bruterley.

'Well, never mind; it was a long time ago. Presumably your husband shared your views?' said Willow.

'Jim? Oh yes, poor old Titch had rather a passion for him, you see, just like everyone else in our year, and she did tend to follow him about a bit and insisted on inviting him to things in the holidays. In the end,' her voice sank to a conspiratorial whisper, 'he had to write her a letter. Our group heard about it, and we did feel a bit sorry for her then.'

'Really?' Willow hoped that her one word did not sound quite as antagonistic as she felt.

'Yes,' said Miranda. 'It was a very cruel one, but it did the trick. She never spoke to him again. I say, what did happen to Titch in the end?'

'She has become a very successful patent agent – earning a great deal of money,' said Willow with enormous pleasure, 'and is about to get married to a kind and very intelligent man.'

'Golly! How unlikely. Still I am glad, especially about the money,' said Miranda. 'It just goes to show, doesn't it?'

'And,' said Willow, yielding to temptation, 'she's not in the least fat now, has a markedly good complexion and dresses very well.'

'Perhaps it would have been better for us all if she had managed to get Jim,' said Miranda. Willow remembered that the woman had just lost her husband and deserved sympathy for that, whatever her values and views on other women.

'I do feel for you,' said Willow. 'I hope that his partners are helpful.'

'Oh yes. John Swaffield is being absolutely sweet.' Onto Miranda's pretty tear-stained face there slid a secret smile. 'You could stay and meet him if you like. He always drops in around four – before evening surgery – to see how I am.'

'I'd better not,' said Willow. 'I've taken up far too much of your time. But can I ask you something else before I go?'

'What's that?'

'Not to tell anyone about my idea that your husband's death might be connected with Simon Titchmell's? I really don't want to cause any fuss or persuade the police into asking any more questions. You've been bothered enough – and so has Caroline.'

'All right. But can I tell John? I tell him everything; I really do. He keeps me going,' said Miranda with a wistful little smile on her swollen lips.

'I expect he'll understand the need for discretion to stop you being bothered any more,' said Willow. Miranda nodded.

'Well I must go. Thank you for being so frank. If you do think of anything that might have connected the two of them, will you give me a ring or drop me a note? Here's my address.' Willow scribbled it on a page from her notebook and gave it to the reluctant Miranda. She accepted it with another shrug and escorted Willow out of the room.

As they walked through the hall, Willow stopped in front of a painting that looked like a Stubbs.

'This is lovely,' she said, turning to smile at Miranda.

'Yes, isn't it? It was one of Jim's better buys. Luckily the beastly burglars weren't interested in that sort of thing.'

'Oh, have you been burgled?' asked Willow, delighted that the subject had introduced itself. 'I was quite recently. It's vile, isn't it?'

'Horrid!' said Miranda. 'And this was worse than usual.'

'Really?' said Willow picking her coat up off the chair where she had left it. 'What happened? You weren't here when they broke in, were you?'

'Oh, no, thank God! But after the last one the insurance company had insisted that we have an alarm installed,' said Miranda and then put her index finger in her mouth and worried at the edge of the nail with her teeth. 'Jim was absolutely livid with me, but I had to tell him . . .' Her voice broke off. Willow thought that she could hear both resentment and exculpation in it.

'After all,' said Miranda, 'I'd only just popped out to collect the children from school. I'd sort of forgotten that it was Maria's day off.'

'And you didn't set the alarm?' suggested Willow.

Miranda nodded.

'It was foul of Jim to be so unkind. And so bloody unfair! After all, I told him that I'd pay for the broken window and replace everything that had been stolen. It wasn't going to cost him anything.' Her eyes filled with tears again and Willow felt some sympathy for her once more. Bruterley really did sound as though he had enjoyed tyrannising his wife. Perhaps, Willow thought, he had minded the fact that she was so much richer than he and was trying to get his own back. She also began to wonder whether perhaps Miranda's fury at the memorial service was directed more towards her dead husband than his killer.

'And they didn't come back again, the burglars?' Willow asked, hoping to discover an unreported break-in when the whisky might have been poisoned. 'When you were away?'

'Not as far as I know,' she said drearily. Willow thought that she ought to go, but before she said goodbye finally, she had one more question to ask.

'At the funeral I talked quite a lot to Andrew Salcott. He . . .' Miranda made a face. 'Don't you like him?'

'Not really. He was one of those coarse, rugger-playing medical students and he's never grown out of it. Although in fact it was always mountaineering rather than rugger. But he's so . . . huge and obtrusive. No, I've never liked him,' said Miranda, actually shuddering.

'He spoke very well of you,' said Willow rather mischievously. Once again Miranda smiled her secret, self-admiring smile.

'Well he would. He kept saying he wanted to marry me, for years really. When I wouldn't he took up with Agnes to spite me. Only he was spiting himself, wasn't he? Because it hasn't worked out.'

Willow left the house. As she was pulling out from the kerb, her car was almost hit by the wing of an enormous dark blue Volvo swinging across the road as though its driver owned the whole town. Swerving and braking sharply, Willow avoided a collision and looked curiously at the driver. He was a large, dark man, perhaps about forty, looking furiously angry.

Willow reversed to the gateway and watched in her rear mirror as the Volvo took its place in the drive. By reversing further, she could see right up the drive to the front door, and she watched the Volvo driver get out of his car and enfold the grieving Miranda in his arms.

Willow drove back to London with a lot on her mind.

As soon as she reached the flat she rang Tom Worth. As usual he was out and she was forced to leave another urgent message on his answering machine. That done, she listened to her own messages. There was an almost hysterical one from Richard Crescent, who had heard of her illness from Mrs Rusham and was desperate to know if she was all right and where she was and who was looking after her.

Willow dialled his number, touched that he should mind so much but irritated too by his apparent assumption that she was incapable of looking after herself and that there was no one else in her life who might be concerned enough to care for her.

Unlike Tom Worth, Richard answered the telephone himself and Willow did her best to allay his anxieties.

'It was only a bad oyster, Richard,' she said. 'Terrifying at the time, but it's all over now. Thank you for ringing. How did you know?'

'Mrs Rusham told me.'

'I see,' said Willow, the annoyance taking precedence over the gratitude again. 'But why did you telephone her?'

'Oh I didn't. She rang me in a terrible fluster because you'd disappeared and it was obvious that you had been . . . er . . .'

'Sick,' said Willow too crudely for Richard. They talked for a few more minutes, before Richard invited her to dinner.

'I'm sorry, Richard,' she said without much real regret, 'but I'm dining with a doctor tonight.' She agreed to telephone him on Thursday evening when she got back from the hairdresser and then rang off. She was beginning to suspect that Mrs Rusham might not be the wholly incurious, wholly discreet paragon she had always seemed.

Trying not to think of the damage an inquisitive, talkative housekeeper could do to her double life, Willow played the rest of her telephone messages, learning that Martin, her interior designer, had ordered the materials, agreed a schedule of work with Mrs Rusham, and was ringing to alert Willow to a wonderful bureau-bookcase in a shy little shop off Bond Street. Amused as always by Martin's phraseology and pleased to be distracted from her personal relationships and her investigation alike, Willow wrote down details of the piece and the dealer and then continued playing the rest of the messages.

There were only two more. One from her poor agent, who was still desperately trying to get Willow to disgorge a synopsis for the new novel, and the other from Tom, saying that he hoped her expedition had not worn her out, that she was feeling as well as possible and explaining that he had to go out on a case that afternoon but would call her at about eight to see how she was.

Smiling a little, Willow went to have a bath before changing to go out to dinner with Andrew Salcott.

It did not have the usual calming effect. As the scent from the bath oil filled the lovely yellow-and-white room, Willow was confronted once again with her mental picture of the murderer. She wondered, feeling slightly sick, how much she had already betrayed herself. Three times already she had been been afraid that the killer had found her and each occasion had been a false alarm, but at moments like this, when she had nothing else to occupy her mind, the murderer seemed to taunt her with the ability to lie in wait for the victims and poison them probably before they were even afraid.

Willow managed to pull herself together, get out of the bath and dress in a tightly belted black skirt and a grass-green shirt made of heavy silk. She brushed out her damp hair and then took it back from her face in two wings, which she skewered with antique jet combs. With mascara brushed on her pale eyelashes, a little blusher on her cheeks and some pale apricot lipstick, she thought that her face would pass muster. A heavy gold bracelet round her right wrist and a jewelled pin instead of the top button of the shirt added the finishing touches.

The dressing and painting had soothed her enough to appear calmly at the Chelsea restaurant Salcott had suggested. He looked very closely at her as they were sitting down at their table and she wondered whether he could diagnose her state of mind.

'You look almost as though you've been ill,' he said. Willow laughed in relief.

'A bad oyster,' she said simply. Salcott's face cleared.

'Poor you, that can be really unpleasant. What happened?'

'Oh, I was disgustingly sick, passed out, was sick again and then got an ambulance. They took me to St Thomas's,' said Willow.

'You were in good hands then,' he said. 'Well you'd better eat very simply tonight. Shall I choose for you?'

Willow was about to inform him crisply that she was quite capable of selecting suitable food for herself when she remembered that she was going to pump him for information and so she smiled sweetly and waited while he ordered for both of them.

'As a gastroenterologist, I am qualified,' he said with a smile that suggested he understood her first unspoken protest.

'I hadn't realised that was your speciality,' said Willow, interested. 'Presumably if you're doing it at Dowting's you have to teach as well as practise?'

'Actually I'm more involved in research than in teaching,' he said. 'Good, here's your soup. Eat up.'

Willow gave him a look from under her eyelashes that made him laugh.

'I can tell that you must be a tyrannical father,' she began, planning to move the conversation quickly on to questions about Jim Bruterley's paternal capacities.

'Not at·all,' Salcott protested and, forestalling her questions, asked one of his own: 'Was yours? Is that why you so dislike authority?'

'I hadn't realised that I did,' said Willow, laying down her spoon and looking across the table at the thick-skinned, square face of her host. 'I dislike people who have none trying to exercise it, but I don't think I resent the genuine article . . . much. Perhaps he was.'

'Tell me about him,' commanded Andrew Salcott, picking up the first of his langoustines.

'He was a scientist,' said Willow thoughtlessly, 'at Newcastle University . . .'

'Really?' said Salcott with a smile. 'Perhaps I've met him. I go up there four times a year to lecture.'

'I doubt it,' said Willow, aware of several dangers all at once. 'He died many years ago.' She wanted to ask when Salcott was last in Newcastle, but did not dare. Instead, she wrenched the conversation clumsily round to the Bruterleys, hoping that he would accept that she did not want to talk of her father. For once she did not care at all whether he put that reluctance down to an Antigone complex, penis envy or any other Freudian fantasy.

'Do you think,' she asked slowly, 'that poor Mrs Bruterley really knew nothing of her husband's love affair? I gather that he was always rather a Don Juan.'

'It's extraordinary what women will believe if they want to,' he said, as the waiter came to clear away

232

their first-course plates. 'She's pretty stupid and so it is possible.'

'You sounded far more sympathetic about her when we talked on the train,' said Willow, really surprised by the venom in his voice. He shrugged his massive shoulders and she wondered whether he still played rugger.

'I was in a pretty sentimental state then,' he said mildly and then added with a burst of fierce feeling, 'and I hadn't then read a letter she's written me.' Willow raised her eyebrows instead of actually asking the question.

'She said that Jim had left me all his books and any of his paintings that I wanted,' he said. 'That was fine. I was just thinking it was good of her to write instead of leaving it to the lawyers when I got to the next sentence.' He paused as though to control his fury. 'She said that since she couldn't bear the idea of seeing me would I please arrange to have the books collected and write and tell her which pictures I didn't want.'

'That seems rather cruel,' said Willow. 'I thought you were old friends.'

'So did I,' he said. 'But she obviously bears some kind of grudge that I knew nothing about. It's an unpleasant feeling.'

Or perhaps, thought Willow for the first time, she suspects you of killing her husband.

The waiter put a plate of fish in front of her and when he had gone she started to chew the first mouthful. It seemed to turn to cottonwool in her mouth and she found it almost impossible to swallow. Forcing herself to recognise that no public restaurant would poison a client's food even at the behest of someone like Salcott, she managed to swallow the chewed fish.

She knew that she had a splendid opportunity to ask questions, but in her residual weakness, she found that she could not bear the idea of sitting eating opposite a man who might have poisoned at least four people. Laying

233

down her knife and fork, Willow held her forehead in her right hand and murmured:

'I feel most awfully sick. Do you think they could get me a taxi?'

Salcott insisted on driving her home himself in his blue Citroen, leaving his own dinner unfinished. When they reached Chesham Place, he tried to escort her upstairs to her flat to make certain that she got into bed safely. Willow, still concealing her fears from him, managed to keep him outside her front door only by promising to telephone the following day to report on her health.

Chapter 15

*I*T WAS only half-past nine when Willow shut the door behind Andrew Salcott and so she went straight to her answering machine. There was a message from Tom asking whether he could drop in and see her, and since it was still early she rang him to ask him to come there and then. While she waited for him she went into her pale-grey writing room to fetch pen and paper so that she could write an account of her inchoate suspicions and sort them into some kind of rational sequence.

Tom's first words when he arrived twenty minutes later were:

'You do look tired. Is it really all right for me to come in?'

Willow smiled as she held the door open wide. Tom grinned and walked past her into the tiny, immaculate hall. Mrs Rusham had arranged a glass bowl of early roses on the little oak chest, the floor and furniture gleamed with beeswax and turpentine and the glass in front of the two paintings was pristine. Willow watched him as he looked appreciatively at it all. His dark eyes were soft and for once his mouth looked very gentle.

'Come on in and help yourself to a drink,' said Willow,

leading the way into the drawing room.

'May I pour you one?' asked Tom. Willow thought for a moment and then asked for a white wine spritzer, explaining that there was a half bottle of hock in the fridge.

'What my grandfather always called hock and seltzer,' he said as he returned carrying two glasses. He handed her the taller of the two.

'I suppose you don't look too bad,' he said when he had examined her face minutely, 'considering.'

'I'm glad to hear it,' said Willow astringently. Thinking of the the terrors that had been tormenting her since she had insisted on involving herself in his investigation, it seemed a little unfair of him to damn her with such faint praise.

'I meant in terms of your recent illness,' said Tom, 'as you very well know. But never mind the compliments now: do you want to tell me or shall I tell you first?'

'You first,' said Willow over the brim of her glass as she sipped the white wine and soda water. 'Mmmm, this is just right. Your grandfather taught you well.'

'Well, I can tell you that you really must be a witch. Claire Ullathorne did have an allotment. It's the most unlikely thing I've ever come across, but it's true. The whole place is smothered in weeds now, of course, but there are rows and rows of colchicums planted like vegetables, as well as a great variety of medicinal herbs. She must have grown them so that she could dose herself with her own concotions.'

'It's not proof that she overdosed herself, of course,' said Willow.

'No,' agreed Tom, 'but it's highly suggestive.' He looked at her as she lay back against the over-firm sofa cushions, her red hair curling about her perfectly painted face and her green eyes intent.

'I wonder,' he said slowly, 'whether I've wasted all this time of yours and the whole thing was a wild goose chase after all.'

236

Willow picked up her glass again and raised it as though she were toasting him. Then she drank and laid her head back to let the fizzy diluted wine trickle back down her throat. When she had swallowed it all, she said:

'No, I don't think you have. I am still not quite sure who the killer is, but I am certain that there is one.' She laughed abruptly; there was no happiness in the sound. 'All the people I've been talking to have secrets or discreditable pasts to hide, and lots of them seem quite capable . . .' Her voice died as she asked herself whether any of the people she had met were really capable of killing another human being.

'Who seems capable of murder?' asked Tom. Willow thought of giving him the lists she had been compiling before his arrival, but decided to talk instead.

'Well, if I had to choose from instinct alone, I'd give you a doctor called Mark Tothill,' she said, thinking back to Caroline Titchmell's dinner party. 'There's absolutely no evidence that he's killed anyone and I haven't turned up any motive for him, but he's a vile man, extraordinarily resentful about perfectly ordinary people . . . and angry. I don't think I've ever seen anyone show anger quite so obviously before.'

'Who is he?' said Tom. 'I don't think I've ever heard the name before.'

'The husband of a friend of Caroline Titchmell,' said Willow. 'But, as I said, I've only my dislike of him to go on and I've probably slandered him.'

'All right. Ignore the unpleasant doctor. Who else?'

'Consider Miranda Bruterley for a moment,' said Willow. Ignoring Tom's expression of half-contemptuous amusement, she went on: 'You know that you told me Dr Bruterley's senior partner had drunk some of his whisky after she had gone away with her children?'

'Precisely,' said Tom. 'Therefore she could not have poisoned it.'

'I take it that the partner is John Swaffield?' said Willow. Tom merely nodded.

'Well in that case, I do wonder whether he was lying,' said Willow. 'He's definitely consoling the widow at the moment and it did occur to me as I was driving back to London that he might have been simply protecting her, which would mean . . .'

'That the breaking-and-entering could have been the occasion for the poisoning of the bottle after all. I'd better have a word with the Cheltenham boys. What's the matter?' Tom demanded as Willow's face changed. She looked as nearly shifty as she ever looked, and very much younger than usual. 'What have you done?'

'I feel as though I'm blushing,' announced Willow annoyed with herself, 'and I don't see why I should.'

'Tell me,' commanded Tom, but there was a note of such affection in his deep voice that Willow let herself smile reluctantly back at him.

'I told Miranda Bruterley that I thought there might be a connection between the murder of her husband and Simon Titchmell,' she said rather quickly. Tom's face hardly changed, but Willow thought that if she were one of his suspects she would find his new expression quite frightening. There was no gentleness left in it at all. Willow turned away to drink a little more spritzer and then put the glass down on the small mahogany table beside her.

'Damn you, Willow,' said Tom after a moment of grappling with his temper.

'It was the only way I could ask her anything useful at all,' said Willow. 'I don't actually think I need to excuse myself, but I made absolutely no suggestion that I had any contact with the police and I impressed on her that it was entirely my own idea and that Caroline Titchmell did not know what I was doing.'

Tom said nothing. Willow thought of asking him how on earth he expected her to solve his problems if he hobbled her ankles and put a blindfold over her eyes.

'I suppose,' she said, struggling to be fair to him, 'you thought that I could sit here and spin fantasies that might have some bearing on your crimes. But there just wasn't enough information to do that.' Tom stood up. Looking down at her, he seemed enormously tall and powerful.

'Would you believe me if I told you that the only reason I didn't want you to go involving yourself physically in these cases was because I didn't want you to risk yourself?' he asked. 'Or is that worse? Patronising?'

Suddenly feeling weak and almost tearful – shamingly like the heroine of her last book – Willow shook her head. Her fears were too vivid for her to object to anything Tom might do to try to ensure her physical safety. But she knew that there was really nothing he could do to guarantee it, which is why she never told him how bad the terrors were. Despite her determination to keep them hidden, she shivered.

Tom leaned forward to look at her more closely.

'You'd better tell me now,' he said at last.

'Tell you what?' asked Willow, wondering whether it was her imagination or her reason that had created the fear. She had made a fool of herself over the suspect bomb already, and built up the Clapham burglary into far more than it might have been, but at least she had done that in private.

'Something you learned in Cheltenham is upsetting you,' said Tom, looking closely at her. He seemed to have mastered his anger completely. 'Is there another connection with Caroline Titchmell?'

Realising that he did not yet know quite how afraid she was, Willow became determined to behave as though the fear did not exist.

'In fact there is, although it's not enough to explain murder.'

'Tell me,' said Tom.

'It seems that when they were all at school, Caroline Titchmell was in love with James Bruterley and he spurned her rather cruelly. But, Tom, that must have been sixteen years ago at least. She's found all kinds of satisfactions for herself since then and so why would she need to kill . . .?'

'Perhaps having found the satisfactions she has become confident enough to take revenge?' he suggested, playing devil's advocate. He had never believed in Caroline as a possible killer.

'These murders started very recently . . .' he began. Willow interrupted.

'As far as you know, but you did say that a lot of poisoning must go undetected. I cannot believe that a woman like Caroline . . . it would be easier to believe that Miranda did it, with or without the help of John Swaffield. Miranda is a highly suitable name for her, now I come to think of it.'

'"Fit to be admired"' said Tom, surprising Willow, who had assumed that he knew no Latin. She made a face at him, which he did not see, because he had got up off the sofa and was walking slowly around the room.

'Why should she have killed her husband? Miranda, I mean?' asked Tom, pulling aside one of the heavily lined curtains and peering out into the street.

'Having discovered about Sarah Rowfant, perhaps,' said Willow, remembering that Miranda had appeared to be more upset about her husband's mistress than about his death. 'Or perhaps she just couldn't stand him any longer. He sounds the most appalling tyrant: not allowing the children to make any noise or bother him; locking up his decent whisky and making his wife drink something less good; being vilely unpleasant about the burglary even though it was hardly her fault.'

'But she knew nothing about Rowfant until after the murder,' protested Tom, ignoring the question of blame for the burglary. Willow shook her head.

'She could easily have been lying,' she said. Her eyes narrowed to glistening green lines between her darkened lashes as she developed the story. 'John Swaffield is being "absolutely sweet" to her; it is quite possible that he lied about drinking the whisky to protect her; it is more than probable that he has been coaching her in what to say to the police and warned her not to admit to knowing about the mistress because that would have given her a motive. How I wish I could interview them all face to face!'

'I can imagine how frustrating it is,' said Tom, coming back to lay a hand on her shoulder. Willow put up one of hers to cover it.

'And then there's Andrew . . .'

Before she could tell Tom anything more the telephone rang. He moved away from the sofa at once.

'Don't worry about it,' said Willow, rather annoyed that he was attempting to answer her telephone. 'It's probably my agent. The machine can take a message.'

'I think it may be for me,' said Tom. 'We're in the middle of something important and so I left your number. May I answer?'

'If you must,' she said as he was picking up the receiver. She heard him give his name, listen, ask two sharp questions and then say:

'I'll be there in ten minutes.' He put down the receiver and was on his way to the door when he added: 'I'm sorry, Will. We'll have to continue later.'

'Tom,' she said quickly. 'There is just one thing I need to . . .'

But he was already out of the drawing room and a moment later she heard her front door bang. She followed him more slowly and relocked the door behind him. Then she went back to the sofa. Ignoring the notes she had made about Caroline Titchmell and Ben Jonson, about Sarah Rowfant, Mark Tothill, Miranda Bruterley and John Swaffield, she re-read what she had written under the heading of 'Andrew Salcott'.

Means: Poison. As a gastroenterologist he would know precisely what dosages to use. He has research facilities at Dowting's, where he could prepare the poisons. He has access to hypodermics and scalpels for inserting poison unobtrusively into boxes and bottles.

Opportunity: Goes to Newcastle four times a year. (Check whether he was there just before Edith Fernside's death.) He could also have lectured in Gloucestershire and taken a detour to Cheltenham; or he could have stayed with his old friend Bruterley while Miranda was away – he admitted that Bruterley would have got out the whisky for him, and he could have poisoned it then. With no teaching responsibilities at Dowting's, he could have slipped away in time to perpetrate the burglary on Titchmell's house in the middle of the afternoon with no one at the hospital knowing where he was.

Possible motives: Once wanted to marry Miranda. His own wife is losing interest in him; perhaps he believed Miranda would marry him if he were divorced and Bruterley dead. Alternatively, he stands to inherit Bruterley's paintings; one is a Stubbs – are the others even more desirable? No apparent connection with Simon Titchmell, although he has known Caroline, but perhaps he was involved in Titchmell's drug habit. Might have known Edith Fernside when he was at school. Perhaps he was the father of the scandalous baby and his anger at my asking about its father was not caused by fear of a scandal about Bruterley.

Observations: Was unexpectedly emotional on the way to Bruterley's funeral and claimed tears as the result of hay fever, but the pollen count was particularly low. Known to be a mountaineer, therefore burglaries would not be difficult.

Reaching the end of her notes, Willow thought of the hour she had spent with him that evening and shivered. He was by no means the only suspect, but at that moment she was almost convinced of his guilt. She clipped all her notes together, folded them and put them into her Clapham handbag ready for the following morning. There was nothing more she could do that night and so she undressed and went to bed.

242

After an hour and a half of fruitless effort, she realised that she was not going to sleep naturally and got up to take two sleeping pills. They calmed her over-active brain eventually and she slept heavily until the following morning, when her alarm clock woke her at six o'clock.

With a thick head and gummy eyelids, she forced herself out of bed and splashed cold water over her face until she felt awake enough to face the day. Then, dressed in her jeans and sweater, she set about making the change from one life to the other.

Having packed her red nylon parachute bag with underclothes and washing things as camouflage, she transferred all Cressida's identification documents, cheque book, credit cards and the Cartier gold watch to the safe at the back of the wardrobe. Retrieving Willow's documents, her much more ordinary watch and the keys to the Abbeville Road flat, she put everything she needed into the worn black-leather shoulder bag that always accompanied her in Clapham.

Then she let herself out of the flat, locking it carefully behind her. She stood for a moment on the top step outside the front door, checking the empty street for watchers. The trees and glossy parked cars and tall white houses looked almost unreal in the cool, slightly hazy light of the early May morning. There was no one about to witness her transformation and she set off towards the bus stop, swinging her parachute bag and striding along, determined to ignore her worst fear that the killer knew of her existence, watched her and planned to dispose of her if she came close enough to pose a threat.

It would be relatively simple to find out whether Salcott had been in Newcastle at the relevant time, she thought, and if he had been to pursue some enquiries there. He could have no way of knowing that the woman he had met as 'Cressida Woodruffe' was also Willow King and so even if he were her quarry and aware of what she was doing, she would be safe for the next three days.

When she had unlocked the door of her flat in Abbeville Road, she checked that there were no signs of forced entry anywhere and then made herself some breakfast and went through her usual routines of getting ready for DOAP. Half an hour later, dressed as Willow King again in a plain, unbecoming grey suit, she walked to her office and immersed herself in the piles of papers that Barbara had arranged on her desk.

By the time her staff arrived she had plenty of tasks to distribute among them, and as soon as she was sure that they were all immersed in work she went back to her office, shut the door and made a series of private telephone calls. The first was to Newcastle University and eventually elicited the information that Dr Andrew Salcott had been there three weeks before Edith Fernside's death. The second was to her publishers to find out whether there were any photographic libraries that specialised in not particularly famous people. Her editor sounded puzzled as she said:

'What sort of people?'

'Doctors,' said Willow promptly. 'A friend of mine who wants to be a freelance journalist is preparing an article about the medical profession and wants to have all the necessary illustrations to send out with his piece.'

'Oh,' said the editor. 'Well, I don't know of anywhere, but I'll get on to our best picture researcher and let you know. OK?'

'Wonderful. If I'm not in, would you leave a message on the machine?'

'Sure,' said the editor and rang off. Willow then telephoned Jane Cleverholme at the *Daily Mercury*. Keeping her voice as low as possible, so that no denizen of DOAP should hear her identifying herself, Willow said:

'Jane, Cressida here. I badly need something that I think only you could provide.'

'Are you still going to give me a story?' said Jane with considerable acerbity in her hoarse, smokey voice.

'If I can,' said Willow, 'but there may not be one after all.'

'Well I suppose that at least your honesty is in your favour,' said Jane. 'What do you want this time?'

'Just photographs of the various people involved in that Cheltenham poisoning case,' said Willow, detecting more brittleness in Jane's manner than usual. 'You are the only person I know who is likely to have them.'

It took a great deal of persuasion to make Jane agree even to check whether the paper had any photographs of the Bruterleys or Sarah Rowfant, but in the end she said that she would, adding:

'You'll owe me a lot of stories for this.'

'I know,' said Willow, wondering whether she might be mortgaging her own protective secrecy.

'All right then,' said Jane. 'How urgent is it?'

'Fairly. Why don't I ring you back in a while to find out whether you have got them and then I can get them picked up?' said Willow, realising that she could hardly ask Jane to deliver them to DOAP if she wanted to protect her double identity for a little longer. The complications of her life were impinging as they had never done before.

Three hours later, having sat through a meeting with the Minister and the Permanent Secretary, dictated twelve letters and found a builder who was prepared to come and assess the damage to her flat and quote for repairing the roof, Willow rang the *Mercury* to discover that Jane was having a full set of prints made. Willow thanked her, said she would get a messenger to collect them and then telephoned Richard Lawrence-Crescent.

With a certain amount of resignation in his voice, Richard agreed to arrange to have the package picked up. Once it was delivered to his office, he would re-address it to Willow King and post it to the Clapham flat.

'I've given up asking what on earth you're up to,' he said when she also asked him to send her a photograph of Caroline Titchmell. 'But how on earth do you expect me to get hold of that?'

'I know you can if you want to,' said Willow caressingly. 'Please, Richard?'

'Oh all right,' he said. 'Look, I'm too busy to chat. I'll see what I can do.' Willow thanked him and, in some relief, went back to her proper work.

Before the end of the afternoon she rang the answering machine of her Chesham Place flat and listened to her messages. Her editor had left a message with the name and telephone number of a photographic agency that might be able to supply portraits of uncelebrated doctors and she telephoned them with her list of names. They promised to go through their files and send a pro-forma invoice for any prints they had.

'It's a bit too urgent for that,' said Willow. 'Couldn't I give you my credit card number instead?'

'Well, we don't usually . . .' said the young female voice to which she was speaking.

'But there's no reason why you shouldn't now,' said Willow as firmly as she had spoken in the meeting with the Permanent Secretary. Eventually she managed to persuade the young woman and dictated details of her credit card.

Two hours later she left the office to walk slowly back to her flat. Feeling tired and yet surprisingly restless, she took off her coat and shoes and let down her hair. She was bored with spinning ever-more fantastic stories and asking sidelong questions to try to solve Tom's mystery and wanted to take some direct action to identify the murderer before anyone else was killed, but there was nothing she could do before all the photographs arrived.

Chapter 16

W ILLOW was very tired when she reached Newcastle after eleven o'clock on Thursday night, but she was happier than she had been for some time. Tom had left a message on her machine the previous evening to say that the 'Cheltenham boys' had persuaded Dr Swaffield to admit that he had lied about drinking malt whisky with Bruterley. Tom had added that Swaffield had obviously done it to protect Miranda Bruterley, and that 'things are unrolling nicely'. Willow had looked at the glossy black-and-white photographs she had collected and considered telling Tom what she was planning to do, so that there would at least be one person who knew where she was. She had tried to telephone him, but was answered by his machine and so she merely thanked him for his message.

She took a taxi to a large, impersonal hotel in the middle of Newcastle and signed the register as Willow King. After a good night's sleep and a large breakfast, she took the photographs she had collected out of their cardboard envelope and put them into her briefcase, together with an official-looking notebook, the novel she was planning to read and a newspaper for bulk, and set out for the retirement homes where Edith Fernside had died.

As she had expected the warden showed some irritation when she introduced herself as a relation of Miss Fernside, anxious to discover the identity of a mysterious visitor of whom the old lady had written in several letters before her death. Willow, who had invented and rejected various cover stories during the train journey from London, explained that Miss Fernside had written in such glowing terms that various members of the family wanted to meet the visitor to thank him or her and offer a keepsake from her few possessions.

It was a fairly thin story, but the alternative of impersonating a DOAP inspector looking into reports of maladministration of pensions in the area would be too easy to disprove. The warden seemed to accept it, but mentioned caustically that it was surprising to find Miss Fernside's relations so scrupulous after her death when none of them had shown the slightest interest in her while she was alive. Willow found herself blushing, as much for the real relations as for herself, and wondered at her apparently ever-increasing sentimentality.

'I should like to show you some photographs and ask whether you recognise any of the men or women,' she said, reverting to her familiar coolness.

'All right,' said the warden, shrugging. 'Anything for a quiet life.'

Willow took the prints out of her briefcase and fanned them out on the table. The warden took his time, stopping and going backwards and forwards among the pictures, but in the end he denied ever having seen any of the people before except for Miranda Bruterley, whom he thought he recognised.

'But I'm not a gatekeeper. I only meet visitors by accident. They might all have come and I could easily have missed them,' he said, pushing a hand through his thinning, greasy hair.

'Pity,' said Willow economically. 'In that case I wonder

if I could speak to one or two of your residents in case they can tell me any more?'

'That's not for me to say,' he said, glaring at her. 'They're not children, or prisoners either. Up to them whether they'll talk to you or not. Who do you want to see?'

'Whoever might have seen her visitors,' said Willow. 'How about the people living either side of her?'

The warden escorted her across a pleasant, lawned quadrangle and pointed the way through a brick arch. Willow thanked him and went on her way alone. When she knocked at the door of the house to the right of Miss Fernside's a rather quavery female voice called:

'Who is it?'

Willow checked over her shoulder that there was no sign of the warden and then said gently:

'My name is King. I'm a niece of Miss Fernside and I wondered if I could talk to you about her. I've just come home from Australia.'

The door was opened at once and a woman in her late seventies, dressed in a baggy tweed skirt and toning green cardigan, stood there smiling.

'Come in,' she said. 'Come in. Poor Edith. How she would have loved a visit!'

The woman, who must have been in her late seventies, introduced herself as Stella Browning and insisted on making a pot of tea for them both before they settled down. Willow waited as she boiled a kettleful of water and made the tea. She loaded a tray with the big brown pot, a jug of milk, bowl of sugar and two saucers and carried it into her front room. Willow noticed that there were no cups and asked whether she should fetch them.

'Oh dear, yes, I'm getting so absent minded,' said Mrs Browning, looking anxiously behind her as though she expected to see the cups following her. Willow went out to the kitchen to fetch them. When she returned, Mrs Browning said:

'Did you say you'd been in Australia, dear? I don't think

poor Edith ever mentioned anyone living there.'

'I went out there when my parents died,' said Willow, 'and I rather lost touch with the rest of the family. I only heard about Aunt Edith when a lawyer wrote to me.'

'She didn't have much to leave you though, did she, dear? I always understood she only had her pension,' said the old lady, sounding much brighter than she had earlier.

'She didn't leave me anything,' said Willow truthfully. 'But I had to go to see them about something else and they told me then. I wished I'd been able to see her again. Did you know her well?'

'Not especially well,' said Mrs Browning, pouring out two cups of of tea. 'I only moved in here nine months ago.'

Willow smiled, relieved that she was not deceiving someone who would have been personally distressed by Edith Fernside's death.

'I just wondered how she was, and whether my cousins visited her and . . . well, really just that. I hate to think of her being alone when she was ill.'

'Well she wasn't exactly ill, you see,' said Mrs Browning, her faded blue eyes sharpening with interest. 'It was terrible when she died, and ever so sudden. But she didn't have many visitors. There was a lady, who she said had been at a school she once worked in, and there was one young man who was here a few times in the winter just before she died, but she never said he was a relation.'

'I wonder if he could have been my cousin Andrew,' said Willow, fishing in her briefcase. When she had put the photographs away after showing them to the warden, she had stuffed them inadvertently between the pages of her book and so she pulled out the whole book, put it face down on the highly polished coffee table and spread out the prints. 'Do you recognise him?' she asked, holding up the photograph of Andrew Salcott.

Mrs Browning looked at it for a long time, but at last she shook her grey head.

'No, dear. I don't think I've ever seen him before; and he's got a striking face, hasn't he? I think the young man I saw was thinner somehow . . . not so strong-looking.'

'I see,' said Willow. 'What about the others? Do any of them look familiar?'

Mrs Browning went through the pile of photographs and then looked doubtfully up at Willow's face.

'I didn't see him at all clearly, dear. Just through my nets while he was waiting at Edith's door or when she was saying goodbye to him,' she said. 'And my eyesight isn't very good. Perhaps I ought to get my spectacles.'

After an anxious search, she found them under a cushion in the chair in which Willow was sitting and put them on. Then she went carefully over all the photographs.

'I'm sure I've seen her before,' she said, picking out the one of Miranda Bruterley, 'and he looks quite familiar,' she added holding another print close to her eyes. Willow put out her hand and was surprised when Mrs Browning put into it the photograph of Mark Tothill. Despite what she had said to Tom Worth she had no real reason to suspect him and had asked the picture agency for a photograph of him just to complete her set.

'Oh, and him, too,' said Mrs Browning. Willow put down the photograph of Mark and saw that the old lady had picked up her book and was staring at the dramatically lit photograph of Ben Jonson on the back. 'He's ever so handsome, isn't he? I'm perfectly certain I've seen him.'

'When did you see him, Mrs Browning?' asked Willow gently, thinking that her impression of Ben Jonson in the flesh was that he was far from handsome.

'D'you know, dear, I'm not really sure,' said Mrs Browning. She looked so worried that Willow felt reluctant to press her. Then the old lady's face cleared. 'Perhaps it was on a library book,' she said. 'I always look at their faces before I choose a book. I was in the library only last week.'

Since that explanation seemed all too likely, Willow straightened the photographs on the shiny table and asked again whether any of the others looked familiar at all. Mrs Browning shook her head.

'I'm sorry, dear, but my memory is not what it was. Now she looks nice,' she said, looking at Caroline Titchmell's face. 'I wonder? Perhaps . . . No, I don't think so. And I'm not sure about him, after all,' she said, staring at the portrait of Mark Tothill again.

'Never mind,' said Willow. 'You've been very helpful, and I'm glad Aunt Edith had a neighbour like you.' She put the book and all the photographs away in her briefcase.

Mrs Browning came to the door with Willow and indicated a shortcut out of the little estate, which would take her quickly back to the bus stop. Willow was delighted that she would be able to get out without passing the warden's cottage, but she wanted to talk to Miss Fernside's other neighbour first.

There was no answer to her knock on the front door of number 38 and when she looked round she saw that Mrs Browning was peering at her through the net curtains of her front room. Willow waved and smiled, and was just about to knock on the door of the next house when she caught sight of the warden appearing through the brick archway. Afraid that he might have telephoned whoever had wound up Miss Fernside's estate to check her story, Willow made her escape.

Her direct action had had only disappointing results, but she decided to pursue Mrs Browning's vague identifications a little further. It was more than likely that her recognition of the publisher's artificially glamorous photograph of Ben Jonson had come from another book, but Willow thought that she should at least find out whether he had been in Newcastle just before the date of Edith Fernside's death.

Remembering that he taught a class of creative writing in South London, she decided that her first source of information should be the university. After some frustrating misconnections and delays, she spoke to a man in charge of arranging summer schools and casual vacation courses.

'Hello,' she said, 'my name is Cressida Woodruffe. You won't have heard of my books, but . . .'

'But of course I have, Miss Woodruffe,' said the slightly nasal voice at the other end of the telephone. 'How can we help you here?'

There was a touch of sarcasm in that question, which annoyed Willow enough to make her ignore the cover story she had invented, and so she came straight out with the question she had planned to disguise.

'I want to know whether Ben Jonson ever teaches at your creative writing courses,' she said. There was a slight laugh.

'Yes, he does indeed. But I ought to warn you that his style is not really compatible with yours.'

'I know that perfectly well,' said Willow, wishing that she had used her other name after all, despite her reluctance to let any old family acquaintances at the university know of her presence in Newcastle. 'All I want to find out is whether he was here last winter – in, say, February?'

'Let me see, I don't think so. Just a moment.' There was the sound of riffling paper. 'No. He was last here in the Christmas vacation. He teaches in London during term time. He will be flattered to hear of your interest.'

'Thank you,' said Willow. She did not like to think of the contemptuous amusement she had just caused. She cut the connection, thinking that if Edith Fernside had died in late February, the Christmas vacation seemed a bit too early for the poisoning of her sloe gin.

Willow then dialled directory enquiries to ask for the number of Miranda Bruterley's mother, who was said to live in Northumberland. Northcote was an unusual name and although Willow could give neither initials nor address she was lucky. The operator had only two possible numbers listed. Willow took them both down, tried the first and quickly discovered that it was wrong.

At the second attempt she was successful, asked to speak to Miranda and managed to elicit the fact that she had been staying with her mother for the first two weeks of the previous February. That sounded much more useful.

Willow wanted to ring Tom Worth at once to tell him, but was told by a woman in his office that he was unavailable. Unable to think of a way of disguising her message that would still tell him all he needed to know, Willow said she would ring again later and refused even to leave her name. Then she took a taxi back to the railway station and found that she had just missed a train to London. There was another one due in two hours and so she went and bought the day's newspapers and took them to read over some sandwiches and coffee at the station buffet.

Two hours later, settled in a window seat in a first-class compartment, Willow took out of her bag the novel Ben Jonson had given her, which she had still not read, and applied herself to it. It was called *Fair Cecilia* and she expected it to be a clever pastiche of one of his namesake's works.

By the time the train pulled out of York station, she had read almost a third and realised that the title provided the only allusion to his seventeenth-century namesake. She also saw exactly what her editor had meant about Ben's writing. He had obviously been impressed by the fashion for exploring the reactions of inadequate people to the cruelties of fate, and had produced a novel that Willow found almost unbearable to read. Ben's undoubted skill and style rendered his characters' misery so effectively that she felt personally depressed by it. The book was very clever, but Willow understood why it had not been popular and wondered why Ben spent his real talent on a literary genre that was horrible to read and that seemed so unsuited to him.

There was a sudden shriek of brakes and the train slid to a halt. Willow looked up from the book in surprise.

There was no sign of any station. The other people in her compartment rustled their newspapers in irritation and one or two asked futile questions. The loudspeaker crackled and after a moment a voice became clear.

'Ladies and gentlemen, this is your guard speaking. There has been an incident further down the line involving the collision of two trains. There has been no loss of life or injury, but I am sorry to say that there will be a considerable delay before the line can be cleared.'

Five hours later the train arrived in London. Willow and all the other passengers were in a state of acute boredom seasoned with violent frustration. They streamed towards the taxi queue like thirsty wildebeeste scenting water after migrating across a vast riverless plain. Willow was not quite angry enough to get to the head of the queue and so it was half-past eight before she was actually standing in Chesham Place, on the pavement opposite her flat, paying the driver.

As he drove off she picked up her briefcase and parachute bag and looked quickly up to her own windows before crossing the road. There was a light shining where no light ought to be and she stopped moving, staring upwards in appalled surprise. Mrs Rusham would have been long gone and no one else had keys to the flat.

Willow's mind went inexorably back to the last invasion of her home and she could hardly bring herself to step off the kerb. There was no one else in the street. Not even a cat moved. At last, recognising that not knowing what had happened to her flat was perhaps even worse than seeing the damage, she walked out into the road.

The stillness of the warm night was broken by the sound of a roaring engine and squealing tyres. Willow looked quickly to her right to see a large dark-blue car tearing down the street towards her. For a moment she was distracted by the driver's face as the car drove under a streetlight. By the time she realised the danger she was in, the car was almost on her. She backed, slipped on something slimy in the gutter and fell awkwardly backwards.

There was a ferocious blow against her legs as they shot out from under her, and she felt the bite of metal on her flesh and the heat of an engine. Her head struck the hardness of a lamppost and as she ricocheted sideways, her face scraped against the damp, rough tarmac of the road. The last absurd thought in her mind as she lost consciousness in a whirling fury of agony, terror and belated understanding was a memory of her headmistress's one piece of worldly wisdom:

'Always wear clean knickers, girls, in case you're run over in the street and have to be taken to hospital.'

When Willow regained consciousness she was lying flat on her back surrounded by whiteness. She knew with part of her brain that she had been awake and talking – or at the very least groaning – for some time, but she could remember very little. There was a furious pain in her head as well as in her legs. She put up a trembling hand to her forehead, only to feel the fibrous softness of bandages. Bringing her hand back in front of her eyes, she saw that it was covered in scratches and grazes, already beginning to turn crusty. Her eyes focused on two monstrous white shapes suspended in front of her and gradually worked out that they must be her legs. For a while she could not think what had happened to her.

Ambulance men came back to her memory, and she thought they had rescued her after the bad oyster, but that did not seem quite right. She closed her eyes. Slowly some memory began to return.

There was a picture in her mind of herself swearing at a nurse who was standing by while someone did something extremely painful to her legs, and she thought that there had been someone she knew, a man she knew, who had said something worrying. Then she remembered the huge, dark-blue car.

Willow raised a hand to push the hair off her forehead as though that might help her to think, already forgetting the bandages. All she could make her mind concentrate on were the extraordinarily unpleasant sensations in different parts of her body, the idiotic sight of her long legs hoisted up in front of her eyes, the feel of the weights dragging on them, and the hospital smell all around her. It was not particularly unpleasant, just a mixture of disinfectant, polish, over-hot recycled air and too many flowers in stale water.

'Hello there,' said a voice that seemed vaguely familiar. Willow raised her weighted eyelids and swivelled her sore head in the direction of the voice. Through the pain-killing vapours in her mind she knew that she should recognise his face. She smiled feebly.

'Hello,' she said, wondering why the sight of him should send such shivers of warning through her. He was wearing a white coat and there was a stethoscope hanging around his neck. There was also a blue plastic label on his left breast pocket. Willow narrowed her eyes, trying to read it, but it was too small. Something was plucking at her memory.

'I made a bit of an ass of myself,' said the doctor cheerfully, dragging up a chair. 'I thought I recognised you as a woman I'd recently met at a memorial service for a friend. She looked awfully like you, but she was called Cressida Woodruffe. When we opened your bag we found you were quite different. You probably don't remember much of our conversation.'

'I don't think I do,' said Willow, pushing ineffectually at the bandages that covered her head. The words 'memorial service' triggered her memory and she knew that she could put a name to him. 'What did I say?'

'Whenever I addressed you as "Cressida" or even "Miss Woodruffe" you called me "Aunt Agatha". It was very odd,' he said with a slight smile.

'Heavens! I must have been hallucinating,' said Willow.

Most of her mind was beginning to work again. She knew precisely who she was, and who he was and why they had met, and she silently thanked whatever Furies were involved in her fate for keeping her discreet about herself. If she had to be tied to hospital with broken legs it was better that she should be there as Willow than as Cressida and so it seemed almost miraculous that she should have chosen to go to Newcastle without substituting Cressida's documents for Willow's.

'How bad are my legs, doctor?' she asked.

'Not all that good, I hear, but I wouldn't know,' said the doctor. 'I'm not in charge of putting people back together again. My name's Salcott, by the way. I'm a gastroenterologist, but I happened to be in the corridor when you were brought in. Your doctor will be up here again in about half an hour – Georgina Wakehurst. I'll look in again when I'm passing.' He left and Willow felt a weight lifting from her mind as she watched him go.

When Doctor Wakehurst appeared, Willow had drifted off into sleep again, but she was woken by a nurse to hear the verdict delivered in a crisp, sensible voice:

'You needn't worry too much about your legs. They're not nearly as bad as some I've seen. The car seems to have flung you very hard against the ground and they're badly bruised as well as broken, but the breaks are surprisingly clean. I can't imagine how anyone can have been driving fast enough on a road like that not to be able to stop.'

'Perhaps I wandered out into the road,' said Willow, trying hard to remember what had actually happened. 'Although I can't think why I should have done any such thing. I wish my brain was working.'

'It'll come back,' said Dr Wakehurst with a smile. 'Don't force it, whatever the police try to make you do.'

'Police?' Willow asked. The doctor explained that the police were anxious to find out exactly what had happened and whether Willow could give them anything to identify the hit-and-run driver.

'What time is it?' she asked suddenly. 'And where am I?'

'You're in Phyllis Ward in Dowting's Hospital on the river and it's half-past eleven on Saturday morning,' said Dr Wakehurst. 'Don't be anxious about your office; we found your identity card in your bag and will telephone DOAP first thing on Monday. They will know what's happened and where you are.'

But Tom doesn't, thought Willow, beginning to remember a little more. She asked for a telephone trolley. The doctor promised to ask one of the nurses to bring one as soon as possible; then she asked Willow how she was feeling, did various tests and left her with the devastating intelligence that her legs would have to be suspended from that weighted pulley system for the next four weeks at least.

Willow could not imagine how she was going to keep her dual identity secret for that long. With a little snort of painful laughter, she admitted that she also did not know how the Permanent Secretary was going to be able to cope with his rage at her absence for that long either, and foresaw a series of visits from members of her staff with problems, papers and policy documents.

Her amusement died as she began to think about what else she had been doing. If Tom had wanted to ensure that she could use only her brain and imagination on his behalf and refrain from any more direct interference or questioning, he could not have done a better job than the driver of the car.

As Willow articulated that thought in her mind, she began to think about the accident and tried to remember what it was that she had understood as it happened. All the terror she had felt in the split second between the impact of his car on her flesh and her loss of consciousness came back to her in a sickening, horrible tide that washed

259

through her brain and left every nerve tingling, but there was something vital that she could not dredge up from the depths of her mind. She put a finger on the bell to call a nurse and kept it there until a harrassed first-year student came to stand by her bed and ask her to desist.

'I must have a telephone,' said Willow through her teeth, suddenly becoming aware that amongst all her other more serious injuries she must at some stage have bitten deep into her own tongue. It felt swollen and sore, and by experimenting with it on her lips she could tell that the indentations made by her teeth were still there.

'Now, now; you're still not quite yourself,' said the girl accurately but infuriatingly. 'As soon as there's a telephone free someone will bring it to you, but you mustn't excite yourself. There's nothing so urgent that it can't wait a little while. After all,' the student nurse went on, trying a soothing smile that sat badly on her frightened face, 'you're going to be here for quite a while yet. We mustn't let ourselves get too impatient, now must we?'

'I don't much care whether you get impatient or not,' began Willow, 'but I . . . Never mind. Please do your best for me.'

The young woman scuttled away on her squeaking shoes, leaving Willow feeling very much worse than she had when she had first woken. She closed her eyes and tried to achieve a calm that would help her to deal rationally with her fears, but it was beyond the reach of her battered mind or body.

The familiar sound of rubber soles squeezed against polished vinyl made her open her eyes and smile a little in anticipation of a telephone and the possibility of reaching Tom Worth, but all she saw was a pair of tree-trunk-like thighs dressed in dark-blue serge trousers. Raising her eyes, she saw a silver-buttoned tunic and a crested helmet.

Higher than that was a fresh young male face and a pair of anxious blue eyes. Willow felt extraordinarily relieved by the existence of this young, but protective-looking policeman.

'Do you feel up to answering a few questions?' said the constable sympathetically. 'The doctor said it would be all right to ask you some now.'

'Have you been here long?' asked Willow.

'Since they reported the hit-and-run, yes, Miss. Now, can you tell me everything you remember?'

Willow knew that Tom Worth had to have all her information first and so she decided to be sparing with the truth.

'I can hardly remember anything. I heard an engine revving and the tyres, but I thought it was just some stupid driver who had nothing to do with me,' she said. 'I'd stepped off the pavement and did not realise that I was at risk at all until he had hit me. By then it was too late to look. I'm awfully sorry.'

'No registration number, I suppose?' asked the policeman.

'Sorry,' said Willow shortly.

'And now, may I ask what you were doing in that part of London, Miss? That might help us because I understand that you live in Abbeville Road, SW12 and work in Clapham High Street.'

Willow thought for a while, put a hand to the bandages covering her aching forehead and shut her eyes.

'I simply don't know,' she said, lying easily. 'I can't think straight. Can you persuade them to let me have a telephone? I really must make a call – an urgent call.'

Watching the young policeman's face, Willow saw suspicion pouring into it and even more she longed for Tom Worth.

'I'm sorry,' she said to the constable. 'When I've cleared my mind a bit, I'll do my best to tell you some more. Will you be here?'

'If there's more to come I suspect I'll be here,' he said wryly. 'I must make my report now.' He left without thanking her or expressing any kind of sympathy for her injuries and she knew that he had put her down as a trouble-maker or worse.

When she did eventually manage to get a telephone trolley, Willow tried Tom's office only to be told that he was 'unavailable'. She left a message, explaining where she was and saying that she needed to speak to him urgently, and then dictated a fuller one on to the answering machine at his flat. Before she had finished doing that, she was presented with a disgusting-looking meal that had obviously been cooked hours before.

Willow picked up the stainless steel knife and fork that had been laid on her tray and cut a small piece off the dried-up slab of liver on her plate. She had just raised it to her mouth when she felt herself gag and retch as violently as she had after the bad oyster.

On the tray in front of her was a piece of card with her name and the number of her bed. Anyone could have put anything they wanted into the food that had been allocated to her. Controlling the nausea her ideas had brought her, Willow dropped the cutlery back on the tray. In that moment she became determined not to eat anything provided by the hospital that had been lying around with her name on it.

When a middle-aged nurse came to collect the tray she remonstrated like a nanny, but eventually accepted Willow's explanation that she simply could not face eating anything. She was just about to go when Willow grabbed her wrist.

'What is it, lovey?' she asked, kindly detaching Willow's grasping hand.

'Can I have some pillows?' she asked pathetically. 'I hate lying flat like this.'

'Of course you can't,' said the nurse. 'Your legs are weighted. In a few days they may be able to adjust the pulleys, but not yet. Do you want anything before I go?' Willow shook her head slightly, wincing. 'Shall I leave your curtains shut or would you like a bit of company?'

That was the first time Willow realised that she must be in a ward of other people. The blue-and-green checked curtains that hung from the ceiling about three foot from her bed had given her the illusion of being in a room on her own. She realised that her senses must have been even more disordered by the accident than she had thought.

'Leave them shut, will you?' she said. 'I don't feel up to company yet.'

Lying back, wishing that someone would come and visit her and bring her some wholesome fruit she could eat, Willow began to hear the other women on her ward chatting happily amongst themselves. They discussed their treatment or their injuries, their children, their husbands, their hysterectomies and the workings of their bowels, about which they spoke in terms of extreme – and graphic – frankness.

The sound of their inoffensive voices began to grate against the pain in her head and she wished that they did not exist. She reminded herself of Marcus Aurelius's injunction to accept whatever experiences the fates bring you and settled down to wait for Tom.

He did not come. A nurse came round with a trolley offering her patients a variety of hot drinks. Willow refused them all, although she was tempted by the Horlicks, which she had not tasted since childhood. Then came the pill trolley and a new batch of painkillers for Willow, which she did accept as she watched the nurses tipping them out of a large bottle. She could not imagine anyone poisoning a whole bottle of painkilling drugs and putting the entire hospital at risk.

Chapter 17

*T*HE FIRST non-medical person Willow saw after her accident apart from the young policeman was the patient in the bed next to her own. Willow had refused her depressing supper of breaded, fried gammon chop and watery vegetables an hour and a half earlier and had been trying not to think how hungry she was. There was only circumstantial evidence to suggest that the driver who had run her over was the poisoner, but she decided that she had taken enough risks with her life.

Lying with her eyes closed she became aware that someone was standing beside her bed, quite near her head. Willow decided that it was not a nurse: it neither smelled nor sounded like a nurse. She opened her eyes and saw a dumpy woman in a quilted nylon dressing gown standing there looking at her with kindly curiosity.

'Feeling a bit better now, dear?' she said, obviously hoping for a lovely chat. 'My name is Marjorie, by the way.'

'How do you do?' said Willow coldly. 'I am better, thank you, but still very tired.'

'Oh, I'm sure you are,' said Marjorie, 'and I won't

disturb you. But I did notice you were asleep when the newspaper trolley came round this morning, and I thought you might like to have a lend of mine.'

Willow struggled to find the patience and civility that she owed the inoffensive woman.

'Thank you,' she said at last. 'That's very kind.'

'That's all right. I'll just pop to my locker and fetch it.'

A moment later the *Daily Mercury* was lying on Willow's chest. Still trying to show a modicum of appreciation, she picked it up and held it above her eyes. The first thing she saw, in huge black lettering on page one, was:

'Private catering company director found poisoned in Wimbledon.'

Willow looked up to see her fellow-patient staring at her face intently. She smiled.

'Isn't it awful, dear? That poor woman was just eating her sandwiches and she died.'

'Awful,' agreed Willow, turning back to the paper. She realised why Tom Worth had been unavailable for so long and read on to discover that it was Sarah Tothill who had died after eating water hemlock. Willow stared up at the paper appalled. The muscles in her arms felt suddenly weak and she let them relax, dropping the paper on to her chest.

For the first time she had met and talked to one of the victims and she felt stricken with guilt. She found it unbearable to think that if she had worked a bit harder, she might have been able to prevent Sarah's death. Her hunger disappeared and in its place was a sickness and a distress that seemed to absorb all her energies.

To control the immediate instinctive horror, Willow forced her mind to work. Either the effort or the shock she had suffered was effective and at last she remembered the one vital piece of information. She tried to imagine what Sarah might have done to deserve such revenge and wondered whether she had eaten something intended for her unspeakable husband.

'I must make a telephone call,' she said abruptly, pushing the sheets of newspaper off her bed and reaching for the bell.

'Must you, dear?' said Marjorie, who had been watching her with bright-eyed interest. 'Shall I see if I can fetch you a trolley then? I expect you want to ring your boyfriend?'

Her hopes of confidences were quickly dashed by Willow's blank stare of incomprehension, but even so she went away to find a nurse and a telephone. When she came back with both she was wearing a peculiarly arch smile, which became her far less than the curiosity she had shown so obviously.

'I'll draw your curtains, dear,' she said coyly, 'so that you can be private.'

'How kind!' said Willow and waited until she was lying in relative privacy to dial the number of Richard Crescent's flat. She was lucky to find him in, he told her, since he had innumerable multi-million-pound deals just coming to the boil and was about to go to the office again.

'I'm so sorry to disturb you,' she said, her voice all synthetic honey. He laughed and she remembered why she had always liked him.

'OK, you win,' he said, sounding like the man he was and not the banker he usually pretended to be. 'What you do you want?'

'I just thought,' she said, half-way between Cressida and Willow, 'that you might prefer to hear this from me and not Mrs R: I've broken both my legs and am in Dowting's Hospital.'

'I wish you wouldn't joke about things that really matter,' said Richard, sounding peevish.

'I'm not. I have two broken legs, hung up in front of me like bandaged poultry carcases,' said Willow. 'And, tied by the heels as I most genuinely am, I need your help again.'

'May I come and see you?'

'Yes, if you like, and if you promise to be discreet, if you see what I mean, but . . .'

'Ah, Willow or Cressida?' he asked intelligently.

'The first,' she said. 'But before you come, I need a piece of information.'

'What do you want to know?'

'You know the woman we met at Caroline's dinner last week?' she began.

'Sarah Tothill,' said Richard in such a cheerful voice that Willow knew that the murder could not have been reported in *The Times*.

'That's right. How long have she and Caroline known each other and have they ever quarrelled?' said Willow.

'That's two bits of information,' said Richard. 'And I'm afraid I can't be much help. I think they were at school together, but I'd only met the Tothills once before that embarrassing dinner and didn't really take to them. D'you want me to go and pump Caroline?'

'Absolutely not!' said Willow so quickly that Richard was alerted.

'I'll look in to see you later,' he said in a voice that sounded almost dangerous.

'All right,' Willow was saying as the green-and-blue curtains were dragged aside and she saw Chief Inspector Worth standing there with a blaze of light behind him. His face was taut and his eyes were bloodshot with tiredness and very anxious.

'I'll see you later then. Thank you.' Willow put down the telephone and was gratified by the speed with which Tom reached her bedside.

'Will,' he said, grabbing both her hands. 'Oh Will.'

'Thank you for coming, Tom,' she said in a low voice that held a warning. She gestured to the other beds beyond her curtains. All chatter in the ward had stopped.

'Even if the curtains don't keep the sound of our voices down,' he said loudly, 'at least they give a measure of privacy.'

Almost at once several self-conscious conversations were started between the occupants of the other beds in the ward.

'Tom,' said Willow urgently and quietly, 'I must tell you . . .'

'No. Wait, Willow. Your doctors have said that you're going to be all right, which is the most important thing, and I need . . . I need to ask you some questions.'

'All right,' she said, 'but . . .'

'My superiors have at last decided that there is a serial poisoner at work,' said Tom, ignoring her protest, 'and I'm in charge of the investigation. I'm about to apply for a warrant and I need to clarify what you've told me about Caroline.'

'Aha,' said Willow, her eyes and her voice hardening. 'I had wondered if Sarah Tothill died by mistake – instead of her frightful husband – but obviously not. What had she done to Caroline?'

The bleakness of Tom's face made her shiver. When he spoke his voice had lost all colour and character.

'One of Sarah Tothill's first large catering commissions was to supply the food for Simon Titchmell's twenty-first-birthday dance,' he said. 'Something went badly wrong and almost forty per cent of the guests suffered food poisoning. One of the worst affected was Caroline, and because of it she was so ill that she couldn't take that year's exams at university and had to retake the whole year's course . . .'

'How odd that she should have even considered using Sarah to do her wedding food, then,' said Willow before she could stop herself. Tom's face hardened even more.

'Not at all,' he said bitterly. 'She obviously needed an excuse to keep track of Sarah's movements and to get into her house in order to poison the horseradish sauce. . . . That's how it was done, you see,' he added, seeing that Willow's expression was puzzled. 'There was an enormous amount of grated water hemlock root in the horseradish sauce she put in her cold-beef sandwiches. Her husband never ate it. Luckily – for us – the jar was a relatively new one and so there was plenty of sauce left for us to test.'

'But no finger prints, of course,' Willow said slowly and very quietly.

'She knows far too much to leave prints,' he said impatiently. 'I've already checked that none of the ones on Bruterley's malt whisky bottle were hers.' Willow stared up at him as though she could not believe what she saw.

'What's the matter?' he asked irritably. 'I know you liked her, but . . .'

'Tom, you don't mean that you think Caroline killed them all?' said Willow. He made an odd gesture with both hands, as though he were brushing aside her protest.

'Look, I know that we both believed no one could be mad enough to do what she's done, but the evidence has mounted up horribly . . . besides, there was a witness to your so-called accident, Will. The description of the car fits hers – and so does the registration number. I'm afraid that she must have done it.'

'But she hardly ever drives,' said Willow, unable to believe that Tom had so badly misunderstood what had been going on. 'And surely you know by now that she's not mad at all, that she's had nothing to do with any of the deaths except for providing unwitting incitement?'

'What?' said Tom, screwing up his eyes and peering at Willow. He sounded exhausted and at the same time absolutely furious. 'What on earth are you talking about?'

They were interrupted just then as a firm hand swished back the checked curtains and a posse of white-coated doctors appeared.

'These are some of my students, Miss King,' said Doctor Wakehurst. 'Do you mind if they ask you some questions?'

'Doctors must be trained,' said Willow conscientiously, 'but would it be possible to do it later? Chief Inspector Worth is asking me some questions of his own just now.'

'Don't worry, Will,' said Tom quickly. 'I'll have another

269

word with the chap outside and come back when you're finished.' He got up.

'Don't go,' she said, wishing that she were not imprisoned by her weights and pulleys. 'We must talk.'

'Yes we must. I'll be outside. You won't be long, will you doctor?'

'Quick as we can,' answered Dr Wakehurst crisply.

The young students were too embarrassed to look Willow in the eye and confined most of their remarks to their teacher. After a while Willow got tired of lying like a piece of meat for their inspection and started to give them a few explanations and instructions herself. Quite soon after that the doctor led her charges away. Before Tom could reappear, Marjorie put her head through the curtains.

'A film is just starting on television. Shall we get the nurses to wheel you into the day room?'

'No, thank you,' said Willow. She managed to put more gratitude into her voice than she had earlier as she realised that she and Tom would probably have the ward to themselves for the next half hour. As soon as the woman withdrew, Tom took her place. Before Willow could say anything he said:

'Now you must tell me what you mean.'

'Of course I will,' she answered. 'I've been trying to tell you ever since they brought me in. Come and sit down.'

Before Tom could settle himself in the visitor's plastic-coated chair again another hot-drink trolley was pushed through the ward. Willow declined again and the nurse told her that she really would have to start taking food and drink soon.

When the heavy, clattering trolley had been pushed away, Tom said curtly:

'Why aren't you eating or drinking?'

'Because I daren't until Ben Jonson is in custody,' she said.

'Ben Jonson? You must be mad,' said Tom. Then he came back to her bedside and put one of his hands on her scarred one again. He looked down at her battered face, with the bruises yellowing at the edges and the cuts and scratches dark red.

'You're still frightened, aren't you?' he said much more gently. 'But you mustn't let it distort your judgment, Will.'

'Will you just shut up for one moment, Thomas?' said Willow coldly. 'There is nothing the matter with my brains any longer, even though my head aches foully and my legs are so painful that there are times when I would like to cut them off. I can cope with that, but I cannot cope with your brushing aside what I say as though I were an idiot. Wait, ask questions, and *listen* to the answers, if your ego will let you.'

'My ego is at your disposal,' said Tom with resignation. 'Tell me why you think Jonson should have done it – and how he could have.'

'He loves her,' said Willow, 'really desperately. He looks up to her. He wants to make up to her for everything she has suffered before she met him. He is kind to her, she once told me, terribly kind.'

'That all sounds admirable,' said Tom, 'but I still can't see him doing all this for her even if she wanted him to.'

'She didn't, you clot. I told you she's completely inno-cent. But she's obviously told him about her past and he must have decided to take revenge for her on all the people who have hurt her.'

'That's absurd,' said Tom. Willow paid no attention to his protest.

'He's a very angry man, you know: angry, chippy, and much poorer than she is. He thinks he has nothing to offer her that she could value, because he doesn't value himself, just as he doesn't understand her or what she needs.'

'How do you know that he is angry?' asked Tom, completely serious and at last apparently willing to believe her, but having some difficulty in following her thought processes.

'I can't remember,' said Willow, putting a hand to her bandaged forehead, 'if you ever talked to him?'

'Never,' said Tom.

'He has the softest voice I've ever heard in a man,' said Willow, 'but it's a voice of fantastic control. I hadn't thought about it before, but you can almost hear the effort he exerts to make it sound light, gentle, calm. Even when he was throwing Sarah Tothill's husband out of his house, he sounded gentle. That makes me suspicious to begin with. But have you read any of his books?' Tom did not even bother to answer that question; he merely shook his head.

'Well, I read one on the way back from Newcastle,' said Willow. 'I'd been meaning to read it for ages and ages, but never got to it until then. If only I had, I might have realised what was going on and stopped it before Sarah Tothill . . .' Her voice broke, but she recovered herself after a moment and went on as coolly as though she were delivering a report to the Permanent Secretary.

'Would you pass me my handbag?'

Tom obediently picked up the shabby black leather bag and handed it to her. Willow took out Ben's book and opened it at the place she had marked with a clean paper handkerchief.

'Listen,' she said.

'I'm listening,' said Tom. Willow cleared her throat.

'"*Martin sat, impassive, at her feet. She had no idea that in his mind he had bound her like one of Hans Bellmer's dolls with tight, straining wire, so that her flesh bulged out in plump, quilted squares. In his mind, she was controlled. The wire would hurt her; but, better, it would keep her there. While her clacking, nagging voice tore into his brain, shredding his eardrums, he had her where he needed her.*"'

'That's horrible,' said Tom, looking almost as sick as Willow had felt. 'No wonder his books don't sell.'

'Yes I know,' said Willow. 'But it's far more revealing than that.'

'Cruel, certainly,' said Tom, looking at Willow through narrowed eyes. 'But what makes you think that these deaths could have been caused by someone like him? There's been no physical brutality, no tying up or rending . . .'

'You didn't listen properly,' said Willow. 'Concentrate, Tom. The woman in that paragraph wasn't tied up, she wasn't in pain, she wasn't "where he wanted her". She was clacking and nagging at him. Only in his mind was she in his control. The whole book is like that. You haven't time to read it, so take in on trust: the story itself is simple and very little happens outside the mind of the "hero". Within that mind, though, the most appalling fantasies are unwound.'

Willow put the book down and took a deep breath. She realised that to someone like Tom Worth, whose interest in other people appeared to have nothing to do with the possibility of controlling them, Ben's compulsions could seem incredible.

'Ben's mother wanted him to be like her brothers, who died in the war. He announced at dinner that she did everything she could to make him like them, but he turned out quite different, meaning us to think that he was the gentle, shambling creature he pretends to be. Think how inadequate he must have felt all his childhood as he failed to live up to the toughness she wanted of him.'

'All this is very interesting,' said Tom, 'but it's hardly evidence. He . . .'

'He was in Newcastle in the Christmas vacation,' she said, stopping his protests effectively. 'He was teaching a course of creative writing there. I had thought that January was too early for anyone to have poisoned the sloe gin until I remembered your original notes: you wrote then that she made her stock of sloe gin once a year when the sloes were ripe.'

Tom's eyes had lost their disbelief and looked alert again.

'And Miss Fernside's next-door neighbour recognised the photograph of him from the back of this book,' said Willow.

'How do you know?' he asked sharply.

'Because I went up to Newcastle myself on Thursday night and talked to her on Friday. I also telephoned the university and talked to the man who organised Ben Jonson's teaching there. I think that if you interview him you'll discover that he found it so funny that Cressida Woodruffe had been asking questions about Ben Jonson's courses that he rang Ben to tell him about my questions. He must have put two and two together and decided to run me over. Unfortunately he recognised me.'

'Willow, it's so unlikely. You must see that,' said Tom.

'As clearly as I saw him at the wheel of that car,' she said slowly.

'You saw him?'

'Yes.'

'Then why in God's name didn't you tell me at once?' Tom demanded, justifiably furious with her.

'I tried,' she said, 'as soon as my mind started to work again, to get hold of you.'

Tom sat silently at her bedside, looking down at her scarred hands lying on the white cellular blanket. His mind was full of the danger she had been in, the terror she must have been feeling, and his own struggle to believe in her reasoning.

'I still don't understand why he should have wanted to kill them all,' he said. 'Even if everything else is as you say. It's very thin, Willow. I can't see the Crown Prosecution Service being convinced.'

'Tom,' said Willow and her voice was so gentle that he was almost shocked. 'Last time we worked together you managed to get the killer to make a confession. I know you hated doing it, but you did without much more direct evidence than you have here. Couldn't you do it again?'

'I don't know. What else is there that makes you think he did it?'

'To recap,' she said, reverting to her formal voice: 'We know that Caroline suffered under Miss Fernside over the meningitis business; she was forced to take drugs at her brother's party; she was in love with Bruterley and he shook her off with extreme verbal cruelty; the latest victim once made her so ill with food poisoning that she failed some important exams. You agree that each of those people has injured her in one way or another?'

'Yes,' said Tom, his face filled with a perplexed expression that sat oddly with the broken nose that gave it such a distinctive attraction or with the firmness of his mouth. 'But what about Simon's girlfriend?'

'I'm sure that was an accident,' said Willow. 'I read but didn't pay proper attention to your first notes when you told me that Simon and the girl were not living together. When Ben poisoned the cereal he must have thought that only Titchmell would be there at breakfast time. She should never have eaten the muesli.'

'All right,' said Tom. 'I'll accept that for the moment.'

'Caroline was in love with Ben; she would have told him everything they did to her. He must have decided to kill them for her. It was something he could give her that she could never get for herself, and it was also a way of making himself superior to her, whatever her success, her money and the possessions she bestowed on him. He could still feel good about himself, too, because he made himself believe that he was doing it because he loved her, to make up for the cruel things people had done to her.'

'It still sounds far fetched to me,' said Tom, noticing that the dark-red scars on her face were almost the same colour as her eyebrows.

'Well it isn't,' said Willow. 'He fulfils all the criteria we listed that day in your flat, even down to being a model-maker.'

Tom's head snapped upwards and he looked at her.

'How do you know?'

'Another of those things I hardly noticed at the time. When I first met him, he was discussing with the girl on his other side how he was working on the accurate staging of one of his namesake's masques.'

'And?' said Tom, when Willow stopped speaking and closed her eyes.

'I was trying to remember his exact words, but I can't. The effect of what he said was that the original design was by Inigo Jones and there are records of it and that he was – yes: he was "reproducing it in miniature".'

'Do you know the name of the person he was talking to?' Tom took a notebook out of his breast pocket.

'Emma Gnatche,' said Willow. 'I know her and I can give you her address if you need it. There is more,' she added as Tom nodded. 'When I went to Caroline's house for dinner she told me that most of the rooms were sparse and under-furnished because a lot of their belongings were still in store. The decorators had not finished and until they were well clear of the house she had not wanted to risk Ben's "masque sets". I didn't register at the time, but that's what she must have meant. She said something proudly about their being "exquisite". Haven't you got enough at least to pull him in and talk to him?'

'Perhaps. Have you said anything about this to anyone? That psychiatrist fellow you talked about?'

'Certainly not,' said Willow. 'But, Tom, be quick. He's obviously mad, clearly dangerous. You must stop him.'

'I'll try, but it's all circumstantial . . .'

'Take this,' said Willow, handing him *Fair Cecilia*. 'Ben gave it to me and signed it for me. You ought to be able to get clear prints from the laminated jacket. Perhaps they'll match one on the malt whisky bottle.'

The film must have come to an end, for Willow's ward-mates came trooping back to their beds, each woman dressed in a similar quilted dressing gown and fluffy nylon slippers. Tom cast them a look of horrified surprise that irritated Willow, even though she shared his distaste for their uniform.

'I must go.'

'You will tell me what happens, won't you?' said Willow.

Tom nodded. 'And don't be afraid. There'll be a man of ours outside all the time. Would you like me to have food sent in for you?'

The relief of being able to be certain that what she ate was not contaminated would be wonderful, Willow thought, and so she thanked him and accepted his offer. It also occurred to her that anything Tom provided would be healthier and taste better than the hospital meals she had seen so far.

He was already walking towards the swing doors out of the ward when Willow called him back.

'Perhaps he thinks he's killed me,' she said softly to comfort them both. 'After all, he ran over Cressida Woodruffe . . . If he's asked for her in any of the hospitals he'll have been unlucky.'

'That's a thought,' said Tom. 'Keep your pecker up, Will.' He bent down and kissed her scarred cheek and left her alone.

Willow watched him go and began to turn ideas over and over in her mind. There were one or two nasty ones that stuck like emotional burrs in her brain. Try as she might, she could not get them out.

Chapter 18

W ILLOW lay on her back waiting for her bones to knit
and Tom to appear with the proof he needed. Her
only distractions were visits from Richard, from Barbara,
who came with minutes for approval and problems for
sorting, and from Michael Rodenhurst, who came with
flowers and fruit and dangerous questions about her
detective story.

It was Thursday before Tom came again to tell her
that Ben Jonson was being investigated. He arrived
before the official visiting time, during the showing
of *Neighbours*, when he knew that the ward would
be empty except for Willow. His face looked bruised
with tiredness and his eyes held a curious mixture
of superiority and distress. He stood by Willow's bed
waiting until she woke and looking down at her healing
face. The bandages round her head were lighter than
the ones he had seen when he had first come to
the hospital, her black eyes were fading to an ugly
yellow, but she looked very much better than she had
when he had last seen her. Her red eyelashes fluttered
upwards.

'Tom?' she said slowly and smiled up at him as she battled with the remnants of sleep that were clouding her brain.

'Yes, it's me, Will,' he said gently. He had never seen her so relaxed and so obviously pleased to see him. 'You look much . . . much more human.'

'You've a great skill with a compliment,' she said, rapidly returning to her usual form. 'But you don't look particularly well yourself: are you all right? Sit down.'

He shrugged his broad shoulders and then went to fetch a chair.

'I suppose,' he said, 'that I'm rather tired.'

'I can imagine,' said Willow, her voice and face softening again. 'Are you . . .? Is he . . .? What stage have you reached?'

'Not very far,' said Tom. 'There were no finger prints on the whisky bottle that matched those on your book.'

'Damn!' said Willow. 'And so?' Tom shrugged.

'Everything else you told me has been confirmed and I've tried to get a warrant to search his house and the rooms he uses in his various adult-education colleges . . . but they say there isn't enough evidence.'

Willow looked carefully at Tom, trying to decide what he was thinking. At last she said:

'You look as though you do think it's him, though.'

'Yes,' he said reluctantly. 'The more I've thought about it, the more I've come to accept your analysis. That's why I've done nothing to pursue Titchmell. But we've nothing to go on. We'll just have to wait until he does it again, and . . .'

'Tom! You can't,' said Willow. The anger in her voice sounded like a call to action. 'You simply cannot sacrifice another innocent person to his obsessions.'

'There isn't anything else I can do. We need actual, physical evidence, and there is none. No fingerprints; no fibres to identify because in each case he was there days or even weeks before the deaths and so the rooms had been cleaned; no possibility of any victim's blood on his own clothes or in his house. Nothing,' said Tom. He got up from the orange plastic chair by her bed and paced up and down. At last he wheeled round.

'I must go, Will. I'm not doing any good here, and I'll only stop your bones knitting with my bad temper. I'll see you soon,' he said.

'When?' she asked, beginning to see a way through the impasse they had reached. Tom smiled to think that she might be so impatient to see him that she actually asked for a date.

'What about tomorrow? Same time? During *Neighbours*,' he said with a laugh. 'Then we can at least be private.'

'Wonderful, Tom,' she said with a sweet smile. 'I'll be waiting.' She kissed her hand to him as he parted the checked curtains and disappeared.

As soon as she was sure he was out of the ward, she rang her bell and demanded a telephone. When it came she dialled the number of Caroline Titchmell's house. As she had hoped, Ben Jonson answered it.

'Could I speak to Mr Jonson?' Willow said in a voice that held more than a trace of a Newcastle accent.

'This is he. To whom am I speaking?' he asked.

'Dr King,' said Willow, still with a northern roundness in her voice. 'At Dowting's Hospital. I'm calling for a patient, a Miss Woodruffe.'

'Oh yes?' said Ben sharply into the telephone. 'Is she all right?'

'She's fine, Mr Jonson, but very anxious to see you.'

'As I am, doctor,' he said. 'Where exactly is she?'

'She's in theatre at the moment,' said Willow, who had worked out which the most inaccessible parts of the hospital would be, 'and will be spending tonight and most of tomorrow in Recovery. But she should be up in Phyllis Ward by about half-past five tomorrow. She'd very much like to see you then.'

'I'll be there,' he said. Willow could not help hearing menace in his light, pleasant voice then. She put down the telephone and spent the rest of the evening watching the ward doors and planning precisely what she was going to say when he appeared. Only when the outer doors of the ward were locked, after the night staff had come on duty, did she relax and accept her usual quota of sleeping pills.

The following morning she woke apprehensive but determined and found that the day dragged by even more slowly than usual. Her only real distraction was a visit from Barbara soon after four o'clock with a memo from the Permanent Secretary that was so infuriating that it wiped everything else from Willow's mind. By the time Barbara had gone, there was only another fifteen minutes to wait.

Willow acknowledged that she was afraid. She had turned herself into a tethered goat to trap a tiger and she had no guarantee that Tom would arrive in time to save her. But it was the only way. The police were not allowed to trap a suspect, and if Tom knew what she was doing he would have stopped her.

Trying to make her breathing deep and slow, she could feel sweat gathering all down her spine and within the plaster that encased her legs. She felt light-headed, too, and hoped passionately that she would be able to control her mind enough to do what she had to do.

All around her was the sound of her fellow-patients getting themselves out of their beds and into their dressing gowns and slippers for their daily dose of *Neighbours*, and she knew that she would be alone with her tiger. She pulled the bell closer and tucked it under her bedclothes, keeping her forefinger beside the button so that she could press it in need.

It was impossible not to think of the time it could take the over-burdened nurses to answer a patient's bell.

There was the sound of footsteps beyond her curtains. She quickly checked her watch. It was exactly half-past five. Willow gripped her upper lip between her teeth. The blue-and-green curtains parted and Ben Jonson stood there, looking just as friendly, untidy and unthreatening as he had always done. Willow unclamped her lip and smiled at him.

'You found me,' she said pleasantly. 'I am glad. It's very good of you to come.'

'Not at all,' he answered in the same, courteous social tones as she had used. 'Had I known you were here, I'd have come days ago. I wanted to see you.'

'Really? How kind. I had the stupidest accident, but I'm getting on all right now.'

'What happened?' asked Ben, pulling up the chair and sitting down so close to Willow that she almost flinched.

'Oh it was too silly. I was exhausted after a long and infuriating train journey and on my way home simply didn't look where I was going and walked straight into the path of a car. God knows why I wasn't killed!'

'Did the driver bring you in?' Ben asked, giving Willow hope.

'No,' she said, looking at him as directly as she could from her supine position on the bed. 'Apparently it was a real hit-and-run. No one saw the accident and no one really knows what happened.'

'You look as though you're listening for something,' Ben said, sounding less gentle than before. 'Are you expecting someone?'

'No,' said Willow. 'But I want to make sure of privacy for what I'm about to say to you.' She checked her watch. If Tom were really coming, he ought to be on his way up to the ward.

'Ah,' said Ben with a smile that would have looked charming in any other circumstances. 'Now we come to it.'

'Yes,' agreed Willow, edging her finger nearer to the bell. 'Has it ever occurred to you that the police might think it was Caroline?'

Ben said nothing, and he did not move. Willow slightly relaxed her finger and took another deep breath.

'They do, you see. They've worked out why all those people died, and they think that Caroline has been taking revenge. They are getting a warrant out for her arrest. You know what will happen then, don't you?'

There was still silence. Ben's eyes looked as though he were doing complicated sums in his head. Suddenly they focused on Willow's pale face and she knew that none of the fear she had felt in her life had been the real thing.

'They'll put her in a cell in a police station,' she said quickly, 'and leave her there. One telephone call – that's all. She'll have a bucket as a lavatory and a cement bench as a bed.'

Willow had never seen a police station cell and had no idea whether her description was accurate.

'She'll be strip-searched and humiliated; terrified; and quite, quite powerless.'

Ben said nothing. His eyes were still staring at her face and his hands were taut and shaking. They looked almost like claws. Willow knew that she had to precipitate whatever was going to happen. Saying a quick prayer to a god in whom she did not believe, she did it.

'And you will have put her there. Is that what you wanted to do all the time? All that love was really hate, wasn't it? She had everything you had ever wanted, and you couldn't bear it. She was everything you had ever wanted to be and you had to humiliate her. That was it, wasn't it? You wanted to make her suffer, and . . .'

Before Willow could finish, the claw-like hands had lifted from the grey-flannel-covered knees and were on her throat. Strung up on the pulleys, unable to move, Willow was completely defenceless. Choking against the grip on her neck, with her head boiling and a fog clouding her sight, she heard:

'You bitch! You fucking bitch! You have no idea. I love her. I love her. I love her. You bitch. You sodding, fucking, bitch. You c . . .'

'Enough!'

The single word ripped through the stream of insult and Willow felt the clutching hands pulled from her throat. Opening her tear-drenched eyes she saw Tom. Choking, gagging, she tried to breathe.

'Tom,' she said. But no sound emerged. She brushed the tears away and saw that he had Ben Jonson in a ferocious arm lock and gave up the struggle to do anything but breathe.

Twenty minutes later, uniformed officers had Jonson in handcuffs and Tom was sitting by Willow's bed, stroking her red head over and over again.

'You fool,' he said gently. 'You idiotic, dangerous, brilliant fool. Oh, God, Willow, don't ever do that again. Promise you won't ever to that again? Darling fool, you must promise.'

'All right,' she said painfully. She could not imagine letting herself go through any such thing again and could not understand how she had done it even once. Only the sensation of Tom's hand on her head was stopping her from screaming out her terror and her relief that she was not dead.

Four days later her throat felt better, although swallowing was still painful. Tom was sitting at her side once again and Willow was slowly drinking the peach nectar he had brought her.

'Has Ben confessed yet?' she asked.

'To the murders? Not to us. We had hopes that he would have admitted something in a letter he wrote to Miss Titchmell, but he didn't.'

'You mean you read it?' asked Willow, sounding absurdly shocked. 'Could I have a glass of that water? This stuff is delicious but a mite sickly.'

Tom stood up and poured some water out of a plastic jug into a tumbler and handed it to her. Willow drank some, but it was warm and tasted slightly stale although one of the nurses had refilled the jug earlier that morning.

'Why are you so shocked? We asked her first,' said Tom. Willow's face cleared.

'I thought you'd been intercepting his mail,' she said drily.

'All letters to and from remand prisoners are private, Willow. You know that,' he answered. 'But one of my men went to see her to ask if he could read it.'

'And what was in it?' she asked with half-reluctant curiosity, handing him the glass to put down for her.

'A Shakespeare sonnet – number 50, I think,' Tom answered.

'I don't know that one,' said Willow. 'Can you remember it?'

'I never saw it,' said Tom, 'and I don't know the sonnets by heart. If you like I'll bring you a Shakespeare next time I come in.'

They were silent for a moment, listening to the faint sussurus from the day room, where *Neighbours* was feeding the other patients' starved fantasies, and the efficient sounds of the nursing staff as they bustled about the six bays on the ward.

Worth stood up and half turned to look out of the wide windows at the London skyline. The weather had broken and the newly emerged leaves and flowers were being lashed by unseasonable rain. The clouds outside the windows were heavy and black. Neither Tom nor Willow spoke, both absorbed in their thoughts of what had happened and what effect it was going to have on everyone involved.

'Tom,' said Willow at last, 'have you seen Caroline?'

'No,' he answered. 'I know she has talked to the Legal Aid people for him, but that's all I know.'

'She must be in a frightful state,' said Willow, betraying only some of the anxiety she felt. 'I've tried to get hold of her through Richard Crescent, but he doesn't seem able to make her answer the door or the telephone. He says that there are lights on in the house whenever he knocks on the door, but that no one ever answers the bell.'

'The lights could be on time switches to baffle burglars,' suggested Tom. 'Perhaps she has gone to stay with her mother or gone away.'

'I don't think so,' said Willow, putting a hand to her head as though it ached. 'I don't think that would be in character. I think she is in there, trying to deal with it all on her own and I think she should be got out. I can't go and batter on the door while I'm strung up like this.'

Tom got out of the chair and walked to the foot of Willow's bed. He turned, put both hands on the steel bars of the bedstead and took a deep breath.

'That's not really in your style is it, Will? Trying to make people express their emotions for their own good? Shouldn't she be left to deal with them as she sees fit?'

'You're right about a lot of things, Tom, but this time I think the need might be so severe that it would justify interference. Don't look at me like that, Tom,' said Willow, seeing mockery where perhaps there was only a dawning hope that she might one day be able to face the fact that he, too, had severe emotional needs – and she herself as well.

'Do you want me to bring her? I imagine she's too embarrassed by what he's done to you to come here without some forcible reason.'

'Would you?'

'Yes,' he said. 'If you really want her. I'll try to bring her tomorrow.'

'Good,' said Willow. 'Oh, before you go, Tom, did Swaffield's confession of his lies produce any real information about him and Miranda?' Tom's face changed. 'I can't help being interested,' said Willow. 'Please tell me.'

'All right.' Tom laughed. 'It was a simple enough story. According to Sarah Rowfant (whose mental trouble, by the way, turned out to be a relatively mild case of anxiety treated with a short course of valium some years ago), Miranda and Swaffield had been playing platonic lovers for a year or more. Bruterley did not particularly mind . . .'

'I should think not!' exclaimed Willow. 'When he was unfaithful and probably had been since his wedding day.'

'It does sound as though he had had a girlfriend on the side since the second year of his marriage,' Tom admitted. 'But he had noticed Miranda's growing predilection for his senior partner and he was worried that she might divorce him.'

'Ah, and she was the one with the money,' Willow said.

'Precisely. And when Bruterley went to Swaffield to warn him off, Swaffield in turn . . .'

'Blackmailed Bruterley with the fact that Sarah Rowfant was a patient of the practice,' said Willow hardly aware that she had interrupted him. 'I see. And fearing for his matrimonial home and income, rather than for his professional standing, which was not really at risk, he told her that he was going to have to stop their affair?'

'Just that. And she, devastated, fled to the wilds of northern Scotland and the telephoneless croft, poor girl.'

'Poor girl, indeed,' agreed Willow, 'but silly girl, too. He was married. What a mess emotions cause!'

'On that note, my dear Will, I'm off,' said Tom with a grin. 'Is the food in those boxes all right?'

'Wonderful! Thank you for sending it, but now that Jonson has been restrained, you don't really need to go on,' said Willow.

'But don't you prefer the picnics to hospital food?' Tom asked, and when she smiled and admitted that she did, he added, 'Well, I'll carry on then. Goodbye.'

She watched him go, thinking that he looked more like his usual tough self than when she had first woken and seen him staring down at her with that slight smile on his lips and the bruised expression in his eyes. Sighing a little for the energy that caring about him took from her, Willow twisted sideways as she had learned to do and picked up a new book Michael Rodenhurst had brought her. But she could not concentrate on it. There were so many loose ends left in her knowledge of the case, but she knew that she would have to wait until the trial itself to hear about the police work that had turned her leaps of imagination and analysis and guesswork into solid, provable forensic evidence.

She heard nothing of Caroline for two weeks and during that time learned to relax properly. Dr Salcott visited her every day on his rounds and she wondered how she could ever have suspected him. He seemed as he had done when she first met him on the train – amiable, loquacious, unthinkingly sexist and conventional – but as her body repaired itself under Georgina Wakehurst's care she recognised, too, that he must be a good doctor, able to instill the necessary confidence in his patients as well as diagnose their gastroentestinal diseases.

Members of her DOAP staff came daily, too, and gradually she felt herself growing back into her own professional life as she assessed their problems and gave advice and the occasional admonishment. Her terror that the two sides of her life might coalesce grew less as she rediscovered the discipline and order of her Civil Service work.

By the time Tom did bring Caroline Titchmell to the ward, late one Friday afternoon, Willow felt that she was herself again. Her legs were still strung and weighted, but her mind was once more in order; and she was no longer afraid.

Caroline looked terrible. Her skin was grey and her remarkable eyes seemed dimmed and deeply sunk into their sockets. Her mouth was pinched and looked as though she had been chewing her lips and tearing little bits of skin of them with her teeth and fingers. She had obviously lost a great deal of weight and her clothes seemed to hang from her shoulders as though from a cheap wire coat hanger.

'Your summons surprised me,' she said to Willow by way of greeting, 'but I understand from Chief Inspector Worth that you were instrumental in sorting out what was happening.' Her voice sounded hoarse, as though she had rasped her throat with weeping or perhaps with talking. She looked round, but Tom had tactfully disappeared.

Willow wanted to tell Caroline that she felt guilty for ruining her happiness with Ben, but she could not do it. Guilt there was, but only for asking questions in the guise of a friend. Ben had had to be stopped. There were a lot of things she wanted to say to Caroline, but Caroline had to speak first. Willow waited for some time.

'He seemed so gentle always,' Caroline said at last. 'That's what I still can't understand. I've never known anyone as gentle and considerate in my life. But how could I not have known what he really was?'

'Because when he was with you he was gentle,' said Willow. There was more to say, but she knew that she would have to wait until Caroline had let out everything she had been bottling up as she fought her own feelings.

'But when we lived together, when we . . . made love together. Do you realise that I lay in bed and . . .' her voice hardened until it sounded as ugly as the euphemism she used, 'and *screwed* a man who killed my brother and the others?'

There was horror in her voice, which Willow could well understand, and a look of sick pain in her dark-blue eyes.

'Sexual intercourse,' said Willow at her driest and most didactic, 'does not bestow second sight on people. You could not have known anything about him that he did not want to show you. It's not your fault, Caroline.'

'But it is my fault. I found him, I loved him, I leaned on him, brought him in contact with my family, I told

289

him all the buried slights and miseries of my past and he took them to be far more important than they were and out of misguided . . . love, I suppose, he killed the people involved. I turned him into a murderer.' Her voice rose higher and higher with each word she spoke and Willow recognised the first signs of hysteria. Relieved that Caroline had obeyed her instruction to come to the ward during the transmission of *Neighbours*, Willow decided to try to prevent the incipient hysteria from turning into the real thing.

'Stop there, Caroline,' said Willow, letting herself sound viciously angry. Her sharp voice had much the same effect as a slap across the face. Caroline gasped and was silent.

'He was a psychopath, Caroline,' Willow said clearly. 'The fact that he is not known to have killed anyone else before he met you may be merely that he was never caught or that he had not fully recognised his desire to kill. Everyone complains to people who love them about their past unhappiness, because in the new love they feel so secure that they think they can never be hurt again and it becomes safe to tell. You did nothing that ninety per cent of the population has not done before you,' said Willow. Then she added in a dispassionate voice: 'Did you read any of his books?'

Caroline shook her head. 'I was afraid that I might not like them or that I might hurt him by some crass comment. I thought it better not to risk it.'

Willow did not say aloud the thought in her mind: 'And so you did not completely trust him. Did you feel that there was something wrong with him after all?' But she could tell that Caroline had thought the same thing. No wonder she looked just as the Spartan boy with the fox gnawing at his vitals must have looked.

'They were all my victims, you see,' said Caroline painfully, 'and so was he.'

'That's nonsense. He was trying to control you. What he did gave him power over you, which is what he wanted.

His job gave him power over his students, his books gave him power over anyone he wanted to chastise, and his crimes gave him power over you – as well as over his victims. Everyone one wants power and the most obsessed with it are not always the strutting Mussolini types . . .'

'How do you know so much about it?' asked Caroline, sounding interested.

'I don't,' said Willow, glad to see that Caroline was thinking of something beyond her own feelings. 'But lying here I have been thinking over and over the whole business. I've remembered what he said when he told me that I must put part of myself in my own books. I'd never let myself see it before, but he's right. In the books I manipulate and take revenge and re-order the universe to my own satisfaction – and from what I have learned about myself and the way I do it, I think I can see how his mind worked.'

Caroline turned her head away to hide her face; her shoulders started to shake slightly.

'But how could he have thought I wanted him to kill them?' she said at last and broke into really violent sobbing. Willow thought it indecent to watch someone in such paroxysms of grief and looked away. Over Caroline's bowed head Willow saw Tom Worth walking back towards them both.

Dressed informally for once in old dark-green corduroy trousers and a Guernsey sweater, he looked so sane, so much himself that her heart lifted. But he too liked power, as she well knew. Perhaps his saving grace was that he was afraid of his own response to it.

The sound of Caroline's whooping sobs had eventually reached the nurses' desk and one of them came to investigate. When she saw the state Caroline was in, the nurse lifted her from her chair by Willow's bed and took her away.

Tom took her place at Willow's bedside.

'Did that hurt?' he asked.

'My confession?' said Willow. 'Yes it did. I've realised that we're none of us free of the desire to rearrange circumstance and other people. It's terrifying when you think of the implications.'

'Not really,' said Tom in a voice that carried comfort although it was not at all soothing. 'For most of us the balance between the satisfying of our own needs and those of other people is more nearly held. The trouble comes when a man's own needs seem to him so much more important than other people's that even their deaths count for nothing in the scales.'

'Yes, I know,' said Willow. 'Has he confessed yet?' Worth nodded his dark head.

'Yes. I was afraid for some time that the sonnet he sent to poor Miss Titchmell would be as near a confession as he was prepared to get. I've got a copy here.' He pulled out of his pocket a small, old edition of Shakespeare's sonnets, bound in rubbed green morocco and gave it to her. 'I've marked it.'

Willow opened the musty-smelling book and read:

'How heavy do I journey on the way,
When what I see, my weary travel's end,
Doth teach that ease and that repose to say,
"Thus far the miles are measur'd from thy friend!"
The beast that bears me, tired with my woe,
Plods dully on, to bear that weight in me,
As if by some instinct the wretch did know
His rider lov'd not speed, being made from thee:
The bloody spur cannot provoke him on
That sometimes anger thrusts into his hide,
Which heavily he answers with a groan
More sharp to me than spurring to his side;
For that same groan doth put this in my mind:
My grief lies onward, and my joy behind.'

When she reached the last couplet, Willow looked up.

'Melodramatic bastard!' she exclaimed. 'He's enjoying it all, isn't he?'

'I think he is,' said Tom. 'He's the kingpin at the moment. How could he resist playing his part to the hilt? It must have been bitterly frustrating for him when he could be the only one allowed to know what he was doing. Perhaps that's why he finally gave in and told us all about it, unable to bear the thought that no one would ever know for certain that it was he who had made the kills.'

'It's horrible,' said Willow, thinking of the broken woman who had just been taken away from the ward, of her mother and all the other secondary victims of the murders. 'I wish I'd never . . . How do you cope with it, Tom? Do you just ignore it?' She put one of her hands on his arm and felt the rough wool of his sleeve.

'You can't pretend not to have been through any experience, Will,' Tom answered gently. 'You have to absorb it and do the best you can with it. With luck, it'll be useful to you one day.'

At that echo of Marcus Aurelius, Willow smiled and took away her hand. She wished that she did not look and feel so ridiculous with her legs strung up before her in their heavy plaster casings. There ought to be a grand gesture, she thought, to finish the case, but she was in no position to make one and grand gestures were not much in Tom's line.

'You're a bit of an old Stoic yourself, aren't you, Tom?' she said.

'Yes,' he agreed and allowed himself a hint of teasing in his smile. 'It's lucky, isn't it, given the way things are with us?'

Knowing that he was not talking about the policing of society any longer, Willow felt like frowning at his mockery. But something had happened to her during the case and her long weeks in hospital. At last the appropriate action occurred to her and she made her grand gesture.

As Willow stuck her tongue out at Tom Worth, a smile of rare pleasure swept aross his craggy face.